JEC PUBLISHING COMPANY
2049 E. Cherry Street, Suite 100
Springfield, Missouri 65802
(800) 313-5121

Copyright © 2008 by Todd Dull

Library of Congress Control Number: 2009925353

ISBN: 978-0-9816282-9-5

Author: Todd Dull

Cover design by: Tracy Jones

Prepared for Publishing by: JE Cornwell and Tom Dease

Printed in Canada

Author's Bio

Todd Dull was born in Springfield, Missouri, he was raised and still lives near there. He has worked on a farm, a ranch, in several factories, at a saw mill, and in a lumberyard.

Destiny called when he followed in his father's and both his grandfather's footsteps and started driving a truck.

Also like his father and grandfathers, he is a huge John Wayne fan. Todd holds a 1st degree black belt in Tae Kwon-Do. Scalper is his first novel.

Acknowledgements

An acknowledgement needs to go to the Greene County Lending Library in and around Springfield, who has a very large collection of audio books, of which I listened while driving a truck.

Thanks to my stepdaughter, Dixie, for letting me use her name.

Thanks to my best friend, Mike Allen, a thirteen-year veteran of the Navy Seals (he refers to the navy as Uncle Sam's Canoe Club), for answering my endless questions about the time he spent in the service of defending this great nation.

A very special thanks goes out to all of the Viet Nam veterans who were patient with me and humored me by talking to me. They all agreed that putting two mini-guns on the nose of a Huey helicopter would make for a nice visual effect at night when both guns opened up, but wouldn't be very practical, and they all listed several reasons: One being that there wouldn't be enough room in the helicopter to carry the ammo for two min-guns. They all agreed that mini-guns fire around three thousand rounds a minute, and to make a double pass as described in this story would take about eight crates of ammo. Another reason was the recoil factor. They all agreed that the recoil from double mini-guns would impede if not stop the forward progress of a Huey. One veteran told me the only aircraft he saw equipped with double mini-guns was Puff the Magic Dragon—and that when it flew over with both guns opened up, it could put a bullet in every square inch of a football field in one pass. He went on to say that when both mini-guns opened up, the pilot of the plane would have to compensate for being pushed sideways because of the recoil of both guns. He also said that there would be two guys in the back with scoop shovels, scooping spent shells out the side door as fast as they could shovel. When I stated that I would change the story and only put one mini-gun per helicopter, they all agreed that I should leave it the way it is; they thought that idea was far out.

A very, very special thanks and acknowledgement goes to J.E. Cornwell for breathing life into this project when I thought it was dead.

Dedication

To Pat Van Epps, my friend, co-worker and biggest fan.

Inspired Quotes

"Greater love hath no man than this, that a man lay down his life for his friends." Jesus Christ, The Gospel according to St. John, Chapter 15, verse 13.

"Missouri is called the mother of outlaws." Author Forrest Carter in his novel 'Gone To Texas', which was later made into the movie, "The Outlaw Josey Wales'.

"Catch me if you can." Jack The Ripper.

Introduction

In the fall of 2003, the Department of Transportation (DOT) announced it was changing the hours of service for motor carriers and commercial vehicles. No one in the trucking industry had a say in this, and in fact some of the larger trucking companies voiced their protests, but to no avail, and the changes were made. Again, in the fall of 2005, the DOT announced yet another change in the hours of service for truck drivers, who again had no representation. The trucking industry has had to adjust to the changes imposed upon it. Early in American History, there were a group of individuals who met in Boston Harbor and had themselves a little tea party because their government imposed laws upon them without their representation.

This story takes place prior to the fall of 2003. It is my first novel. One of the main characters in it, Jason, is a man much like me. I would like to think I would react in much the same way Jason does in the same situations.

This is a work of fiction and is set in a very real place, the queen city of the Ozarks, Springfield, Missouri. I have taken the liberty of changing Springfield to fit the needs of my story. I meant no insult or injury to the feelings of those who live in or around Springfield. The people who live in and around the communities of Springfield are some of the nicest people I've met in the country, and while driving a truck coast to coast and border to border in this country, I've met a lot of them.

Chapter 1

He woke slowly and asked himself the same series of questions he always asked himself when he was on the road. Did he know where he was? Yes, he did, Kingman, Arizona. Did he know what he was doing in Kingman? Yes, he knew the answer to that one too, he was on his way home. Did he know what time it was? He rolled over and looked at the Panasonic clock/stereo face which stated it was eleven-thirty P.M.—that's Central Standard Time. Yes, he knew the answer to that one too. Hot damn, he was on a roll, he thought to himself as he stretched and blinked sleep from his eyes. Did he know his name? Yes, he did: Jason Fox. All right, batting a thousand, so far. Did he know what day it was? Well, shit, he thought that was one answer he didn't know right off the top of his head, he would have to give that one some study.

He sat up, looked outside, and was satisfied to see that he was parked in the same parking spot of the same parking lot of the same truck stop as last night. That was a good thing, no surprises there. What day was it? He thought back, and briefly ran through the last few days in his head. He had left his home in Strafford, Missouri, a small town about ten miles east of Springfield, Missouri on Saturday morning, delivered in City of Industry, California on Monday morning, reloaded in Ontario, California on Monday afternoon, so that would make this Monday night-almost Tuesday morning. He felt better about that.

Jason was forty-two years old, and he drove a truck over the road. He stood five foot, seven inches, and weighed in around one hundred and ninety pounds. Not all of the weight was muscle, but a good portion of it was. It seemed the more he tried to take off the weight, the more he packed it on. His belly hung out over his belt a bit, and he was fond of telling folks that if you have something important, you built a shed over it. His hair, which was starting to recede and vacate his head, was a sandy shade of brown, which he kept cut above his ears and short also on top. His eyes were a dark, steamy brown, and he kept a close cropped beard.

He came from a trucking family. His mother's four brothers at one time had all been truckers, his mom's dad had been a trucker. His father and paternal grandfather had been truckers, two of his father's brothers had been truckers. Three maternal cousins and two paternal cousins were currently truckers. So to say he came from a trucking family would be an understatement.

The conversation with his wife, Diane, earlier that night had been disturbing. She had been watching the local news on the television as she talked to him and had stated that a young woman from Ontario, California had been found dead on the front steps of a trucking company in Springfield early that morning. After they had finished their conversation and he had hung up the phone, he had wondered about the murdered girl. Murdered? Diane hadn't said anything about the girl being murdered, she had said the girl had been found dead. He hadn't thought about it much more then, he had been tired, hungry, and in need of a shower. He had eaten supper in the truck stop restaurant, walked outside to his eighteen wheeler, climbed in the sleeper, and gone to sleep. Now, it was time to take care of that shower thing and after that start making his way along the interstate eastward toward home. With a little luck, he could be home by early Thursday morning.

He grabbed his duffle bag of clean clothes and his shaving kit and climbed out of his truck into the cool, clean night. He had gotten to the truck stop fairly early that afternoon, so parking hadn't been a problem. Most of the time, if a driver pulled into a truck stop in the middle of the night, finding a parking space could be a problem as truck stops seemed to start filling up in the middle of the afternoon. He smiled to himself as he thought, Travel Centers, not truck stops, that's what they preferred to be called now. He would try to keep that in mind—not. Old habits are hard to break, and he should know, he had smoked his last cigarette on the thirty-first of December, a kind of late Christmas gift to Diane—and himself. Being a twenty-year smoker, it hadn't been easy, but he had stuck to it, reminding himself what was really important to him in his life. Yes, he knew all about old habits, just like he knew he would always call them truck stops instead of travel centers.

He stepped inside the truck—travel center—it didn't feel right, so to hell with it, the truck stop, and walked up to the driver kiosk. He pulled a small wallet out of one of his back pockets and retrieved a points card. Almost all truck stops—another smile to himself as he thought the old dogs and new tricks saying his grandparents had been so fond of repeating whenever the

9

situation arose—gave truck drivers a free shower with the purchase of fifty gallons or more of fuel, which was good if said driver needed fuel, if not, the cost of a shower was about seven dollars, the system would ask the driver to swipe his points card also. Most truck stops had these systems, and the gallon amount was converted into points, usually a penny a point, and added to the existing balance of the card. It also added a shower for each fuel amount of over fifty gallons, but only one per purchase, please.

Jason swiped the points card through the slot provided in the kiosk and brought up the appropriate display on the touch screen. He chose a shower with the touch of a finger, and the kiosk printed him a confirmation number onto a small slip of paper which it slowly spit out to him.

He checked the overhead screen to match up his number. In some truck stops—another inner smile—instead of handing out keys, they have installed electronic locks on all the doors. When one is issued a shower, that person is given a slip of paper with two sets of numbers on it. One number is sort of a receipt number, and the other is the lock combination to be entered into the keypad to open the door. When he looked at the screen, his receipt number showed up next to another number, and that number listed the shower number.

Jason toted his duffle bag to the shower door that had his number on it, so to speak, and entered the lock combination. There was a slight buzzing sound, and then a small click as the lock released. Jason applied pressure to the door handle and pushed the door inward. He brushed his teeth, undressed, showered, and shaved. After he dressed, he stuffed his dirty clothes in the netted bag he carried for the purpose. He gathered his duffle bag, dirty clothes bag, shaving kit, and exited the shower, leaving the towels and washcloth in the sink.

Jason stepped outside and walked toward his truck. The truck wasn't hard to spot, it was a 2001, white, model 387 Peterbilt, but the most charming thing about it was the stuffed Wile E. Coyote strapped to its grill. If a person looked closely, and the glare on the windshield wasn't too bad, that person could see the stuffed Roadrunner mounted on the dash. The truck was powered by a 600 Signature Series ISX Cummins, double over-head-cam motor, an eighteen-speed transmission, with 3:36 ratio rear ends, and twin straight stacks, of course. The trailer he pulled was a fifty-three foot dry van, filled with fishing poles, lures, and tackle, all of which weighed just over fifteen thousand pounds. He was taking it to the main yard of the company that he drove for, Blanket Transportation. He would unhook it, or drop it there, and a local-city driver would take it to the major sporting and hunting goods store main warehouse in Springfield to be unloaded at their leisure.

To say he had a sense of humor would be correct as evidenced by the stuffed animals and the bumper stickers on the sleeper windows that read GOD BLESS JOHN WAYNE. He received a lot of comments on his choice of truck decorations. Everyone enjoyed the stuffed animals, but not everyone enjoyed the bumper stickers. To each his own, Jason thought.

He dug in his jeans pockets again and pulled out his key to unlock the truck door. After unlocking the door, climbing into the truck, and stowing his bags, he pulled out his logbook. Well, he thought, the fun is over. He opened it up and took a look at what he needed to do in order to get home. Probably the best thing to do would be to leave the truck parked, buy an airline ticket, and fly home. Since that wouldn't get the truck home, he needed to figure a way to get home in the next two days. The problem was he needed about twenty hours to get home, but he only had sixteen hours available to him on his logbook. In other words, he had enough time on his logbook to show getting to Oklahoma City, Oklahoma, and then he would have to sit for twenty-four hours before driving home. The only thing for him to do was drive to Eric, Oklahoma, take his time off, drive to Oklahoma City, Oklahoma, and decide what to do from there.

Jason sighed and put his logbook away. He would figure out something between now and then. He climbed into the driver seat and opened the driver side door. He climbed down out of the tractor, picked up the twenty-eight ounce claw hammer and a flashlight he kept by the driver seat. The hammer was to thump the tires, and the flash light was to check wheel seals, brake pads, air lines, air line connections, tractor and trailer undercarriage, and the like. Thumping tires is not an exact science, but with a little practice, a driver could distinguish between a tire that is low on air, fully inflated, or flat just by thumping tires, listening to the sound, and feeling the recoil. Before closing the door, he reached up into the tractor cab, turned on the parking lights, and flipped on the hazard flashers. Jason walked around the tractor and trailer, checking that all the lights worked, that all the turn signal lights worked, giving the equipment an overall observation with the flashlight, and thumped the tires as he did his walk around inspection. He paused momentarily at the drive tandems of the tractor on the driver's side. He bent forward from the waist and looked at the fifth wheel release handle to make sure it was still retracted. In recent years, disgruntled drivers, or just plain trouble makers, sometimes stalked around truck stops releasing fifth wheel couplings. Then later the unsuspecting driver of the same truck, not checking the coupling, drives out from under his trailer, dropping its retracted landing gear onto the ground, and sometimes ripping air lines loose from tractor and trailer. Jason had never had this happen to him, knock on wood, he thought, but he had seen the effects of it. The embarrassment of the victimized driver was usually bad enough to make that driver see red and want to fight. Jason didn't want to become a victim of such an act. After completing this, he put his hammer away, and turned off the flashers and the parking lights. Next, he pulled the hood release and raised the hood. He checked all the belts, checking for tension and frays. He checked for oil leaks and checked all the water and air hoses and lines. Satisfied with everything he saw, he secured the hood again and climbed back into the cab behind the steering wheel. He depressed the clutch and rotated the ignition key. The whole cab of the tractor rocked as the huge diesel motor turned over and started. He sat and listened to the motor idle looking over the gauges for anything abnormal, satisfied that everything was as it should be.

Next, he fastened his seatbelt and adjusted it to his comfort. He then turned his attention to his CB radio. The CB (short for Citizens Band) is a main lifeline to the American truck driver. From it the driver can obtain traffic information, road and weather conditions, local directions, and sometimes help if stranded on the side of a major roadway. That was the intended use printed on the side of a new CB radio box, but the more common use was to give Smoky Bear (highway patrol and DOT) reports, the current status of scale houses, discuss the latest global or national gossip, and to alert other drivers of what certain female motorists were or were not wearing. Jason reached over to the CB, and turned the volume up a little. He took a hold of the microphone, pulled it to his mouth to speak into it, and depressed the call button.

"Break one-nine," he said into the microphone, "how about a radio check? Can anyone hear this little ol' radio?" Most truck drivers monitored channel nineteen on the CB, unless they were in certain parts of California where Interstate 5 and Highways 99 and 58 were close together. Drivers would get confused from contradicting reports, so a system was devised among the drivers that regularly drove those roads designating which channel they monitored, nineteen, seventeen, or fifteen.

"Damn it, driver, that radio sounds loud and proud," came a voice over the CB speaker. It's worth noting that in the nineteen seventies, truck drivers called each other "good buddies", but somewhere along the line, homosexual men started monitoring the CB radio, and whenever they would hear one truck driver call another one good buddy, they would get on the radio and talk about some variation of how they would be a truck driver's "good buddy", so truckers started calling each other "driver". If one trucker called another one a good buddy, it was meant as an insult, literally calling the other trucker a homosexual that wanted to have sex with any same sex trucker, usually orally.

"I appreciate that, driver," Jason teased. "Now I can mark in my logbook that my vehicle inspection is complete."

"How does this radio sound on that end?" asked the same voice that had answered Jason just a moment before.

"It sounds like shit, driver. You'd be a lot better off throwing that piece of shit out the window, but tell me where you throw it out so I can get it," Jason teased, and let go of the mic. The CB mic was attached on one end by a small, thin bungee chord that fastened to the back of the mic, the other end of the bungee chord was attached to the compartments above Jason's head with the curly cord that resembled the cord of a telephone. This gave the CB mic the freedom to swing back and forth, to and fro, and it also kept the mic about mouth level all the time.

"Ten-four," the same voice laughed through the speaker.

The CB radio is a piece of electronic equipment that can have its power boosted. The CB radio that Jason had in his truck was a rare model called a President Lincoln, that he had taken to a CB radio shop to have it peaked and tuned, or in other words had the power boosted.

Jason took a hold of the gear shifter, depressed the clutch, and pulled the shifter into the fifth gear position. Next, he pushed in a knob on the dash that released the parking brakes which were air powered. He eased the clutch out and pulled slowly from the parking space heading for the parking lot exit. He made his way onto the deserted street and headed for the entrance ramp for Interstate Forty. As he made his way to the end of the ramp, he constantly checked the driver's side rearview mirror while slowly gearing up. By the time he reached the end of the ramp and merged onto the interstate, his speed had reached sixty miles per hour. He settled back into his seat, pushed the accelerator petal to the floor, and listened to the engine's whine climb with intensity. As the RPM needle touched the seventeen hundred mark, Jason eased up on the accelerator pedal, pulled the gear shifter into the neutral position, waited for the RPM needle to back down to the fifteen hundred mark, and pulled the gear shifter into the seventeenth gear position, all without using the clutch. When the engine RPMs rose again, Jason flipped a button on the shifter knob, eased off the accelerator pedal, and the truck shifted into eighteenth gear. He pushed the accelerator pedal back down to the floor, and watched the speedometer rotate around to the eighty-mile-per-hour mark. The speed limit in the state of Arizona on the interstates was seventy-five miles per hour, and he felt comfortable at this speed.

"Okay, you big white bitch," Jason muttered to himself and his truck, "it's hammer time, let's haul ass east toward home."

Not quite eight hours later, he took the exit ramp at the two hundred seventy-seven mile marker on Interstate Forty in New Mexico. Not bad he thought to himself, five hundred seventy-seven miles in just under eight hours, he would take that average anytime. He pulled into one of the truck stops there and found a place to park. He backed into the parking space he had selected, pulled the knob to set the tractor air brakes, and shut the motor off. He climbed out of the truck, stretched, shut the truck door, locked it, and walked toward the truck stop restaurant. As he entered the restaurant, he looked for, and found, a booth with a phone. He slid into the booth, dug into a pocket, and pulled out a phone card. The waitress came and left a menu as Jason ordered coffee. Jason was ready to place his order by the time the waitress returned with the coffee. He ordered, handed the menu back to the waitress, thanked her, and picked the phone up and put the receiver to his ear. He entered the numbers in on the key pad to access the phone card, and then dialed his home phone number.

Diane answered the phone on the third ring with a soft, pitiful hello that sounded more like a question than a greeting.

"Honey?" Jason said. "Are you all right?"

"Yeah," she said trying to force the sleepiness out of her voice. "What time is it?"

"It's eight o'clock," Jason answered. He never changed the time on his watch or the clocks in the truck, but kept them set on Central Time.

"I went up and spent most of the night with Sally last night. The time got away from me, and I didn't get home until after midnight," she explained, even though she knew Jason wouldn't need or necessarily require one from her. Selena, or Sally for short, was Diane's closest friend from childhood and Diane's sister-in-law. She was also the night time dispatcher for the

Blanket Transportation.

"I see," he replied. "You had me worried there for a minute, I mean a country girl like you laying abed when the sun is up, and the day is half over." He loved to tease her, especially when she was like this, groggy, and her mental defenses down.

"Yeah, right. The day is half over maybe for you," she retorted, knowing what he was doing, and starting to wake up enough to play along. "When you called last night, you were in Kingman, and if I know you, you took off at midnight. So where are you, Oklahoma City?" It had taken her a few months to get used to his rare sense of humor, but once she had, she found that she loved it, and loved him that much more for it. She could play this little game too.

"You know me too well," he was just starting to rev up. "I was in Oklahoma City, but when I looked at my logbook, I saw I couldn't legally be there, so I turned around, and came back here." Just let her try to top that one. He heard her softly laughing, but trying to keep him from hearing her.

"Where are you?" she finally asked as her last chuckle escaped her.

"Santa Rosa, New Mexico," he answered. "I'm gonna have breakfast, climb back in the saddle, and dig my spurs in."

"Damn it, driver," she said lowering, and softening her voice even more, knowing what that did to him. The trucker lingo was another thing she loved about him. The first time she had gone with him for a week, she thought he was speaking a foreign language whenever he talked on the CB radio, but, by the end of that week, he had her talking the talk, so to speak, and not only that, she knew what most of it meant. "I miss my truck driver," she said in that whispery voice Jason called her sexy voice.

"I talked to him earlier, and he said that he couldn't make it home this weekend, and told me to come in his place," Jason teased her again.

"No one but my truck driver will do," she said sounding serious. "When will you be home?"

"I'll either be home late tonight or early in the morning," he replied, and then asked. "When do you work again?"

"I have the brunch to dinner shift today," Jason heard the sound of bed covers being flung aside and heard the sound of her stretching in her voice.

"Okay," he said. "I'll call you tonight and let you know where I am."

"All right," she said, then spoke sternly into the phone, "you be careful."

"Yes ma'am," he replied briskly, and then added in a more subdued tone, "to quote Dirty Harry, 'A man's got to know his limitations,' and I know mine."

"I know you do," she said, using that sexy voice on him again. "Come home to me safely."

"I will," he said, then added, "have a good day. I'll talk to you again later."

"Okay, honey," she said. "I love you. Bye."

"I love you, too," he said smiling. "Bye-bye."

He hung up the phone just as the waitress approached with his breakfast. Jason ate his breakfast without incident or interruption. He left a two dollar tip on the table for the waitress, paid for his meal, and returned to his truck. He got back onto the interstate and headed east again. Just over an hour later, he exited the interstate at the small town of San Jon, New Mexico, and found a place to park at one of the two truck stops there. He needed some sleep, and here was as good as place as any.

He slept for about four hours, woke, got his insulated coffee mug and shaving kit, and went inside the truck stop. He entered the restroom and did his usual tour of using the facilities, washing his hands, and brushing his teeth. He hadn't always taken the time to take care of himself, but as of late, he was taking the time to do so. He exited the restroom, got himself a cup of coffee at the self-service counter, paid for it, and returned to his truck. Old habits were hard to break, and Jason was a creature of habit, but he also had a keen sense if something seemed wrong or out of place. He put his coffee on the floor mat of the cab of the truck, picked up his hammer, and performed the V.I., or vehicle inspection, as he had done earlier that day.

Satisfied that everything on the truck was as it should be, he started the engine and made his way back onto the interstate, again heading east. Jason had been a long time fan of Stephen King, and when audio books became popular, it helped ease the boredom of the road. He kept the volume of the CB radio adjusted to where he could hear the audio book and also monitor the CB. Jason preferred the books that Mr. King read himself, but if Mr. King didn't read his own work, then the combination of Stephen King as writer and Frank Muller as reader was pretty awesome too.

He continued listening to the current work by Mr. King and settled in for a four-and-a-half-hour drive to Oklahoma City, Oklahoma. The only two sites of concern for Jason were Shamrock, Texas, and El Reno, Oklahoma.

Shamrock was the site of a permanent weigh station, and El Reno the site of a place where portable scales could be set up. Both were closed, or "locked up" as truckers referred to it.

Jason arrived in Oklahoma City and found a place to park in one of the many truck stops in the city. He would stay here for a while before completing the last leg of his trip home. He climbed into the sleeper to rest for a bit and had no sooner put down when there was a knock on the driver's side door. He leaned out of the sleeper and looked out the window of the door to see a man in his mid-thirties standing there looking back at him. Jason pressed the button for the power window to lower it.

"Hi," the man said, "I hate to bother you, but I was wondering if you could donate a couple dollars to help a fellow brother out to buy a sandwich or something."

"If you're hungry, I can fix you a sandwich," Jason said, not believing a word of this sad tale. He had been driving a truck over the road for about fifteen years now, and it hadn't taken that long to catch on to the people that hung around truck stops to beg. He could usually tell when someone was sincere or not, and there were people that on occasion that really were in need of a helping hand from time to time, and he could usually tell the difference, but Jason could smell the deception coming off this guy.

"What?" the guy was taken aback.

"I can fix you a sandwich," Jason repeated. He and Diane had installed a refrigerator in the truck a couple of years back. Jason continued, "I can fix you two if you're really hungry."

"You have meat in packages?" The man asked.

"Yep," Jason said, "beef and turkey."

"Can I have a whole package?" the man asked.

"No," Jason said. He remembered something he had read in the Bible about treating strangers with kindness because you never knew when you were entertaining angels. Jason also remembered reading that in every case in the Bible when an angel had appeared to someone, that angel had identified itself as an angel, and that they weren't prone to lying or begging.

"Man, are you broke?" the man was indignant.

And there it was, just as Jason suspected. This guy wasn't hungry, or an angel, just a hustler. This obviously wasn't this guy's first time out, and Jason wasn't a rookie.

"No, I'm sorry, I don't think I can help you," he said patiently, no need to be rude, he just wanted to be left alone.

"Oh, please, I really need some help, and anything will do," the guy insisted.

This still didn't add up, Jason thought, this guy is telling his story of woe with nothing to back it up.

"I'm sorry," Jason repeated. "I can't help you."

"Oh, come on," the guy's tone had changed now, he was becoming more indignant.

"Sir," Jason said, keeping his tone cool and even, "I've been nice twice. If I have to get out of this truck to make you leave me alone, I won't be nice. Now beat it while you still can move on your own." Jason could back up what he said, he had earned his first degree black belt in Tae Kwon Do in nineteen ninety-six. That had been a number of years ago, and he had put on more than a few pounds, but the knowledge was still there.

The guy never said a word, but Jason could tell he was seething inside. Jason powered the window up, keeping a steady and unwavering gaze on the man. When the window was up all the way, Jason eased back into the sleeper and lay down again. He would definitely do another walk around inspection on his truck before he left here. He faded off to sleep and awoke two hours later. He went inside the truck stop to use the restroom, did his walk around inspection on the truck, and headed for the interstate.

Three interstates cross in Oklahoma City. Interstate 40 goes east and west, I-35 goes north and south, and I-44 runs a diagonal course across Missouri and Oklahoma. Jason followed I-40 East, took the exit for I-35 North, and veered onto I-44 East. Interstate 44 is a toll road in the state of Oklahoma. Jason left Oklahoma City, and arrived in Tulsa, Oklahoma about an hour and a half later. He made his way through Tulsa and headed for the Missouri state line.

Jason was almost halfway to the Missouri state line when he ran up behind another Blanket Transportation truck. The other truck was rolling along at a speed of about seventy-two or seventy-three miles per hour. The speed limit on Oklahoma's interstates was seventy miles per hour, and the speed limit on most of its toll roads, or turnpikes was seventy-five. Jason was still maintaining his speed of eighty miles per hour when he passed the other truck. Jason could tell that the other truck was a company truck.

"Hey, big white Peterbilt," a voice said over Jason's CB radio, and he knew immediately that it was the driver of the company truck. "I thought the company turned all of the trucks down to seventy-five."

Some companies hooked their truck motors up to a computer and had software to set their trucks to whatever speed they chose. Some companies set their trucks' speed at sixty-two miles per hour, some at sixty-three miles per hour, some at sixty-five miles per hour, and so on. The company Jason drove for set most of their trucks' speed at around seventy-five miles per hour, but if a driver decided to go on the lease-to-own plan like Jason was on, then the company almost never restricted those trucks, as was the case with Jason's truck. He didn't know how fast it would run, but he knew it would do over one hundred miles per hour, or in trucker talk, it would do triple digits.

"I'm gonna turn you in to the company. I didn't get your truck number, but I'm sure they will know who I'm talkin' about when I describe the truck," the other driver's voice said over Jason's CB speaker.

Jason was still in the passing lane, or hammer lane, and checked his side-mounted rearview mirrors. Seeing that no one was directly behind him, he pulled his foot off the accelerator pedal, and turned on his Jake brake, or engine brake. He waited until the company truck passed him on the right, then Jason turned on his right turn signal, and eased in behind the company truck. He pushed the accelerator pedal to the floor, and started gaining speed again.

"Well, if you're gonna turn me in, then I'm gonna make sure you have plenty to talk about," Jason said into the keyed CB mic, and then asked, "Did you get my truck number that time? I wouldn't want you getting my truck confused with someone else. Get ready. Don't blink, now. Make sure you get your story straight, I wouldn't want you getting someone else into trouble and embarrassing yourself because you couldn't recall my truck number."

Jason let the CB mic go to let it swing freely on its bungee cord, and turned on his left turn signal. He checked his left rearview mirror, saw nothing there, and merged into that lane. The last time he glanced at his speedometer, it had gone past the last numbers it registered, and was approaching the six o'clock position. Jason estimated his speed to be close to ninety-five miles per hour when he passed the company truck.

"I'll see you down the trail, pilgrim," he said into the keyed CB mic doing his best John Wayne impersonation. Jason looked into his rearview mirror again, and was astonished to see another truck right on his tail. Jason turned on his right turn signal, and merged into the right lane.

"Sorry about that, big truck," Jason said into his keyed CB mic. "I didn't see you behind me."

"That's all right," said a hollow voice over his CB speaker. "I heard what went on back there, and I don't blame you a bit. That was pretty funny."

Jason eased off the accelerator pedal, and backed his speed off to eighty miles per hour again. When the other truck came alongside him, Jason glanced over at it and saw an almost duplicate truck to the one his best friend Keith was leasing to buy through Blanket Transportation. It was a black 379 model Peterbilt just like Keith's except this one had a sleeper that could almost be considered a small apartment. The other truck passed Jason, and Jason flashed his headlights at the other truck driver to let him know it was safe to merge back into the right hand lane. The other trucker thanked Jason by turning on his hazards, and letting them blink a couple of times.

The rest of Jason's trip to Springfield was uneventful. He thought no more about the twin to Keith's truck, and he figured he would catch some heat for what he had done to the company driver, but it wouldn't happen today, he could be in Strafford, have the trailer dropped at the company yard, and be on his way home by the time the company driver got there. What if the company driver had a cell phone, Jason thought. That was easy, he knew Sally, or Sal, as he called her would be on duty by now, and maybe she would get a chuckle out of it if the company driver chose to tell her.

Jason arrived at the yard around seven-thirty P.M. that night, found an empty space for the trailer, backed it into the spot, and dropped it. He drove by the dispatch office, which had huge glass panes set into the wall directly in front of the dispatchers so they could see which trucks were arriving and leaving, and gave Sally a blast from his air horns and flashed his lights at her. His only mission and concern now were to go see Diane at work and get something to eat. He would worry about mouthy company drivers and turning in his paperwork for the week tomorrow, and that's exactly what he did.

Chapter 2

Diane hung up the phone after talking to Jason. She smiled to herself as she headed for the shower. He said he would call her tonight, but she doubted that. It would be just like him to show up at her work before she finished her shift at the truck stop restaurant tonight. She thought of a song that had been popular in the eighties. She couldn't remember the name of the song, or even who sang it, but the opening line was "I'd drive a million miles to be with you tonight," and that was Jason hands down. If there was a way, he would find it. She had been with him on the truck when he had to cover incredible distances in impossible time periods, and frankly she didn't know how in the hell he did it. His stamina behind the wheel was astounding as it was in other areas, but for her own sake, she had better not think about that, or her morning shower would need to be a bit cooler than she liked.

Things hadn't always been this good for her. After she had graduated from high school, Diane had worked for awhile with a family friend who had helped get her a job at one of the two truck stops near her home. One night a friend of her older brother, Dewey, came by the restaurant. Whether the attraction had always been there or not she couldn't say, but his visits became more regular, and soon they began to date. His name was Mark, and the two of them became a serious item fairly quick. They were soon married and settled down to a quiet life together.

The first two years were good, as they got used to living together. Diane's father, and favorite uncle convinced the newlyweds to build a house, helped them get the loan, hire the labor, secure the materials, and gave them the value of their experience. The house was built on a large scale for its time, but it would never become a home.

After the completion of the house, Diane became pregnant and worked as long as she could. Two weeks after their daughter was born, Diane returned to work at the truck stop, where she did a variety of jobs. Sometimes she waited tables, other times she worked the fuel desk, still other times she worked the register for the gift shop and gas counter. She had worked in the kitchen cooking and washing dishes, and had even measured

21

the amount of gasoline and diesel fuel in the holding tanks by sticking a long pole into the tanks to get the measurement. While this job might not take a lot of thought or energy, the boss had usually picked the darkest and coldest night to ask her to do it.

While Diane was doing her part to keep her small family together and make ends meet, Mark became distant. Although their sex life wasn't anything to give Diane earth-quaking orgasms, it wasn't the worst she could imagine either, but that was the first change. It was as if Mark had not only lost interest, but when they did have sex, it left her feeling empty and wanting more. Not just wanting more sex, but wanting more closeness, feeling, and at least he could act like he wanted to be there with her at that moment. Was that too much to ask? She didn't know, maybe it was just her being too sensitive. She heard other women talk about their men, most of which it seemed, lived throughout the week giving their women just enough attention to pacify them, and think nothing of every weekend watching football or stock car racing on television, with the occasional professional wrestling matches thrown in. Mark did all of this. Diane tried to put some zing back into the marriage, but Mark resisted her all the way.

If she planned a quiet night out for just the two of them, he called from work to tell her he had to work late. If she met him at the door with little or nothing on, he lightly kissed her on the cheek as he walked past her. If she made the first move to initiate sex, he rolled away from her, and mumbled something under his breath about being tired and having a long day tomorrow. Not only was he ignoring her sexually, he was little or no help when it came to finances. He basically bought what he wanted and had very little interest in maintaining a budget. He lived for the moment and caused Diane and their daughter to do without things they really could have used. When he drove to work, if his pickup truck was low on gasoline, he drove her car and brought it home nearly on empty also. He gave every indication that he did not want the same things that she wanted, mainly a loving marriage and relationship, and a stable home life. It seemed to Diane that he went out of his way to show her acts of unkindness. Then he started coming home from work late, sometimes he had been drinking, and later the phone calls in hushed tones late at night—but on the nights he wanted sex, she was expected to be the good wife. She had been young and hadn't had much experience in such matters.

With all of this going on in her marriage and home life, it was amazing to her when she became pregnant a second time. She hoped the news would somehow bring Mark back closer to her, it hadn't. After he stomped and paced around the room, he stormed out of the house to return some three hours later drunk. He roused Diane out of bed, started shoving her around, and calling her all sorts of names. He accused her of cheating on him with the lowlife truck drivers where she worked. At first she denied the accusations, but when he persisted that the baby couldn't possibly be his because he couldn't "get it up for her anymore because of all her bitching and nagging," she started to cry and to plead with him to at least calm down. She tried to tell him that she still loved him and wanted things to be the way they used to be between them. He laughed at this and told her things would never be like that between them again. He went on to tell her that he was sleeping with two other women besides her, and she would just have to get used to sharing him with them. At this she began to sob, he had just broken heart without showing her any remorse at all, and she made to leave the room. He grabbed her roughly, and screamed at her that she was going to stay and be the good little wife he expected her to be. She asked him to let her leave, but instead, he hit her with his fist, giving her black right eye, and knocking her to the floor. The amount of alcohol and the momentum of the swing pulled him off balance and sent him sprawling over the back of a padded easy chair.

Diane lay still for a moment. She was shocked that Mark would do such a thing to her. She had suspected he was having an affair, but she never imagined in her wildest dreams he would ever be capable of hitting her like he just did. She gingerly touched the throbbing part of her face where he had hit her, and was satisfied that nothing was broken. She started to get to her feet to check to see if Mark was injured when she saw her three-year-old daughter looking at her, starting to cry. Diane forgot about checking on Mark and hurried around the house gathering up things she would need for a few days away from the house. She loaded her daughter and their belongings into her car and hoped to God she had enough gas in the car to make it to her parents' house.

When she arrived at her parents' home, no words needed to be spoken, and Diane broke down and cried like she never had before on both her parents' shoulders. Dewey happened to be there that night visiting his father about a cattle deal the two of them were thinking of partnering up on, and he witnessed his sister's pain, shame, and anguish. When their father decided he would go pay his son-in-law a little visit, Dewey stopped him, and told him that it had been him, Dewey, that had sent Mark to the truck stop that night to fix him up with his sister, and he, Dewey, would clean up this mess.

When Dewey got to his sister's house, he went in like he owned the place, not bothering to knock. Mark was sitting at the kitchen table with his head lying on his arms that were folded across the table, passed out. Dewey got a quart plastic tumbler from the sink drainer, and filled it with cold water. Next he walked up behind the sitting Mark, pulled his head back by his own hair, and splashed the water full force into Mark's face. Without missing a beat, Dewey returned to the sink, and filled the tumbler again. This time he didn't have to wrench Mark's head up, Mark was still trying to cough out the last bit of water from his airway. Dewey waited until Mark looked up, and then splashed the second wave into his face. Dewey refilled the plastic tumbler a third time.

"Wait! What the fuck are you doing, Dewey?" Mark screamed at him.

"I'm helping you sober up, so you can feel every bit of this ass kicking you're about to get," Dewey said in a matter-of-fact tone as he splashed the third wave into Mark's face.

Dewey did as promised. He gave Mark the most severe beating of his life. Dewey broke Mark's nose, knocked out two of his front teeth, and fractured three of Mark's ribs, while he also bruised up his own knuckles. Next, Dewey hauled Mark outside, put him behind the steering wheel of his own pickup truck, and gave him this one warning.

"If you even think about fighting my sister on a divorce, I'll beat you 'til it'll hurt you to walk. If I catch you at this house, I'll do the same thing. You will give Diane an uncontested divorce, you will pay for both attorneys, and the court costs, and any child support the court deems is fair. You will not talk to or touch Diane again, unless she wishes it. Am I making myself clear?" Dewey said.

"The state of Missouri won't grant us a divorce if Diane's pregnant," Mark said. With his missing teeth, and broken nose, he talked with a lisp.

"I don't give a damn," Dewey said, his voice taking on an edgy tone that Mark didn't much care for. "Since you couldn't treat my sister decent while being married to her, you will make up for it now. You will release any claim you have on the house, and the land it sits on to Diane. When you need something from here, you will call me, no discussion, period. Now get out of here, and don't ever come back."

After Diane had her second baby, another girl, the divorce was granted, and Diane returned to work. After a few years, she tried dating again. Most of the men she met were associated with the truck stop in some way. She dated a couple different truckers at different times, and then she had a steamy relationship with a salesman, until she found out he was married. She had been tempted to see if Dewey would perform an encore, but she thought better of it. Through the years, friends had set her up with men they knew to be single, divorced, or widowed. Most of them seemed nice, some were not too bad-looking, but none excited her the way she always had dreamed it should. Then Sally had suggested she might try the local singles line. It took a lot of convincing to get Diane to join the singles line, and when she did and started meeting some of these potential dates, she was sorry she had joined.

Her experience wasn't a good one. Most of the men she met had some deep-rooted personal problem that she just didn't want to have to deal with. All of this was many years after her divorce from Mark. Her oldest daughter, Megan, was married and living about fifty miles away. Her youngest daughter, Christine, was active in sports through her school, she played volleyball, basket ball, tennis, softball, and was on the track team.

It was on one of these outings, when Christine was still too young to drive herself, that Diane was driving to pick her up after that season's sport practice. She was running late and nearly ran over a man crossing the street. She stopped to ask if he was okay, and sometimes life's little meetings work out for the best. The man's name, of course, was Jason Fox, and he said he was pretty shaken up, but thought he would start feeling better if she would show him some kindness and write down her phone number for him. At first, she was concerned, all of the men she had dated she had been acquainted with or set up with by a friend or family member. For all she knew, this guy was just another loser. It was his eyes that convinced her that he was a gentleman, and she gave him her phone number.

Jason took the phone number and stuck it in a shirt pocket after looking at it. He thanked her for not crippling him for life and said he would be around for a while if she was so inclined to spend a little time. She had been inclined, but other matters needed to be tended to first. Her daughter, Christine, first and foremost, and she had been seeing one of the deputy sheriffs lately, and really didn't want to get something started with someone else while she was in that relationship.

Jason hadn't given much thought to the phone number Diane had given him. For all he knew, it could've been the phone number of an area nursing home. Then one night, around eight o'clock, when he was sitting by himself in an all-but-empty truck stop restaurant, feeling miserable because it was the first year's anniversary of his second divorce, he happened across the phone number Diane had given him. It had been a couple of weeks since she had given him the number, and he thought, What the hell, nothing to lose. He dialed the access number for his calling card, and then dialed her number.

"Hello?" she had answered on the second ring.

"Hello." Jason had been shocked for some reason to catch her at home. "Is this Diane?"

"Yes," she said slowly.

"Hi," Jason said. He was starting to sweat. "Uh, you probably don't remember me, but I almost got run over by your car a couple of weeks ago." What in the hell was he doing, he asked himself. He was just calling her to maybe talk for a while, not to see how fast he could make the biggest fool of himself.

"Let me see," she said slowly again. Of course she remembered him, she had not thought of much else since. She had wondered why he hadn't called, had even spent some nights trying to will the phone to ring, but she was going to be damned if she let him know that. In fact, she was going to see just how far she could play out this little drama. Then she continued, "You were crossing the street in front of the bank, right?"

"No, I was crossing the street in front of the video store," he said a bit perplexed. What did he have here, a crazy lady that tried to run so many men down a week that she couldn't keep them straight?

"Right, right, the bank sets kind of caddy-corner from the video store," Diane said, smiling to herself. She was so happy that he had called, but it would be better to play it cool.

"Did I catch you at a bad time?" he asked. "If so I can call later."

"Oh, no," Diane said, "this is fine, but I won't be able to talk too long."

"Okay, I won't keep you long, I just wanted to call, and say hi, and see how you were doing," he said. Why was he so damned nervous?

They talked for a while longer, almost for about an hour. The more Jason heard, the more he liked, but he wasn't going to be so quick to tell her that. In the coming months, they talked quit a bit on the phone. Jason told her that he wasn't really looking for a relationship, but with being on the road, he just wanted to have someone, a woman, to talk to. On the rare occasions that Jason made it through Springfield, usually every other weekend, he and Diane would meet for dinner or coffee.

Diane told him about her dating a cop, and he was nice enough, but he wanted to take the relationship to the next level, and she didn't know if she wanted that, or if she wanted that with him. Jason did the best thing he could have ever imagined for Diane in the next few weeks, he listened to her. He didn't offer unsolicited advice, he didn't offer another man's point of view. He did the one thing she needed and that she had never experienced with a man, he listened, he listened, he listened. While he listened, he learned, and the more he listened and learned, the more he liked. Before long, he felt something he thought he never wanted to feel ever again. He wanted to tell Diane how he felt about her, he thought he loved her, but what if he told her that, and she never wanted to speak to him again.

Finally, on the night he called to tell her, she told him she was going to have to back off a little. It seemed that her boyfriend, Gary, had tried to call her on several occasions, only to find her line busy for hours at a time, and quite frankly he wanted to know what was going on. Diane told Jason not to stop calling, but instead of calling four times a week, to only call once a week. She went on to explain that her boyfriend had been really understanding through all of this, but he was starting to feel neglected. Jason could hear the excitement in her voice when she told him that her boyfriend had really eased off on the pressure he had been putting on her, and that maybe there might be something there with him after all. Jason told a little white lie, and told Diane that he understood, and wished her happiness. He also gave her a phone number, telling her that it was his dispatcher's phone number at work. He also told her his truck number, and that if she needed, or just wanted to talk to him, that was how she could get into contact with him.

When Jason had hung up the phone, he was saddened by this turn of events. He reasoned it was better that he hadn't told her how he felt. She had said once a week, he thought. The following week would seem like a month long. He was wrong.

The third day after talking to Diane, the message light lit up on his highway master as he was heading west on I-70 in Ohio. The message was from his dispatcher, of course, and it read, "Some woman named Diane called for you. Wants you to call her. Says you have her number. Says the sooner the better."

Jason was at the twenty-mile marker when he received the message. He exited the interstate at Exit Ten and found a parking space at one of the two truck stops there. He all but ran to get to a phone. His hands and fingers didn't want to work fast enough to suit him, but he finally got her number dialed.

"Hello," Jason heard Diane almost blurted into the phone as it was snatched it up on the first ring.

"Diane, is everything okay? Are you all right? What's happened?" Jason asked rapidly, hoping he didn't sound like a blithering idiot to her.

"Where have you been? Why haven't you called me? Where are you? When can I see you?" she was hoping he wouldn't hang up on her for being so blatant, and demanding.

"Diane," Jason said puzzled, "I haven't called you because you asked me to limit my calls to once a week. I thought I was doing the right thing."

"I know," she admitted, "that was my fault. I've been miserable not hearing from you. I've missed talking to you. I want you in my life, Jason."

"What about the cop?" Jason had to know.

"He made a comment last night about how stupid, fat, and lazy truck drivers are, and that every one of them is a disease-carrying skirt chaser," she told him, her anger starting to mount.

"Well, he's not too far from the truth," Jason said, hating to admit it.

"Jason," Diane said in a low soft, sexy voice. Jason had never called a 1-900 phone number, but if he had, this is the voice he would have wanted to hear. Diane continued in the same voice, "I know one truck driver that isn't like that. When I talked to your dispatcher today, he said you were heading in for a couple of days. If you are so inclined, Mr. Fox, I want to dominate most of your time."

Jason was about to take off like a rocket. He had never been this excited his whole life. Did she know what she was setting herself up for? He was speechless, but he knew he needed to say something. Something intelligible would be nice, and he would just as soon as he got his breathing under control, so he could make his voice be heard over the pounding of his heart. An image of Red Skelton in one of his acts where he was trying to clear his throat came to mind. That's what helped him to break his silence because thinking of Red Skelton loudly clearing his throat over and over while he crossed his eyes made Jason snicker.

"Jason?" Diane asked. Jason heard the reluctance in her voice, "Are you laughing at me?"

"Absolutely not," Jason sobered quickly. He knew she was sensitive and delicate right now. He needed to tell her something to ease her mind. "Diane, I've missed you, too. I really want to see you. I'm going to hang up now and head that way, but I want to say this, and then hang up the phone. If you don't want to see me after this, then I will understand. I love you." He hung up the phone before she had the chance to react or respond.

It's approximately five hundred and twenty miles from where Jason was to Strafford, Missouri, and it normally takes eight to nine hours for a truck to make the trip if the driver obeys the speed limits for the different states. Jason drove it in seven and a half hours.

If there had been any doubts Jason had about how Diane would react to his proclamation of love for her, she dismissed them soon enough, not with words, but with actions. Now two years later, she couldn't be happier, she had found her true love and soul mate.

After she showered, she dressed, did her hair, and applied just enough makeup to bring out her natural highlights. That was one of the things Jason loved about her, she didn't wear a lot of make up. "Low Maintenance" was the term she preferred to use.

She stood in front of the mirror one last time and looked at herself. Diane was about five foot six, and since it's not polite to ask a woman her weight, suffice it to say she was not skinny and by no means overweight. She had light brown hair, with blond highlights. She had an hourglass figure with full hips. Her eyes were blue with a tinge of green. Probably her most striking features were her breasts. They weren't artificially enhanced, she had developed early, and they had continued to grow throughout puberty. She had become very self-conscious about them when she was in high school and had hid them behind books as often as she could. Her other striking features were her bright smile and lovable personality. People who knew both Diane and Jason, often told him that he was the best thing that ever happened to her, and he was quick to reply that it ran both ways. There were very few people that didn't like Diane, most of the time she had a smile on her face and a kind word on her lips. She decided she had enough time to go to the tanning bed before she started her shift, so pulling the locked door behind her, she closed it. She started her car, a navy blue 1994 Ford Thunderbird, and drove to the tanning salon.

After tanning, she drove to work and clocked in. The day was clear, and not too hot for it to be the first week of August. Diane started her shift by checking her station, then she wiped off the unoccupied tables assigned to her and made sure she had coffee and tea brewing.

As mentioned before, Diane was a happy, friendly, gregarious person. She had been waiting tables off and on most of her life, and with that came experience. Not on the job experience, but rather after-the-job experience. She knew that most truckers were just lonely, Jason had been a good example of that, but there were others who were different. Diane learned early not to make excessive eye contact with certain men. For some reason, some of these truckers thought that if a waitress or any woman made eye contact with them or even showed a bit of a smile, something in that trucker's brain told him that that woman wanted them. In her life, she had had more than one driver wait for her to end her shift because he took her meaning wrong. She would make her rounds with the coffee and iced tea. She would speak kindly to her customers, and maybe call them sugar or darlin' or hon', but what they seemed to not realize is that was how she earned her tips, by being attentive, maybe say a kind word, showing a brief smile, or listening to a joke. When she did these things, she was doing her job. When she wanted sex, there was only one man that would do, and he probably had his ears laid back and was hauling ass across Texas right now. By the time he left to go out on the road again, he would be walking like John Wayne if she had her way about it.

The waitress staff always kept a small television set turned on to catch bits and pieces of favorite programs, and to watch the news broadcasts, especially the weather. The old timers that frequented the truck stop and used it as their meeting place like a small town coffee shop were fond of saying of Missouri weather, "If you don't like the weather, hang around a couple of days, maybe it'll change to something you do like." The older generation would nod almost in unison at this as if it were the gospel right out of the New Testament. Some of them even amended this by saying, "A couple of days, hell, just wait a couple of hours, and it'll change."

It was time for the six o'clock news cast, and the dining area was not too crowded. The top story was still the young woman that had been found dead on the front steps of one of the trucking companies in the Springfield area. Authorities weren't releasing too many details as of yet, but what they did release was her name, age at the time of her death, and current address. The reporter went on to say that all the police were releasing at this time was that her throat had been cut, and she had been found wrapped in a large piece of plastic. The girls on the waitress staff all exchanged glances then went about their work.

A little over an hour later, Diane saw a familiar white Peterbilt with a stuffed Wile E. Coyote strapped to the grill pull onto the truck stop parking lot, headed towards a place to park.

Chapter 3

The previous week on a truck stop parking lot, in the early morning hours in Ontario, California, a shadowy figure was making his final plans. The figure, Jack, waited in the shadows of a building where he could see the employee's entrance. He was patient, knew the young woman he intended to victimize well enough to know her shift would end in the next fifteen minutes. He had been here before many times, had seen her, but had never spoken to her, and had tried to stay out of her eyesight. He knew that sometimes after her shift, she would go across the street and sell her body to any trucker willing to match her price. She did not always do this, but only on the times when unexpected expenses arose as they sometimes do.

She had two small children that she was raising on her own with the help of her retired parents. She was a good mother, she didn't beat her babies or neglect them or make them feel unwanted, and after this morning, they would miss her terribly. She married young, her parents granted her permission to marry the guy that she became pregnant with when she was in her junior year of high school. She dropped out of school, reluctantly, and devoted her time to preparing for the baby and adjusting to married life. The guy she married was a few years older than her, and this wasn't his first marriage—or baby.

After the birth of their baby, the young couple started working on baby number two. When the deed was done, and baby number two was conceived, the young woman's husband was killed in a work-related accident. His employer's insurance carrier paid the claim, and the young mother moved back home with her parents, after they all but begged her to do so.

She started trying to put her life back together. She was working full time at the truck stop, going to night school to get her G.E.D., and coping with the loss of her husband. Although theirs hadn't been a perfect marriage, few, if any are, he did love and provide for her and the one baby he had fathered. She refused to be a burden to her parents, they were retired and living on a fixed income. Anyone who has children knows their needs are constant. Their clothes never fit for long, as well as their shoes, and then there are the diapers, and the formula, sometimes it seems the list never ends. She refused to apply for the state help. Being Hispanic, she figured, she would be typecast, and she didn't want that for herself or her babies. So when things got tight, she turned to prostitution.

Jack had seen her more than once climbing in and out of trucks, selling herself, and it made him sick. His plan was simple, kidnap her, use her as often as he could in the next few days, and then dump her body after he had taken her life. He had the perfect dumping ground, a city that had more trucking companies inside its limits than any other city of its size in the country. What was more, she wouldn't be the only one. He had plans for other women, or whores as he thought of them, that he knew were doing the same thing as this one. As the small window sticker says, "So many women, so little time." He would treat them all the same—and dump their corpses in Springfield, Missouri.

Although this wasn't the first time he had killed, it would be the first time he would do it in this manner. He had killed for Uncle Sam during his military service for years, and shortly after being asked to leave the service, he had taken his anger out on some unsuspecting women in this country, moving from state to state, city to city. Those victims, he thought, had been unfortunate casualties, and now he had a chance to redeem himself.

When he had been young, growing up, his stepfather had driven a big truck. Sometimes he had gone over the road with his stepfather, learning all he could about this career in case he ever needed to fall back on it.

When he was a child, his mother worried about the sudden appearance of his invisible friend. His stepfather told her not to worry, most children had imaginary friends.

The whispery voices started in his head when he entered puberty. They were relentless. Sometimes they overlapped, other times they chanted the same message in unison. One voice would suggest something, and the other voices would cheerfully agree, saying things like, "Go on. What will it hurt? No one will find out, we will protect you. We are your friends."

One of the things the voices had suggested was that he kill his stepfather. He balked at this, but the sly whispery voices convinced him it was all right and God's will. They said, "Go on. Help God along. No one will miss him. Do it! Do it! Do it!" So before going into the military, he had done away with his stepfather. His stepfather's only crime was to become useless to this killer, and besides this killer didn't want his stepfather sleeping with his mother anymore. So on a lonely stretch of road, late at night, he waited for his stepfather to pull over to the shoulder of the roadway to relieve his bladder, and he had sprung his trap. He had been following his stepfather in a borrowed pickup truck, and waited for his stepfather to finish "squirting the dirt" as he was often fond of saying. As his stepfather made ready to climb back into the semi, Jack simply drove the driver's side of the pickup truck passing by the driver's side of the semi and held a long sharp blade out the window. The blade made a clean cut, cutting deep into his stepfather's neck, severing muscle, tissue, blood veins, and nearly decapitating the unsuspecting truck driver. Of course, the most rewarding part of this was the recognition in the eyes of the stepfather as he realized who his killer was. Jack simply drove away, leaving his stepfather to bleed to death. Afterwards, the cleanup hadn't been much, and he had gotten away with it.

Now he waited for the young woman to emerge from the building. He had watched her before, as mentioned, and she never varied from this part of her routine. She stepped out the door, calling a farewell over her shoulder to an unseen coworker, and before she had turned to face the direction in which she was walking, a man's hand holding an ether-soaked rag clamped itself over her mouth from behind. She overcame her shock and tried to struggle, but he wrapped his other arm around her waist, yanked her backwards into him, and shoved his own crotch forward so she could feel his erection.

Her eyes were so wide from fear, they seemed in danger of popping from their sockets. She tried to twist away from the hateful stiffness she could feel pressing against her buttocks through her jeans. The hand across her mouth kept hard pressure, and the horrible odor from the rag made her weak. She kicked, tried to scream, tried to bite the hand across her mouth, tried to stomp on her attacker's feet, and even flailed with her arms and hands, but nothing worked, and now she was starting to weaken from the ether. She turned her head enough to see her attacker's face, and was puzzled to see that her attacker strongly resembled the character that Patrick Swayze portrayed in the movie Point Break. Before she went completely out, her attacker pulled her close and tightly to him, and whispered to her, "Good morning, my name is Jack, and we're going to have such a good time while it lasts."

That was the last thing she heard or felt before she passed out. What she experienced the next few days before her death was unlike anything she could have ever imagined.

33

What the police weren't releasing was the fact that the young woman had been alive until just a couple of hours before she was found. She had been wrapped in a piece of thick, clear plastic. Her naked body had been rolled up inside the plastic, much like the way a person would wrap something breakable inside a rug or blanket. The ends of the plastic had been taped shut with duct tape. Her hair was wet as if she had just stepped out of the shower. All of her clothes had been washed, dried, folded neatly, and left beside her corpse. All of her personal belongings had been likewise left beside her clothes with a note that was later determined to be in her handwriting and on her own stationary. The note simply asked that whoever found her, would they please send her things back home to her family in California.

The police called in the FBI when it was confirmed that the dead woman was who her ID proclaimed. Her personal belongings were gone through. Her wallet contained fifty dollars in varying denominations of U.S. currency. She had two credit cards, both of which were at their maximums and a few photographs of children that'resembled her in looks. The remaining contents of her purse were nothing out of the ordinary, a comb, two tubes of lip gloss, a makeup compact, an address book, a pack of chewing gum, two ink pens, and a few unused tissues. Two unused condoms still in their wrappers were the only unusual items. All of her personal effects were fingerprinted, and the results would take a few days.

Forensics went over the body, looking for foreign hairs, fibers, blood. They took swabs of all of her body orifices and cavities. They scraped her fingernails and checked her skin for fingerprints, and they awaited those results also. An autopsy was performed, although no one disputed what had killed her. Two of the details the police had asked the press and news media to keep quiet about was that not only did this poor woman die from having her throat cut, whoever did it, cut her throat to the spine and nearly decapitated her. The other was what the killer referred to as scalping, the hair and skin of the pelvic area was cut away. One reason for the autopsy was to try to find some clue of how she had traveled from California to Missouri. Maybe it was only wishful thinking, but nothing out of the ordinary turned up.

Next, the FBI started looking into her background. She had been in her late twenties, Hispanic, a single mother of two toddlers that stayed with her when she was at work or on her rare occasion out. She had been employed at a truck stop in Ontario, California. She had been reported missing two days prior to her body being found. Only a few witnesses could remember her leaving work, but one of the girls she worked with said she had been seen talking to a man at her car several nights after she had clocked out to go home. This witness didn't think too much about this since her friend was attractive, friendly, and popular with the guys. The description the witness gave of the man at the car was sketchy, she said he was about five foot nine or ten, not overweight, was pretty sure he was white. He had shoulder length hair that he pulled back with a rubber band, and it was dark but couldn't tell for certain of the hair color. The FBI thanked her and moved on to her car, which had been parked behind the truck stop, instead of out front where the employees parked. The witness had stated she saw her friend get into her car, but then she had gotten busy and had to return to work. They went over her car with a fine-toothed comb and found some amazing results. There was foreign matter in the car, all right, but not all belonging to one individual.

When they investigated further, the FBI found that to supplement her income to help feed her children, sometimes she turned to prostitution or running drugs for dealers.

When the other test results came back, only her prints were on the condom packages, but there were multiple prints on the other items. The other fingerprints were small, like a child's print. They checked the prints against the prints the victim had on file in case her children ever came up missing.

The swabbing test results were no help. Whoever had committed this crime had washed the victim's body—at a car wash is what the evidence pointed to—and washed the victim's clothes at a public laundry. It would take some time, but everyone connected with the case was determined to solve this crime.

Then there was the note, a computer printout. The note read:

Dear boss,
    Some have said that if jack the ripper were alive today, he would definitely be caught. Let's put that to the test. Here is your first victim. More will follow. I will make it as easy for you as I can, I will bring them to you. It will be like an Easter egg hunt, you will know they are here, but you will have to find them. There will be at least one a week. My trademark will be the scalping of the pussy area. So begins our game, wish me luck.
    Your new friend,

Jack
Catch me if you can.

The FBI called for help, preferably someone with knowledge of the Jack the Ripper murders. Their request was answered in the form of Dixie Crenshaw.

Dixie Crenshaw was thirty, five foot ten, slender, brunette, very attractive, and all business. People who knew her well knew she was lonely, not a loner, but lonely. She had attended high school in Dandridge, Tennessee and had gone into the marines after graduation where she served as an M.P. After her four-year hitch with the Few and the Proud, she went to college on the G.I. Bill, getting a degree in criminology and psychology. From there, she applied and was invited to work with the FBI, and she had accepted.

While in high school, she had written a report for one of her classes on the Jack the Ripper and White- chapel murders. She had stated a lot of facts, such as dates, places, and the Scotland Yard list of suspects, but offered no opinion as to the killer's identity. Instead, she stated that she thought it important to learn from these crimes, because history might someday repeat itself. She had gotten an A on the report, and Jack the Ripper was linked to her from that time on. She wasn't obsessed with the crimes, but people who knew her or worked closely with her, knew it was one of her interests. Now, she was being called on to put her talents and theories to work, and she had no clear idea how to go about getting started. The letter that the FBI had received was right out of the past. She was determined to do her part.

Although she had never been to this part of the country, she had researched the area. Springfield is situated near the heart of the Ozark Hills, about thirty-five miles north of Branson, Missouri. Branson has a double claim to fame, the first being made famous by Harold Bell Wright and his story of the Matthews family in the book The Shepherd of the Hills, and the second being local talented entertainers opening and operating music theaters along the famous Hwy. 76 in Branson. Some of country music's well-known entertainers moved to the area and opened theaters there. Then there were the amusement parks in the area, one of which could seemingly transport a person back in time.

Laura Ingalls Wilder came through the area and settled in Mansfield, Missouri where she wrote the Little House books.

During the time of the Harold Bell Wright novel, there were vigilantes, known as the Baldknobbers, that roamed the Ozark Hills.

During the Civil War, George Todd, Bloody Bill Anderson, and Quantrail's Raiders operated along the Missouri-Kansas border. Dixie remembered her father telling her once that there was fighting along the Kansas-Missouri border seven years before the Civil War was officially under way.

Frank and Jesse James were from Missouri. Missourians referred to them as the James Boys. Along with the James Boys, Thomas Coleman Younger and his brothers were from Missouri. The James/Younger gang robbed banks, trains, and stage coaches. Jesse and Frank evaded capture for sixteen years until Jesse's death on April 2, 1882.

Some famous Missourians included the thirty-third president of the United States, Harry S Truman, science fiction writer Robert A. Heinlein, the music group, Ozark Mountain Daredevils, Brad Pitt, Bob Barker, golfer Payne Stewart, Sheryl Crowe, Mark Twain, NASCAR drivers Jamie McCurry and Carl Edwards to name a few.

The largest battleship ever built by the United States was named the U.S.S. Missouri.

Dixie did all of her research of Missouri, Springfield in particular, from Quantico, Virginia looking for any similarities between Springfield, Missouri and London, England. She found none. She could have seen comparisons between say Seattle, Washington and London, England. Both of those cities shared the same type of climate, rainy, and foggy in the early morning hours. Seattle, also in some form, seemed to draw serial killers, the Green River Killer and Ted Bundy to name a couple, but she did not see any similarities between Springfield and London.

Three things became blaringly apparent to Dixie as she did her research about Missouri. Number one was the location of the state, it was positioned near the center of the country. Number two was that Interstate 44 was a major alleyway for moving goods. Part of the interstate followed the famed Route 66, and provided a link from the Northeast to the Southwest. Travelers going east or west had the option of using I-44 to connect I-70 and I-40 without going through Kansas City, thus saving them hundreds of miles. And, number three was the trucking industry. Springfield, Missouri, along with the surrounding communities of Strafford, Nixa, Ozark, to name a few, had more trucking companies within their city limits per capita than any other American city of the same size. Dixie counted over one hundred trucking companies that were either based around Springfield, Missouri, or had terminals there. The combination of the location of the city and state, and I-44, made Springfield, Missouri a midway point for the trucking industry hauling freight from Los Angles to the New England states, for example.

Dixie drew no conclusions, but she had her suspicions. If there was a killer who fancied himself to be the likeness of Jack the Ripper (the name Jack hinted a suggestion to that), then time would tell. Jack the Ripper had committed half a dozen grizzly murders in London, England's East End known as Whitechappel, between the months of August and November of the year 1888. The murders commenced and ceased without warning, and stood unsolved for over one hundred years. Novelist Patricia Cornwell had written a very convincing book claiming to reveal the identity of Jack the Ripper. Dixie had read the book and agreed with the conclusion.

Dixie came to Springfield via flight. She arrived in the city on the afternoon after the young woman had been found. Her hotel accommodations had been prearranged for her by the FBI not far from the airport. Upon arriving, her contact, Special Agent Thomas Bradford, met her at the airport and chauffeured her to the hotel.

"Any idea why the killer picked this area as his dumping ground, Agent Bradford?" Dixie asked, as they drove out of the airport, she readjusted her wrist watch to Central Time.

"None, and please call me Tom," he answered simply. Thomas Bradford had been with the FBI for close to thirty years. Like Dixie, he had military training. He had joined the army after high school and had been in the Special Forces in Viet Nam. He did two tours of duty, went to college on the G.I. bill, and applied to the FBI, being accepted not long afterwards. He was of average build, in his early fifties, standing about five foot nine inches, and weighing around one hundred and ninety pounds. He had a full head of salt-and-pepper-colored hair that was cut conservatively. He wasn't a native of Missouri but had lived there for the past ten years.

"Okay, Tom," Dixie said smiling. "When can I see the body?"

"I can take you there after we get you settled in, if you like," he answered her.

"Yes, that would be nice," she said. She noticed a wedding band that circled the ring finger of his left hand. In fact, the twirling motion he did with the thumb and little finger of the same hand to the ring drew Dixie's attention to it. At first, she thought it was a nervous habit, then she saw he was actually spinning the ring on his finger with the motion. She said, "If that will interfere with your family plans, I can find my own way over there."

"What?" he asked perplexed, giving her a quizzical look. Then, realizing she had spotted his ring, he said, "No, that won't interfere with anything like that."

"I wouldn't want to be a burden," she said.

"You won't," he said. "I lost my wife about four years ago. She was murdered, much like the way this victim was. I have a personal interest in this case. The FBI is allowing me to be your shadow and your liaison to local law enforcement for as long as you're in town, to offer you any assistance I can, in any capacity I can. I still wear the ring as a tribute to her and her memory."

"I'm sorry," Dixie said. "I had no idea."

"That's all right," Tom reassured her. "Every day gets easier. Now, I need to give you a word of caution. Not every agent assigned to this area is happy to see you here. I think they feel they are capable of handling this case without outside help. Just something to keep in mind."

"How many agents are we talking about?" Dixie inquired.

"Six, seven counting me," Tom answered. "I'm not one of the groups unhappy to see you here. I will help you as much as I can."

Later that night, she viewed the body of the victim and couldn't believe the cruelty of her murderer. Dixie went through all the evidence and the personal effects found with the body. Although, this young woman had turned to prostitution, she couldn't remember any state that punished such a crime with death. Her job as profiler had begun, and she would embrace the opportunity.

Chapter 4

Selena, or Sally as Diane called her, sat at her desk looking at her computer screen. As part of her job, she was given a list of drivers and their corresponding truck numbers. She then entered those truck numbers into a computer program that tracked that truck through a satellite tracking system. The system gave tracking updates every fifteen minutes of every truck in the system, or every truck in the Blanket Transportation fleet. The system also tracked the drivers' input into the system. For example, every driver was required to input data as to his or her current status under the load he or she was assigned. The system's main menu offered several choices for this purpose, but the ones the drivers mostly used were load confirmation, arrived at shipper, loaded, arrived at consignee, and empty.

She sat in her swivel chair with her right leg pulled underneath her left, and the shoe of her left foot barely dangling on the end of her toes while that leg made little arching motions. She would do this most of the night switching legs alternately. When she got to Jason's truck number, a small surprised laugh escaped her because he was almost to Springfield. She noticed that his load data input was current. She knew from watching his progress in the past and talking to Diane that when he got in the mood to run, neither hell nor high water would hold him back. When she entered Keith's truck number, she saw he was in Youngstown, Ohio. He was scheduled to reload there later that night, and then head this way. She crossed through both truck numbers with a lead pencil as she had done with the previous truck numbers she had entered into the program.

Selena was five foot seven with black hair, dark eyes, clear skin, and like Diane, she wasn't really skinny but by not means obese either. Like Diane, she was a very attractive woman, and also like Diane, she didn't think of herself as attractive. Both women felt this way about themselves, and to men like Jason and Sally's husband Billy, that added to their beauty. Jason had always thought Selena resembled Catherine Zeta-Jones.

Selena had moved to the Springfield, Missouri area from the Tulsa area with her family when she was around eight years old. She was enrolled into school, met Diane, and the two became the best of friends. They were together as much as their parents allowed. Diane was raised on a farm and had certain chores to do every morning before school and every afternoon after school. Selena's parents wouldn't allow her to help Diane in the mornings with the chores, but had no objections with her helping with them in the afternoons once her parents had met Diane's parents and were satisfied they were good people.

As the years went by, the girls still remained close. They traded secrets on make up, hair care, clothes, and, of course, boys. They even double-dated when they both were old enough by their parents' standards. When they were in their junior year of high school, Selena's father was transferred back to Tulsa by his employer. It was a tearful parting for the two girls, and they promised to stay in touch with each other, and they had.

After she graduated from high school, Selena went to college in Tulsa to earn a business degree. One night, while walking from the literary library to her car to go home, she was attacked and nearly raped. She fought back and escaped. That very night, she reported the incident to campus security, and the woman that took the report told Selena about a self-defense seminar that was very good, offered that week. Not only did Selena take the seminar, she liked it so much, she joined the Tae Kwon Do school, or Do-Jang as it's called in Korea, where the martial art originated. Two and a half years later, Selena graduated a first degree black belt.

After college, she moved back to Springfield, Missouri. She and Diane had remained in contact through the years, in fact when Mark had abused Diane, Selena had driven to be with Diane and had offered to do to Mark what Dewey had done.

One day not very long after moving back to Springfield, Selena was at the mall and accidentally bumped into Billy, Diane's younger brother by two years. After apologizing profusely, he calmly said her name. She looked at him and maybe really saw him for the first time. He bought her lunch that day, even though she protested that they could go Dutch, but he wouldn't hear of it. They began to date, and two years later, they were married. They had remained married for twenty years, and had two children, a girl and a boy. Both of their children were in their teens, and the girl was about to graduate high school.

When Diane had met Jason, started seeing him, and broke off her relationship with Gary, Selena had questioned Diane's sanity. Although Selena had never been around truck drivers before, she had always heard the old stereotypes and was fearful that Diane was setting herself up for a painful disappointment. In fact, Selena had taken the time to drive to Diane's home one night after work to talk with her best friend and sister-in-law.

"What do you really know about him?" Selena asked as the two of them sat at either ends of the sofa, both drinking iced tea. The evening was cool but comfortable, and Diane had opened the bay windows of the living room where the two women sat.

"I know he respects me," Diane answered. "When Gary had gotten so upset about Jason calling so often, I asked Jason to back his calls off to once a week, and he did."

"Being around someone once every two weeks is a lot different than being with someone constantly," Selena had protested.

"He's honorable, thoughtful, funny, and cute," Diane said, "and when I am around him, he never fails to open doors for me, pays for things when we go out, and pays close attention to details of our conversations and what's important to me."

"It could be an act, be careful." Selena warned, then added, "Diane, I've known you for a long time, and I love you like a sister. I know you, of all people, deserve to be happy, and I've seen the way you've been treated by other men. I just don't want this to be a repeating behavioral pattern that you're stuck in. This guy could be like all the rest."

"I understand you're concern, Sally," Diane said, smiling slightly, "really, I do, but Jason is not like anyone I've ever met. On top or everything else, you know how sensitive I am about the size of my breasts?"

"Yes," Selena said, feeling a bit uneasy about talking about such a subject. She knew how Diane felt about her breasts. It had always bothered Diane when a boy approached her to talk to her, and he had acted as if he were talking to her breasts because that's where his eyes remained the whole time. "I can't imagine how frustrating it is for you. Even now when we're in our forties, do you still encounter that?"

"All the time," Diane confessed. "Gary refused to keep his hands off of them. The rest of the men I've been with were the same way, they acted like they tolerated me to get to them."

"And you're telling me that this guy, this Jason, isn't like that?" Selena asked as if she didn't believe any of this.

"That's exactly what I'm saying," Diane said. "Oh, don't get me wrong, he knows they're there and what to do with them, but he doesn't push the rest of me aside to get to them. He has never failed to take the time to listen when I've had the need to voice my opinion. I've never had a man do that for me."

"Diane!" Selena exclaimed. "Are you saying you've already slept with him?"

"Yes," Diane admitted, a bit embarrassed. "I have, and it was unlike anything I've ever experienced."

"What?" Selena asked, sounding a little sarcastic. "Does he have something other men don't?"

"Well," Diane hesitated a moment, her cheeks turning pink again. "All I can say is that he's a true gentleman. He thinks of me first, even in sex. He has never pushed me any further than I want to go, he has never degraded me, and he takes 'no' for an answer. I've never had that with any man."

"So he's considerate and good in bed," Selena said. "What about his personal habits, and does he keep himself clean?"

"He doesn't go around filthy. He has all of this teeth, from what I can see. He's not really fat, but he does have a little bit of a belly. He does smoke, but he doesn't smoke in the house or my car. He can cook and knows how to wash the dishes. He even knows what the clothes washer and dryer look like, what they're used for, and how they work. Not even Mark did all that," Diane said, counting each point off on her fingertips. "He's even-tempered, doesn't make it a habit to downgrade people, and even takes the time to talk to Christine, and doesn't ignore her. On top of all that, he raises the seat on the toilet when he pees, and puts it back down when he's done."

"I just don't want to see you get hurt again, Diane," Selena said, trying to convey her feelings of concern to her friend.

"I know you don't, Sally," Diane responded, then added. "Haven't you ever met anyone, man or woman, that you felt so comfortable around? It's like that with Jason, I feel comfortable with him. He respects my wishes and doesn't take me for granted."

It was pleasantly different having this type of conversation with Diane, Selena thought. Most of the time, hell 99.99 percent of the time, Diane acted as if she didn't have a serious bone in her body. Diane was a fun-loving person, most of the time she had a smile on her face. Selena also knew Diane to be quick with a joke, and would be the first to laugh at herself. On top of all this, Selena also knew Diane wasn't easily fooled by people. Another thing Selena knew about Diane was she wasn't prone to talk badly about people, in fact, Selena could count on one hand the number of times Diane had said a bad word about Mark. In fact, Diane and Mark had gotten along better in the last few years than they ever had. All totaled, Selena knew

Diane was well-rounded. She knew Diane was lonely and wanted to find someone to be happy with, but Selena also knew Diane would never compromise herself to that end.

After talking for a short while longer about a variety of other subjects, Selena left for her own home, feeling a little better about Jason. While she had been doubtful about him before she met him, she was his biggest supporter when Selena finally met Jason and had the opportunity to get to know him. She actually liked him being around for family dinners at Diane's parents' house on the holidays and special events such as birthdays. He tried to bring Diane something every time he came through Springfield, and it seemed he tried to remember other people as well. When her daughter had gone through her phase of collecting rocks, Jason had helped her by bringing her rocks from the various states he passed through. It was small things like that that made one like this guy. Jason and Selena also had the Tae Kwon Do in common, although neither of them worked out that much any more. Selena did stretch every so often and perform a few moves to keep the rust worked out.

When Diane and Jason announced their engagement, Selena was all but their head cheerleader. In fact, when other family members or close friends of the family questioned if Diane knew what she was doing by marrying a truck driver, Selena was quick to point out that Jason wasn't just any truck driver. Jason had come a long way also, Selena thought. She knew part of his history, about the two previously failed marriages, and the children that didn't want anything to do with him. What Selena knew most about Jason was that he loved and adored Diane, and she knew she didn't have to worry about Diane as long as Jason was around.

After checking all the truck numbers off her list, Selena stood up and stretched. She walked to the soda machine, bought a diet soda, and sat back down at her desk. She had seen the same newscast that Diane and her coworkers had seen earlier, and wondered who the young woman could have been and what circumstances had brought her to this end.

Selena became busy by answering phone calls from various drivers. Some drivers complained that their "Highway Master" system wasn't working properly. For these drivers, she looked up the information they needed on her computer and relayed that information over the phone to them. Some drivers complained of having to sit where they were until morning for their next load information. To these drivers, she calmly replied that she could not give them something she did not have, and that every effort would be made to get them loaded and on the move as soon as possible. These drivers usually grumbled something about how she wouldn't like it if she were made to work all night and not get paid for it. Selena sympathized with these drivers, but in truth, her hands were tied. If there were actually loads to be dispatched, she would have dispatched them, but there weren't. On some occasions, there were loads to be hauled but with a hold order on them. Maybe a load had been promised to a certain driver because of special circumstances. Maybe there was more than one driver sitting in a certain area with one load going to a destination hundreds of miles away. If one of those waiting drivers lived near the delivery area, it made sense to dispatch that driver on that load. On other occasions, it depended on the freight of a certain area. If the freight was slow in an area, it made sense to lay a driver over until the next morning to try to get a load from that area, rather than ask that driver to drive possibly hundreds of miles for another load. The problem there was that not all drivers got lay over pay, and Selena understood that, but didn't necessarily agree with it.

She had a small radio at her desk tuned to a local station that played light rock. She also had a television set at her disposal that she could watch as long as she kept her work up. Selena wasn't one to watch a lot of sports, but on occasion, she did watch a football game with Billy. To her, it was more fun to see if she could get Billy to bet with her on the outcome of the game. The bet wasn't what bothered Billy, it was the payoff if he lost. So far when Selena had won, his debt had been to do the supper dishes after the kids were in bed wearing nothing more than an apron, or to vacuum the carpet the same way, or wearing only his cowboy boots and cowboy hat. She could be ornery at times, and she took as well as she gave. She never welshed on a bet, and Billy could come up with some pretty humorous stuff too. She smiled to herself at these memories and thought how nice it was to be in love with someone like Billy, who trusted her completely, and there was no doubt or question that she trusted him. They had been married for nearly twenty years, and in this day and age, that was saying a lot. They didn't always get along or see things the same way, but they always respected, trusted, and, of course, loved each other. When Billy wanted to go hunting for a weekend, Selena found other things to occupy her time until his return, and likewise, Billy never questioned her motives for doing what she wanted. They were good together and good for each other. Yes, Selena thought, it was very good to be in love.

Selena hadn't worked here very long, she had always worked at banks.

One day while talking with Jason, she mentioned how there was a scandal at her workplace, and she was being set up to take the fall. Jason told her of an opening for the 3:00 P.M. to 11:00 P.M. shift for a dispatcher at Blanket Transportation. She had applied, and at first the owner of the company thought Selena was overqualified for the job, then he made her another offer. He told her that if she would try this position for a short time, and she got comfortable with it and was good at it, he would give her the chance of her own dispatch board with her choice of drivers, and the chance to make the kind of money she was making at her last job. Not only that, he offered her the option of advancement through the company by way of sales and brokerage. Selena was puzzled by this man's attitude, a man she had never met before this morning was making her such a tremendous offer.

"Sir," Selena asked, "why would you make such an offer to me, someone you know really nothing about?"

He smiled as he leaned back in his chair to answer her, "You're qualifications are very good. You have an excellent list of references, and Jason Fox has told me quite a bit about you, all of which was good, by the way. Besides, I play golf with your former boss when I have no choice, and I have to play with him. He's a horrible and lousy cheat. You will do fine here."

Selena smiled to herself as she thought about that memory. She had worked here now for a couple of months, finally getting settled into her new job. Selena had been reluctant at first to try this new venture, but Jason had been a big supporter. It was almost as if he were trying to repay her for her support of him.

Selena smiled to herself at these memories. She felt a special friendship with Jason, he was funny and she liked to laugh. She saw a movement outside the window and recognized it as Jason's truck. He pulled through the lot to find a space to drop the trailer, and then he would be off to see Diane. Selena smiled to herself at the thought of this. She knew she wouldn't be talking to Diane this night, not because Jason wouldn't allow it, but out of respect for their privacy. Soon his truck roared in front of the window again, and he let loose with a blast form his air horns.

Selena liked Jason and loved Diane, and was so very happy that Diane had finally found the happiness she deserved. She sat back in her chair hugging herself. A sly little smile tugged at the corner of her mouth as she realized Jason was home early by at least twenty-four hours, and she knew he had done that to see Diane.

Chapter 5

Jason found a parking space, set the air brakes, shut the motor off, and walked into the truck stop restaurant. He walked directly to Diane, took her in his arms, and kissed her long and hard.

"Hi, baby," she whispered as she strove to recompose herself after such a greeting. "It's about time you got here," she teased. "What took you so long?"

"I was peddling as fast as I could," he said, kissed her on the nose, then turned and headed for a booth with a telephone.

"Do you want some coffee, sweetheart?" she asked him before he made it to the booth.

"You know that stuff keeps me awake," Jason said, turning to face her, she was several paces away, and Jason was aware there were several pairs of ears listening to them. He was aware the owners of the ears were paying more attention to Diane than to himself, maybe that was why he let his ornery streak have a loose rein.

"Unless you have plans to keep me up half the night," Jason continued, showing her much humor with his eyes, "I had better pass."

Diane immediately looked down in embarrassment, and then looked slightly left and right to see who all might be watching and listening. Damn it, she thought to herself, the whole damned room was waiting to hear and see her reaction. Jason would ultimately pay for this, she would see to that.

"I guess I should show you how much I plan to keep you up," she said, raising her face to show him her own ornery streak. Two can play at this little game, she thought, as she tilted her chin a bit higher, and turned from him. She was keenly aware that ninety percent of the patrons in the room were men, and that they were all watching her. It was bad enough that they watched her every move anyway, now they watched her with what seemed like a voyeuristic expectation of sexual excitement, as if by their imagination they could somehow be a part of the festivities that would take place between Diane and Jason later that night. She worked really hard to keep a straight face as she made her way to Jason's booth and placed the full two-quart insulated coffee mug on the table directly in front of him. The total look of surprise in Jason's eyes as he looked at her was what Diane was striving for. She turned and wiggled her backside at him as she walked away, glancing over her shoulder at him. There were a number of muffled laughs and snickers as Diane resumed the work she had been doing before Jason had arrived.

Jason grinned, pulled his phone card out of a pocket, and picked up the telephone hand set from its hanger. He entered the access code, then entered Keith's cell phone number.

When Keith answered his telephone, his "hello" greeting sounded more like "low?" This was how he answered his phone on the second ring now.

"Where ya at?" Jason asked, not expecting to have gotten through to his friend, but rather expecting to have gotten his voice mail.

"Hey, little man," Keith answered his friend. "I'm just now leaving Youngstown, Ohio."

"Oh, lucky you," Jason said with a sarcastic tone. "Are you coming home for the weekend?"

"Yessir," Keith said, "I should be home tomorrow sometime."

"Have you had a good week?" Jason asked.

"Yep, pretty good. You?" Keith answered with a question of his own.

"Not bad," Jason answered, he could hear the whine of the big diesel motor in the background as Keith was up shifting. "It sounds like you've got your hands full. Give me a call tomorrow evening after you've had a little R and R with the little woman."

"Will do," Keith said. "Are you home already?"

"Yes…I…am," Jason said punctuating each word. In Jason's mind, Keith bore a strikingly strong resemblance to the character Stuart Wilson played in the movie No Escape.

"Damn it, boy," Keith teased, "when I grow up, I want to be just like you."

"You mean if you grow up," Jason shot right back. "Listen, I won't keep you tied to the phone, so you take care and be careful. Call me tomorrow."

"Okay," Keith said. "Say hi to the missus for me, see you later. Bye."

Keith pressed the end button on his cell phone, folded it back onto itself, and clipped it back onto its holder on the dash of his truck. He settled in for the long drive back to Springfield, Missouri. He had no illusions about how long it would take him and was determined to make the best of the long, drawn out trip. The main reason it would be such a long trip was the speed limit for trucks across Ohio, Indiana, and Illinois. The speed limit for trucks in Ohio and Illinois was fifty-five miles per hour. The speed limit for trucks in Indiana was sixty miles per hour, while the speed limit for cars and pickups, or four-wheelers as truckers called them, was sixty-five miles per hour. The states that had one speed limit for big trucks and another speed limit for four-wheelers claimed it was a safety issue. Most truckers didn't believe a word of this, but rather chose to believe this was a money-making scheme by certain states targeted at truckers. In most instances, if governments targeted certain people because of culture, color, race, religious beliefs, or jobs, that was called discrimination.

It's a little over eight hundred miles from Youngstown, Ohio to Springfield, Missouri, and Keith estimated it would take between twelve and thirteen hours to make the trip. Of course, DOT regulations wouldn't allow him to drive the total distance at one time, so Keith knew he would need to take an eight-hour break by the time he got to Saint Louis, Missouri. As he mentally formulated a plan to get himself home safely, his mind slipped into the past where he didn't always like to go.

He was born Keith Doyle on February 9, 1960. Like Jason, he came from a family of truck drivers. His father died when Keith was four years of age. His mother remarried two years later to a man who drove a cattle truck. Keith remembered him and his younger brother going on runs with their stepfather. Keith could recall sitting on the passenger seat of the truck while his stepfather put it through the paces. It was nothing for his stepfather to reach speeds in excess of one hundred miles per hour. In fact, he had heard his stepfather brag that his truck would run about one hundred forty miles per hour. Keith also remembered how his stepfather was in life. He remembered his stepfather being a good financial provider, but not much in the emotional support department. Keith supposed this man that his mother had married actually loved her, but he knew his stepfather only tolerated him and his brother. Keith and his brother were never allowed to cry unless his stepfather was the sole reason for the crying. If they did cry, their stepfather would tell them he would give them a reason for it.

As the years passed, and Keith grew into his teens and later manhood, he never forgot or forgave his mother or stepfather for their treatment of him and his brother. Keith rarely talked of his memories of when he was a boy, but with Jason it was different. Keith found the man was not only easy to talk to, but trustworthy enough to tell his darkest secrets. After high school graduation in nineteen seventy-nine, Keith joined the U.S. Navy, and shortly after joining, he set his sights on the Seals. It took him two tries at the swimming portion to be accepted into the Seals school, but he never gave up, and passed the test to be admitted into the highly-selective instructional facility.

Keith spent fifteen years with the Navy Seals, and in those years he saw some action and was asked by his country to kill in her name. He was in Somalia, Bosnia, Desert Storm, and a few other exercises the American public probably didn't know about. He was trained in the art of explosives, fighting hand-to-hand combat, with guns and knives, and stealth. He remembered his unit's motto which was "Catch Me If You Can", and that was the way the unit had been trained. Their training taught them the best escape was evasion and avoidance at all costs. Keith had been very good at what he did for the Seals and was given a small command of his own. It was during his last action for the Seals that he had been asked to sacrifice some of the men in his command for the good of the whole. He tried to go over his immediate commander's head to his next superior, to no avail. His commander somehow convinced their superiors that Keith was insubordinate, and soon was brought up on charges as such. Although he didn't have to face a court martial, he was given the option to leave the service quietly with honors. Keith took the discharge, and tried to get on with his life.

Shortly after joining the Navy Seals, Keith met and married his first of three wives. They had two children together, but after the Seals asked him to leave, Keith became hard to live with. He never raised a hurtful hand to her, but he soon made her feel neglected, and she refused to live like that. They were soon divorced, and Keith began to roam and wonder. He returned to his original home in Texas for a short while to visit his mother and brother. It was here that he went to work for a local trucking company, hauling dry goods coast-to-coast.

It was during this period of his life, that he met and married his second wife. They were happy for a while and had a child together. There is an old saying that states in some variation: What goes around comes around. Such was the case with Keith, his second wife did to him what he had done to his first wife. They were soon divorced, and a friend of a few years' acquaintance asked Keith to move to Missouri and to take a job team driving with him. Keith did so, not relishing the thought of staying around that area of Texas any longer.

In this time in his life, Keith began to give up hope of ever finding the happiness he so craved. He saw other people who had been able to find their own portion of happiness and started to wonder why God had dealt him such a hand in life. He finally realized that much of what had happened to him in his adult life was the result of his own choices. Yes, God had dealt him a hand, but it was his own choice to keep the cards he chose, and the ones he threw away, hoping for better cards the second time around. Then in a moment of real enlightenment, he realized that God would never gamble. Keith theorized that throughout time since the Creation, God had empowered mankind with free will, giving mankind the choice of good and evil, and since God had dealt so severely with Adam and Eve, why should the Creator deal with him any differently. It was then that Keith began to live his life differently.

Keith contacted his first wife, expressing his desire to make amends for the wrongs he had done to her. At first, she was concerned that this was a scam of his, and that he was after some unnamed accolade. He assured her that he was not. The next thing she worried about was that he wanted a second chance, and although she still felt deeply for him, she did not wish to subject herself or their children to any situation that was not a sure thing. Deep down, even though she still felt strongly for him, the trust had been lost. He was patient with her, explaining that he just wanted the chance to apologize for the hurt he had put her through and nothing more. She relaxed, and they began to communicate often with each other.

When Keith tried to do the same thing with his second wife, it didn't turn out same. She was so fearful that he was out for revenge that she filed a restraining order against him. She moved without leaving a change of address, and for all intents and purposes, hid quite effectively from him. It would be years before she rethought her decision and contacted Keith. He agreed to meet her, and he told her he didn't harbor any ill will against her.

After he had made amends to his first wife and was trying to do the same toward his second wife, he met a young woman that changed his life completely. Her name was Katrina Huddleston, and she showed him something he had never experienced before: unconditional love. By this time, he was nearing his fortieth birthday and had decided he was never going to get close enough to another woman to be tempted to marry once more. The adage about never say never was true here. After seeing each other for a couple of years, Keith and Katrina were married.

Keith and Jason met one sunny morning in the city of American Canyon, California. By this time, they were both driving for Blanket Transportation and were both on the lease-to-own plan, or the rent-to-own plan as they jokingly called it. They traveled together, or ran together as truckers call it, back to Missouri. On the way, they became acquainted, and soon became the best of friends. Often the two of them would badger their dispatchers until they got loads going to the same place at the same time. It became well known around the company that they were close friends, some even theorized they were gay, but not to their faces. Those who knew the two of them knew there was no truth to this rumor. Keith often told Jason stories of his experiences while with the Navy Seals, or Uncle Sam's Canoe Club, as Keith called it.

Keith thought of all of these memories as he traveled east on I-76. At the intersection of I-76 and I-71, Keith pulled into a truck stop to empty his bladder and to purchase a soda. He returned to the highway and merged onto I-71 southbound, heading toward Columbus, Ohio.

Keith thought of Jason and how he simply liked being around the guy. Jason was comical, witty, but also very insightful which was why he liked Jason's company. Also, Jason had listened to his stories of his Seals adventures and the stories of his past life without even a hint of passing judgment. Jason just listened, and that was something Keith had noticed right away about Jason, the man was observant. Keith noticed, more than once, that Jason could describe, in fairly accurate detail, any scene he saw at a glance. Not only that, he could have a brief conversation with someone and tell what made that person tick, with very few exceptions. If anyone had missed his calling in life, in his opinion, it was Jason Fox. Keith made a mental note to call Jason tomorrow after he got home to see where he was delivering his first load for next week. It had been several weeks since the two of them had run together, and he at least wanted to try to see about getting them two loads going the same way.

It was Thursday night, Keith thought, as he was headed home, and he would be there tomorrow afternoon if nothing bad happened. He took his break at a rest area in Illinois just east of East Saint Louis, Illinois, and went to sleep for about six hours.

Keith awoke, grabbed his shaving kit, and walked toward the men's restroom. He had a routine much like Jason's. He would use the restroom, wash his hands and face, and brush his teeth. As he was doing the latter, he regarded himself in the mirror above the sink. Since he had been discharged from the navy, he had grown a beard which he kept trimmed as neatly as possible and had let his hair grow to about shoulder length. Most of the time he kept his hair pulled back from his face with a rubber band. He was taller than Jason by about three inches and outweighed him by an estimated twenty to thirty pounds.

Keith finished his routine in the restroom and walked back toward his truck. He opened the driver's side door and tossed his shaving kit onto the drivers seat. He then took out his tire buddy, a short wooden or fiberglass club of about two feet in length with a thick metal band around one end, used to thump tires. He completed his vehicle inspection much the same way that Jason had done. Not all truckers did their inspections in the same order. Some might do the walk around, thumping the tires first, while others might check the lights and hazards first. Different strokes for different folks, as the old saying goes, Keith thought as he climbed behind the wheel of the black 379 Peterbilt he drove.

Keith arrived in Springfield at about the time he had estimated. He dropped the trailer at the company yard, or terminal, and made one more stop before going home. He stopped at a coin-operated car wash.

Chapter 6

Jason left for home a couple of hours before Diane's shift ended. He arrived home, parking the Peterbilt in the driveway in its usual place. He got his shaving kit, logbook, dirty clothes bag, duffle bag, and laptop computer. He had to make two trips from the truck to the house to get all of the items carried inside. Christine, Diane's youngest daughter, wasn't at home, but probably still at work, or maybe out with friends, either one was likely. Jason checked the telephone answering machine on his way to the shower. There were three messages.

Message One: "Christine, hi, it's me Rob. Sorry I missed you, please call me when you get this. Bye." Rob was a young man that Christine had gone out with a few times, and Jason actually liked what little he had seen in Rob. He didn't delete this message, but let the machine automatically save it. Christine could get it later.

Message Two: "Hello, it's me." Jason recognized the voice of Diane's father. "I just called to see if anyone has heard from Jason. I haven't heard where he is, how he's doin', or if he'll be home for the weekend. Someone please let me know something, bye." Jason mused to himself that it must be strange for this down-to-earth family to have an over-the-road-trucker in their family. Diane's parents had never been anything but nice to Jason and had embraced him as one of their own. He would return this call after he took his shower.

Message Three: "Hey, you two. Why don't we get together this weekend. I don't know how much longer this fair weather will hold out. Why don't we barbeque or something this weekend. Call me, I'm still at work, I don't get off until eleven, and, Jason, I know you know the phone number." Jason smiled as he finished listening to Selena's voice on the machine. He wouldn't return this call until after Diane got home. With him being on the road and gone through the week, he didn't know if Diane had anything planned whenever he got home. He wasn't the type to dictate what they would do with their limited time together. Instead, he would leave the message for Diane to listen to, and then discuss their plans together. He knew some men would consider him henpecked for taking such a view. Let them think what they like, Jason thought.

Jason took a nice, warm, relaxing shower, brushed his teeth, and shaved. He put on a pair of black, nylon shorts, and a gray cotton T-shirt. After putting his dirty clothes in the basket for such clothes in the utility room, he sat down on the sofa in the living room with the cordless phone and entered Diane's parents' phone number on the keypad.

"Hello?" Diane's father always made the greeting sound like a question.

"Howdy," Jason answered, "I got your message and decided to call you back myself."

"Well, I'm glad you did," his father-in-law said. "Did you have a good week?"

"Yea, pretty good," Jason responded, and then added. "I didn't tear anything up, and I didn't get any tickets. I'm gonna say that was a good week." They both laughed at this.

"Where did you go this last week?" Diane's father asked, then said. "Since Diane went back to work, I don't get my updates on you like I used to."

"I delivered in City of Industry, California on Monday morning and reloaded in Ontario, California Monday afternoon," Jason answered, he knew that Diane going back to work wasn't an issue with her father, he just wanted to feel involved. They talked for a few more minutes, and after he clicked the telephone off when their conversation ended, he made a pitcher of iced tea, knowing Diane would want a big glass of it before she took her bath. He went into the living room, turned on the television, sat down on the sofa, and waited for Diane to come home.

Not quite two hours later, as he sat watching one of his favorite T.V. shows that Diane had taped for him earlier that week, he heard the motor on the garage door engage and knew his wife was home. He got up from the sofa and went into the kitchen. Jason retrieved a drinking glass from the cabinet to the right of the sink and moved to the refrigerator with the ice box on top. He dropped a handful of ice cubes in the glass and poured the tea into the glass over the ice. The ice popped and cracked in the glass, and Jason could feel small tremors vibrate the sides of the glass as the ice split.

Diane came through the door that connected the utility room to the garage and exhaled heavily. Jason handed her the glass of iced tea as he took her purse from her. She leaned against the wall adjoining the door and drank deeply from the glass.

"Oh, thank you, honey," she breathed, and straightening from the wall, placed the tea glass on the corner of the clothes dryer. She started to kick her shoes off, but before she could, Jason had slipped his arms around her waist, pulling her off balance toward him. She gasped and made a little sound as she was drawn up next to him. Before she could voice a protest that she wanted to get cleaned up, he had her in a tight embrace and was kissing her firmly on the mouth. She forgot about the protest and encircled his neck with her arms, pressing herself closer to him.

"Damn it, girl," Jason said, using the trucker lingo on her, "I missed you."

"I missed you, too," she returned, and then added, "you are such an ornery shit. Almost every truck driver in that room had something to say to me after you left."

"You knew I was ornery when you married me," he said grinning. "If you're hungry, I'll try my hand at cooking."

"No, that's all right. I'm not hungry," Diane said. She knew he could cook, and although he was no chef, he did manage quite well. Then she asked, "Were there any calls?"

"Yeah," he answered. "Rob called for Christine. Your dad called, and I already called him back, and Sal called, asking if we want to cook out sometime this weekend."

"Did you call her back?" Diane asked. She was all but stripping in the utility room now, throwing her discarded clothing into the opened washer.

"No," Jason simply said, watching her and smiling.

"Isn't there something on T.V. you would rather watch besides me?" she asked, looking up at him, feeling a little embarrassed.

"Are you kidding?" he said, feigning disbelief. "They don't show anything like this on prime time television."

"Well you've seen all of this before," she said, now starting to feel the orneriness come back.

"I won't ever pass up a show like this," he said, capturing her face between his hands and looking into her eyes. Then he kissed her and, releasing her face, turned to leave the room.

"You're so sweet," Diane giggled, as she stepped toward him and patted his behind.

Jason walked into the kitchen, opened the refrigerator, and retrieved the tea pitcher. She padded through the kitchen barefoot. In fact, the only piece of clothing she wore was her panties. He took the glass from her and poured tea into it filling it to just below the rim. He extended the glass of iced tea toward her, but instead of taking it, she took the cordless telephone off the charger and turned to face him. He saw the playful look in her eyes as she stuck her tongue out at him. When he took a step toward her, she turned to flee. Diane ran from the kitchen into the living room, turned left, bounded up the five steps there to the landing leading into the hallway that led to the rear of the house toward the master bath, all the while shrieking the word, "No!"

Jason let out a low laugh to himself, still holding the glass of iced tea, slowly shaking his head. He stepped into the living room and sat down on the sofa to watch television. He drank the glass of iced tea himself, then pressed the stop button on the VCR remote. He walked back into the kitchen and refilled the glass again.

Jason walked down the hallway to the master bathroom where Diane was bathing. As he neared the door, he heard Diane laughing and guessed she was talking to Selena. The door wasn't latched, so he pushed it open, and stepped into the room. Diane sat in the bathtub looking up at him, smiling. Her eyes sparkled with glee, and Jason couldn't remember anyone ever looking so lovely. She held the phone to her ear listening, laughing, and talking to Selena. Jason set the tea glass down on the rim of the bathtub and reached for the bath sponge, intending to help Diane with her bath. She caught his wrist, still looking at him with those playful, sparkling eyes, and blew him two kisses in rapid succession. He knew by her catching his wrist that she was asking him not to carry through with his intention. He grimaced playfully and dropped the sponge. He leaned forward and kissed her on the forehead before straightening, turning, and leaving the room.

Jason walked back through the house, exiting by way of the garage. He carried a lawn chair out of the garage, set it on the sidewalk that lay in front of Diane's flower beds, then sat down in it. The evening air was turning from sultry to cool as the night progressed. Jason sat and thought about his past life.

His first marriage had lasted twelve years. He and his first wife had had two children together, a son and a daughter, and they were nearly grown now. At first, he made every attempt to see his kids, but his ex-wife was a vindictive sort and trashed him to their children at every opportunity. He resisted this quietly, not speaking badly of their mother in front of the children, but she made it very hard for him to hold his anger and tongue.

Through all of this, he paid his child support and kept the health insurance paid for the children. On the times when he did have the children, he made every effort to show them how much he cared for them without lavishing them with gifts. On their birthdays and on holidays, he mailed them greeting cards and always enclosed his telephone number for them. They never called him.

His second marriage started out well, his new wife was attentive to Jason and his desire to have a good relationship with his kids. His second wife had two young children of her own, and they all made an effort to get along with each other—all except Jason's first wife. She didn't want their children to have anything but bad memories after a visit to their father. She so poisoned their minds that soon they weren't even speaking to him, let alone wanting to see him. His second wife became frustrated. She saw the effect this was having on Jason, and instead of trying to help, she became despondent and withdrawn. Soon, she was seeking diversion elsewhere. She and Jason were divorced after only four years of marriage.

Jason hadn't quite given up hope of ever being truly happy when he met Diane, but he was getting close. After the failed relationships she had had, she also was about to give up. The two of them had talked of this often, and each reassured the other they weren't to blame for those failures. Diane had asked him what he wanted to do about his children shortly after they were married, and he told her there wasn't much to do. He explained he could take his ex-wife back to court, but that would probably have an adverse effect on the children. He felt it was better to pay the child support and the health insurance premiums, and hold out hope that some day his children would become curious enough to come to him. He thought maybe this was an extremely passive attitude, but he didn't want to force his children to be around him.

Jason knew that God had given man the power of free choice. Jason knew people had the power shape their lives by the choices they made. If his children chose not to see him, he would respect their decision, but it didn't mean he liked it. It hurt him to think his children disliked him, but he refused to force his own will on them. If the day came when his children confronted him with their mother's twisted logic of how he never cared for them, then he would remind them of who had paid their child support, who had paid their health insurance premiums, and of the choices they had made concerning him. He would inform them that he had never forced them to see him, he had given them the means to contact them, had made himself available to them, and if they didn't like the way their lives had turned out, then they had two people to blame: themselves and their mother.

Jason leaned back in his chair, extended his legs, and crossed them at the ankles. He closed his eyes, interlocked his fingers across his belly, leaned his head back, relaxed, and enjoyed the night. He thought of Diane and how fortunate he was to have her in his life. Anyone who knew him knew he loved to watch movies—movies of all types, westerns, action, science fiction, comedies, even a few love stories. He had told Diane at one time that she reminded him of three actresses rolled into one.

"Really?" she had said, a hint of disbelief in her eyes, and voice. "Who?"

"You look and act a little like Elizabeth Shue in the movie, Adventures in Babysitting. You look and act a little like Olivia Newton-John in the movie, Grease, and you sound and act a little like Sissy Spacek in The River with Mel Gibson," Jason recited. She had giggled at this and had thrown her arms around him.

She had stayed single for eight years between her divorce from Mark and her marriage to Jason, and that made Jason feel really special. Of the men Diane had dated and been with, to choose him, was no small thing to Jason. He loved Diane like he had never loved another woman. When he left to go out on the road in the truck, she nearly cried tears of sadness every time, and when he returned home, she cried tears of joy. When she spoke of past loves and lovers, she rarely talked bad of them. When they went to family functions, she was the life of the party. She was well loved by her own family and was adored by Jason's family. A smile crept across Jason's lips as he stretched, sighing a sigh of contentment. Neither Diane nor Jason had compromised their standards to be with someone else, and they were truly happy with each other.

This was how Diane found Jason, kicked back in a lawn chair, with his head leaned back and a grin on his mouth.

"So here you are," she said, walking up behind him. "Would you like some company?"

"Whose?" he asked, jokingly.

"Mine, you shit," she said slipping her hands down his chest from behind.

"You bet," he said, taking her hands in his, and kissing them each in turn.

"I can make some coffee," she said. Jason could hear the ornery chime in her voice.

"I think I'll pass," he said, as he maneuvered her around the chair and pulled her onto his lap. He saw she was dressed simply in a thin cotton gown covered by a terry cloth bath robe.

"Both of us will collapse the chair," she protested, as she tried to pull away.

"Then I'll break your fall," he said as he nuzzled her neck with his nose, running his tongue along the bottom of her earlobe. She giggled, wrapped her arms around his neck, and held him tighter as he put his own arms around her waist.

"Come on," she took him by the hand, led him into the house and to their bedroom.

After they made love, they lay entwined in each others arms and legs.

"Why did you wait so long to find me?" she asked. It was a rhetorical question, but she loved the way he made her feel in and out of the bedroom.

"So I would know how to really appreciate and take care of you," he replied, pulling her closer and kissing her forehead.

"It was well worth the wait," she said, snuggling closer to him, completely satisfied.

"I told Sally we would cook out with them tomorrow night after I get off work," Diane said, then asked, "is that okay?"

"Well, of course," he answered her. "I didn't call her back to make plans because I didn't know how tired you would be."

"Thank you, sweetheart," Diane said, tilting her head to kiss him on the neck. One of the things she loved about him was the way he respected her feelings and opinions. She knew he wouldn't commit her to do something without discussing it with her first. If she made plans for them, he never complained unless he had a work commitment, and knowing this was how he was, she never exploited that power.

"You're welcome," he said, "anything for my baby."

"You make me feel so special," she said, giggling, and giving her whole body a shrug against him.

"You deserve to feel that way," Jason told her, moving his right hand slowly down her left side, trying to make the caress feel sensual.

"I love you," he breathed to her between kisses. Where she was caressing him, and the way she was doing it was making his breaths come in gasps.

"I love you more," she responded, smiling. This was a little, harmless game she liked playing with him.

"Two things, Mrs. Fox," he said, seeing her smile in the darkness.

"Number one," he continued, he could play this game too, "that's not possible, and, number two, just remember who said it first."

"You don't play fair," Diane teased.

"That's right, I don't," he said matter-of-factly, as he rolled on top of her.

Afterwards, they lay, again, entangled with each other, this time sleeping. Jason awoke a few hours later. After remembering where he was, he extended an arm and felt for Diane. She wasn't in the bed with him. He looked toward the window and saw the beginnings of morning. He listened for sounds coming from the kitchen, there were none. He flung the covers back and walked into the bathroom just off the master bedroom. He did his usual tour of the bathroom, then returned to the bedroom.

The bedroom door leading to the hallway was open, and he could see Diane's shape in the bed across the hall. He walked to her and, lifting the covers, slipped in behind her. He snuggled up behind her. She moaned and drew his arm beneath her neck, then settled back against him.

"There is no escape. Resistance is futile," he breathed into her ear. He heard her giggle softly, as she wiggled against him.

"I wasn't trying to escape," she explained as she turned her head toward him. "Your snoring was keeping me awake."

"How could you hear my snoring over your snoring?" he asked her, feeling pleased to see her smile at this.

"You are such an ornery shit," she said, rolling onto her back to face him better. Before she could say more, he kissed her.

"I love you, Diane," Jason said to his wife as he looked deeply into her eyes. He knew if he looked too deeply, he could possibly drown. Oh well, there were far worse ways to die. She opened her mouth to say something, and he kissed her again, lightly teasing the inside of her mouth with his tongue. While she kissed him back, Diane shifted closer to him, and he rolled her beneath him.

"My only hope is that I show you how much I love you, the way you show me," she said.

"You show me every day," he told her, "even when I'm hundreds and thousands of miles away, you show me by the way you talk to me on the phone."

"You're not hundreds and thousands of miles away right now, and we're not talking on the phone," she purred. They made love, slowly this time.

"What time do you work today." Jason asked, afterwards.

"Brunch to dinner," Diane answered, nestling in the bed beside him. "As much as I hate to, I better get up and get around."

"Okay," Jason whispered. He followed her to the shower when she headed that way.

"What are you doing?" she asked as he stepped into the shower behind her.

"Helping," he answered simply.

"Helping with what?" she asked, laughing.

"Trouble spots," he said, kissing her.

"Like what?" she asked, stepping under the spray of water.

"Like down here," he said, taking the bar of soap and lathering her buttocks.

"I can reach that," she said, shampooing her hair.

"Oh," he said, as if this was news to him, and then said, "well then here," as he lathered her breasts extensively.

"I can reach those, too," she said, rinsing her hair.

"Damn the bad luck," Jason exclaimed with a hint of sarcasm.

"I really need to get ready for work," Diane said, but was unable to sound convincing. She finished her shower, stepped out, grabbed a towel, and walked into their bedroom. Jason watched her until she moved from his view, then he finished his shower. When he stepped into the bedroom, she was reclined on the bed, waiting for him.

"You know," he said, "I always wanted a wife that had as much of a sex drive as what I do. Now that I have one, I just hope I can keep up with you."

"I promise that I'll be gentle," she said to him, extending a hand to him. He took her hand and lay on the bed next to her.

"What about work," Jason asked, but really didn't care.

"When I went downstairs to make coffee, I called and told them I was running a little late," she whispered into his ear, as she rolled on top of him.

Afterwards, they were downstairs having coffee together, when Christine came bounding downstairs from her room.

"Good morning," Diane said to Christine, as she hugged her daughter.

"I guess," Christine mumbled, as she opened the refrigerator door and rummaged around for the milk and butter.

"Is something wrong?" Diane asked, as she and Jason exchanged glances and smiled slyly. The two of them knew what Christine was possibly going to complain about. This wouldn't be the first time, and as far as the two of them were concerned, it wouldn't be the last.

"I could hear you two last night," Christine said, setting the milk container on the counter top. She opened a cabinet door to retrieve a drinking glass. She opened the bread sack, popped two slices into the toaster, and pressed the button down until it locked in place. "I mean, I know you two love each other. Anyone that comes around here can see that. My friends that come out here all say the same thing, 'Your mom and step dad are always smiling at each other,' and sometimes it's embarrassing the way you two act."

"Do you want us to act more reserved and controlled?" Jason asked her, the playful look never left his eyes.

"Yes," Christine said, turning to face them both. "You've been married now for over two years, and you're both so...so...old."

Diane and Jason both laughed at this.

"We're sorry," Diane said, putting an arm around Christine. "When you find what we've got, you'll understand."

Christine rolled her eyes, shaking her head. She retrieved the toast from the toaster, spread butter on both pieces, and poured herself a glass of milk. She put the milk away and turned to leave the room, but when she turned, she saw Jason holding his arms out to her. She leaned into his embrace, hugging him back. She pulled away, left the room, and scampered back up the stairs to her room.

"I really need to go," Diane said apologetically, putting her empty coffee cup in the semi-loaded dishwasher.

"I know," Jason responded, "but I don't have to like it."

"Come and see me later," she invited, as she slipped on her shoes and slung her purse over her shoulder.

"Okay," Jason said. He kissed her goodbye before she turned away and slipped out the door leading into the garage. He heard the motor on her car start, a 1994 blue Ford Thunderbird, and slowly walked back to their bedroom. He undressed, climbed back into bed, and was soon fast asleep.

Jason awoke two hours later to Christine gently shaking him by the shoulder and softly calling to him. She held the cordless phone out to him like it had an ugly message to tell, and Jason imagined it did. He took the phone from her, blinking sleep from his eyes, and knowing Christine must have felt the call important enough to wake him.

"Hello," Jason said, his voice thick with sleep.

"Hey, Slick!" Keith's voice said into Jason's ear. "What in the world are you doin'?"

"Hey, man," Jason said, stretching. He could tell that Keith was on his cell phone, he could hear the roar of the diesel motor in the background. "I just woke up."

"You?" Keith asked sarcastically. "Asleep this time of day? Come on." Keith made the words "come on" sound more like "cam own."

Jason smiled at this. He knew Keith used the trucker lingo a lot, even when he wasn't talking on the CB. In trucker lingo, the term come on or come back is a term used to signify to the person you are talking to that you are through talking for the moment, and it is their turn to talk. Most truckers speak a slightly different dialect than other Americans.

"Diane had plans for me last night," Jason said yawning.

"Whoa, that's more information than I need," Keith said laughing.

"Where ya at?" Jason asked, adding his own form of trucker lingo.

"Just strollin' along," Keith answered. "I just got off the phone with my dispatcher. He gave me a run to Orlando, Florida for Tuesday morning, and he says there's another one. Why don't you call and see if you can get the other one?" In part of trucker lingo, a run means a load.

"Alrighty," Jason said. "I'll call you right back." Jason pushed the button to disconnect the line, then dialed the number to his dispatcher.

"No, I don't have another Orlando load, but I do have a Suwanee, Georgia run for Monday morning," Jason's dispatcher told him. "You and Keith could run together to Atlanta."

"Okay, I'll take it," Jason said, a bit disappointed, and pushed the disconnect button again. Jason dialed Keith's phone number, held the receiver to his ear, and waited for Keith to answer.

"'Lo," was Keith's standard answer.

"Hey, it's me," Jason said, "I couldn't get the other Orlando load, but he did offer me a Suwanee run for Monday morning, and I took it, so we can at least run together to Atlanta."

"That'll work," Keith said. "We need to start bugging them for next week, to see if they can get us together for a couple of West Coast runs for next week."

"We can try," Jason said. "They act like sometimes they're trying to keep us apart."

"They're just jealous, big boy," Keith said laughing. "I'll call you when I get home. Bye."

"Bye," Jason said as they both disconnected.

Jason listened to make sure Christine was at the other end of the house, then climbed out of bed and headed for the shower. After taking his shower, he dressed in clothes Diane called "Diane clothes". This consisted of tight blue jeans, a western style shirt, cowboy boots, and, of course, a cowboy hat. This was the type of clothes Diane preferred him to wear when he was at home, but she didn't want Jason wearing that style of clothes when he was on the road. Jason didn't mind, it was something he did that made Diane feel good and secure. He had discovered some time ago that since Diane's first marriage and subsequent divorce, she was a little insecure, but not to the point where she was overly possessive. Jason was mindful of her feelings and did what he could to encourage her silently. Besides, he knew from his own past marriages how bad it could be, and he wanted to keep Diane as happy as he could.

Jason drove to the truck stop to see his wife and to have breakfast. As he entered the dining room of the truck stop, he saw three drivers that drove for Blanket Transportation sitting together at a table. Jason nodded a greeting to the group of them, and they invited him to join them. As Jason pulled out a chair and sat down, Diane placed a cup of coffee in front of him.

"Man," one of the drivers said to Diane teasingly, "what does he have that we don't to get that kind of service?"

"My heart," Diane answered, winking to them as she turned away. "What do you want for breakfast, Honey?" she called to Jason over her shoulder.

"Two pancakes, two biscuits and gravy, and two eggs over easy," Jason answered. He all but laughed at her joviality. She was in fine form today, he thought, and he loved her for it. When he made himself look away from her sashaying backside, he realized he was the center of attention of his grinning table companions.

"Do you know how lucky you are?" one of them asked good-naturedly.

"Yep, I sure do," Jason answered, the color of his embarrassment starting to recede.

"Where are you going for Monday, Fox?" another one of the men asked.

"Suwanee, Georgia for Monday morning," Jason answered as he picked up the cup of hot coffee.

"Hey, have you heard from Wolf-Kat lately?" the third man asked. "I haven't seen him in quite a while."

"Yeah," Jason said after he had taken a sip of coffee. "He called this morning. He's on his way in from Youngstown, Ohio. He should be home sometime this afternoon."

Diane started bringing plates of food to their table. The four men started moving items on the table out of her way and scooting themselves around in their chairs to allow her better access to do her work. It took her two trips, but she finally got all the orders to the table, with some good-natured ribbing from the men seated there.

Jason, as a rule, didn't mind the truckers teasing his wife. He generally had a good sense of reading people, and truck drivers are no exception, most are just ordinary people. Besides, he knew these men, and they knew Diane wasn't the type of person to step out on Jason. If there had been any doubt about how far to push the teasing, Diane would have drawn the line, and Jason would have been there to back her, if that's what she had needed. Jason knew how important it was for Diane to be able to fend for herself, he couldn't always be there. She needed to feel she could stand on her own, and what's more, Jason couldn't beat up every man that looked at Diane. She wouldn't want him to, and there was a part of her that secretly enjoyed the looks directed her way, as long as it stopped there. She had never invited more than that from her admirers, and she didn't intend to start now.

The men ate their meals with bits of broken conversation thrown in. They talked about work, the places they had been to lately, and the overall plight of the American truck driver. Diane returned every few minutes to refill cups of coffee or to warm half empty cups to a warmer fullness. Of the men seated there, Jason watched her the most. His eyes strayed from her only temporarily to answer a question asked by one of his breakfast companions, and every time this happened, one of them caught him doing it. They teased him somewhat about this, but secretly, all of them were somewhat envious of the obvious love that resonated between Jason and Diane. When these drivers caught Jason at his palpable watching of Diane, they traced his gaze to see it being returned by her when she wasn't busying herself with something else.

If a poll had been taken of the three men seated there with Jason about how married couples should act toward one another, they all three would have answered, in unison, "Just watch the way they adore each other."

Marriages involving truck drivers usually don't last long, of course there are exceptions. Some married couples, where one member is a trucker, thrive on the aloneness until they are reunited. Others just naturally get along better if they see each other only a couple of times a week or month. For a marriage to work, where one member is a trucker, takes dedication, loyalty, sacrifice, trust, discipline, and a lot of love from both parties. Another problem is where the partner who is the trucker may not have a good idea of everyday goings-on at home, for example, money matters, children's disciplines, or any number of everyday occurrences that most people take for granted. Jason's coworkers seated there didn't know for sure if Jason and Diane had all the bugs worked out of their marriage, but from what they saw, it looked like the two of them had a good handle on it.

Of the three truckers seated with Jason, two were divorced, and the third was in the process of getting one. The divorce rate among truckers seems to be on an equal plane with that of police officers, if not more so. What these three men saw was a marriage between Jason and Diane that had, and was likely to, beat the odds. The one contributing factor to that, they all would have agreed, was the willingness of Jason and Diane to put the other one first in all matters. If given the chance, they all three would have stated that what Jason and Diane had, they also wanted.

With their meals finished, the four of them made their way to the pay counter. Each had left at least a two dollar tip apiece for Diane on the table. They took their turns paying their own checks, and each of the three other truckers teasingly told Diane that if she ever was to become single again, she wouldn't need to be for long. Jason was the last one in line to pay, and instead of teasing his wife, he kissed her full on the mouth before joining the grinning trio as they made their way outside. Jason said his goodbyes, and took his leave, turning again before leaving for home to cast a gaze toward Diane through the huge plate glass windows of the truck stop dining area.

Jason drove to Blanket Transportation and stepped inside the dispatch office to get his paycheck. His dispatcher was on the phone when Jason entered, and before he could sit down, his dispatcher had his check pulled from the stack and slid it across to him. The paychecks came in an envelope, and Jason tore his open. He pulled out the paycheck, looked at it, and nodded a couple of approval nods. Also in the pay envelope each week was a pay settlement, stating the deducted amounts for the truck payment, truck insurance, health insurance, dental insurance, workman's comprehensive insurance, the fuel purchases for the week, the fee for using the fuel card, and the rent on the satellite unit. There were certain accounts that required deductions, there was a tire account, an accident reserve account, and an excessive mile account that helped pay for the balloon payment at the end of the lease on the truck. Also listed were the places Jason had picked up and delivered that week, and the pay miles between each point.

Jason looked his settlement over, put it back into the envelope, folded it over once, and stuffed it into a back pocket of his jeans. He folded over his paycheck, and put it into one of his shirt pockets. He then dug into one of his front jeans pockets and pulled out his key fob. Selecting the appropriate key, he opened the mailbox allotted to him by the company and checked inside. Seeing nothing there, he closed the mailbox door, retracted his key, and put the keys back into his pocket. He returned to stand in front of his dispatcher, who was wrapping up his phone conversation.

"Hello, Jason," he said when he had returned the telephone handset to its cradle.

"Hi, how are ya?" was Jason's standard greeting.

"I'm fine," Jason's dispatcher said. "What are you doing today?"

"I came by to get my check and check on the bills for my next load," Jason said.

"Well, it won't load until this afternoon. Do you want me to call you at home when it's ready? Or have one of the city drivers bring it back to here?" the other man asked.

"Just have one of the city drivers drop it here," Jason said. He would be so glad when Selena got her own board, he would try to move to hers. This was an every week occurrence with this dispatcher. He wanted Jason to go to the shipper and sit with the trailer until it was time to load it, and then go inside and count the freight while it was being loaded. Jason refused to do this, let the city drivers do their jobs. He would help on occasion, but he didn't want to get something started that would soon be expected, and once something like that started, it was hard to get stopped. He got up from the chair, nodded his farewell, and left the building.

Jason then drove to the bank to deposit most of his paycheck. This particular week had been a good one, it paid four thousand miles. After all the deductions were taken out, that left one thousand six hundred fifty-five dollars, and a handful of change. Although that may sound like a good check, and it was, the main deduction hadn't been taken out yet: Uncle Sam. When in a business like this one, where the driver is on a lease-to-purchase plan with a company, that driver is responsible for paying the taxes on those earnings. Jason and Diane knew this and always paid two thousand five hundred dollars in every quarter.

The drive-through windows were doing a healthy business this morning, so Jason decided to go inside the lobby, he preferred this anyway. He filled out the deposit slip, depositing all but two hundred dollars of it to be used as expense money for the following week, and endorsed his paycheck.

"Hi, Jason," the teller, a small young woman, said smiling at him. "How are you and Diane doing these days?"

"Trying to avoid the heat," Jason said, giving her the paycheck and deposit slip. She did all the appropriate business and counted Jason the two hundred dollars back to him.

"Did you run a lot of miles this week?" she asked him. The women that worked in the bank knew Jason was an over-the-road trucker, and often they teased him about bringing bad weather back with him.

"Yep, I sure did," Jason replied in the false robust tone. They had learned from past experience that when he spoke in this tone a rather tall tale was about to be told, and upon hearing him speaking in said tone, several of them paused in their duties to hear what was about to be said. "I ran so many miles this last week, that when I got home, I had to hire Diane as a lumper to help me out of the truck." Lumper is a term used in the trucking industry for someone, who loads, or unloads a truck.

"Jason Fox, you're not right," she said laughing, as other laughter was heard coming from other parts of the bank.

"Oh yeah?" he asked, arching his eyebrows, then said, "I ain't left yet either." She laughed at this one too, as he stuffed the money into his wallet, and exited the bank.

Chapter 7

After Jason returned home, he and Diane lived but a few miles from the truck stop, he checked the telephone answering machine for messages, and seeing there were none, he stretched out on the sofa and went to sleep. Another thing about truck drivers, the ones that run hard, is they sleep quite a bit when they are home. This can lead to hurt feelings by the non-truck driver member of a marriage or relationship. If a married couple, where one partner is a trucker, is not secure in their relationship, they can be on the verge of a marriage meltdown. Jason always tried to show Diane how he truly felt about her, and one way he did this was by being rested when she returned home.

When the two of them realized there was more to their relationship than friendship, they crossed that bridge hand in hand slowly and cautiously. After Diane's divorce from Mark, she had remained single for just over eight years and was very hesitant about entering into another marriage. Jason, likewise, was skittish about another marriage, but he sensed something different and genuine about Diane. That was why it hurt him so much when she had asked him to limit his phone calls to her before their marriage when she was dating the cop. He had missed her terribly and decided that if he were given the chance, he would tell her of his love for her. He had been given the chance, and he poured out his passion on her every chance he was given.

Diane also felt much of the same way as Jason. She had never met anyone who loved her wholly the way Jason did. He wasn't like the men in her past who had taken certain parts of her to love and discarded the rest, he took every part of her and loved her completely. She didn't have to work outside the home for financial reasons, Jason's income kept them comfortable. In fact, he told her once, that if she wanted to work outside the home, it was her choice, and that he never wanted it to be a necessity. Diane chose to work outside the home because if she didn't, Jason would get no rest when he was at home. She had never been treated this way, and quite frankly, she loved it, and she had her own passions she wanted to pour out onto Jason.

Jason woke to the sound of music from the stereo in the kitchen. He sat up on the sofa, took a deep breath, then stretched as he stood up. Diane had wanted a small stereo to place on the counter in the kitchen, and this was the source of the music. Jason knew she was home by the type of music coming from the stereo; she enjoyed listening to the station that played the "golden oldies". The fact that she was singing along with the song that was emitting from said stereo confirmed to Jason that Diane was home. He heard her moving around in the kitchen and smelled the aromas of cooking food.

Diane was standing at the stove, rhythmically swaying to the music, singing, and alternately stirring the contents of two boiling pans. She had her back to him, and he stood and watched her for a moment. The heat in August in Missouri is sweltering, to say the least, most of the time it stays in the upper nineties or is not uncommon to reach the triple digits, which, with an equally high humidity level, can be very miserable, as was the case on this afternoon. Diane had obviously come home, entering the house quietly, taken her bath as normal, dressed, and returned to the kitchen without waking Jason. She still stood facing away from him, dressed in a pair of bright red nylon shorts and a white pullover, sleeveless T-shirt, and no bra. She was barefoot and had her shoulder-length hair pulled back and up off of her neck with a hair clip.

There were times when he was awed by her, and this was one of them. As stated before, Diane as well as Selena, were attractive women, but neither of them would ever be accused of flaunting that. The attitude that Diane had about herself, to Jason, was attractive in itself. He watched her swaying to the music, dressed as she was, and felt his passion starting to rise. He took a step forward as she turned and caught sight of him. She stopped singing and smiled brightly at him. Jason was unsettled for a moment, he loved to hear her sing, she had a beautiful singing voice, but he also loved to see her smile. He decided that he would shake off the unsettling feeling by holding her.

"Hi, Honey! Did you have a good nap? Did I wake you? Do you still feel up to going over to Billy and Selena's tonight? I'm just finishing up the potato salad!" Diane was chirping like a bird. She had said all that, seemingly without taking a breath. When she did stop talking long enough to take a breath, Jason made his move.

He stepped in close to her, slipped his arms around her waist, and pulled her snug against him, as his mouth locked over hers. He kissed her long and sensually, his arms remaining around her as his hands moved to the back of her head and grasped both hands full of her hair. She responded to him by pressing herself tighter against him. She was pleased to feel his impassioned response to her, as she pressed her loins even more firmly against his, and at the same time she pulled his upper body against her more than ample breasts.

"From now on, you're taking a nap every afternoon when you're home," Diane breathed when they both came up for air. Life with Mark, or Gary had never been this good. Without saying a word and smiling, Jason reached to the two control knobs that were in the "ON" position on the cook stove, and turned them off.

"Sir! What are your intentions?" Diane said in her best Southern belle imitation, batting her eyes at him rapidly.

"You, ma'am, have been conquered and are about to be ravaged." Jason returned, mimicking the same accent.

"Damn! Why didn't you say so!" Diane snapped, dropping the southern accent and bounding for the steps that ended at the hallway that led to their bedroom.

"You can run, but you can't hide," Jason called after her, switching to a John Wayne accent, as he broke and ran after her.

"Who's hiding? If you can't find me, I'll make enough noise so you can!" she called back over her shoulder to him, flinging off her shirt as she darted into their bedroom. He heard her splash onto the bed a moment before he joined her there.

Two hours later, Diane and Jason drove to Billy and Selena's house for the barbeque. When Jason had joined Diane on the bed, they had made love. Afterwards, they had lain in each other's embrace, talking, laughing, kissing, and cuddling, and made love again. Diane then took a quick shower, dressed again, and went back to the kitchen to finish the potato salad. After Diane had taken her shower, Jason took his, and by the time he had dressed, Diane was ready to go. Jason dressed in the familiar "Diane's Clothes" of the cowboy look that she loved, complete with tight black jeans, gray western style shirt with snaps instead of buttons, tan cowboy boots, and a brown cowboy hat.

They arrived at Billy and Selena's, and Diane parked in the driveway. Jason wasn't an overly-demanding person, but one of the conversations he and Diane had had was concerning who would drive when he was at home.

"I won't mind driving every so often," he had told her. "I will probably drive more miles in one week than you would normally drive in a month. So I would just as soon you do the most of the driving."

Diane had agreed, a bit perplexed. Here was this man treating her like she was actually worth something more than a warm body, and what woman wouldn't want that? She knew she did, and that was another reason she loved him. He did his share of the driving when he was at home, if she asked him to, but she never quavered about his request for her to do most of the driving. Besides, if he wasn't driving, that left his hands free to do other things to her. Another reason she loved him, he couldn't seem to keep his hands to himself when he was around her. He was usually touching, lightly stroking, or caressing her arm, face, or leg when they were in the company of others. If they were ever walking in a crowd, she always felt his presence because of the hand he would either put on the small of her back or in her hand. She had never felt so loved, so desired, so protected, or so honored by another man in all her life, and that was another reason she loved him. When he did drive, he usually opened her door for her when they entered the vehicle. He did this even on the occasions when she went with him on the truck, even though he had given her a door key of her own. That was another reason she loved him.

When they got out of the car, Diane came around the front of the car and took the bowl of potato salad from Jason that he had held on his lap with one hand; he had used the other hand to explore Diane's leg, arm, and neck. She kissed him as she took the bowl from him, and he softly patted her rump when she turned toward the house.

Billy was on the concrete carport, standing in front of a smoking barbeque grill. Jason walked closer to Billy, raising a hand, and speaking a word of greeting to his brother-in-law who in turn responded likewise. Billy and Selena's home was a tall structure that sat on the side of a hill. Its roof was high and steep, reaching toward the sky, and almost touching the ground. They had built the house themselves with the help of Dewey and sub-contractors they knew. It had a combination two-car garage and basement, the ground level was the kitchen, living room, children's rooms, and main bathroom, and the upper level was more of a closed off loft, containing their bedroom and bathroom.

"Grab a seat," Billy told Jason, motioning to a patio chair.

"Thanks," Jason responded, but before he sat, asked, "does Selena have tea made?"

"Yeah, probably so," Billy said fidgeting with the glowing coals in the bowl of the grill. "If she doesn't, there's beer in the fridge."

"Okay," Jason said, heading for the kitchen door, "which one do you want?"

"I'll have iced tea when we eat, but right now I'd like to have a beer," Billy said, then added, "Sal's supposed to have some meat ready, tell her I'm ready out here whenever she is, as long as you're going."

"All right," Jason said, opened the kitchen door, and stepped inside.

The two women were standing at what could be described as a staging area of the kitchen counter. They had been talking in low tones and laughing. They sobered somewhat when the door opened and Jason stepped over the threshold. Diane's blue eyes flashed as his own eyes met hers, he knew that look.

"Have you been telling all my secrets, woman?" he asked Diane in a tone of mocking sternness.

"No," Diane said, her eyes starting to dance now. How did she get her eyes to do that? Was this a result of the effect he had on her? He hoped so because she was absolutely beautiful to him. How had he gotten so lucky?

"Just the juicy ones," Diane said, then giggled when she saw the color of his embarrassment escape the collar of his shirt and spread across his face. His eyes left Diane's and met Selena's gaze as a second wave of embarrassment rushed up to reinforce the first one. Selena tried to stifle a giggle of her own by covering her mouth with her hand at Jason's embarrassment, but it still escaped her lips.

"Do you have iced tea made?" Jason asked Selena, trying to regain his composure, "and Billy says he's ready for the meat."

"Yes, I have tea made," Selena said, still showing her delight at his obvious discomfiture. Then as she slyly glanced at Diane, she said, "I will bring the beer and tea, if you will take the plate of meat to Billy, you Conquering Hero, you."

His face felt like the color red now. Both Diane and Selena were laughing outright, relishing in Jason's awkwardness. He lowered his head, laughing himself. When he felt his face returning to the cooler shades of flesh, he plucked up the plate of meat, and made his retreat.

"Selena said she would be out shortly with drinks," Jason told Billy, as the latter took the plate from the former.

"Tough room?" Billy asked, sporting a bemused look of his own.

"Yep," Jason said. "You know you're sister."

"Don't I though," Billy said nodding. "Diane has a big heart, but keeping a secret isn't one of her strong suits." The two men shared a laugh of their own together over this common knowledge of Diane. Jason, Billy, Dewey, and even Keith would have fought to the death for Diane, with no hesitation, or no questions asked, yet they all knew this about her, and even loved her for it.

The two women came through the kitchen door, Selena carried a six pack of beer and a glass of iced tea, and Diane carried two glasses of iced tea. Billy was busy loading the grill with the contents of the plate Jason had brought to him, and Selena opened a can of beer for him. He took it from her with one hand, and setting the plate down, encircled her waist with the other arm. He pulled her close and kissed her full on the mouth.

"Wow," Selena said, "we'll have to have them over more often." Billy smiled at her, winked, and gave her a squeeze.

Jason and Diane were seated together on the patio chairs, each sipping their tea and holding hands. Billy and Selena joined them.

"I will be starting up my own board in a couple of weeks," Selena told them, referring to her dispatch job, "and I've been given the opportunity to select some of the drivers that will be on it, and I would like to have you on it, Jason."

"I would like that, too," Jason said, nodding. "Thanks."

"You're quite welcome," Selena said. She then asked, "Do you think Keith would be willing to make the change to my board?"

"I couldn't say for sure, but I don't know why he wouldn't," Jason told her.

"Have you heard from him, lately," Diane asked her husband.

"Yep, he called this morning before I came up for breakfast," Jason said. "He said he was going to call again when he got home this afternoon, but he probably got side tracked."

"He didn't call when I was there," Diane informed him.

"He's going to Florida next week, and I'm going to Suwanee," Jason said.

"Will you get to run together any?" Billy asked. he wasn't certain where Suwanee was.

"You will run together to Atlanta, Georgia, won't you?" Diane asked.

"Yep," Jason said, using his standard affirmative answer. "You just might make a trucker's wife yet." She beamed at him, and locking her arm through his, squeezed closer to him.

"If I can get you both on my board," Selena said, "I might be able to run the two of you together more often, if that's what you would want."

"That would be nice," Diane said, before Jason could respond. "I wouldn't worry about him as much," Diane said this last part to Selena.

"Oh, hell," Jason said. "I'm fine."

"I know you are," Diane said, inflecting a double meaning, "but I also know how you run whenever you have to be at a certain place at a certain time."

"How many miles can you legally run in a week's time?" Billy asked, not trying to derail his sister, but seemingly asking his question before he forgot it.

"Legally, in a seven-day period, forty-two hundred miles is about the limit," Jason said. "There are exceptions, of course. If you ran across most of the western states where the speed limit is seventy-five miles per hour, you could log more miles."

"Just out of curiosity, how many miles do you like to run a week?" Selena asked Jason.

"I'm comfortable with thirty-five hundred to four thousand," Jason answered her.

"That's good to know," Selena said.

"You know I'm right about how you run," Diane said to Jason. "I've been on the Jason Fox Express a few times when you've had to run hard."

"Hopefully, I can help change that," Selena said to Diane. "In Jason's defense, whenever he is dispatched on a load, no one in that dispatch office worries about that load anymore. I've seen that more than once in the short time I've been there."

"Thank you," Jason said to Selena.

"Everyone tell me how well done you want your meat," Billy said getting up from his chair and moving to the grill. The three of them agreed that medium was the unanimous choice, and Billy cooked the cuts of meats accordingly. After the meat was pulled from the grill, the quartet moved inside the house and ate together.

After the meal, the four of them sat together in the living room, Jason and Diane on a love seat together, and Billy and Selena on the sofa. They talked about a variety of things, and eventually their conversation turned to the young woman from California who had been found dead in Springfield.

"Does anyone know how she ended up here?" Jason asked, to no one in particular.

"If anyone does know, they aren't saying," Selena said.

"I can't imagine how terrible that must be for her family," Diane said, snuggling closer to Jason.

"We may never know how she got here, or why she was picked," Billy yawned.

"Surely with today's technology in forensic medicine, they can find most, if not all the answers," Selena pondered.

"Maybe," Jason said, then to Diane, "are you ready to go?"

"Yes, I am," she answered, hopping to her feet. Selena got to her feet also, and the two of them went into the kitchen. They had already loaded the dishwasher, so all Diane needed to do was retrieve her bowl of leftover potato salad. There wasn't much of it left, but anyone who knew Diane, knew she saved everything. In her mind, when you're a single mom, raising two kids, and on a limited income, you take nothing for granted, and you save everything.

Billy and Jason shook hands and said goodnight. Diane and Selena hugged and said goodnight. Billy and Diane hugged, and said goodnight. Jason and Selena hugged, and said goodnight. Jason expected someone to call from another room, "Goodnight John-Boy!" and he involuntarily chuckled under his breath.

Diane and Jason returned home and went to bed, but it was over an hour before they drifted off to sleep.

Jason awoke the next morning to a truly wonderful surprise, Diane was still in bed with him. Most nights when he was at home, Diane commented that Jason's snoring kept her awake, so instead of interrupting his sleep, she would simply go across the hallway to the spare bedroom and spend the rest of the night there. He was lying on his back, and he could tell he had slept with his mouth open by the tacky feeling there. His right arm was under Diane's neck, and he would have loved to leave it there, but the urge to urinate was powerfully strong this morning. She lay on her side, with her back to him, and her legs pulled up slightly. She wore the usual, old, faded cotton nightgown that she usually wore to bed, with nothing on underneath. Jason knew this, and the knowledge wasn't helping ease the pressure on his bladder. He shifted slightly, and Diane stirred, moaned softly, raised her head ever so much, and Jason removed his arm from under her.

Jason slipped from the bed and looked down at his wife. A ghost of a smile showed itself on his lips, as he remembered the old joke about going to bed with ugly women. The next morning, if you have your arm under their necks, you have to chew it off to get away. Some called it the "Beaver Arm" syndrome. This wasn't the case here, Jason found Diane very attractive. He could see the bare skin of her legs, the curve of her shoulders and hips, and what he couldn't see now, he had committed to memory. He wanted to climb back in bed with her, snuggle in behind her, wrap his arms around her from behind, press himself close to her, and do things. Then he remembered why he had gotten out of bed in the first place and headed for the bathroom.

He did what he needed to do, washed his hands, brushed his teeth, splashed water onto his face, and put on deodorant before returning to bed. He slipped in behind Diane as he had wanted to do, and after slipping an arm under her neck again, he wrapped his other arm around her, and held her tight. She was intoxicating to him, and before long, he was asleep again.

The next time he awoke, she was gone, and he had to pee again. After doing his usual tour of the bathroom again, he set out in search of his wife. He found her on the living room sofa, watching a Sunday morning news program on the television, and nursing a cup of coffee. She smiled her greeting to him as he went into the kitchen to get his own cup of coffee. After he had done so, he joined her on the sofa. She still wore the old nightgown, but now wore a blue terrycloth bath robe as well. He had thought to pull on a pair of athletic shorts before leaving the bedroom.

"You started something that you didn't finish this morning," she cooed at him, showing him a playful flash of her eyes.

"I came back to bed with the full intention of making love to you, but when I climbed in behind you, I just wanted to hold you there forever," Jason said soberly, and then kissed her.

"Wow," she whispered. Diane was about to explore this more in detail when they heard footsteps coming from the stairway leading to the bedroom on the third level of the house.

"Are you two decent?" Christine called down to them. It intrigued, stunned, and embarrassed her to think of her mother actually having a sex life. She loved Jason like he was her biological father, but how long could these two keep it up. Then she stifled a giggle at the "keep it up" phrasing. Jason and her mother acted like they were still on their honeymoon. They had been married a few years now, and they showed no signs of slowing down. On the other hand, she didn't want them to slow down. Christine, being the younger of the two daughters, had seen the way most of the guys her mom had dated had treated her. Christine knew Jason loved her mother, and she loved him for it.

"Yes, we are," Diane said, then giggled as Jason blew a soft, steady, stream of air along the baseline of her neck.

"Come on, you guys!" Christine had resumed her descent, then stopped again at the sound of her mother's giggles. "I have to pee!" she called out blatantly, she had no bathroom of her own upstairs on the third level.

"Well, then, come on down," Jason called up to her. "It's not like you have to look down here at us."

Christine considered this. Then asked herself what was that the name of the woman in the Bible that hadn't resisted the temptation to look back at that burning city. Could she in fact walk past the living room without looking into it? Probably not, but she doubted she would be turned into a pillar of sugar—or was it salt?

"Okay, I'm coming down," Christine called out to them.

"Wait!" Jason called to Christine. Christine froze. Jason covered Diane's mouth with one of his hands. She had seen the mischievous look in his eyes, and he had seen that she had seen, and he didn't want her laughing out loud, as it looked like she was about to do.

"What?" Christine called back to them, her tone that of exasperation.

"How do we know you're decent? I haven't had breakfast yet, and I don't want to be sick because I saw you naked," Jason called back to her.

"Oh!" Christine blared out, then bounded down the rest of the stairs and dashed down the hallway to the main bathroom.

"You are such an ornery shit," Diane said, laughing when Jason uncovered her mouth with his hand.

"It's her own fault," Jason said in mock indignation. "Just because she may think we don't look decent when we're naked, doesn't mean we aren't." Diane's eyes danced at this, her laughter coming easily.

"How about some breakfast, now that you've mentioned it?" Diane asked.

"Okay, where would you like to go?" Jason asked her right back. Part of the money he had held out of his check was for such an occasion as this. Neither one of them owned a credit card, the closest thing Jason had to one was his fuel card for the Peterbilt.

"How about we cook?" Diane arched an eyebrow at him.

"Pancakes?" Jason asked; it was probably their favorite breakfast food.

"Yes," Diane answered. "While you're doing the pancakes, I'll scramble some eggs, make toast, and maybe even some biscuits and gravy," she enticed him.

"All right," he said. He got to his feet, extended a hand to her, and helped her to her feet. He embraced her and kissed her again. "I'll be right back, I want to get a shirt."

Later, in the kitchen, they cooked together. Jason had the free-standing griddle going, cooking three pancakes at a time. Diane had one skillet on the stove, with scrambled eggs slowly cooking. She had a small plate of toast started and a pan of biscuits in the oven.

They had the stereo on, and a slow song came on. Jason put down his spatula, and circled his arms around Diane's waist from behind. He started the swaying from side to side. Diane let herself be drawn into the moment, she loved it when he did this. They were lost in the moment when Christine came into the kitchen.

"Don't you two ever give it a rest?" she wanted to know.

"Hey, I had something going on here until you showed up," Jason said humorously, then kissed Diane on the back of the neck as he released her.

"Tease," Diane said to him accusingly, as she faced him, obviously wanting more.

"You two don't ever stop," Christine accused. "What can I do to help?"

"You can finish up the toast," Diane told her daughter, as she divided the scrambled eggs on three plates. Christine accepted the post as "Master Toaster Operator" graciously. Diane melted a half a stick of margarine in the skillet, previously occupied by eggs, set it back down on the same burner, waited for the margarine to melt, reduced the heat, added flour, stirred, then slowly poured in small amounts of milk until she had the desired thickness. With the gravy made, she turned the burner off, and pulled the biscuits out of the oven, turning it off as well. Christine finished spreading margarine on the sixth piece of toast she had just plucked from the toaster. Jason was ladling the last of the pancake batter onto the griddle. Diane and Christine filled their plates and sat on barstools at a breakfast bar. Jason soon joined them, and the two women made room for him.

"What time do you need to leave today?" Diane asked. She was going to try to keep her spirits up, this was the part of the week she hated the most. Jason would leave sometime today, and Christine would be leaving for work herself this afternoon, leaving Diane alone.

"What?" Christine asked expressively, her head coming around to look at Jason. "You're leaving today? It seems like you just got here. I never get to see your ass anymore."

"My ass has been around here most of the weekend," Jason said, winking at Diane. "I probably better call Keith and see what time he wants to leave."

"Tell him I said hi," Christine said, dismissing herself and putting her plate and eating utensils in the dishwasher. She dashed out of the room and up the stairs to her room, singing the words to some song Diane and Jason had never heard, and probably didn't want to. Jason picked the cordless phone up off its charger and punched Keith's phone number in on the keypad. Diane had put their dishes in the dishwasher as Christine had done, stepped around behind Jason, and wrapped her arms around him from behind. Jason put the phone to his ear with one hand and clasped one of Diane's with the other. He was kissing her palm, when Katrina, Keith's wife, answered the telephone.

"Hello," she greeted, Jason knew she knew who was calling because of their caller ID unit.

"Hi," Jason said, "how are you?"

"I'm fine," Katrina answered. "Have you enjoyed your time off this week?"

"Yes, I have," Jason said, pulling Diane's arm forward until he could feel her breasts pressing into the back of his neck. "Considering this is the shortest part of the week."

"I'll second that," she said. "I suppose you want to talk to my good looking man?"

"Well, no, actually, I wanted to talk to Keith," Jason said mischievously. Diane and Kat both burst out laughing in his ears, Kat through the telephone connection, and Diane from behind him.

"That was one of your better ones," Kat told him after she started to sober a bit. "Hang on, I'll get him." Jason could still hear her chuckling.

"Hey, Slick! What in the world' you doin'?" Keith asked through the telephone into Jason's ear.

"Oh, you know me, my favorite pastime—making fun of you," Jason said, pulling Diane tight against his back again.

"Yea, I heard," Keith said. "I'm glad you're my friend, I'd hate to see what you could do to me if you were my enemy."

"Hey, all seriousness aside, what time do you want to leave today?"

Jason asked. He was finding it hard to concentrate, because, presently, Diane had the back of his neck notched between her breasts, and she was swaying side to side. He knew that she knew what she was doing and how it was affecting him.

"I guess I need to leave around noon, two o'clock at the latest," Keith answered.

"Well, you have the furthest to go, so you tell me," Jason said, he was just itching to get off the telephone.

"Let's split the difference and say one o'clock," Keith suggested.

"Okay, I'll be there," Jason said. "I'll see you then, bye."

"Bye," Keith said, and they both hung up.

Jason came off the barstool in one quick, fluid motion, and cornered Diane in the kitchen. She backed into a corner created by the joining of two perpendicular countertops and bent forward slightly, anticipating Jason's advance upon her. She held her hands out in front of her, and she was laughing. Her eyes were alive and sparkling, she was forty-five years old, and she couldn't ever remember being this happy. Jason crouched down like a knife fighter, keeping his arms and hands wide, and slowly moved in. Diane continued to laugh, and she started twisting in place on her bare feet, drawing one leg over the other, squirming like she needed to go pee. Jason got within a few feet of her, then he dropped down on this hands and knees, and growling, sought the back of Diane's knees with his tongue. Just as he made the contact of Diane's desired body part with his desired body part, Christine's voice came from behind him.

"What in the hell is going on here?" Christine exclaimed. She was ob-viously heading out the door. She had her purse slung over one shoulder, digging her car keys out of it. Her sunglasses were propped on top of her head, she wore a sleeveless pull-over T-shirt, a pair of blue jean cut-offs, and flip-flops. On the other shoulder, she was trying to keep a work uniform propped there on a clothes hanger. She had heard the commotion from the kitchen and was utterly surprised when she stepped around the corner, and saw Jason on his hands and knees, backing her mother into a corner, trying to lick the back of her knees, at least that's what she thought she saw. She shook her head, as if to clear it.

"Never mind," Christine said presently, "I don't want to know."

"Christine, help me!" Diane called in mock horror and fright.

Christine started to open her mouth to say something like, "you got yourself into this, now you get yourself out," or, "you knew what he was like when you married him," but before she could say anything, Jason turned on her, growling, baring his teeth, and took one doggy step toward her. Christine screamed, "Mommy!" her eyes alight with humor and excitement, and bolted for the door. Jason barked his satisfaction at the fleeing Christine, then resumed his stalking of Diane. It was time to attack the back of her knees and her ankles simultaneously, and as he hunkered down for his second attack, Diane sprang over him, and darted for the bedroom.

Diane halted halfway down the hallway to see if she was being pursued. She was, but not by a four-legged ankle licker, now she was being pursued by a two-legged ankle licker. She squealed with delight and dashed into the bedroom. Jason found her waiting for him, lying on the bed.

After they had made love, she lay curled up next to him. He had his arm around her, lying on his back, looking up at the ceiling. She watched him silently, and she knew secretly what was running through his mind. She had been with him on the truck several times before, and she knew of the personality change he went through. It wasn't as severe as a Dr. Jekyll and Mr. Hyde metamorphosis, but like most people, Jason was a little different at work than at home. Even she, Diane, knew she was different at work than at home. She definitely knew she wouldn't let anyone at her place of employment chase her around on all fours, trying to lick the backs of her knees and ankles. Just as she was secure in the knowledge that Jason wouldn't chase anyone but her like that. They had both been through hard emotional times and lonely times, and what's more, they both knew what they had now would never be duplicated or replaced.

Jason was, in fact, thinking of life on the road. One day blurring into another, sleeping and eating when he could, and never once taking his inner eye from his goal: Get the job done, and get home. He hadn't always had people at home that cherished him, but now he did, and he loved the feeling of being loved. Life on the road could be all-consuming. Jason had seen many varieties of this road consumption. Truck drivers hooked on sex, spending all their money on prostitutes until they were broke. Truck drivers hooked on drugs, spending all their money and time getting high. Truck drivers hooked on gambling, spending all their money and time in casinos until they had lost everything. If there was a vice out there on the road, there were truck drivers indulging themselves, at any and all costs, even sacrificing the love and trust of their families, but, in all honesty, most career-minded truck drivers don't do anything on the road they wouldn't do at home, they are just people who have chosen a different lifestyle.

Jason closed his eyes and drifted off to sleep, still holding Diane close to him. She curled as close to him as she could, snuggled tightly against him, and relished in the knowledge that she had finally found the love she had craved for so long. She followed her husband off to sleep with that thought on her mind and a smile on her face.

They woke a few hours later, a few minutes before twelve o'clock, and didn't want what the rest of the day had to offer: the absence of each other's company. Diane got up and busied herself with packing Jason's items for the week, duffle bag of clean clothes, laundry bag, laptop computer, shaving kit, and, of course, his logbook. She gathered these items and carried them to the truck, a couple at a time, while Jason took a reviving hot shower.

Jason and Diane met in the kitchen. He held her tenderly and stroked her hair as she laid her head on his shoulder. She clung to him, wishing she had him to herself just a few more hours, but realizing that when that time was up, she would want more time.

"I won't be gone forever," Jason whispered to her.

"You better not be," Diane choked out.

"Kiss me," he said, not completing the whole sentence. When they were first married, he had told her once, "Kiss me like you'll never see me again."

She had, but had asked him to never use that phrase again. She had been with him on the truck enough to know how easily he could be taken from her, mainly by impatient motorists who had no respect for the amount of skill or patience it takes to pilot eighty thousand pounds of machinery through all sorts of traffic and weather conditions. She kissed him, hugged him, then kissed him again. He pulled away from her, put a hand on the side of her face, smiled, winked, then turned, and walked out the door. A few seconds later, Diane heard the truck start and drive away.

Chapter 8

At the same time Jason and Diane were at the cook out with Billy and Selena, a black model 379 Peterbilt driven by Jack was making its way toward Springfield, Missouri. The entity inside Jack had kept its part of the bargain, and he lacked nothing. Lately, though, the man's desires were getting in the way of the demons' "work".

When the driver did stop, it was always in a secluded spot, a deserted rest area, a parking lot late at night, but rarely did he stop at a truck stop. He was presently stopped on an access ramp to I-70 in Ohio, west of Columbus. It was time to sample the delights of his latest victim.

She was a young woman, white, average build, and pretty. Until yesterday, she had planned to be married in a couple of weeks. She was nineteen, a year out of high school, and until yesterday, she lived in the Seville-Lodi area of Ohio. She had taken a job at a truck stop, waiting tables after graduating high school. She had quit the truck stop, and went to work at a truck wash in the same area as the truck stops. The owner of the truck wash wanted someone, preferably female, to work behind the counter, answering the telephone, taking money, and talking on the CB to the truckers. This had worked so well, that he decided to stay open twenty-four hours, and to do that, he would like to have two more girls to fill those shifts. The young woman here, Rachel, worked the graveyard shift of 3:00 P.M. to 11:00 P.M. Around 9:30 P.M. the previous night, she had stepped outside to enjoy the night air and thought she heard something like a puppy barking. When she stepped around the corner of the building to investigate, someone attacked her from behind out of the darkness. That was the last thing she remembered until now.

Rachel lay in what could only be described as a padded box. She felt her bare skin touching everywhere in the box and assumed she must be naked. It was dark, and she heard a noise, as well as felt a vibration, both were low. She had experienced these sensations before, but in a different way, she recognized these ambiances, but couldn't quite put her finger on it. Presently, whatever she was lying in rocked gently, then the "lid" of the box she was in lifted.

Rachel squinted her eyes to the point of closing them, and brought her hands up to help shield the light, which wasn't much. She saw a figure standing over her, but all she could see of him was from mid-thigh up. After seeing her captor, she realized she was naked, and tried unsuccessfully to cover her breasts and pubic area with her hands.

"Oh, please, don't," said a rich, mild, pleasant male voice. "I've seen the naked female body many times, and yours is truly among the finest."

Rachel blinked, perplexed, but made no verbal reply. She was still trying to cover herself, and she raised her head slightly to peer around. It was dimly lit, and she couldn't be certain, but she thought she was on the inside of a truck sleeper. She had never been inside one before, but that was the only thing that came to mind. Now the vibration, and the noise she had experienced earlier made sense. She was terrified to say the least, and she had no idea where she was, who her captor was, or how long she had been here, wherever here was.

Rachel used the hand that had covered her breasts to grip the edge of the box, only to find the top edge flush with another surface. She sat up and recovered her breasts. What she saw confirmed her belief that she was indeed inside a truck sleeper. The walls of the sleeper were padded, and it had a ceiling high enough for her captor to stand erect. He was holding the "lid" of the "box" she was in open with one hand, and his other hand was holding a much larger "lid". He let go of the larger "lid" and offered that hand to her.

"I am many things," that rich masculine voice said again, "and among them, I am polite."

Rachel ignored his hand, and stood to her feet on her own. Now that her eyes had adjusted to the light, which wasn't much, she could see her surroundings and her captor. Her surroundings were claustrophobic by some standards, and the opening between the sleeper and the cockpit of the truck was covered by a heavy vinyl curtain that looked to be zipped up the middle. Her captor was of medium height, she guessed him to be close to five feet nine or ten inches. His hair was dark brown? Dark blonde? Black? She couldn't tell in this light. His eyes were his most striking and memorable feature because they actually glowed slightly, a shade of red, not much, but enough to catch people's attention. If she had to describe him, that description would be the character that Keifer Sutherland had portrayed in the movie, The Lost Boys.

"If you would please step down here beside me," he said.

Rachel did, using the sides of the sleeper wall for balance. Once she stood beside him, he lowered the "lid" to the "box" she had been in. The box was, in fact, a recessed area shaped like a rectangle, large enough for a human body, that had been placed into the sleeper bunk with the "lid", when closed, flush with the bunk, and with the mattress of the bunk in place, no one would ever know of its existence. Next he lowered the larger "lid", it was hinged so that it swung downward with the help of two gas filled cylinders, to its resting place atop of the "box" Rachel had been in just moments before. She looked at him, not hiding her look of surprise.

"It's my own design," he said, showing her a brief smile. Then he sobered, and turned to face her. Rachel cringed when he reached toward her, then past her, and she heard something go click.

"I'm sure you would like to use the restroom, and freshen up a bit," he said, "and the restroom is right behind you. It isn't much, but it does the job."

"I'm not doing anything until you answer some questions," Rachel said defiantly, finally finding her voice.

"Of course," he said, and he sat down on the end of the bunk furthest away from her, showing her no signs of aggression. "I'll answer any question you have for me."

Rachel's mind was racing. This didn't make any sense. She couldn't remember ever seeing him before, he didn't look or sound like anyone she knew. Nothing about him stirred any obscure memories. She quickly ran a silent inventory of all the men she had ever come into contact with, and came up with nothing.

"May I please have my clothes back?" she asked, testing the waters.

"No," he said simply, smiling what looked like a comforting smile. Rachel waited to see if he would add anything, an explanation, perhaps, but he said nothing more on the subject, as if to say the case was closed.

"Who are you, and what do you want with me?" Rachel asked, shaken a little by his comforting smile and his no-nonsense manner.

"You can call me Jack," he said, extending a hand of greeting toward her, she ignored it, and he placed it in his lap. "You are going to become my second victim." His eyes flashed bright red momentarily at the name of Jack. It was so brief, that Rachel silently questioned whether it had actually happened. She didn't know anyone named Jack.

"When will you let me go?" Rachel asked, still turning the name he gave her over in her head.

"I won't," Jack answered simply, still smiling, and now he was looking at the parts of her body that she wasn't able to cover.

"Why?" Rachel tried to hold back her tears.

"You're mine," Jack replied, still smiling, and now he was tilting his head from side to side, slowly, but keeping his eyes on her.

"Please don't hurt me," Rachel pleaded, she was openly sobbing now.

"That's not a question," Jack said, still enjoying himself.

"I want to go home," Rachel said through her tears, she was starting to hitch her breaths like a child does when crying. "Will you please let me go home?"

"That's out of the question," Jack said, he was starting to sober. "You can't go home naked, and I won't give you your clothes back, so you will have to stay with me—for now." He stood, and she noticed for the first time that he was about two inches shorter than her. She was still crying, but not as hard now, and she showed only defeat when he gently took her by the arm, turned her toward the bathroom door, tenderly put her inside the small enclosure, and closed the door behind her. He listened by the door and was satisfied when he heard her urinating into the small toilet. He quickly shed his own clothing and stood waiting for her to come out.

Rachel quickly assessed her situation. This was kidnapping, and he obviously knew it, and wasn't bothered by it. Her lack of clothing concerned her the most, this was either a control tactic to keep her from trying to escape, or he meant to rape her. If it was sex he was after, she wasn't a virgin, but she also wasn't vastly experienced either. She had lost her virginity four years ago to a boy one year older than herself. She had continued to date him for a few weeks longer, then broke up with him, after becoming bored with his ever-repeating request for sex. She had had several more boyfriends since then, but had been sexual with only three, including the one she was planning to marry. There had also been Stewart.

Stewart, or Stu, to most people who knew him, had been her boss at the truck stop. He had caught Rachel and another waitress, Darla, in the back, intimately kissing and touching. The solution was simple; they would each start giving him blow jobs once a week for his silence. Rachel knew that news of her having an affair with another woman would not only hurt her parents, but would also disgrace them in the small community they lived in, so she consented.

After the third week of Rachel giving Stu his extortion blow job, Darla's boyfriend paid Stu a little visit. Darla's boyfriend found Stu demanding his "payment" at Darla's car door. What happened next wasn't pleasant. Darla's boyfriend didn't kill Stu, but instead he beat him much the same way Dewey had beaten Mark. As Stu had lain on the ground in horrible pain, bleeding, bruised, and fearing the beating wasn't over yet, Darla's boyfriend bent down over Stu.

"If I ever hear of you trying this shit again on Darla, I'll be back, and I'll hurt you next time," Darla's boyfriend told Stu in a friendly tone, then added in the same tone, "I know Rachel's boyfriend, and I'm sure he would want to try to convince you of the error of your ways."

"Fuck you," Stu said, "that's none of your business."

Darla's boyfriend had kicked Stu hard in the crotch. White pain had exploded through Stu's testicles. He cried out in pain, and covered his crotch with both of his hands, and before he could pull his knees up and roll away, Darla's boyfriend stomped hard onto Stu's hands. Stu's top hand was crushed, and the force of the stomp, cracked his pelvic bone. Stu was convinced; he never bothered Darla or Rachel again after that, and he never fathered children after that either. A few days later, Rachel went to work at the truck wash.

Rachel and Darla had remained friends, though now they didn't kiss and fondle each other. Darla still worked at the truck stop, and Stu had not only quit his job there, but had completely left the area. Darla's boyfriend had also gone AWOL; he had left a couple of days after that. Darla changed boyfriends every few weeks, and Rachel had only seen this one that night. It had been dark, and he hadn't been there that long. Rachel would not have recognized him if she had ever seen him again.

These memories came to her as she finished in the small bathroom. She was by no means inexperienced when it came to sex, but she wasn't worldly either. She steadied herself for the possibility that this man was going to demand sex and opened the door.

Rachel blinked as if not registering what she was seeing. The smile was still on Jack's lips, and his eyes were glowing again. Rachel glanced at his face only briefly, then returned her gaze to the stiffening organ protruding from Jack's crotch. She gasped in fright, tried to back into the bathroom again and close the door once more. Jack caught the door, wrenched it open, grabbed a handful of hair on Rachel's head, and yanked her out of there. He roughly threw her onto the sleeper bunk and crawled onto it after her. She was scrambling away with nowhere to go.

Jack knelt on the bunk and reached for her ankles. Rachel tried to kick at him, but he was too fast and too strong for her. He soon had an ankle in each hand and jerked them hard toward him, spreading her legs as he did so. She had been on her rump facing him, and now she had her legs involuntarily on either side of him. He reached around her, and placed each hand on her buttocks. She was crying again and trying to get away, but he held her firm. She was trying to hold herself away from him by pushing against his chest with her hands.

"Please, God, help me," Rachel pleaded, trying to find anything resembling compassion in his glowing eyes, but she found none. Instead what she found was an end to his patience.

Jack tightened his grip with one hand on Rachel's buttock, and moved his other one up her back. He pulled her toward him with enough force to knock the wind out of her, and while she was gasping, and trying to get her breath back, he laid her onto her back. He stopped for an instant and was still, as if listening. His facial expression changed to one of confusion.

"What's happening?" Rachel asked in a croaky whisper. She had expected to be impaled by him, but he had suddenly stopped.

"Damn it!" he swore. Rachel chanced a quick look and saw that the erection he had threatened her with a moment ago was gone.

"I don't know what—" she started, then stopped, looking at his slowly pulsing red eyes. "If this is about—"

"You made the choice," Jack said simply. "You didn't have any qualms about doing good ol' Stewart." He was looking at her now, his eyes glowing with more intensity now. She gasped in reflex to his comment, not knowing how he could have known that. Her reaction brought a smile to his lips and a chuckle from his throat, which soon turned into the sound of a growl.

"How did you know about that?" Rachel whispered in horror.

"Remember, little girl, somewhere, someone will see or hear, and that someone may talk. If you want to act like a whore, there are people willing to treat you like a whore," Jack said still looking at her, his eyes never stopped exploring her nakedness.

"I made a mistake," Rachel whimpered, feeling the tears coming again.

He loosened her out of his grasp, and Rachel retreated to the farthest point in the sleeper away from him. She just wanted to hide in a place where there was no place to hide. She her legs pulled up to her chest, trying to make herself as small as possible. She would not take the time to marvel at how the survival instinct took over in these kinds of situations. Presently, Jack's face returned to normal, and he turned his attention to preparing the truck for travel.

A few hours later, on a lonely access ramp of I-70 in Indiana, Jack attempted to rape Rachel again, without success. He didn't understand, everything was working the way it was supposed to, but when the time came to penetrate, he couldn't. Rachel didn't know how much more of this she could take, and she did something she hadn't done since she was a little girl, she started to pray silently. She didn't pray for rescue, but for God's salvation and everlasting mercy.

The load that Jack was hauling went to Cape Girardeau, Missouri, so after entering the state of Illinois, he continued on I-70, and, at the city of Effingham, Illinois, he merged onto I-57 South.

On yet another quiet access ramp, Jack tried to rape Rachel again, with the same result. He cried out in frustration, and cursed venomously. He finally gave up, eased off the bunk, and angrily got dressed.

"Get yourself cleaned up," Jack told her, obviously from the lack of anything else to say. "We'll be stopping again when we cross over into Missouri."

Rachel's only response was a silent prayer to God, thanking Him for his protection.

Jack grabbed his logbook, opened it, and brought it up to date. He released the air brakes and left the access ramp. He drove down I-57 South to exit 30, and turned onto Illinois State Highway 146 East, and fifteen miles later, he turned south onto Illinois State Highway 3. About twelve miles later, Jack turned east again onto Illinois State Highway 146, and crossed the Mississippi River into Missouri. Jack drove to the industrial park of Cape Girardeau and parked in the street. He stood up from his seat and turned to Rachel.

"Get up," Jack ordered her. When she complied without responding, Jack angrily grabbed her by the hair of her head, opened the door to the bathroom, and shoved her in there, slamming the door after her. He then raised the bed of the bunk, and raised the door to the small compartment under the bunk. When he heard the toilet flush, he wrenched the door open, yanked her out of there, and forced her into the compartment.

Rachel went into the compartment, although she didn't want to. She lay down and closed her eyes.

"Don't get too comfortable, we won't be here very long," Jack chided her. Rachel ignored him, she had started making her peace with God, and nothing he could do to her now would make any difference to her. He low-

ered the lids and drove to the warehouse where he was supposed to un-
load. He checked in with the shipping and receiving department, and the
shipping/receiving clerk, not knowing exactly why, assigned him a door
promptly.

That was one of the perks of having a demon for backup, Jack thought
to himself as he opened the trailer doors and backed the tractor/trailer unit
into the appropriate door space. When Jack was a young child, his grandmother had taken him to church with her. He had loved his grandmother
and had gone with her without complaint, until her death when he was in
his teens.

When his grandmother was diagnosed with stomach and intestinal cancer, Jack's imaginary friend had appeared to him in a dream in the form
of a beautiful woman. Jack knew the beautiful woman was his imaginary
friend, dreams were funny like that.

"My name is Sultry," the woman in the dream told him, "and this is what
you need to do…"

When Jack had awakened the next morning and considered the dream,
he had rejected it. Sultry appeared again in a dream as before, and this time
promised Jack that if he would join forces with her, she would give his
grandmother a merciful, quick death. The next morning, Jack agreed, and
the demon moved in, possessing Jack. As the weeks went on, Jack's grandmother still lingered, suffering horribly. Jack called upon the demon by way
of a mental page, he had come to think of it. Although Sultry couldn't read
Jack's mind, they were mentally linked, it was confusing to think about.
The demon would make its presence known in Jack's mind by way of a sort
of mental tap on the shoulder, or when Jack wanted the demon, he used
this mental page. Although Jack had discovered the demon couldn't read
his mind, it came whenever Jack sent out this mental page.

Jack confronted the demon, reminding it of the promise of a quick
death for his grandmother.

Jack could catch a hint of humor in the demon's response as it said,
"To immortals, a thousand years is but a blink of an eye. When we made
our little deal, you did not specify what perception of time we would go by,
yours or mine. I'm more comfortable using mine, and with this said, her
suffering will be short."

Jack was furious. He had felt a rage unlike any he had ever felt in his
life. In a moment of religious weakness, he had sought to help his grandmother end her suffering. Instead, he had made the situation worse because

she would have small remissions, only to be worse than before.

"I suppose I could speed the process up by putting a thought into her head to kill herself," Sultry suggested.

"No!" Jack screamed. He knew where suicide victims spent eternity, "I'll kill her myself before…" he trailed off, guessing what the demon would suggest next.

"Funny you should say such a thing," Sultry said. "Seeing as how you are willing to trade your everlasting soul for hers, and I am in need of a blood sacrifice anyway, who knows, maybe the Creator will forgive you in the end."

Jack didn't waste any time, he loved his grandmother very much, and knew now with what a liar he had aligned himself. Oh sure, what the demon had said about perception of time was true, but he still felt like he had been lied to, and he would certainly watch his ass more closely next time. Jack went to the barn behind the family home and drew a substantial amount of a sedative used on cattle into a large syringe. He found his grandmother asleep in her bed and tearfully injected her with the sedative. She died peacefully in the night.

With the help of Sultry, Jack wrote a suicide note, convincingly in his grandmother's handwriting. When the autopsy was performed and the note read, Sultry used her unique gift of influence on the authorities to rule out foul play.

As the months passed, the demon made no demands of Jack that he could tell. What the demon was doing in actuality was slowly bending Jack to its way of thinking. By subliminally suggesting thoughts to Jack and then watching Jack's reaction, the demon knew what Jack wanted most. One day while communicating with Jack, Sultry asked if there was any change Jack would make on himself.

"Well," Jack said thoughtfully, "you will probably think this funny, but I would love to have all kinds of women."

"I find no humor in that at all," Sultry lied, and had a very high suspicion that this would be the answer.

"You can do this?" Jack asked, wanting to believe. It felt as though his simple life of the passed was falling away.

"Of course," the demon said. "Just say the word."

"Consider it said," Jack told the demon, grinning evilly.

Sultry simply sent women under its control to Jack, women who were addicted to drugs or alcohol, or women who would do most anything for money. Sultry pressed Jack to take on all the women it sent him. Not all of the women were attractive or appealing, but Sultry insisted Jack have sex with them all, and Jack surprisingly found that deep down he wanted to have sex with all of them. Most of these women wore blank expressions and had hollow countenances, but there were some who were attractive and vivacious. These women, Jack noticed, had eyes that glowed red from time to time. This unnerved him, but it also charged him with a sexual excitement that he had never felt before.

Sultry also gave Jack its vast knowledge of the best lines women wanted to hear. The demon had thousands of years of experience of compiling these lines, and they all worked. What the demon didn't tell Jack was it also increased his sex drive and added a violent nature toward women.

As the months passed, Jack realized the demon had lied to him again. Jack became bitter, withdrawn, and increasingly violent toward women. The demon, of course, was subliminally suggesting these thoughts and emotions to Jack. After a short term in the military, he was given a medical discharge, and he turned to the one thing he felt he could fall back on, being an over-the-road trucker.

What Jack found was that about the only women willing to have sex with him were prostitutes. Jack didn't like taking no for an answer—and didn't. The prostitutes that refused to render him their services Jack simply raped or sodomized or beat or did any combination of the three. Sometimes, these prostitutes offered him oral sex instead, and he accepted, but most of the time, that wasn't enough, and Jack would demand more of the oral sex or rape them. In Jack's mind, he reasoned these victimized hookers wouldn't go to the police, and he was correct in his way of thinking, although he sent more than one to the emergency room with the beatings he dished out.

As Jack traveled the country, driving a truck, the demon used Jack's disillusionment about sex, and slyly suggested that Jack should rid society of as many of these hookers as possible. Sultry also mentally overwhelmed Jack with the notion that all women sold sex in one form or another. Jack fought this, but after being bombarded with these suggestions for so long, he consented, and that brought him to the present day.

After the unloading of the trailer was completed, Jack drove south on I-55 to the city of Sikeston. Again he drove to the industrial park and found the warehouse where he would be loading. The load was scheduled for the next day, but Jack smiled to himself as he mused about how persuasive he could be. He found the warehouse, parked, opened his trailer doors, and backed into a dock door. Jack left the motor of the truck idling as he exited the truck and headed for the shipping/receiving door. He left the motor idling so Rachel could still receive fresh air through a duct that pumped fresh air into the "box" under the sleeper bunk. The weather determined whether the fresh air was cool or slightly heated. Jack didn't want Rachel to die on him, he still had use of her body, and he wanted that body alive.

After Jack checked in with the shipping clerk, a tall, heavyset man in his late forties, the clerk shook his head dejectedly.

"That load is scheduled to load tomorrow," the clerk said.

"Yes, but I'm here now," Jack replied.

"And you'll be here in the morning if you're picking up this load," the clerk said, adding a tinge of irritation to his voice.

"Is the load ready?" Jack asked, keeping his tone even and his voice calm.

"Yes, it's ready, but you don't seem to understand, you won't be loaded until in the morning," the clerk said, sounding very defiant.

"Is there some reason you can't load me now?" Jack asked, he maintained a tone of patience, although his patience was peeling off him like a banana peel.

"Yes, there's a reason. Your appointment time is in the morning, and that's when you will be loaded," the clerk raised his voice slightly, as his face started to redden from anger. He had been sitting behind his desk in an open area called "shipping", but now he was on his feet and moving toward Jack, obviously thinking to intimidate with his size. What the clerk didn't know was the demon was busily at work in this situation. As soon as Jack had entered the building, there had been a half a dozen people in the shipping area, and the demon had sent suggestions to each one, suggesting that each one would later give different descriptions to the police of the man they saw, what was said, and what had been done. None of them would even agree on the description of the truck.

"Are you short handed with no one qualified to operate a fork lift?" Jack was barely remaining calm.

"No, I am not short handed," the clerk hissed. Jack could feel the tension building, and could hardly conceal his delight at the coming activity. The clerk continued, taking an ill-advised step toward Jack, and adding, "You will wait, because I say you will wait, and that's the end of it."

Well, Jack thought, if I can't fuck, maybe I can fight. The clerk heard the fist driving toward his face before he saw it, and then it was too late as the fist smashed into his face, squarely between the eyes. The blow rocked him off his feet, as another equally devastating blow connected with his temple, sprawling him face first onto the concrete floor. He lay still for a moment, then slowly got to his hands and knees, shaking his head, he couldn't remember ever being hit so fast and so hard. As he started to move, Jack took one step toward the clerk, and kicked him hard, driving his foot between the clerk's buttocks. The clerk sprawled face first again, this time howling in miserable pain, and unsuccessfully trying to reach the injured area with his hands. Jack took another step, and planted his same foot in the same area of the clerk's anatomy. The clerk went limp, his howls of pain turning into sobs of pain. Jack reached for the clerk, grabbing a handful of the clerks thinning hair, and pulling the man to his knees. Jack cocked his free arm back, and chambered his whole body for the next blow. Jack uncoiled, twisted from the waist, bent his knees, and put his body weight behind the punch, which scraped across the bridge of the clerk's nose, laying it over onto the man's cheek. As the clerk sprawled onto the concrete floor for the third time, Jack didn't let up. He stepped close, reached for the clerk, and yanked him to his feet.

"Now," Jack said, keeping his tone even and icy, "we tried things your way, and as you can see, it hasn't worked. So, if you will be so kind, climb your cock-sucking ass on that forklift and get me loaded, or this will just be the beginning. Do you understand me, you fat piece of shit?"

"I-I don't know th-th-that I can s-s-sit," the clerk whined, he was on the verge of sobbing.

"We all have our crosses to bear," Jack told the clerk in a mild tone. "You should have thought of that before you opened your fucking mouth. You have thirty minutes to get me loaded before I completely stomp the dog shit out of your fat cock-sucking ass."

The clerk started to sob as Jack shoved him toward the forklift. The clerk painfully climbed onto the seat of the forklift and started the motor. Jack walked to the clerk's desk and rummaged through the papers stacked there. After a few seconds of searching, he found the bill of lading and handed it to the clerk.

"You now have twenty-nine minutes," Jack said simply. Thirty minutes later, Jack pulled away from the dock, closed and sealed the trailer doors, and drove away. He turned onto the access ramp to U.S. Highway 60 and drove toward Springfield, Missouri. About three hours later, Jack pulled onto the parking lot of the closed westbound scale house on U.S. 60 between Cabool and Willow Springs, Missouri. He had stopped shortly after leaving Sikeston, let Rachel out of the compartment under the sleeper bunk, and she had remained quietly in the sleeper. At first, she had rummaged through every closet and drawer she could find, trying to find some clothes. She would have been satisfied to have found clothes other than her own, but the closets and drawers she could open held no clothes or anything she could use as a weapon.

Rachel could tell they were stopping again by the changes in motion and the sound of the motor. She peeked out of the opening between the sleeper and the cab of the truck, but all she saw was a dimly-lit parking lot of some sort. This was the first and, unknown to her, the last trip to Missouri she would ever make.

Jack parked the truck and set the tractor air brakes. He stood up from the driver's seat, stretched, and took the few steps to the sleeper. He didn't utter a word, but instead, started to undress. He took off his boots first, then his socks. Next, he pulled off his shirt, all the while watching Rachel. In another time, he thought, he could have possibly fallen in love with this young woman. She was pretty, slim, and supple. When he unbuttoned his jeans, Rachel cringed, and tried to put as much distance between herself and Jack. He lowered his jeans, relishing the look of resigned terror in Rachel's eyes as she watched him. He hooked his thumbs in the waist band of his underwear, shoved them down to his knees, and stepped out of them.

Jack tried, unsuccessfully, for the last time to rape Rachel. Instead, he lay beside her. He held her roughly and tightly close to him, wrapping his arms around her, and squeezing hard, to the point that he almost hurt her. The demon prevailed, and Jack's desire for Rachel was at full mast.

"Your ass is mine!" Jack hissed at her, the light of victory showed in his eyes and erection. He shoved her onto her back and climbed on top of her. As he started to penetrate her, she spoke.

"Jack," Rachel said softly, and put her arms around him, "if you can hear me, I'll pray for you."

The demon inside Jack's head screamed in pain, fear, and anger. It yanked Jack to his feet, away from Rachel. It regrouped, and Rachel realized what had happened before her eyes.

He was in a rage when he got dressed again. Jack drove about a mile west to a small truck stop there and pulled onto the east end of the lot where there was a coin-operated self-service car wash with a truck bay.

It was late at night by this time, and Jack knew from past experience that there wouldn't be anyone watching his activities. Rachel saw the lights of the truck stop, sprang painfully off the bunk, and tried to make a break for the passenger side door. Jack caught her movements out of the corner his eyes and slammed his right elbow into her midsection.

Jack parked the truck next to the truck bay, set the air brakes once more, and angrily got to his feet. He exited the truck and opened a side box, pulling out a roll of plastic and a roll of duct tape. He laid these items on the floor of the truck bay, and went back inside the truck after Rachel. She raised her hands in protest, but Jack never flinched, he hit her hard with his fist across her cheek and jaw, knocking her unconscious. He caught her in his arms before she fell to the floor. She was facing him, her head hung back, and the outside light dimly illuminating her face. Jack took a moment to really look at her and saw how pretty she really was. He lowered his head to hers and softly, passionately, kissed her on the mouth, then as the moment passed, he maneuvered her out of the truck.

When she awoke, Rachel saw she was lying on a sloping, concrete floor with a drain in the center of it. She recognized it as a floor of a car wash. She was still naked and one side of her face hurt. She looked around and saw Jack standing a few feet away holding a large-bladed knife. She suspected that her life was about over. She slowly got to her knees, put her hands together in front of her in a prayer gesture, lowered her head, and began her last prayer.

Jack rushed to her, wrenched her head back, and pulled the blade of the knife across Rachel's throat, cutting the flesh of her neck to her spine. The blood rushed out of the wound in a great torrent, but Jack didn't stop there. He was in a violent rage and started stabbing her. His rage came from his own action of kissing her and being aroused by it. She was a whore, and come to think of it all women were some sort of whores, Jack thought. When Jack finally regained his senses, he had unknowingly stabbed Rachel forty-five times. He stood over her with the knife grasped loosely in his hand. She still sat on her knees, leaning against his legs, her head tilted back, and her dead eyes "looking" at him.

He placed Rachel's body on its back and cut around her pubic area, then lifted away both skin and hair. He called this scalping. He would take this small patch of hair and skin, stretch it, scrape it, tan it, and hang it on a wall of the sleeper. Next, he fed coins into the receptacle and took the wand from its holder. Jack washed Rachel's body and rinsed it. Next, he wrapped her corpse in the plastic and duct taped it securely. Jack got back into the truck and changed his clothes. He retrieved her clothes from the truck, and along with the clothes he had worn until he stripped them off, he burnt them together. When he dropped her body off in Springfield later, the protection of the demon would prevent there being any evidence linking him to Rachel.

Jack loaded Rachel's wrapped body into the truck carefully. He drove to Springfield and reverently laid her lifeless body on the front steps of one of the many trucking companies there, with an attached note:

Dear boss,

As you can see, I've brought you another one for your consideration. As you can see, this one was special to me. I'm now two for two.
Sincerely,

Jack
Catch me if you can.

Chapter 9

Jason drove to Blanket Transportation's terminal, found the trailer with his load on it, hooked the tractor to it, and sat waiting for Keith. As he sat there, he reflected a bit on his past life. He had met Diane at a time in his life when he had thought love was a thing of the past for him. She had done more for him than she would probably ever know. His one thought, as he prepared to leave for the week, was to run the miles asked of him, and get the hell back home to her.

Jason took out his logbook, opened it, and made sure it was up-to-date. He had the stereo on and was also listening to the chatter on the CB radio, and looking over his logbook when he heard a familiar voice on the CB

"I'll have to catch you next time, neighbor," Keith's voice came from Jason's CB speaker. "I'm running a little late, and I want to try to beat my buddy over here. I'll take you up on the offer of the visit later."

Jason grinned mischievously. He loved getting his digs in on Keith, and in all fairness, Keith had gotten his digs in on Jason before. Jason took the CB microphone in his right hand, brought it to his mouth, and depressed the talk button.

"Is that you, WolfKat?" Jason asked into the microphone.

"Yeah," Keith's voice came over the CB speaker. "Is that you Fox?"

"Yep, it sure is," Jason answered into the microphone.

"What's your twenty?" Keith's voice asked over the CB speaker.

"Sitting over here at the terminal, waiting on you... as usual," Jason said into the microphone, grinning, then added, "Is this the way it's going to be all the way to Georgia?"

"What do you mean?" Keith's voice asked over the CB speaker.

"Where you at, WolfKat? Come on, try to keep up. Did you stop back there?" Jason said into the microphone in a mocking tone, trying to keep from laughing. Jason could imagine Keith laughing, sighing, shaking his head, rolling his eyes, knowing he had been had again.

"You dog," Keith's voice sounded over the CB speaker again. Jason could tell Keith was trying to keep from laughing.

"Com on," Jason teased into the microphone, "the A.M. will be P.M. by the time you drag your slow ass over here."

"All right," Keith's voice came over the CB speaker, injecting a false tone of exasperation, as Jason saw the familiar black 379 Peterbilt turn onto the terminal lot.

"Well, it's about time," Jason said into the microphone, feigning impatience. Jason watched Keith drive by him, keeping a straight face, and raising his hands up shoulder height, palms turned skyward, shrugging his shoulders as if to say, "What the hell?" Keith laughed at this, and shook his finger (the pointer finger) at Jason. He drove on by Jason and found his trailer. Keith hooked on to it. He turned on the truck running lights, pulled the lever to activate the emergency flashers, and jumped out of the truck. After making the air lines and the electrical cord connections from tractor to trailer, Keith walked to the rear of the tractor/trailer unit, checking that all the lights worked, thumping the tires of the trailer and tractor as he went. Keith also visually checked the brake pads of the trailer. In addition to this, Keith checked the document box on the front of the trailer to make sure the paperwork for the trailer was legible and current. This was known as a walk around inspection, and every commercial driver was supposed to do one at the beginning and end of every day and every time a trailer was changed. Keith and Jason combined had done millions of these, and to the untrained eye, it looked as if they were taking a leisurely stroll around the tractor/trailer unit. Soon Keith pulled alongside Jason.

"Are you ready now?" Jason asked into the keyed microphone of the CB radio.

"Not quite," Keith's voice returned over the speaker, "I have to fix my comic book." Comic book was one of those trucker slang terms for logbook. Keith busied himself with bringing his logbook up to date.

"Okay, I'm ready," Keith's voice commented over the speaker. Although they were sitting side by side and could see each other, they conversed over the CB radio.

"Are you sure?" Jason asked into the CB microphone, feigning irritation.

"Yeah," Keith's voice replied.

"You need to go pee?" Jason asked into the keyed microphone, he lived to tease Keith.

"No," Keith's voice answered with humor.

"Need a drink of water?" Jason asked into the keyed microphone, trying to keep from laughing.

"No!" Keith's voice answered with conviction, he was about to crack up laughing.

"Why don't you two good-buddies take that to another channel," said an unfamiliar voice over the CB speaker. Most truckers monitor channel nineteen, and any conversation taking place on channel nineteen could heard by anyone with a CB radio.

"We were on another channel, but Houston asked us to leave the astronauts alone," Jason said into the keyed microphone.

Jason looked at Keith, raised his eyebrows as if to ask his friend if he was ready. Keith laughed, nodding, and raised his right hand about shoulder level, elbow bent slightly, palm vertical, fingers and thumb together. He extended his right arm to its extent, then bent the elbow, raised the hand a bit, and brought his hand and arm back to its original position, as in the Native American hand sign to proceed, or go forward.

Anytime Jason and Keith ran to Atlanta together, they had two arguments. The first one had already been settled which was what time to leave. The second was about to begin which was which route to take: to go through Arkansas, Memphis, and Birmingham, or to go through Kentucky, Nashville, and Chattanooga.

"Are you gonna weigh?" Jason heard Keith's voice over his CB speaker.

"Yep, my bills say this load weighs forty-two thousand, so I better weigh," Jason said into his keyed microphone.

"I'll follow you there," Keith's voice said from Jason's speaker.

Jason drove to one of the truck stops and pulled onto the scales. He opened his door and stepped onto the running board of the truck. He pressed the call button next to the speaker there and waited. The speaker had always reminded Jason of a drive-through speaker at a fast food restaurant, and was often tempted to order a burger, fries, and drink whenever the attendant answered.

"First weigh, or reweigh?" asked the female voice from the speaker.

"First weigh," Jason answered.

"Okay, I've got you. C'mon in," said the feminine voice.

"Thank you," Jason said into the speaker. He didn't know if she heard him or not, but he always thanked the speaker voice. Jason pulled off the scales, pulled through the fuel island, and parked. A few moments later Keith weighed, then parked next to Jason. They entered the truck stop after a friendly argument of age before beauty, and who was going to hold the door open for whom. They paid for their respective scale tickets, and exited the same way they had entered: in a friendly argument. Once outside, they compared scale tickets.

"How's yours?" Jason asked Keith.

"I'm looking pretty good, my gauge said the same thing," Keith answered. On some trucks, there was a pressure gauge for the drive tandems that read the approximate weight of the load over those axles. On Keith's truck, when the needle of the gauge pointed to the sixty pound mark, it corresponded to about thirty-four thousand pounds. Jason had no such gauge on his truck.

"That's a matter of opinion," Jason teased, glancing toward his friend.

"Smart ass," Keith growled. "What about you?"

"I'm a little heavy on the trailer," Jason said. "I'll slide the trailer tandems back one notch."

"I'll help ya, although it's beyond me why I should," Keith muttered.

Jason grinned at Keith and walked to the cab of the truck. As he climbed into the cab, Keith positioned himself next to the trailer by the release lever for the tandem slide. Keith pulled the lever out, releasing the lock pins and locked it into place, then signaled Jason with a wave that he was ready. Jason set the trailer brakes, and pulled forward slowly. Keith released the slide lever when the trailer slid forward on the tandem frame one notch. When the pins and lever snapped back into place, Keith signaled Jason again with a wave.

"Are you gonna follow me to Paducah?" Jason asked as he climbed out of the truck cab.

"You always do this," Keith said exasperated. "Every time we run to Atlanta together, you always start this argument."

"I hate going through Birmingham," Jason said simply.

"If I say no one of these times, are you gonna pout?" Keith asked.

"No," Jason answered, "I'll cry." They both laughed at this.

"Yes, I'll follow you," Keith said, "you big crybaby."

They climbed back into their respective trucks and made ready to leave. Jason folded his scale ticket thrice and slid it behind a strap on the driver's side sun visor. Jason looked through the passenger side window of his truck into the driver's side window of Keith's truck at his friend. Their eyes met momentarily, and Jason raised his eyebrows in a wordless question, asking Keith if he was ready to go. Keith answered wordlessly by nodding, and Jason led the way out of the truck stop.

Jason and Diane lived in the small town of Strafford, Missouri, just a few miles east of Springfield on Interstate-44. Keith and his wife Katrina lived a few more miles east in the small town of Marshfield, Missouri, which had its own claim to fame, by way of President Bush Senior having visited Marshfield on a Fourth of July celebration in the not-so-distant past. Blanket Transportation was located on an outer road that paralleled I-44 in Strafford. All three of the truck stops, the one Diane worked at, the one Jason and Keith weighed at, and the national chain one were also located in Strafford.

When Jason led the way from the truck stop, he turned south onto Missouri State Highway 125. Eleven miles to the south, they came to a traffic light where Highway 125 and U.S. Highway 60 crossed. When the traffic light turned green for Jason and Keith, they both turned left, heading east onto U.S. Highway 60.

"Did you make it through there?" Jason asked into his keyed microphone. He knew Keith had made it through the traffic light, he had seen Keith make the turn by looking into his rearview mirror. Jason had approximately seven hundred miles to pick on Keith, and he was starting early before Keith could start picking on him.

"Right on your donkey," Keith's answer came over Jason's CB speaker. Donkey was trucker slang for tail or behind.

"Okay," Jason said into the keyed microphone. "I would hate to lose you, Kat would never forgive me."

"You dog," came Keith's familiar voice and response over Jason's CB speaker.

Kat was Katrina's CB handle. As far as anyone knows, the word "handle" comes from the American Cowboy slang word meaning name. When a person decides to converse on the CB, that person should have a handle or nickname. A person can pick his or her own handle, or someone else can appoint them one. A handle can come from a variety of sources. It can reflect a person's personality, such as Diane's handle, Gabby. It can reflect a person's attitude, such as Keith's handle, Lone Wolf. Keith later shortened this to just Wolf, and still later added Katrina's handle, Kat, to his own, making it WolfKat, which is what everyone saw printed on the doors of his truck and what most people called him on the CB. A CB handle can also reflect a person's past profession, such as Doc or Zookeeper for example. It can describe a person physically, such as Tiny for a two- or three-hundred-pound trucker, or Short-n-Sweet for a lady truck driver. A handle can be taken from animals, such as Jackrabbit, Roadrunner, or Blue Jay. Another source can be from movies or songs, such as Bandit, Snowman, Rubber Duck, White Knight, or Phantom 309, to name a few of the ones that few truckers use anymore. Most of the more conventional handles taken from movies might include Mad Max or The Road Warrior. Some handles include the name of the driver's home state, such as the Kentucky Ridgerunner, or the Tennessee Hillbilly. If a driver walks with a limp, some of his friends might start calling him/her Gimpy, Sashay, or the ever-popular Chester from the character of the well-liked T.V. show Gunsmoke. The best CB handles reflect an aspect of the person. Jason was a rare exception in that he used his last name as his handle. A few years ago, he had known a trucker named Todd who used the handle Fox because the literal translation of the name Todd means Fox. That is something else that is sometimes common, two truckers who might live hundreds of miles apart, unknowingly using the same handle.

"How 'boutcha, westbound?" Jason said into his keyed microphone to any trucker ready to answer, as he and Keith went through the green light at Rogersville. "What'dja leave behindja?" This was the trucker lingo that Diane had heard Jason use before, causing her to think he was speaking a foreign language.

There was a moment of static, and then a voice came over the CB speaker, "Haven't seen a thing since the sixty-three split, the coups were locked up on your side." Translation: We have not seen any police since the junction of Highways 60 and 63, and the weight scales on the eastbound side were closed.

"We appreciate it, westbound," Jason said into his keyed mic. "We just jumped on there at Highway 125, we can't help you much, 'cept to say be careful and Godspeed."

"Right back atcha, driver," responded the voice over Jason's CB speaker.

"Let's go, Wolf," Jason said into his keyed mic.

"Take off, I'm right behindja, buddy," Jason heard Keith's voice over his CB speaker.

Jason and Keith conversed about several different subjects as they drove eastward on Highway 60, including the price of fuel, the highest and lowest they had paid per gallon the previous week. Jason and Keith would both spend about one thousand dollars in fuel purchases alone each week, that's not including meals, sodas, coffee, and anything they chose to purchase for their wives. They told each other what they had done over the weekend and what they were planning in the coming weeks. In short, they talked as most friends do or should.

Between the towns of Cabool, Missouri and Willow Springs, Missouri, U.S. Highways 60 and 63 run together, then split off. Jason and Keith continued to follow U.S. Highway 60. At Poplar Bluff, Missouri, Highway 60 connects with Highway 67, and the two highways merge together for a few miles, then split off again. Highway 60 continues east from that point, following a winding path into Kentucky. Highway 67 runs north towards Saint Louis and south into Arkansas. In Sikeston, Missouri, Highway 60 merges with Interstate 57, where it has one of its starting points, then splits off ten-twelve miles later at Charleston, Missouri. It is here that Jason and Keith made their first pit stop, at a truck stop where Highway 60 and I-57 split off. They pulled through the fuel island, knowing they wouldn't be there that long, just long enough to go to the restroom and get something to drink.

As they pulled back onto Highway 60, going east, Jason heard Keith's voice over his CB speaker.

"You know, I hate crossing these bridges up here."

"Yeah, yeah. I know, I know. Nag, nag, nag." Jason responded into his keyed mic, feigning exasperation. The bridges Keith was referring to are on Highway 60 on the Missouri and Kentucky border and cross the Ohio River and the Mississippi River close to their meeting point. The bridges are arched, they have steel trusses over them, and they are narrow. Two trucks can successfully meet on both bridges, as long as both drivers stay on their respective sides. More than one trucker has lost a side-mounted mirror because another, oncoming trucker took his half of the road out of the middle. Some of these were due to inexperienced truckers crossing the bridges or truckers crossing the bridges faster than they should, veering toward the middle of the road.

Jason made it to the midway point of the first bridge, at the apex of the arched structure, and transmitted an all-clear message to Keith. This was a tactic Keith preferred to use because a few years earlier he had encountered one of the aforementioned road hogs. The damage to the company truck had been minimal, but the other driver had not stopped. That left Keith with the expense of having the driver's side mirror of the Volvo 650 he had been driving replaced. The total bill for the mirror and the labor had been over five hundred dollars, and Keith was not eager to have a repeat performance.

They got across the second bridge the same way, and crossed the state line into Kentucky. At the small town of Wycliff there is a DOT checkpoint. U.S. Highways 51, 60, and 62 merge together there, and the checkpoint is set up there to check trucks leaving Kentucky, although on more than one occasion, Kentucky State Troopers had worked the opposite side of the highway checking trucks going into Kentucky. This was not the case on this particular day, however, and Jason and Keith drove by the checkpoint. They continued on Highway 60 until it crossed Interstate 24 at the city of Paducah, where they merged onto I-24, heading southeast, toward Nashville.

They crossed the scales at mile marker thirty-five without incident, and stopped at the small town of Oak Grove where there are a few truck stops. They both went to the restroom, and they both opted for soft drinks rather than coffee. They merged back onto I-24, drove the less than half a dozen miles to the state line and crossed into Tennessee.

"How 'boutcha, westbound?" Jason said into his keyed mic as they got closer to Nashville. He and Keith had been talking on the CB their whole trip. Whenever someone else called for a break, one or the other of them told the breaker to go ahead. It wasn't as if they had hogged the airwaves, but had been polite enough to offer someone else the opportunity to join in on their conversation, or to call for someone else. Now, however, there came no response.

"How 'boutcha, westbound?" Jason repeated into his keyed mic. He could see the trucks in the westbound lanes going the other direction. He also knew that an increasing number of truckers were listening to audio books. Not only that, but more still were listening to any number of the satellite radios currently available. Jason himself listened to a lot of audio books. Most of the time when he was at home, he would make a trip to the Greene County Library and check out a few selections. There were some that he purchased from book stores or truck stops. Even though he was guilty of listening to audio books, he still kept the volume of his CB turned up enough to monitor it.

"Let's try this," Jason said absentmindedly into his keyed mic. "All of you trucks going toward Kentucky on Interstate 24, you're westbound."

"I thought I was going more north than west," said an unfamiliar voice over Jason's CB speaker.

"Humor me," Jason snapped into his keyed mic. "Did you come through the Guitar?" Truckers have nicknames for almost every state and major city, Nashville has the rare distinction of having three of these nicknames. Most of the truckers call Nashville the Guitar, nicknamed for the country music industry and the Grand Ole Opry there. Others call it the Music City, which is also one of the nicknames for Detroit, Michigan. Detroit, Michigan is also called the Motor City, or more obviously, Motown. The third, less commonly used nickname for Nashville is Nastyville.

"Ten-four, I sure did, driver," said the same unfamiliar voice over Jason's CB speaker. "I came right up through the middle. You've got a clear shot if you're going on through on twenty-four."

"Alrighty. Appreciate it," Jason responded into his keyed mic. "You look good back to the Bluegrass. We jumped on there at Oak Grove." Bluegrass was a trucker nickname for Kentucky.

"Ten-four," replied the same voice from Jason's CB speaker. "Have yourself a good day."

"Ten-four," Jason said into his keyed mic. "Right back atcha, driver."

One of the reasons Jason had asked about Nashville was that traffic in the bigger cities can be horrendous for truckers sometimes, especially on a weekend in a city that sponsors a professional sports team, one or more colleges and their sports teams, and if either is playing at home. The other was because Nashville has three major interstates that cross in its city limits. Interstate 24 cuts a diagonal path across Tennessee, Interstate 65 runs a north/south course through the state, and Interstate 40 follows an east/west route across the state. All three interstates merge and separate in Nashville. Although Nashville does have a loop that goes around the city, it is faster to go straight through if the traffic is moving, and there are no accidents to hold up the flow of traffic. Jason and Keith got through Nashville without incident.

When they got to Monteagle, Tennessee, they pulled into the required brake check area. As they were pulling through the stoplight section of the check area, Keith's voice came over Jason's CB speaker.

"I've got a phone call, Fox." Keith's voice said. "I'll be right back."

"Okey-dokey," Jason said into his keyed mic, letting his friend know he had heard him.

"All right, I'm back," Keith's voice came from Jason's CB speaker after a few minutes. "You gotta copy on me, Fox?"

"Yep, I sure do," Jason told his friend over the CB. "It sounds like you're sitting right next to me."

"Do you remember the last two numbers of the number of the trailer you're pullin'?" Keith's voice sounded harried to Jason as it came from the speaker.

"Yep," Jason answered quickly into his keyed mic, it was thirty-five.

"Go there," Keith's voice said from the speaker. When a trucker does this, he or she is asking the other party to turn to that corresponding channel on the CB. In other words, Keith was asking Jason to go to channel thirty-five on the CB. This would offer them a little more privacy for a conversation and get them off channel nineteen, or what most truckers refer to as Main Street or Sesame Street.

"I'm gone," Jason quipped into the keyed mic and immediately turned his CB to channel thirty-five. Then he keyed his microphone again, and asked. "You make it WolfKat? What's up?"

"Yea, I made it," Keith's voice drifted from the speaker. "That was Kat on the phone, and another body has been found by the Springfield police. She said the story was on the evening news tonight. She said this poor girl was found early this morning, almost the same way."

"I'm sorry," Jason said into his keyed mic when Keith had finished, "but you'll have to fill me in. Diane said something about them finding a dead girl last week, but I haven't been following the news lately."

"What?" Keith asked, feigning indignation. It was his turn to pick on Jason. "What in the hell do you do when you're at home?" Then before Jason could answer, he added, "Never mind, I have a pretty good idea what you do, especially if Diane's at home."

"You stepped into that one all the way up to your neck, didn't you, big boy?" Jason said into his keyed mic, grinning

"Yes, I did," Keith's voice answered over the speaker. "Anyway, the first woman they found was from Ontario, California. She had been raped over and over, and her throat cut. Then her and her clothes had been washed, and she had been wrapped up in a big piece of plastic. They found her and her belongings on the steps of a trucking company. Now, they've found a second woman. This one wasn't raped, but her throat had been cut, and she'd been stabbed a bunch of times. She was found wrapped in plastic, but none of her belongings were found, and she was from Lodi, Ohio."

"Does the police think the same person killed them both?" Jason asked into his keyed mic.

"Don't know," Keith's voice answered from the speaker. "Kat said that was about all the details the news people had to offer."

Jason said nothing for a moment, but just thought as he drove. If this were a serial killer, why did the MOs differ? He knew that 99.9 percent of serial killers in this country were single men and that a high percentage of them were white. He also knew the closest thing to a female serial killer in this country had been Lizzy Borden. He also knew most serial killers killed in a certain area, and then maybe transported the body to a location away from the kill area. He had never heard of a serial killer who dropped his victims in one spot after gathering them from different parts of the country.

"You all right, Fox?" came Keith's voice from Jason's CB speaker.

"Yep, I'm fine," Jason said into his keyed mic. "Do you mind if we stop down here at the rest area south of the Choo-Choo in Georgia? I want to call Diane." The Choo-Choo was the trucker name for the city of Chattanooga, Tennessee.

"Yeah, sure thing," Keith's response came over the speaker.

The rest area Jason spoke of is just across the Tennessee-Georgia state line south of Chattanooga. It is a rather large rest area with a huge space for truck parking. If this rest area were considered to have a sister rest area, it would be the one on Highway 75 in Texas, just south of the Texas-Oklahoma state line. It was after nightfall by the time Jason and Keith reached the rest area and found parking spaces.

Jason pulled out a phone card, as he walked up to a pay phone. He normally carried at least two phone cards. He had found that in certain parts of the country, some phone cards would not work on the phone system of that area, so, as a habit, he carried at least two phone cards. There were times when he would happen upon a phone card that offered a lot of minutes, with no or a very low connection fee, and he would purchase it, even though he might have two phone cards at the time.

Jason picked up the handset for the telephone, held it to his ear, checking to see if there was a dial tone, then dialed the toll free access number printed on the phone card. After hearing the automated voice welcoming him to the company that had printed the card, he followed the prompts, and entered the PIN number or card number to access the long distance service. Next, he dialed his and Diane's home phone number and waited for the connection after the automated voice told him how many minutes he had left on this particular phone card.

The line went silent, then there were a couple of soft clicks, then silence again. He heard the growl in the earpiece of the handset, telling him that the telephone was ringing at home. If he had any doubts about calling Diane late at night, she had put them to rest long ago by telling him that she would rather be awakened by a phone call from him, telling her that he was all right, rather than a call from a stranger telling her that he was injured or dead. He thought about this as he heard the phone at home ring a second time. Although it wasn't that late, Jason knew that if Diane was tired, she would go to bed when the sun did. The telephone at home rang again. Jason checked his watch and mentally scanned his memory to recall anything Diane might have told him regarding whether she would not be home tonight and came up with nothing. The telephone at home started to ring a fourth time when Diane answered it, and a wave of relief flowed over him.

"Hello," Diane chirped in a cheery voice.

"Hi," Jason said, letting his pent-up breath out. "I thought maybe I had missed you."

"No," Diane said, still sounding happy. "I just got home a few minutes ago, and you caught me in the bathtub." Then she broke out in a verse of "Rubber Ducky, You're the One".

"Hey," Jason said, trying to suppress a laugh, and failing miserably, and giving in to it at last.

"What?" Diane asked, her mood still up. Then her mood changed dramatically, and she added. "They found another young woman dead today in Springfield. They said she was from somewhere in Ohio. I'm going to call the women in our families, and tell them all to be extra careful and to keep a wary eye out."

"That sounds like an excellent idea," Jason said. "It sounds like you're on top of things."

"I know what I'd like to be on top of," she teased. Jason thought she sounded just fine to him.

"Careful," he said, in a low teasing voice of his own, "I'm too far from home for you to be talking like that."

"Where are you?" Diane asked, settling down a bit, she loved teasing him as much as he loved teasing her.

"We just crossed over into Jo-Ja," he replied, this was how he pronounced Georgia.

"You gonna make it okay?" she asked.

"Of course," he answered. "Just remember who you're talking to."

"I'm talking to my truck driver," she informed him. "Please be careful. Hope to see you soon. I love you."

"I love you, too," Jason said, knowing she was all right. "It won't be soon enough. You be careful and keep your eyes open."

"I will," she promised. "Goodnight."

"Goodnight, sweetheart," Jason hung the handset of the telephone back on its rack.

Jason walked outside after making a visit to the restroom. Keith was waiting for him beside a bench on a sidewalk that surrounded a flagpole.

"Is she all right?" Keith asked as Jason joined him.

"Yep," Jason answered, "she'll be fine."

"You ready?" Keith asked, as he stretched.

"Yep," Jason responded as he nodded. "Are you gonna fuel when I do, or are you gonna wait until you get closer to Florida?" Jason didn't know the trucker nickname for Florida.

"I'll definitely fuel before I cross over into Florida," Keith stated. The different states have different rates of fuel taxes which directly affects the price of diesel fuel. Not only that, but at the end of the year, truckers like Keith and Jason paid a fuel tax based on the amount of fuel they had bought throughout the year and where they had bought it. Georgia's fuel prices were lower than Florida's, but at the end of the year, even though Georgia's fuel prices might be lower than Florida's, the fuel taxes would reflect the difference. The smart trucker would try to buy some fuel in every state he or she went through on a regular basis. Keith, in this instance, would buy fuel in Georgia, deliver his load in Florida, then purchase fifty to one hundred dollars' worth of fuel in Florida, otherwise, if he were to purchase fuel only in the states with the cheapest fuel prices, then his end of the year fuel taxes would be higher. Keith then asked. "Where you gonna fuel?"

"Down here at Adairsville," Jason said, looking absently around.

"I'll probably wait until I get south of Atlanta before I fuel, but I'll stop at Adairsville with you," Keith said, stretching again.

"Alrighty," Jason said. "You ready to go?"

"Yeah," Keith said unconvincingly, and the two of them walked back to their parked trucks.

After they merged back onto the interstate, they resumed their conversation over the CB until they stopped at Adairsville, and Jason fueled his truck. After Jason fueled, they resumed their southern trek. At the north side of Atlanta, Jason took the exit for Interstate Loop 285 East, and Keith took the exit for Interstate Loop 285 South. Actually, these exits were at the same place, and then split off. Jason and Keith said their goodbyes at this point.

Atlanta is one of those rare cities that don't want trucks to go into its borders, unless making a delivery there, and passed a law requiring trucks to go around the city via I-285. Jason would have taken I-285 East, to I-85 North anyway to go to Suwanee, Georgia. Keith, on the other hand, added miles that he would not get paid for to his trip by having to go around Atlanta.

Jason got to where he was to make his delivery and checked in with the receiving office. The person working the receiving office assigned Jason a delivery door. Jason left the bill of lading with the receiver, went back to his truck, opened the trailer doors, backed up to the corresponding door, chocked the trailer wheels with the rubber block provided, climbed into the sleeper, and went to sleep. He liked coming to this receiver for this reason, he could sleep, and when they had him unloaded the next morning, they would wake him up by knocking on the side of the truck.

The next morning, Jason was awakened, as expected, by three rapid knocks on the door. He thanked his human alarm clock as he was handed his copies of the bill of lading, and climbed out of the truck. Jason kicked the wheel chock out of the way, climbed back into the truck, and pulled away from the delivery door. He set the air parking brakes of the truck again, climbed out of the truck again, and closed the trailer doors. After pulling out of the way, Jason entered his "empty" information into the Highway Master system, and sent that information via satellite communications to his dispatcher. Jason then pulled out his logbook and brought it up to date. By the time Jason had his logbook current, he was receiving the information over the Highway Master concerning his next load. Jason copied the information, noting the appointment times for the pickup and delivery, the company names and telephone numbers of the companies involved, and any directions that were included.

Jason did this on most of the load information he received. In this particular case, however, he knew both the shipper and receiver of this load, and the only information he found necessary to copy was the pickup date and time and the delivery date and time. Jason then typed in a personal message to his dispatcher, thanking him and acknowledging that he had received the information, and that he was on his way.

The load was waiting for Jason in the city of Trenton, South Carolina. It was twelve thousand pounds of clothing being shipped to a certain distributor's warehouse in Junction City, Kansas. Jason headed north on I-85 toward Augusta, Georgia, where he crossed the state line into South Carolina, and drove north onto Highway 25. The shipper Jason was going to was about twelve miles north, on the right hand side of the highway. He pulled onto the parking lot, checked in with the shipping office, was assigned a door, backed up to it, and waited to be loaded. After loading, Jason headed back toward Atlanta, and north onto I-75 toward the Tennessee state line.

It was on the western slope of Monteagle, Tennessee that Jason ran into trouble. For truckers that drive that particular stretch of I-24, they know how close Tennessee state troopers sit and watch there. The speed limit for trucks there was forty-five miles per hour, and the lady trooper that pulled Jason over clocked him at sixty-six miles per hour. Not only did the trooper write Jason a ticket for the speed limit violation, she also wrote him a ticket for the possession and use of a radar detector.

Jason had found from past experience that most state troopers in all of the states were polite as long as they were treated in kind. This was the case here. The trooper explained to Jason why the speed limit for trucks was set at forty-five miles per hour on the down slopes of the mountain. Also, the trooper took the radar detector, recorded the serial number from it, and then gave it back to Jason. Jason had heard of this procedure and knew that if he were to be caught with this radar detector, it would be confiscated, and a huge fine issued.

Jason decided to call Diane from Oak Grove, Kentucky, and it wasn't a phone call he was looking forward to making, he didn't want Diane to be disappointed in him.

"Hello," Jason heard Diane's voice through the telephone, her greeting sounded like a question. He had behaved himself on the drive to Oak Grove, Kentucky and was now sitting in the truckers' phone room of one of the truck stops there.

"Howdy," Jason replied.

"Hi, honey!" Diane said exuberantly.

"Hi, sweety," Jason said, he knew the straightforward way was the best way. "I have some good news and some bad news. The good news is I'm all right. The bad news is I just got two tickets coming off of Monteagle."

"Oh my," Diane said after a moment of silence. Jason thought she sounded as if she had just jumped into a swimming pool of cold water and was trying to catch her breath. He pushed that image out of his mind, Diane breaking the surface of the water, her hair wet and straight, clinging to her neck and shoulders, her swimsuit wet, contouring her body, nipples erect… He snapped out of his little fantasy, best not think about such things this far from home.

"I'm sorry, honey, I don't want to be a disappointment to you," Jason said, trying to get a feel for her.

"You're silly," Diane blurted, she was laughing, "a disappointment? You, my lover, will have to do worse than that."

"Wow," Jason said, truly relieved, "you are really amazing. I was hoping you wouldn't be angry with me."

"Angry? This is your first ticket in what, fifteen years?" Diane asked.

"Yes, that's right," Jason confirmed.

"Well, don't you worry your cute buns over that. Just don't make it a habit," Diane said, keeping her tone light, "and when you get home, I'll kiss it and make it all better."

"Hey," Jason said in mock sternness, "I just pushed an image out of my head of you in a cold, wet swimsuit. I'm too far from home for you to be talking like that."

"A cold, wet one, huh?" Diane said. She wasn't through teasing him yet. "When you get here, I'll give you a warm, wet one."

"Thanks," Jason said, keeping his mocking tone.

"When will you be home?" Diane asked, the teasing tone was still dancing around the edges.

"In the morning," Jason said, wishing he could drive the six hours it would take him to get there, but knowing he needed a break, and to quote the immortal lines of Clint Eastwood, "A man's got to know his limitations."

"You be safe coming home to me," Diane said, her tone more serious now.

"I'm gonna lay down and catch a nap before I head that way," Jason said, but he wasn't going to let her off that easy, "after I take a cold shower."

Diane giggled, then said, "Sweet dreams, and I love you."

"I love you, too," Jason said, in fact, feeling the love.

"Night-night," Diane said.

"Bye," Jason returned, as they both hung up.

Jason took his shower, then his nap, and was on the road again a little after midnight. When he arrived home the next morning, Diane was there to greet him. Christine had already left for work, and Diane and Jason were alone. He wasn't scheduled to be in Junction City, Kansas until after midnight, so they had a few hours until he would leave again. His fantasy of her in the cold, wet swimsuit wasn't discussed. Her promise of kissing and making it all better wasn't discussed. Actions spoke louder than words that morning, as Jason showed Diane how much he appreciated her, and Diane showed Jason how well she could kiss it and make it better.

As Jason and Diane were enjoying each other's non verbal company, Keith was making his way north along I-75 in Florida. After he was unloaded, Keith had placed his empty call to his dispatcher and waited for his reload information. He didn't have to wait long. The reload information sent him north to Lake City, Florida, where he was to pick up a load of Cypress wood mulch, delivering to Indianapolis, Indiana. The load weighed forty-two thousand pounds, and it didn't take long to load. By the time Keith had checked in with the shipping clerk, weighed the empty tractor/trailer combo, got loaded, weighed the unit loaded, signed the paperwork, closed the trailer doors, and sealed the trailer, it took a few minutes over an hour. He then drove north again on I-75 and spent the night just across the Georgia state line at a truck stop in Lake Park, Georgia. By midnight he was on the road again.

The trip north so far had been fairly uneventful except for coming through Atlanta which could always be an adventure. Presently he was just northwest of Monteagle, Tennessee going northwest on I-24. When Keith got to the bottom of the western slope, he saw flashing lights from several state troopers parked along the shoulder of the interstate. Keith immediately slowed, and the state troopers were detouring all westbound truck traffic into the left lane. Keith dropped several gears and rolled through the area slowly.

After crossing the state scale near Manchester, Tennessee, Keith activated his cell phone and called Jason.

"Hello," Diane answered on the second ring.

"Hey," Keith said, genuinely glad to hear her voice. "How's my best friend's main squeeze?"

"Main squeeze?" Diane retorted comically. "I'd better be his only squeeze."

"Yeah! Yeah! Only squeeze!" Keith said laughing. "That's what I meant. His only squeeze. Wow, I'm sorry. I didn't call to get anyone in trouble, mainly me! Is Jason there? Can I talk to him before I stick my other foot in my mouth? Please?"

"Well, all right," Diane consented, "since you're being so apologetic. Just a second, I'll get him."

"Hey, slacker, where are ya?" Jason asked a moment later after Diane had handed him the telephone.

"In the Volunteer, just south of the Guitar," Keith said. The Volunteer was the trucker lingo for Tennessee.

"Ouch," Jason said, "I just gave them about three hundred dollars today. I got two tickets coming off of Monteagle yesterday."

"Ouch is right," Keith said. "What else did you do? They're still stirred up down there."

"I have no idea what you're talkin' about," Jason said, perplexed.

"When I came off Monteagle a while ago, there were a bunch of Smoky Bears at the bottom," Keith explained.

"I wonder what's goin' on there?" Jason pondered.

"I don't know," Keith said. "Nobody's sayin' anything about it."

"Well, where are you headed?" Jason asked.

"The Circle," Keith answered, using the trucker nickname for India-napolis, Indiana. "I figured it was closer and faster to go this way rather than go through K-Town." K-Town was the trucker nickname for Knoxville, Tennessee.

"Yeah, that's the way I always go." Jason said. "I don't even like saying Ohio, much less goin' through it."

"I hear ya, buddy," Keith responded laughing. "What time are you leaving there?"

"Hell, I don't have to be in Junction City 'til after midnight, but as you know it's always a drop and hook there, so I'll leave here in a couple of hours," Jason explained.

"Well, don't get in any hurry, enjoy that home time," Keith advised.

"If I enjoy it too much, I'll leave here walking like John Wayne," Jason said, and they both laughed.

"Your handle should be Duke," Keith said.

"I have too much respect for the man and his memory to compare myself to him," Jason said, doing his best to impersonate the Duke.

"Don't kid yourself, my friend," Keith said soberly. "You're a big man trapped in a little body."

"Thanks," Jason said simply. "I better get off here, and work on that walk-ing like John Wayne thing."

"You dog," Keith said laughing. "God bless, and we'll talk atcha later."

"Take care," Jason said. They both said goodbye and disconnected.

Jason went in search of Diane and found her in the bedroom getting ready to go to work. He approached her, took her in his arms, kissed her, backed her toward the bed as she began to giggle, and he delayed her progress about thirty minutes.

Chapter 10

After Jack had disposed of Rachel's body, he checked into a motel just off of I-44 in Springfield. He took a shower and stretched out on the bed. The demon made its presence known in the usual manner.

"There is a certain truck driver that I've been watching of late that I would love to bring down hard, and as many of his friends and family as possible with him. You, Jack, will help me with this, and in turn you will help yourself to the end for which you seek. Get some sleep, we will get started in a couple of hours," Sultry said to Jack.

"Who was Jack the Ripper?" Jack asked, yawning. The demon's suggestion of sleep hit Jack hard, and all of a sudden, he was very sleepy.

"That's not important," the demon evaded.

"I was just curious who he was," Jack said, lying down on the bed and getting comfortable.

"Sleep," the demon said hypnotically. When it heard Jack starting to snore, it imbedded a strong suggestion in Jack's subconscious to forget about Jack the Ripper. It would wake Jack in about four hours, and until then it had to check the progress of its other hosts.

About four hours later, the demon woke Jack, who showered and got dressed. Jack packed, and the demon instructed him to drive to the terminal of the trucking company he drove for.

"Hi, Jack," said a middle-aged woman sitting behind a desk. The desk was behind a plane of plate glass with a six-inch open space at the bottom. This was a safety feature for dispatchers, protecting them from disgruntled truckers who were intent upon doing them bodily harm.

"Hi, Marcia," Jack replied, as he looked around the room. Springfield was the unofficial trucking capital of the country, there were truck drivers from all over the country that traveled through the city every day of the week. The drivers that didn't live in the Springfield area would have to spend time in Springfield between loads, and when they did, sometimes they would hang out at their company's terminal for a while. Some of these drivers were setting up their next loads, some were having preventative maintenance done to their trucks, and some were just lonely and wanted some human contact. There were three of these drivers in the dispatch lobby at the present time. All three of these drivers knew Jack, and all three greeted him.

"Jack, I haven't seen you for a while," said one of the three extending his hand toward Jack who took the extended hand and shook it, and then shook hands with the other two drivers.

"I've tried to stay hidden," Jack said smiling. "How are you fellas doin'?"

"We're all right," said the one Jack had shook hands with, "we're just laid over waiting for loads to get us home."

"Have you had a long wait?" Jack asked.

"No, our trailers are being loaded now," said one of the other drivers.

"Well, good luck to ya" Jack said as he stepped up to the safety glass to face Marcia.

"What's goin' on Jack?" Marcia asked, looking at him and smiling.

"Not much," Jack answered, then asked with a mischievous gleam in his eyes, "When are you going to give this up and come with me?"

"You're a tease and a charmer," Marcia said smiling. She was an average-built woman who had had a weight problem in the past but now had it under control. She was a true redhead; her genetic makeup had dealt her red hair, pale skin, blue eyes, and freckles. In recent years, she had tried to hide the freckles by going to a tanning bed. The effect had lessened the intensity of the freckles, but one could still tell they were there. The tan, however, couldn't mask the color of embarrassment that assaulted her cheeks. "I'll bet you have women all over the country."

"I always come home to you," Jack said, smiling and winking at her, as he heard chuckles of approval from the men behind him.

"How can I help you, Jack?" Marcia asked, softly laughing herself, and trying to get her embarrassment under control. She was attracted to Jack, not only by his looks, but he was clean, polite, and always friendly.

"I wanted to see if you had anything short that I could run," Jack said, this was trucker lingo, inquiring about a load that didn't have too far to go.

"Well, let me see," Marcia said, looking at her computer screen and tapping keys on her keyboard to bring up the screen she needed. After a few seconds of studying the screen, she said, "I have an Oklahoma City that isn't due there until Monday, but you could run it down there, and bring back another loaded trailer. Down there and back, some decent, quick miles." Some trucking companies have what's called drop yards, or drop lots, where drivers can drop one trailer and pick up another.

"This at the drop yard there?" Jack asked to verify.

"Yes," Marcia answered primly. "The trailer you'll bring back is a loaded trailer that is due back here by Monday afternoon. If you do this one, that will take some of the pressure off."

"I'm your guy," Jack said, the demon whispering in his ear that he would get another blush from her if he used this line on her. The demon was right, Marcia's face flushed the brightest red it had that night. She lowered her face as she felt the blush come on, smiling, and then blushed in embarrassment again as she realized Jack was watching her with a knowing grin on his face.

"I'll send this information to your truck," Marcia said, composing herself as best she could. Her sexual excitement level was higher than it had been in a long while, the demon could see this, and relayed the information to Jack. She tapped more keys on her keyboard, and pressed the send key. After a couple more deep breaths, Marcia raised her eyes to meet Jack's and asked, "Would you like me to send the information for the trailer you're picking up in Oklahoma City now?"

"Yes, please," Jack said, looking into her eyes and holding her gaze.

The sent information Marcia spoke of was satellite communications. Most of the larger trucking companies in America had some sort of this type of system installed in their trucks. It made the transfer of information faster. The cost of such units varied as to the type of system, degree of power, and number of options desired. Although desired by most trucking companies, this type of satellite communications wasn't without its glitches. As with cell phones, if a driver was between towers, sometimes the signal would be weak. If this occurred, the system would automatically resend the information, and depending on the system, would depend on how many times it would resend the information until received. Basically, the more expensive the system, the better the signal.

"Is there something else?" Marcia asked as Jack lingered in front of the window.

"Why don't you come with me?" Jack teased. The demon had fed him the information to pursue this line of teasing and also gave him the probable outcome.

"Oh!" she said, a bit surprised, she hadn't really expected this, or had she? She was starting to enjoy this. After she overcame her giddiness, she playfully asked, "And just what would we do?"

"I would buy a blue, washable magic marker, and starting at your right wrist, I would play connect the dots," Jack said in an even, mild tone, the playfulness still dancing in his eyes.

"Oh," Marcia purred, her sexual excitement rising, as she squirmed in her seat. Her eyes were locked on Jack's almost defiantly, she could feel the animalistic sexuality emanating from him, and if she had dared a look, she felt certain she would have seen evidence of his arousal in the front of his jeans. Then she asked, "Why a blue washable marker, and why start at my right wrist?"

"That's easy," Jack replied easily. Marcia was right, his sexual level was at the erupting point. "After the first time through, if it's not dark enough to see, I can go over it again. Make it washable, so after our shower together, I can start all over. I'll be connecting the dots as I drive, and if I start at your right wrist, you can lay across my lap facing me, or you can sit between my legs, with your back to me."

"Uh-huh," Marcia said, she had her hands clasped together in front of her on her desk to keep them steady. "And what will I be doing, while you're doing this to me?"

"Telling me how good it feels and showing me all of your hidden freckles, I wouldn't want to miss any," Jack said. He shifted his stance and got the desired response from Marcia. She looked and saw the bulge behind his zipper.

"What if the only freckles I have are on my arms and face?" Marcia asked. She was fighting down another round of embarrassment.

"Then I will be truly disappointed," Jack said with all the sincerity he could muster.

"Wow," Marcia breathed, she had been unprepared for this encounter, but she wouldn't be the next time. Most of the drivers that flirted with her were either married, overweight, scraggly, or were blatant about their lusty intentions. "As tempting as you've made it sound, I'll have to pass this time."

"I understand," Jack said with a slight bow, trying to hide his disappointment, "maybe next time." With that, he took the paperwork for the Oklahoma City load Marcia extended to him. He turned away and faced the other three men in the room who had enjoyed this exchange also.

"Better luck next time," one of the other drivers said as he patted Jack on the back.

"Can one of you guys tell me if my parachute came out?" Jack asked, keeping the humor in his voice, and steadily moving toward the door.

"Yep, it sure did," one of the drivers said, as all three laughed at Jack's reference of being shot down.

"Good, that means I can come back, and try it another time," Jack said as he turned to face the men, and catching Marcia's gaze with his, he winked at her. Then he stepped through the door, walked down the steps, and headed toward his truck.

"Jack!" Marcia called. She had come through the side door from the dispatch office and was standing on the small landing just outside the door. As Jack turned, he successfully hid the knowing grin on his lips. Marcia bounded down the steps two at a time, and approached Jack at a brisk walk. She was wearing a pair of jean cut-offs, that showed off her tanned, freckled legs. She also wore a green button up blouse that accented her breasts and the color of her hair, and a pair of sandals on her feet.

"Did you mean all of that in there?" Marcia asked, her eyes were darting over his face, as if the answer was written there. With no barrier of any kind between them, she really felt the sexuality coming off of him.

"Every word," Jack said softly and simply.

"This load doesn't have to go tonight," Marcia made her pitch. "We could get together after my shift is over tonight."

"That is tempting," Jack said, reached into his shirt pocket and retracted a piece of small paper and an ink pen. He began writing on the paper and said to Marcia, "You might think less of me if I backed out of this load now."

She sighed, as Jack offered her the paper he had been writing on. As she took the piece of paper, their fingers brushed, and Jack clasped her hand gently in his own. He softly placed his other hand on the side of her face, and lowered his head to look into her eyes.

"Here is my cell phone number," Jack told her, as she grasped his hand back, and snuggled her face into his palm. "When you get caught up later tonight, call me. When you get off work, call me. When you get home, call me. I should know by then about what time I'll be back here. If you're not busy, maybe we can get together before I leave out again."

"Okay," she whispered. She stood perfectly still and held her breath as he bent toward her, and lightly kissed her on the cheek.

"Mmm," he made the sound in his throat as he straightened to his full height, "I like the taste of freckles."

Marcia blushed and smiled. The blush didn't stop at her face, but ran the length of her body, coloring her red from her head to her feet. Goose-bumps also raised on her arms and legs as her nipples hardened. The lighting where they were standing was enough for Jack to see all of this. He smiled at her, released her, and turned toward his truck. As he opened the driver's side door and climbed upon the running board, he looked at her and mimicked the "call me" signal. She watched him do this, waved, and then turned to go back inside the dispatch office.

As she sat down on her chair behind her desk, she thought about all that had transpired in the last few minutes. Never in her dreams had she ever thought Jack Farley would have given her a second look. She would definitely call him in a couple of hours.

About two hours later, as Jack was heading west on I-44, between Joplin, Missouri and Tulsa, Oklahoma, his cell phone rang. After leaving the terminal, Jack had driven to the drop yard his company used in Springfield and found the trailer he was to take to Oklahoma City. He had hooked onto it, done his walk around inspection, filled out his logbook, and was now on his way.

"Hello," he answered the phone on the second ring. He said this one word greeting in a slow southern drawl, knowing who was calling by his inside information.

"Jack?" Marcia's voice asked from the earpiece of the cell phone, her voice had a magical, musical quality. She was still riding high on the sexual excitement he had fired up in her.

"Hi, Marcia," Jack said, letting his voice settle into its normal tones. After leaving the terminal, the demon had quizzically asked Jack about his actions toward the woman. Jack had responded by stating that in the past whenever the demon had done something for him, a blood sacrifice had been required of him. The demon had then acknowledged this, but had said that it had someone else in mind for the sacrifice that would metaphorically kill two birds with one stone. The demon went on to say that if Jack wished to pursue a relationship with Marcia, that it thought it an excellent idea, offering Jack a distraction from time to time. The demon also reminded Jack that he would have to guard against divulging too much information to the woman, and that since all women are whores, this one would be no different in the end.

"Hi, Jack," Marcia's voice responded. She was doing her best to remain smooth, and calm.

"How are you?" Jack asked. The demon, present now more than ever, remained silent, ready to offer Jack assistance with dialog if needed or wanted.

"I'm fine," Marcia said. "Can I ask you something, Jack?"

"Sure," Jack said.

"How long have you been attracted to me?" she asked, it wasn't common, in her experience, for men to be attracted to her. After she had gone on her diet, started to exercise, and lost her excess weight, men approached her a little more often but were still cautious. Jack had showed no signs of hesitation in talking to her.

"For about two years now," Jack said simply, "even before you lost the weight."

"Why did you wait so long to tell me?" she asked.

"I'm shy," Jack teased, and Marcia laughed at this. What followed was a short ten-minute conversation of two people getting to know each other.

Marcia called again about two hours later, just a few minutes before her shift ended, and just after Jack had hooked onto the trailer he was to pull back to Springfield. Their conversation lasted only a few moments, ending with the promise from Marcia that she would call Jack back in about an hour.

During that hour, the demon sensing Jack's need for the release of his pent up excitement, informed him that he could start paying his blood sacrifice. On the north side of Oklahoma City, there is a cluster of truck stops where I-44 and I-35 cross paths. The demon instructed Jack to go there, and that soon there would be a young woman ready for the taking.

Debra Klinger, age thirty-two, tall, slender, married, and the mother of one two-year-old boy was a school librarian for one of the area grade schools. She was on her way home from her biweekly workout with a couple of her girlfriends, and had stopped at this group of truck stops to put gas in her car and to purchase a cold drink. The gas never got put into the car, and the cold drink was never bought.

Jack acquired the young woman with the help of Sultry who had suggested to Debra that the gas pump on the far end, under the dim light, with no cars waiting in front of it, would be faster. Sultry, of course, was counting on today's culture of impatience. Debra pulled her car to the gas pump on the far end, under the dim light, and the most attractive feature, no waiting. Jack soon had her stripped naked and lying unconscious on the bed in the sleeper. He left the truck stop just as his cell phone rang.

"Hello," Jack said into the activated phone.

"Hi," Marcia said cheerily. "I just got home and called you like you asked me to do."

"I'm glad you did," Jack said smoothly, then told her a lie. "Look, sweetie, I'm pulling into a truck stop to take on fuel and grab a bite to eat. Would you mind calling me back in the morning?"

"Not at all," Marcia said, a little disappointed, but working with truckers enough to know how they preferred to do things. She then asked, "Do you want my phone number?"

"No, ma'am," Jack replied, little did she know that he could have it anytime he wanted it without her knowledge or consent. "I'm giving you complete control in this matter. You get some sleep, and call me whenever you want, if not tomorrow, then whenever you want."

"That's sweet," her voice breathed softly into his ear. "I will call you later this morning."

"I look forward to it," Jack said. "Sweet dreams."

"Bye," Marcia hung up her phone.

Jack clicked off his own phone and returned it to its holder. He had just bought himself a few hours, and he planned to use his time wisely.

The Springfield Police Department, the Greene County Sheriff's Department, and the FBI would find two bodies left by Jack this week. The first was the young woman Jack had in his truck at the moment. They would find that she had been raped at least twice, maybe more, by a single attacker, her throat cut, and her abdomen slashed open. They would find that her pubic hair and skin had been cut away and taken. They would also find that her internal organs had been rearranged, and her reproductive organs removed. They were wrapped in plastic, and left with the body. Both the body and the removed organs had been washed as the other bodies had been. A note had been left with the body that read:

Dear Boss,

As you can see, I've found the time to continue my work. I found her on a parking lot. Who says librarians aren't hot? Her gender plays with men's minds and hearts, so for that, I removed her mommy parts. This is cool, because your head person is a huge fool.

Patiently waiting,

Jack
Catch me if you can.

After Jack deposited the body of his latest victim on the front steps of a Springfield area trucking company, he called the dispatch office of Blanket Transportation. After a short conversation with the dispatcher on duty, Jack was hooked onto another loaded trailer headed toward Atlanta, Georgia. He was going to miss seeing Marcia, but a little voice told him that she would be there when he got back.

Jack drove east on U.S. Highway 60, and after successfully crossing the state scales between Cabool and Willow Springs, Missouri, he exited onto U.S. Highway 63, going southbound. Later, he crossed the state line into Arkansas. A couple of hours later, he merged onto I-55 south, going toward Memphis, Tennessee. In Memphis, Jack merged onto I-40 eastbound, he then merged onto I-240 eastbound, and then merged onto U.S. Highway 78 eastbound. A few miles after crossing the state line into Mississippi, Jack pulled into a truck stop, found a place to park, and slept four hours before continuing on to Atlanta. The rest of his trip went as uneventfully as the first part. He continued on U.S. Highway 78 east, and after uneventfully crossing the state scale, crossed the state line into Alabama. In Birmingham, Jack merged onto I-20 eastbound and headed for the Georgia state line. As Jack entered Georgia, his cell phone rang.

"Hello," he said as he clicked the phone on.

"Hi," Marcia's voice said through the earpiece.

"Hi, how are you this morning?" Jack asked.

"I'm fine." Marcia answered. "Did I wake you?"

"No," Jack answered. "As a matter of fact, I was hoping you would call. After I talked to you last night, a load to Atlanta came up, and I took it. I'll drop this trailer in Atlanta, pick up a loaded one there, and be back there day after tomorrow."

"Oh," Marcia said, a little bemused and taken back by his explanation.

"If you're free anytime in the next couple of days, I would like to see you," Jack said.

"I would like that," Marcia answered.

"Well, hell, I'm coming upon a scale house, and they're open, so I better get off here," Jack lied, he was, in fact, coming upon a scale house, but it was closed.

"All right," Marcia said, this conversation hadn't gone at all the way she had hoped. She had been looking forward to seeing Jack today.

"I really need to go," Jack added a little anxiety to his voice. "Call me later?"

"Okay," Marcia then heard the click of Jack shutting off his phone.

Jack entered Atlanta on the west side. He exited I-20 and merged onto I-285 going southbound. He followed I-285 south, passed the airport, and merged onto I-75 north. Atlanta didn't allow trucks in the city on I-20, I-75, or I-85 inside the I-285 loop, unless the truck driver had a delivery on the inside of the loop. Jack followed I-75 north a couple of miles, where he exited the interstate, and making a few quick turns, was in an industrial park.

Jack parked on the parking lot of the warehouse where he was to switch trailers, and taking the paperwork to the trailer he had brought here, he went inside to the shipping/receiving office. After getting the paperwork signed, and traded, he dropped the trailer he had brought here, found the one he was to take back to Springfield, hooked onto it, did his walk around inspection, and was on his way in about twenty minutes.

He followed I-75 south, merged onto I-285 west, followed it around half of the city, and merged onto I-75 once more, this time going north. About forty miles north of Atlanta, Jack exited the interstate, pulled into a truck stop with a huge parking lot, found a place to park, and slept about four hours.

After his nap, Jack once again headed north on I-75. He merged onto I-24 west at Chattanooga, Tennessee and got through that city without incident.

As he was going down the western slope of Monteagle, he met with the same fate Jason had just a few hours earlier, he was pulled over by a Tennessee state trooper. As Jack sat in the truck, watching in his side-mounted mirrors for the approach of the trooper, the voice of the demon spoke in his head.

"Get ready for a rare treat," the demon said as Jack saw the trooper. A slow smile spread across Jack's face as he watched her approach the passenger side of the truck. The demon continued, "The call she put in to her dispatcher was never heard by them. As far as they know, she's still sitting up there in her little speed trap. The answer she received didn't come from anyone connected with the Tennessee state patrol. Have fun."

As the trooper arrived at the passenger side of the truck, Jack powered down that window. The state trooper, Brenda Brewer, a thirty-three-year old, blonde, married mother of two, stepped up on the running board of the truck and opened the door. She stepped down, swung the door wide, stepped back onto the running board, and into the doorway of the truck, her hands resting on either side of the door frame.

"Hello, officer," Jack said in greeting.

"I need to see your operator's license, your medical card, your permit book, and your logbook," Officer Brewer said, managing a business tone to her voice.

"In that order?" Jack asked, he hadn't moved and sat looking at her.

Officer Brewer had been visually inspecting the interior of the truck, seeing what she could from where she stood. When Jack asked what he had, her eyes locked onto his. She saw a small red flash in his eyes and was a little unnerved, but soon regained her composure when she convinced herself she hadn't seen what she thought she had.

"Sir," she said, her tone still flat, with the tinge of a mother getting ready to scold a child. As she looked at him, she couldn't help but think he had a close resemblance to the bald, character Matthew McConaughey played in the movie, Reign of Fire.

"Fine," Jack cut in. "Logbook first." He turned to his right in the driver's seat and stood up. He stepped between the two seats and half stepped into the sleeper. As he did so, he glanced at the trooper, and saw she was again looking at the interior of the truck. He made his move. Reaching toward her with both of his hands, he hit her with a jab to her nose with his fisted left hand, and simultaneously, wrapped his right hand around the back of her neck. She grabbed at her injured nose with both of her hands, releasing the sides of the door. With his left hand, he grabbed the front of her shirt, and with both his hands, yanked her off her feet, and into the interior of the truck.

Jack dragged her across the passenger seat, and turned his body to the left, and at the same time, turned her body so her back would be pressed against his front. As he completed this move, he also leaned toward the bed in the sleeper. He slammed her onto the bunk face first, and then body checked her with his own body. He heard and felt the air leave her lungs as the wind was knocked out of her.

Brenda tried to fight back but found she couldn't. His body was pressed on top of hers, the wind was knocked out of her, she was weakened by this, and she was scared out of her mind. She tried to reach both her sidearm and the microphone to the portable radio on her belt, but found she couldn't.

Jack kept her pressed to the bunk. He wrapped his right arm around her neck, and squeezed, shutting off the air to her lungs, and covered her nose and mouth with his left hand for the same purpose. After a few moments, she stopped struggling. He kept applying pressure for a few seconds to be sure she was unconscious.

When he was satisfied she was unconscious, he released his hold on her, clambered to his feet, and shut and locked the door she had been standing in just moments before. Next he removed her clothes, stripping her naked. He picked her up, raised the lid of the bunk, rolled her unconscious, nude body into the specially-made compartment, and closed the lid again.

Jack didn't know how long it would be before the Tennessee state troopers would discover that one of their own was missing, and with that in mind, he continued west on I-24. He got past the state scale house, just southeast of Manchester, and a little over two hours later, crossed the state line into Kentucky.

Jack's assumption that the state of Tennessee would miss Officer Brewer was correct. Thirty minutes after Officer Brewer had pursued a speeding truck down the western slope of Monteagle, the state trooper that had shared the sitting spot with her, came looking for her. He, of course, found her cruiser empty, the engine still idling, and the red and blue lights still flashing. It was as if she had disappeared, either on her own or against her will. He put in the call to his dispatcher, reporting what he had found, and requesting backup and instructions. The state troopers were still at the site when Keith came through there.

Jack didn't stop until he was well into the state of Kentucky. He finally pulled into the state scale house, which also served as a truck haven. He and the demon thinking this to be a funny kick in the pants. He allowed Brenda a short recess from her confinement, just long enough to relieve her bladder in the truck's toilet.

"The state of Tennessee won't let you get away with this," Brenda told him, as she exited the toilet stall. She thought she sounded nasally to herself, her nose still hurt, and it was swollen. She was an attractive woman, of average height, weight, and build. Her hair was blonde, her eyes blue, and her skin tanned. She modestly tried to cover her naked body with her arms and hands, while maintaining eye contact with her captor.

"Wow," Jack said, letting his eyes admiringly wonder over her body. "If I wasn't committed to someone else, I might be tempted to keep you for myself."

"What makes you think I would be a willing party to that?" Brenda spat, not caring for his blatant manner. She was still scared but trying to keep her fear in check.

"That's the other reason I wouldn't consider keeping you longer than I have to, you seem to have trouble keeping a civil tongue in your head," Jack said, he was speaking evenly and calmly. "Before I give you up, maybe you can redeem yourself of that sharp tongue."

"Who are you?" Brenda asked in a hushed voice. While he had been speaking, she had seen the same red flash in his eyes as before. She was fighting the terror that would start her screaming at the top of her lungs.

Jack raised the lid to the bunk with one hand, and motioned to the compartment with the other, indicating his wishes for her to climb inside.

"My name is Jack," he said smiling evilly, the demon told him of her fear.

Brenda gasped, the story of the murdered women being found in Springfield, Missouri had just recently made the national news networks. Although the Springfield area law enforcement and investigators, along with the Federal Bureau of Investigation weren't releasing much of the details of the case, they had released enough to make a story. Brenda had heard of the case and of the killer that called himself Jack, and was immediately confused as well as scared.

"I don't understand what you want with me," Brenda stated, her fear could soon turn to terror.

"You must be really naïve," Jack said, grinning and reaching for her.

The next morning Brenda Brewer's body was found in Springfield. She had been raped repeatedly, beaten, and mutilated. Her throat had been slashed wide open, and her tongue removed. A long, deep cut from her sternum to her pelvis, along with half a dozen crossway cuts had made the removal of her internal organs effortless. As with the other women, Jack had removed the hair and skin from her pelvic area, keeping it for a trophy. Brenda's body, like the rest, had been washed and wrapped in plastic. Her organs had been sloppily rearranged inside her. As with the other victims, a note had been left.

Dear Boss,

 As you can see, I ran a two for one special this week. As you may also see, that is if you're paying attention, I'm choosing my girls from all walks of life, a sort of collection, if you will. Of course all women are whores, some make many men happy in their lifetimes, and some make one man miserable their whole life. All sell their bodies one way or another. Your FBI-fools, buffoons, idiots- I was trying to be nice there- are falling off the pace. No matter, I'll keep doing what I'm doing. I'll be watching, and waiting.

 Yours (maybe someday) truly,

Jack
Catch me if you can.

Chapter 11

After Diane left for work, Jason puttered around the house for awhile. He fixed himself a breakfast of eggs, bacon, toast, and coffee. He sat on the living room sofa with his breakfast plate resting on the coffee table directly in front of the sofa and watched the morning news on the television.

The news program he was watching was a national broadcast that combined informative news with guest visits from members of the entertainment world. Soon the national broadcast broke for a few minutes to allow a local news brief.

"The top story at this time is the discovery of yet another body of a dead woman found in Springfield. This brings the count to four," the female reporter said as she seemed to look out of the television screen and talk directly to Jason. "The Springfield Police Department, working in conjunction with the FBI, declined to make a statement at this time, but are asking citizens to report any suspicious activity to the police. The main areas affected are industrial areas, specifically around trucking companies. The police are asking citizens to exercise caution, and not to approach anyone who looks suspicious when they are in these areas."

The newscaster went to the next story, and Jason fell into his own thoughts. Who had these women been? Who could be doing this? Why would anyone do this? How would he, Jason, feel if someone had kidnapped Diane, transported her hundreds or thousands of miles away from home, killed her, and then dumped her body with little or no regard. He would be saddened and angry, and not necessarily in that order, but mainly he would be heart stricken. He could not imagine how devastated the families of these women must be right now. It was beyond his comprehension how he would go on if something like that were to happen to Diane.

Jason finished his meal, and after putting his used dishes and cooking utensils in the dish washer, brought his logbook up to date. Next he pulled a clean sheet of paper and ink pen from the drawer in the kitchen where Diane had kept such items long before she had met him. Jason put pen to paper, leaving Christine a note, asking her to wake him when she got home. Jason knew Christine would be home long before Diane returned home, and he wanted to be awake and rested and have supper ready for her. He left the note where he was sure Christine would find it on top of the telephone. Then he went to bed.

Diane was lying on the ground. It was at nighttime, on a paved parking lot that seemed familiar to Jason, but there was no time to dwell on that. Her breathing was shallow, but regular. Her eyes were closed, and Jason kept throwing short glances her way as he slowly circled her in a stalking, crouched position. He was circling her with his back toward her. He kept his arms and hands loose, but ready to defend. He knew Diane was hurt, and the thing that hurt her was still nearby. He made up his mind he would circle one more time, then try to get her out of there—wherever there was.

The thing that had hurt Diane had flashed a knife or something like it, looked directly at Jason, then stabbed Diane. The instant the blade had made contact with Diane's flesh, Jason had been moving. The thing had stabbed her, then retreated to the shadows, moving deeper into the darkness. Jason wanted to help Diane, knew he had to, but also knew danger was still lurking nearby. Something in the back of his mind kept telling him to not take his attention away from the darkness for very long.

After completing his last circle around Diane, Jason squatted beside her and laid a hand on her arm. Her body was warm, and after satisfying himself that her pulse was still strong, he softly called her name. She replied with a moan, and he looked at her face. Something touched his shoulder, and he whirled around, ready to defend, attack, and—n

"Oh hell!" Christine said in a startled voice, as she jumped back, pulling her hand from Jason's shoulder.

"Shit," Jason muttered as he willed his eyes to focus on Christine's face, then asked, "I didn't hurt you, did I?" Somewhere in the back of his mind a voice sounded off with a low, menacing chuckle. Jason knew he had heard that laughter before, but couldn't put his finger on it. Where had he heard that voice?

"No," she responded, and blinked her eyes a couple of times, "you just scared the hell out of me."

"Sorry," Jason mumbled, as he swung his legs over the edge of the bed, and sat up. "I guess I was in the middle of a bad dream."

"Are you sure you're all right?" Christine asked, as she backed off another step, giving Jason room to stand if he wished.

"That would depend on who you asked," Jason quipped, and shot her a half grin. "I'm fine."

"Are you leaving now?" she asked.

"Not now," Jason responded. "I thought I would fix supper for you and your mom before I left."

"That's sweet," Christine said, "but I called her before I left work, and she said she wanted some takeout Chinese, so that's what I brought home."

"Oh, okay," he fisted sleep from his eyes. "I guess I'll get ready to go, and by the time I'm ready, maybe your mom'll be home."

"All right," Christine said as she turned and took a step toward the bedroom door. She paused and cast another glance toward Jason, and asked. "Are you sure you're all right?"

"I'm fine," Jason said looking at her. "By the time I take a shower and get the truck packed, maybe your mom'll be home."

Jason pushed himself off the bed and stood there for a moment. He headed toward the master bathroom. He stopped at the dresser drawer long enough to empty his pockets and lay the contents there. Next, he shed his shirt and kicked out of his jeans and underwear. The images of the dream seemed more like a clouded memory, and he thought about this as he took a reviving shower. That voice still haunted him. Where had he heard it before?

After showering and toweling dry, Jason selected a clean pair of underwear, socks, jeans, and a shirt. Subsequent to dressing, Jason pulled on the pair of cowboy boots he sometimes wore on the truck and placed a cap on his head. He morosely packed his duffle bag for the superfluous next few days away from home. The images of the dream had embedded itself into the back of his mind, and he was having a hard time ignoring them.

Jason picked up his duffle bag from the bed, and exited the bedroom. He made his way along the hallway, down the steps, and into the living room. He dropped the duffle bag onto the floor next to the wall that separated the living room from the kitchen, and stepped into the kitchen.

"Hey, peach fuzz," Christine said to him as he picked up the coffeepot, and filled it with water.

"Howdy," Jason said, pouring the water into the top of the coffeemaker.

"You know what I haven't done in a long time?" she asked him, a playful glint in her eyes.

"Had a date?" he ventured, opening the cabinet door above the coffeemaker.

"Kiss my butt," she responded, flipping the wet end of a kitchen towel in his direction, making it snap, and laughing at the sound. Jason scattered some of the coffee he was pouring into the filter when he jerked at the sound of the snapping towel, which brought another round of giggles from Christine.

"I don't have that much time to spend," he retorted as he dropped the coffee-filter assembly into the appropriate receptacle of the coffeemaker, and swung it closed with a click.

"No, I haven't done this in a while," Christine said as she advanced on him. She wrapped an arm around his neck, and pulled him close to her. She stood 5'9", about a half a head taller than Jason's 5'7", and it was no trouble for her to rip the cap from his head, and plant a wet, loud kiss onto his forehead, where his hairline was receding.

"Knock it off, brat," Jason said as he half-heartedly pushed her away. "You'll give me your cooties."

"At your age, you should be more worried about having a heart attack rather than getting cooties when a hot, young babe kisses you, old man," she shot back at him, enjoying this banter.

"Who's a hot, young babe?" he asked cocking an eyebrow at her, flipped the switch to the coffeemaker to the on position, then asked, as he pointed a finger toward her, "you?"

"Asshole," she mumbled, and prepared to flick the kitchen towel in his direction again.

"Careful," Jason teased, and picked up the bottle of dishwashing liquid that was setting in its place by the kitchen sink. "I'll wash those bad words out of your mouth with this dish soap."

"You don't have enough hair on your—" she stopped herself before finishing, and noticed the comical, cocked-eyebrow look of Mr. Spock that Jason was giving her.

"Yes?" he asked, the grin still playing around the corners of his mouth.

"I'll be quiet now," Christine said, the twinkles still dancing in her eyes, and threatening to snap the towel in his direction again.

They both raised their empty hands, palms outward, toward each other, in the gesture of mutual consent of backing down. Jason loved Christine as if she were his own. He had never disciplined her with a physical punishment, but he had previously verbally reprimanded her, thinking her mature enough to handle the latter, and too mature to endure the former.

As the coffeemaker started to gurgle, Jason returned the bottle of dish-washing liquid to its place by the sink and winked at Christine. He stepped into the living room, picked up his duffle bag, slung it over his shoulder by the strap, and carried it out to the truck. He sat behind the steering wheel of the truck and thought again of the images from the dream.

He was grateful for the interruption when Diane drove her car up the driveway and parked next to the Peterbilt.

"Hi, honey," Diane chirped as she got out of the Thunderbird. "I thought you would be long gone by now."

"I don't have to be in Junction City until after midnight, and it won't take me but about five hours to get there," Jason said as he climbed down out of the truck.

"Are you gonna get a nap once you get there?" Diane asked, it was her constant concern that he get enough sleep. Life with Jason was everything she had ever hoped for in a relationship, not like the losers she had known in her past, including Mark.

"I'll be fine," Jason said, wrapping an arm around her shoulders, lead-ing her toward the house. "I've been sleeping most of the day, and Christine woke me up about an hour ago when she got home."

"Good," Diane said simply as they stepped into the house.

They ate supper together, the three of them. After Christine waved the two of them outside to say their goodbyes, Jason and Diane walked to the Peterbilt.

"Please be careful," she almost whispered to him.

"I will," he responded, then kissed her. He climbed behind the steering wheel and tossed his logbook into the sleeper. Jason turned the key in the ignition switch to the on position, listened for the buzzing of the fuel pump, then turned it to the start position. The whole cab of the truck rocked as the big diesel engine turned over and then roared to life. He looked down at Diane, she looked up, and blew him a kiss. He reached out with his hand, and mockingly caught it.

"Can I put that wherever I want?" Jason called to her, grinning.

"I'll come up there and put it where you want," Diane called back to him as she flashed a teasing smile at him and backed away. Jason reluctantly shut the door, never taking his eyes from her. She waved to him, and he touched the bill of his cap with his fingertips, while giving her a short nod. Jason depressed the clutch with his left foot, moved the shifter to the fourth gear position, as he saw Diane turn toward the house. He leaned over to his right, pushed in the knob to release the tractor brakes, and eased out on the clutch. He drove to the terminal to reattach the trailer.

Jason had fueled the truck upon his arrival at the terminal that morning. This was an old trucker trick he had learned from his father on how to back up a logbook. Blanket Transportation required their drivers to log all fuel stops within an hour of the actual time of fueling. The time could be confirmed if the DOT wanted to pursue the issue. He found the trailer where he had dropped it, and re-hooked onto it, then completed his walk around inspection. He drove to the front of the dispatch office, parked, and went inside.

"Hi, Jason," Selena said, smiling at him.

"Howdy," Jason returned, then checked the mailbox the company provided for any "propaganda" as Jason called it.

"You all right?" she asked, dividing her attention between him and her computer screen.

"Nothing an hour with Diane wouldn't fix," he said, mischievously.

Selena ignored the computer screen, laughing as she looked at him. She felt the color of embarrassment erupt from her neck, spreading across her face and arms. She knew Jason lived to embarrass her, and she knew he was good at it.

"She is very special," Selena said, trying to turn the attention away from herself.

"Yes, she is," Jason agreed, nodding slowly, then asked. "How about you, are you all right?"

"Yes," Selena said, with a sigh, "I'm okay."

"That was convincing," Jason said, teasing her. He pulled up a chair, spun it around, and sat on it with his chest leaning against the backrest.

"Oh, it's nothing," she said. "I was just thinking about you and Diane when you came in. I was thinking how things have changed for the better over the last couple of years, since the two of you got married."

"Well, I was worried at first," Jason said, a bit reflectively. "I know I wasn't the only guy Diane had been with since Mark, and I didn't want to be a big disappointment to her."

"I know that feeling, being a disappointment, I mean," Selena said. "I've known Diane and her family most of my life, and we've grown up together. I always felt like it was unfair that when we matured, Diane got more than her fair share in the size of her breasts. All the women in her family are like that, her mother, her two sisters, even some of her female cousins have larger-than-average-sized breasts. When Billy and I got serious and started talking about marriage, I was hoping I wouldn't be a disappointment to him in that department."

"That, and you were probably hoping whatever gene made Diane big there," Jason said, with a slight grin, and pointed to his own chest, "got passed on to Billy to make him big there," and he pointed to his own crotch.

The color of embarrassment erupted from under Selena's blouse, up her neck, and across her face. She propped both elbows onto her desktop and clamped both of her hands over her mouth, as if trying to keep in the laughter and hold down her embarrassment . It didn't work, the sound of laughter came through her hands and shone through her eyes, as the color of her embarrassment spread across her face. When her gaze focused on Jason, she saw he was laughing with her.

"Well, I guess I better head out," Jason said. He stood up and returned the chair to its original position.

"Okay," Selena said, wiping the tears of laughter from her face. "Be careful."

"I will. Bye," Jason said, as he reached for the door handle. As his hand touched the door handle, a voice whispered in his mind, "If only things had been different a few years ago, you might be with her now. You could probably still have her if you pursued her." Jason stopped, turned, and looked at Selena.

Selena watched Jason open the door to leave, and she saw him stop as if frozen when a voice whispered in her mind, "If things had been different a few years ago, you might be with him now. You could probably still have him if you pursued him."

Jason and Selena looked at each other for a moment, each unaware that the other had "heard" the same whispered voice. They both blinked and slightly shook their heads. They were both unaware that Sultry was the voice inside their heads.

"Bye, Sal. Tell Billy I said hi," Jason said, trying to shake the effects of the inaudible voice and the dream together, and stepped though the doorway.

"Bye. I will," Selena called after him, as she watched the door close with the help of its automatic closer behind Jason. Like Jason, she was bothered by the effects of the voice she had heard in her head. She loved Billy very much and took her wedding vows seriously. She had never cheated on Billy and disagreed with anyone that cheated on their spouse for any reason. Her feeling was, if things were that bad, clear your head of one problem before creating another. She didn't wish to hurt Billy that way, or any other way, for that matter. She also knew Diane was crazy about Jason, and from what she saw, Jason was head over heels in love with Diane. She loved Diane like a sister and would never knowingly hurt her. As for Jason, she was hesitant to admit to loving him, because in this day and age, it could so easily be misconstrued by so many people. She settled upon a feeling of affection for Jason. From the conversations she had had with both of them about the other, she knew they loved each other, and she didn't want to see that destroyed for any reason.

Jason sat behind the steering wheel of his truck, and thought about that whispery voice that had just run through his mind. The dream of Diane being hurt was bad enough without this on top of that. Jason loved Diane and would never willingly hurt her. He chose not to cross that line and sleep with another woman. Some men said that a stiff dick had no conscience, but Jason's opinion was that was a bunch of crap. His thought was that he wouldn't want Diane to cross that line, so he would show her the same consideration. Besides his penis was not a separate entity but a part of him, and he, Jason, would be conscious of where he put it. He started the engine of the truck, depressed the clutch, and pulled the gear shift into the third gear position. He glanced at the window-paned dispatch office and eased out on the clutch pedal. The Peterbilt slowly rolled forward, and Jason turned left onto the highway that would grant him access to I-44.

Jason gained speed as he drove down the access ramp to I-44. He checked the mirror mounted on the left side of the truck, and when he didn't see the reflection of any vehicle there, he merged onto the interstate. He eased the pressure off the accelerator pedal with his right foot, flipped the button on the side of the gear shifter, and heard the transmission shift into thirteenth gear. He then mashed the accelerator pedal to the floor with his right foot again.

Jason drove westbound on I-44 about ten miles, where at the west side of Springfield, he exited onto State Highway 13 at Exit Seventy-seven. There was a traffic light at the end of the exit ramp, and when he got to it, Jason turned right to head northbound onto Highway 13. As he gained speed and geared up, it started to rain. He turned on the windshield wipers, and settled back for the drive to Junction City, Kansas.

Jason thought about the dream of Diane and the whispery voice. He normally would be listening to an audio book, or to the stereo, or talking with another driver on the CB, but not this night. He thought about both incidents and wondered if they could possibly be related. He made his way though Clinton, Missouri, where he turned onto State Highway 7 and continued north. At Harrisonville, Missouri, he merged onto State Highway 71 and drove passed the sign declaring the weigh station there was closed. At the south end of the Kansas City, Missouri area, Jason exited State Highway 71 and merged onto I-435 westbound, and about ten miles later left his home state of Missouri to enter the state of Kansas. He exited I-435, at Exit Twelve, and merged onto I-70 westbound. Except for the rain and the thought of the dream about Diane and the whispery voice about Selena, it was a quiet drive to Junction City for Jason. A little over three hundred miles, and four and a half hours after leaving the truck terminal, Jason arrived.

He drove to the warehouse where he was to drop the trailer he had and pick up another one, truckers called this a drop and hook. After he stopped in front of the guard shack of the warehouse, he picked up the keyboard of the Mobile-Max unit, keyed in his arrival call, and pressed the send button.

Jason gathered the bill of lading for the load he had, climbed out of the truck, and walked to the door of the guard shack. It was a few minutes after midnight, it was still raining slightly, and Jason thought the rain felt good on his face. He had thought about the dream and the voice the whole trip here, and he thought the rain had a metaphorically cleansing quality.

"Mornin'" Jason said, when he stepped into the guard shack and closed the door behind him.

"Good morning," the female guard replied. She was an African American in her mid-thirties, and Jason knew her name, but couldn't recall it just now.

"Quiet night?" Jason asked, as he handed her the paperwork.

"Yes," she said, smiling at him, and took the paperwork. She laid the paperwork on the work table next to the computer there, and entered the information she needed from the paperwork into the computer. "To tell you the truth, I like it that way."

"It seems like it would get boring," Jason commented.

"You get used to it after a while," the guard said, as she stamped the paperwork with a "RCVD-Subject To Count-Seal Intact" rubber stamp, and handed the top copy back to Jason. She then turned her attention back to the computer screen, and after tapping a few more entries, told Jason onto which lot number and what space number he could drop the trailer.

Jason exited the guard shack and was surprised to see the message light on the truck communication system lit, indicating there was a waiting message. He climbed behind the steering wheel, closed the truck door, and pressed a button on the communication system that displayed the main menu. Next he accessed the waiting load information and began to copy the information onto a steno pad he kept for that purpose. The load information was for a load on a preloaded trailer at the very place he was dropping the current trailer. The load information not only provided a load number, but also provided a pickup time when the load was loaded, a delivery time and place, a delivery or appointment number, and the trailer number. The providing of the trailer number would save him from getting back outside into the rain one less time. When he had been in the guard shack, he had noticed a CB radio mounted onto the work table, and had also observed the channel in which it was tuned. He reached to his own CB, tuned to that channel, called for the guard, and when she answered him via the CB, he told her that he was going to be pulling a loaded trailer from there. He gave her all the information regarding the load, and she thanked him.

Jason drove to the lot she had told him, and found the space where he unhooked the trailer he had brought with him. He found the trailer with his next load on it, and hooked onto it. He climbed out of the truck and into the rain one more time and made the electrical and air hook-ups from the truck to the trailer. He completed his walk around inspection, climbed back into the truck, and drove back to the guard shack.

The guard had the bill of lading paperwork ready for Jason when he reentered the guard shack. He looked the paperwork over, signed the top copy, and handed it back to her. She gave Jason his copies and walked outside with him to see if there was a seal on the trailer doors and to verify the number on that seal matched the seal number on the paperwork. After doing her visual inspection, she wished Jason a safe trip. Jason thanked her and climbed back into the dry interior of the truck cab, while she went back into the guard shack.

Jason pulled away from the guard shack and parked to one side of the driveway. He climbed into the truck sleeper, and pulled out his logbook. He logged his arrival time, noted the dropping of the trailer he brought with him, and also noted the trailer he was taking with him. He also noted the new load number. He logged his departure time and prepared to leave.

The load he was under was to be delivered at a warehouse the following morning in Fort Worth, Texas. He had been to the place where he was to deliver this load several times. He knew how to get to the warehouse in Fort Worth without consulting his direction book, and he knew the highways he would need to travel to get there fairly well. Jason also estimated it would take him about seven hours to make the trip.

Jason left the warehouse at Junction City and drove south on U.S. Highway 77. A few miles north of El Dorado, Kansas, Jason merged onto the Kansas Turnpike or I-35 southbound. He crossed the state line into Oklahoma a little over an hour later. The rain kept coming; it was little more than a drizzle yet less than a downpour. The wipers kept up with the rain, and Jason tried not to think about the hypnotic swishes and thumps they made on every cycle.

Jason first listened to the stereo, then to an audio book, but his thoughts and concentration were continually interrupted by the images of the dream. It had seemed so very real, and it had an ominous feel to it. Jason didn't think he was clairvoyant, but he felt like someone or something was trying to give him a warning.

The one thing that puzzled him was: who would want to hurt Diane? If there were ever a truly loving person, she was that person. He couldn't make himself think that anyone would willingly do her harm. He was thinking along these lines and trying to convince himself that the dream he had had was nothing more than a dream, when a soft mental voice "spoke" to him. This wasn't the same kind of voice that had spoken to him about Selena, but a more bold and commanding, yet soft voice.

"There is someone who can say the same thing about all of the women that have been murdered so far," the voice said.

In a moment of undisputed clarity, Jason knew the voice had spoken the truth. The murdered women had been someone's daughters, possibly someone's mothers, sisters, wives, lovers, aunts, or nieces. He again thought of how he would feel if Diane were to be taken from him in this way, and the thought saddened him.

Jason drove through the night trying to fit the pieces together. Murdered women from different parts of the country were being dumped in Springfield, Missouri, a city close to home, too close. Not only dumped in Springfield, but on the front steps of trucking companies in Springfield. Jason had often heard that the seventy miles that separated Springfield and Joplin, Missouri had more trucking companies per capita than any other part of the country, making it the trucking capital of the country.

As Jason drove, four wheelers, cars and pickups, buzzed around him. Some tailgated him with their headlights on bright, one headlight peeking around the side of the trailer to shine directly into his driver side mirror. Some would pass him, cut back in front of him, barely miss clipping his front bumper, no turn signal of course, then dart off the nearest exit ramp. Some would try to crowd him out of his lane as they attempted to merge onto the interstate, as if they expected him to yield to them even though he had the right of way. Jason always made the attempt to change lanes and give a vehicle room to merge onto the interstate. Sometimes, though, he couldn't because of another irritating habit some four wheelers did, that being to ride alongside a big truck. It seemed to Jason most people in four wheelers had the attitude that everyone else, especially big trucks, were supposed to watch out for them and to yield to them. Jason, as well as most experienced truck drivers, had seen more accidents involving four wheelers and trucks, where the four wheeler was at fault and caused the accident, rather than the other way around. One other thing Jason had noticed about people who drove four wheelers, it wouldn't matter if every state in the union raised the speed limit to 120 miles per hour, there would be more than one who would want to do 130 miles per hour.

Jason gave himself a mental shake of the head and returned his thoughts to the murdered women. If one person was doing this, how was that person getting in and out of town without being spotted. Jason could believe one person could get away with it once, maybe twice, but not this many times. Whoever was doing this was seemingly running circles around the Springfield Police Department, the Greene County Sheriff's Department, and the Missouri Highway State Patrol, all of which were good law enforcement agencies, and it stood to reason, all were on high alert—not to mention the Crime Stoppers network in Springfield which was comprised of citizens helping the police by reporting anything unusual or suspicious.

Then another thought entered his mind. Entered, hell, it blasted its way in, derailing Jason's train of thought. A leak in the investigation had revealed one, maybe more, letters left with the murdered women signed by someone calling himself Jack, and something awoke in Jason, Jack could be close to Jack the Ripper. Then something else occurred to Jason, the word "himself" had been used so readily.

As Jason drove through the rain the song "Riders on the Storm" by the Doors came to mind.

America had its share of cruel serial murderers, and all were young white men. Lizzy Borden was the closest female serial killer the United States had seen, so it stood to reason that Jack was a man. Jason, at one time, had listened to the audio version of John Douglas's book Mindhunter. In it, Mr. Douglas gave his theory of who he thought Jack the Ripper was based on the information and the list of subjects he was given.

Jason tried to recall all he knew about Jack the Ripper. Those murders had taken place in London, England in the late summer and early fall of the year 1888. Jack the Ripper had appeared and vanished seemingly without a trace. His murdered victims were unfortunates that lived in London's East End, known as Whitechappel. He butchered his victims, taking certain body parts. It seemed as though he came and went with the fog. He hadn't been caught. Over the years, theories were developed. These included: Jack the Ripper was more than one person, he was a physician, he was part of the Royal Family, he was a butcher by trade, and so on.

Patricia Cornwell had done a very good in-depth investigation into the identity of Jack the Ripper and had named the killer. Jason owned the audio book and had listened to it several times. One thing that Ms. Cornwell had brought out was disguises, and it was her thought that Jack the Ripper was very good at blending in with his surroundings and that he knew every possible hiding place in his killing area. Jason figured that if this Jack was being undetected by several law enforcement agencies, maybe more, then he was probably good at disguises. He probably knew his way around Springfield, could blend in with his surroundings, and possibly had help.

Jason made himself concentrate on the task at hand which was getting to Fort Worth, Texas. He had gone through Oklahoma City and was presently headed for the Texas state line. It was close to 5:00 A.M. when he did cross the Red River, the natural boundary between that part of Oklahoma and Texas. He was starting to get sleepy, but he knew if he didn't keep going, the traffic going into Fort Worth would be horrendous. After he got to his destination, he could take a nap, and by that time the traffic would have died down quite a bit.

Jason arrived in the Fort Worth area a little before 7:00 A.M. He made his way to the warehouse where he was to drop the trailer he had and pick up an empty one. He stopped at the guard shack long enough to give the guard there the information required to get past the gate. That information included the name of the trucking company, tractor and trailer numbers, appointment number, the number stamped into the trailer door seal, and the driver's name. Jason privately referred to this as jumping through hoops.

The guard, a huge African American man, told Jason where he could drop the trailer. Jason thanked him and complied. They exchanged waves as Jason exited the drop lot and made a right hand turn. It was still raining, making it hard to see at night, but Jason knew where he was going. He followed the street one block down and made a left hand turn at the next intersection. After following that street for two blocks, he came to the drop lot the warehouse used for empty trailers. There were three trailers there that belonged to Blanket Transportation among a host of other trailers that represented about half a dozen other trucking companies. Jason chose one of the two that had an air ride suspension. He hooked the tractor to the trailer and did his walk around inspection. He typed the information required into his Mobil Max system, and entered his empty call, noting the change of trailers.

Jason hefted himself out of the driver's seat and stepped into the sleeper. He sat on the edge of the bunk, hung his cap on the arm rest of the driver's seat, and pulled off his boots. He was on the verge of lying down when the message light indicating an incoming message lit up accompanied by a soft buzzing sound. Jason blinked at it. He picked up the keypad to the satellite communication system and looked at the view screen. On the screen was his next load information.

Jason climbed back into the driver's seat and retrieved his steno pad and an ink pen. He copied the information. It was another drop and hook. He was to drive to Roanoke, Texas, an industrial suburb of Fort Worth, drop this empty trailer and hook onto a preloaded trailer there. The preloaded trailer was scheduled to go to Brook Park, Ohio for the following week. Jason knew he could drop the preloaded trailer at Blanket Transportation's home terminal, and someone else could make the delivery.

Jason climbed back into the sleeper and opened his logbook. After a few calculations, he brought the logbook up to date. He set his alarm clock for three hours, and lay down to get some sleep. It seemed as though he blinked, and the alarm clock was sounding off.

Jason picked up the alarm clock, looked at the face of it to see if he had set it incorrectly, confirmed that he had not, and shut it off. He sat up, ran a hand through his thinning hair, and reached for his boots. He pulled his boots on and dug around in his duffle bag for his toothbrush and toothpaste. He stepped out onto the running board of the passenger side door and brushed his teeth, using some bottled water to rinse. He stood there for a moment, enjoying the splash of the rain on his face. He stepped back into the cab of the truck, and checked his logbook one more time, after he put his toothbrush away.

Jason drove to the warehouse in Roanoke and jumped through the hoops at the guard shack. He dropped the empty trailer beside the trailer he was to hook onto and made the switch. He did his walk around inspection and brought his logbook current, noting the change of trailers. He then walked to the shipping/receiving office and called Diane. He knew he had probably missed her this late in the day, but he left her a message on the answering machine. He told her that he was all right, where he was, what he was doing, where he was going, and that he would be home sometime later that night.

Jason left the warehouse lot around 11:00 A.M. and headed for I-35 west northbound. Interstate 35 splits north and south of the Dallas/Fort Worth area. The leg that runs through Dallas is called I-35 east, and the leg that runs through Fort Worth is called I-35 west. Interstate 35 also splits the same way north and south of the twin cities of the Minneapolis/St. Paul area.

Jason's plan was to follow I-35 north to the town of Gainesville, Texas, where he would follow U.S. Highway 82 east to Sherman, Texas and merge onto U.S. Highway 75 north. U.S. Highways 75 and 69 run together from the Texas/Oklahoma state line to Atoka, Oklahoma, and it was here that Jason would follow U.S. Highway 69 north. It was on this route that Jason arrived at the truck stop in Eufaula, Oklahoma about three and a half hours after leaving Roanoke, Texas. He fueled the truck in the rain, paid for the fuel with cash, found a space to park, and planned to take a three-hour nap. The images of the dream of Diane being stabbed, the echoes of the voice tempting him with Selena, and thoughts of Jack, turned his nap into a three-hour wrestling match with himself.

Three and a half hours later, Jason was headed north on U.S. Highway 69 again. He drove through the towns of Muskogee, Wagoner, and Pryor. At the small town of Adair, Jason turned right at the traffic light there onto Oklahoma State Highway 28. About twelve miles later, he turned left at the traffic light in Langley onto Oklahoma State Highway 82. About twelve miles later, Jason merged onto U.S. Highway 60, headed eastbound. It was here that Jason finally ran out of the rain. Jason followed U.S. Highway 60 and crossed the state line into Missouri. A few miles west of the town of

Neosho, Missouri, Jason turned north onto U.S. Highway 71, and about fifteen miles later, merged onto I-44 headed east.

Jason exited I-44 a little over an hour later at exit 84. He turned right at the end of the exit ramp, and then turned left at the stop sign about a hundred yards away. He dropped the trailer at Blanket Transportation's main lot and walked to the dispatch office.

Jason entered the office and checked his mailbox; it was empty. He then turned, walked to stand in front of his dispatcher, and seated himself there. His dispatcher was currently on the phone with someone and nodded a greeting at Jason as Jason sat down. Soon he hung up the phone.

"Jason, how are you?" the dispatcher asked.

"I'm fine," Jason answered, he heard his own weariness in his voice. "What do you have for me next?"

"I wanted to talk to you about that," the dispatcher said. "Keith Doyle requested that you be placed on a California run for next week, he has one also. The two of you would deliver at the same place in Stockton, California, and your appointment times would only be an hour apart."

"Sure," Jason said, he always enjoyed going to the western states, especially when he could run with Keith.

"Fine, I'll put you on it," the dispatcher said.

"Thanks," Jason said as he rose from the chair. "Have a good weekend."

"You do the same," the dispatcher called to Jason's retreating back.

Jason drove toward home. He was tired to the point of exhaustion, and he just wanted to get some sleep. He drove on by the truck stop where Diane worked, and a few minutes later parked the truck in the driveway of their home. He gathered up his laptop computer, logbook, fuel receipts, paperwork, and shaving kit. He entered the house, dropped these items onto a corner table in the living room, and walked to the bedroom. He stripped off his clothes, pulled back the covers, and climbed in. As he drifted off to sleep, he thought about the circle he had just completed. There was no way he could legally log those miles in the time he had driven them. He would have to redo his logbook later when he woke up, but now he needed to get some sleep.

Jason woke about three hours later. He knew Diane was there because when he had gone to bed, he had left the bedroom door open, and now it was closed. His clothes were gone, and the items that had been in the pockets were now on the dresser. He swung his feet to the floor and sat on the edge of the bed. He sat there a moment, trying to collect his thoughts. He had had the dream again, and it had seemed all the more real every time he had it. He shook his head, stood from the bed, and headed for the doorway that separated the bedroom from the bathroom.

After emptying his bladder, brushing his teeth, shaving, and showering, he slipped on a pair of athletic shorts and went downstairs. Jason went to the kitchen where he found Diane washing dishes, singing along to her favorite radio station, and dancing to the music. He stepped up behind her, slipped his arms around her, and held her close. She leaned into the embrace, closing her eyes, and grasped his clasped hands in hers.

"I love you," Jason whispered into her ear.

"I love you, too. Hold me," Diane said. She broke his hold on her, and turned to face him. She snuggled into his embrace, and said, "Keith called while you were asleep."

"I'll call him back in a little while," Jason said. He stood there holding Diane close. He closed his eyes and breathed in her essence. She wore one of his oversized button up shirts and not much else. He knew from past experience that she would have headed for the bathtub as soon as she got home. Jason was resigned to the fact that he was married to a mermaid. He smelled the fragrance of the bubble bath she used coming from her skin, the shampoo she used on her hair, and the small amount of perfume she occasionally used. He squeezed her tighter and tried to melt into her when he felt his embrace being returned.

"Are you all right?" Diane asked, pulling away from him just enough to look at him. "You were sleeping hard when I got home. Are you hungry?"

"I'm fine," Jason answered. He held her face between his hands and kissed her.

"Wow," Diane breathed, "I love it when you do that."

"I love it that you love it when I do that," Jason was smiling at her now.

"Tell you what," Diane said, "I'll finish these dishes and fix you something to eat while you call Keith. We'll get done about the same time, and the rest of the night will be ours."

"All right," Jason agreed.

Jason called Keith and spent about ten minutes on the phone with him. Diane finished washing the dishes and had a supper plate ready for him when he got off the phone. Later, after they had made love, Jason lay awake, the memories of the dream about Diane and the nagging voice about Selena still lingered. He couldn't shake the feeling that their lives were on a collision course with impending disaster.

Chapter 12

FBI Special Agent Dixie Crenshaw sat on a four-legged barstool at a long table. Across the table from her on the same type of stool sat Forensic Doctor Beverly Mattingly. They were looking over the results of DNA samples of semen taken from each of the victims. Dixie was on the verge of pulling her hair out, this was frustrating. The first set of results showed a single donor, but the same results showed multiple donors. The DNA samples tested human, but the same samples tested not human.

What was so frustrating was they had taken one set of samples, and tested that set here in Springfield. They had sent another set of the same samples to the Jefferson City, Missouri Crime Lab. They had also sent another set of the same samples to an FBI forensic lab. The results of all three tests were back, and all three agreed. The donor was the same person, yet different. The donor was human, but not human. The results of the tests pointed to the donor being human, but didn't confirm it.

"Can you make any sense out of this?" Dixie asked of Dr. Mattingly.

"Not really," the doctor answered, she was checking and rechecking test results.

"I need your opinion, Doctor, what are we dealing with here?" Dixie said.

"Please call me Beverly, Special Agent Crenshaw."

"All right, Beverly, I'm Dixie."

"You'll probably think I'm crazy, but I have two theories."

"Please, tell me. As far as crazy, I'm on my way, and for me it will be a short trip."

Beverly took a deep breath and said, "Okay, the DNA test results point toward a human donor with some anomalies. The three labs that tested the samples reported the same findings, as you know; there's no need for me to rehash all of that. So here goes, theory one, we are dealing with alien DNA that has grafted itself onto human DNA with the ability to change at will to prevent us from locking onto it and identifying it."

"Aliens...from outer space?" Dixie asked to clarify.

"I said you would probably think me crazy," Beverly said shrugging.

"You said you had two theories."

"The other theory has to do with an advanced terrain form of DNA that has the ability to shift from one form to another, keeping us off balance."

"You'll have to explain that one to me, Beverly, I'm just a simple country girl from Tennessee," Dixie said.

"All I mean is we are dealing with an advanced culture that has the ability to manipulate its own DNA, and throw us off balance," Beverly offered.

"Okay," Dixie said slowly. "What are you saying?"

"I think we may be dealing with someone from the future or from another dimension," Beverly said all at once as if she were afraid she would lose her nerve.

"Beverly," Dixie said, shaking her head.

"I know it sounds ridiculous, Dixie, but there seems to be no other explanation," Beverly offered. "The people at the other labs that tested the same samples have no idea what could have caused the results we've gotten. At first we all thought the samples had been contaminated by a foreign substance, and we retested to make sure we were seeing what we were seeing. Then, all three labs called for new samples, and we tested those. We all agree that the samples were not contaminated, and then we sat up and paid attention when we got the same results the second and third time we ran the tests."

"All right," Dixie said, "but there must be some other explanation, isn't there?"

"If there is, I sure would like to hear it," Beverly said. "Neither one of the other labs would have even told you anything close to what I did."

"What do you think they would have told me?"

"Probably something along the lines that the test results were inconclusive," Beverly offered Dixie a brief smile. "I don't want to believe what I've told you, but that's what the evidence points to."

"So let me get this straight," Dixie said, "it's your opinion that we're dealing with either extraterrestrials or time traveling people from Atlantis."

"Like I said before, if you have a theory, I would love to hear it," Beverly said.

"There must be something else," Dixie said. "There must be something the labs missed, another test that can be run, or another lab that can do the testing."

"No," Beverly shook her head. "The Springfield lab, the Jefferson City

Crime Lab, and the FBI Lab are all three good labs. Although mistakes could have been made, there is no way the same mistakes could have been made at three different labs on the same tests of the same samples."

"I suppose you're right," Dixie said letting out a sigh. "I just find it hard to believe that in this day and age we have to grasp at straws on a case like this."

"I agree, Dixie," Beverly said. "With all the medical training I've had, it was hard for me to actually tell you what I did."

"I'm sure it was," Dixie confided. "Tell me something, Beverly, will you be able to identify this type of thing again? Let's suppose for a minute that there are X amount of unsolved rape/murder cases that can be compared with what we have here. Could you be confident enough to match the results?"

"That's one thing about this DNA strand, it seems to have the ability to take different shapes, kind of like a shape shifter," Beverly said, "but it still has its own kind of signature, and I think I could spot it."

"Okay, Beverly, thank you. I'll be in touch," Dixie said and stood to stretch her legs and back.

No sooner had Beverly left the room, than Special Agent Tom Bradford entered the room and sat on the stool that Beverly had vacated. Dixie noticed Tom's particular way he played with the wedding band on his left hand.

"Well, where are we?" Tom asked, as Dixie sat back onto the barstool.

"I wish I knew," she said and began scanning papers again. Then a thought occurred to her.

"Tom," she said, "didn't you tell me that your wife had been murdered a few years ago?"

"Yes, I did," Tom confirmed. He twirled the ring more with the thumb and little finger of the same hand.

"Would it be too painful for you to tell me about it?" Dixie asked, looking at him.

"No, she was leaving work one night and was raped and killed," Tom said, and his eyes welled up. He wiped at his eyes, sniffed, and then continued. "The police ran DNA testing on the semen samples like what you've done, but couldn't match the test results with any known offenders. The case stands as unsolved."

"Tom, I don't want to reopen any old wounds any worse than what I have, but would you permit Dr. Mattingly and me to compare your wife's test results with the ones we have here?" Dixie asked. She didn't know where this might lead, but she wanted to see if there might be a random match in the DNA structures.

"I wouldn't mind," Tom did a sort of half shrug, continuing to twirl the ring. "Do you think you're onto something?"

"I don't know," Dixie shook her head, then looked at Tom. "It's just a hunch right now, but I'm having a hard time believing the interpretation I was offered of these test results, I want something similar to compare them to."

"What can I do to help?"

"Get me your wife's file and the test results."

"Consider it done," Tom said as he slid off the stool and headed for the door.

Tom returned about thirty minutes later with the file and gave it to Dixie. Dixie opened the file, read through it briefly, then went to the sheet of paper with the results of the DNA tests of the semen samples. A small smile danced at the corner of her lips.

"You found something?" Tom was anxious, he was spinning the ring on his left hand with the thumb and forefinger of his right hand.

"It's nothing concrete, Tom, and I don't want to get your hopes up, but we may have a hit here. I need to get Beverly back in here to see what she thinks. I can do small comparisons, but Beverly is the expert here," Dixie said. She tried to convince herself that Beverly was an expert, but after hearing Beverly talk about extraterrestrials and time traveling beings she wasn't so sure. One thing she was sure of though, the fact that Beverly seemed confident in her own ability to be able to identify this odd DNA structure. Dixie reached for the desk phone resting not far from her and paged Beverly.

"I'm pretty sure our killer is a truck driver," Dixie said.

"The Yorkshire Ripper?" Tom asked, referring to the serial killer England had a few years ago who turned out to be a truck driver.

"It's definitely a possibility," Dixie said. "The way he travels the distances he does in the time frame he does."

When Beverly entered the room, Dixie explained to her what she had done, and what she had found, and what she wanted of Beverly. Beverly studied the DNA test results from Tom's wife's attacker, and swore softly under her breath.

"It's a match," Beverly said. "There are slight differences from these test results and the ones we're comparing them to, but the ones we're comparing them to are not carbon copies of themselves either. The structure is the same, whatever the donor is, it's the same donor."

"All right, here's what we need to do," Dixie said. "First of all, Tom I need you to get on the FBI computer and send out a kind of all points request, asking for any unsolved rape/murder cases where DNA semen tests were found to be inconclusive. Ask them to include places and dates of the attacks. You should probably include the military."

"Okay," Tom said, he was taking notes as Dixie talked.

"Beverly, I need you to go through the test results we are going to receive. If you need to, get a couple of your associates that you trust to help with the sorting," Dixie told Beverly.

"All right," Beverly said.

"The first thing we need to do is eliminate the test results that don't match the profile we've established here," Dixie said. "Then we can concentrate on the ones that do match our profile and see where, how long, and how often our killer has been around."

"You think this killer is just some ordinary serial killer?" Beverly asked. Her tone had hints of disbelief.

"Beverly, I don't think there's anything ordinary about this killer. I think whatever else this killer may be, it's not ordinary, and I won't rule out supernatural just yet," Dixie confided, "but my daddy was a backyard mechanic, and he would work on other people's cars as a sideline job. I heard him say more than once to eliminate the simple stuff first. That's what we're going to do here. We are going to eliminate the cases that don't match our profile and concentrate on the ones that do match our DNA profile. Whenever you feel we have a hit, we will mark it, and go on to the next one.

"I think this killer has a past, I don't think he just started raping and murdering women a few weeks ago but has been doing it for years. I don't think he has committed these same crimes as often as he has now. He has probably perfected his crime to the point he feels he can't be caught. What we are going to look for is patterns in occurrences, time of day, how far the victims were away from home, if they were traveling or on vacation, and so on. We will consider all possible explanations, even people from outer space, or time traveling people from Atlantis, or even dimension jumping people. Fair enough?"

"Fair enough," Beverly nodded, a bit embarrassed, but smiling.

Tom looked at Dixie, raising an eyebrow. She shook her head slightly at him.

"One more thing we need to address is why Rachel was treated differently than the other victims," Dixie stated as she picked out Rachel's file. "There was no evidence of rape, but the cutting of the throat along with the multiple stab wounds, the scalping, and the way the way the body was wrapped in plastic, points to our killer's MO and signature."

"Maybe Rachel reminded the killer of a sister, a cousin, a niece, or his mother," Tom stated.

"Could be," Dixie said, "but I'm inclined to think this killer picks his victims in advance, rather than at random."

"Or it could be that she did or said something that prevented him from raping her, but also infuriated him to the point to change this killing to a crime of passion," Beverly put in.

"That's definitely something to consider," Dixie said, then asked. "If that's the case, then what was said or done? And if it was a crime of passion, why didn't he destroy her face? This killer is far different than any normal serial killer, if there is such a thing."

"I'll be in the computer lab if you need me," Beverly stated as she stood. "Tom, I'll send you my web address via email."

"Okay, thanks," Tom answered as he finished writing his notes.

"Okay, let's do this," Dixie said. What she hadn't told Beverly and Tom was that her superiors in Quantico were leaning on her hard to crack this case, and she wasn't used to giving up.

Later, after Tom had completed the task that Dixie had asked of him, he approached her.

"Can I ask what that was all about?" Tom asked, he twirled the ring.

"Beverly has a theory that may swing toward the X-Files, and we're at the point that we need to go slow and examine all possibilities," Dixie explained. "I don't know if we are in fact dealing with alien DNA, but whatever we are dealing with can alter its DNA enough to make it look different every time it shows up. We need to know who or what this killer is. We need to know if this killer has a preferred hunting ground. We need to know how this killer selects its victims. We need to know how this killer transports its victims here and why. We need to know if there is more than one killer."

"More than one?" Tom looked at her sharply.

"That was one theory about Jack the Ripper, that there was more than one person doing the killings," Dixie said.

"You're shittin' me," Tom said, his tone noted disbelief.

"No, that was one theory, and since our killer has kind of named himself after Jack the Ripper, we should not overlook any possibilities. No matter how irrational they may sound," Dixie said.

"Yeah, the name itself, Jack, and the letters," Tom asked. "Could they offer us some clues?"

"That's what I mean," Dixie said. "We need to consider any and all possibilities. We need to come up with some sort of formula to punch all of our findings into, and at the same time we need to catch all of the obvious clues that come our way. This killer is a cool customer, every note is sent on the same type of paper that our lab hasn't been able to identify."

"I think your daddy was right about eliminating the simple stuff first, but I wouldn't be a bit surprised if our killer trips up on something simple and gives himself away," Tom stated.

"If that happens," Dixie said, "I hope it happens before any more women have to die."

"Me, too," Tom agreed.

"I'm gonna go back to the motel and get some sleep. Let me know if anythin' happens," Dixie said, her Eastern Tennessee accent usually surfaced whenever she started to get tired.

"What about the lab personnel working on the letters?" Tom asked.

"I'll check with them when I come back, I just need a few hours' sleep right now," Dixie said.

"All right," Tom said. "Dixie, you did good work here today. I know the uppity-ups at Quantico are leaning on you, but don't let them get you down. This is a high-profile case, and none of them wanted to tackle it, that's why they sent you."

"And I thought it was my good looks and charmin' personality," Dixie said, letting her Eastern Tennessee accent run amuck on purpose now, as she smiled at Tom.

"Well there is that, too," Tom smiled at her and added a wink. He was twenty-plus years her senior, and although he found her attractive, hell he found her absolutely gorgeous, he felt nothing more than a brotherly interest in her. He didn't watch her walk away.

Dixie drove to the motel where she was staying in her rental car. The motel the Bureau had chosen for Dixie was close to her work. It was small, but clean and quiet. She let herself into the room and removed her suit jacket. She pulled her hair down and brushed it out. As she stood in front of the mirror, she thought about her parents.

Her mother had been killed in a head-on crash with a drunk driver when Dixie was six years old. The emotional scars were still visible at losing her mother at such a young age. Her father had never remarried, but had had several girlfriends, a couple of them quite serious. Dixie lost her father eleven years after losing her mother to cancer. She missed them both terribly and thought of them often.

"What would John Wayne do, Daddy?" Dixie asked the darkened room as she lay in bed. John Wayne had been her father's favorite western actor.

"What would John Wayne do if he had come up against Jack?" Dixie asked again, then smiled as she answered herself. "He would have shot him full of holes like he did George Kennedy in Cahill U.S. Marshall or slung him into a mud hole like he did his own son Patrick Wayne in Big Jake or knocked him out like he did Robert Mitchum in El Dorado, that's probably what he would have done."

Dixie was back in the lab after about a four-hour nap and a shower. She felt refreshed and revived. The truth was she hadn't been sleeping well. She had lost weight since her few weeks' stay in Springfield, and it wasn't because of the quality of the food. This case had taken its toll on her. She had been involved in a couple of murder investigations before this where the perpetrator had transported the victim across state lines, but nothing that compared to this. She knew she was close to solving some aspects of the case, she could feel it. She just needed a slight nudge in the right direction or enough of a lead to point her that way.

The technicians at work on the letters looked up and greeted her as Dixie entered the lab. She returned the greeting and poured herself a cup of coffee. The letters were arranged side by side on a countertop. Each one was in a sealed, clear plastic-type freezer evidence bag. On each bag was a space where information had been written, identifying each letter to the victim with which it had been found.

"Dana, Brandon," Dixie said, calling each lab technician by name, "I don't want to seem ungrateful or to seem pushy, but I need answers, like yesterday. What can you tell me about the author of these letters?"

"He's sneaky and smart," Dana offered after a moment's hesitation and exchanging a glance with Brandon. "The paper is an old grade. I think he's playing with us by using this type of paper and changing his style of writing. The letters in the words in the letters are made with brush strokes, much like the original Jack the Ripper letters. This person thinks he's Jack the

Ripper reincarnated."

"What about physical evidence?" Dixie asked.

"I'll take this one," Brandon spoke up. "We dusted for fingerprints. What we got was unlike anything we've ever seen before. We sent the fingerprints to the FBI, and they couldn't come up with anything more than what we did."

"Meaning?" Dixie asked after a moment's pause.

"Meaning," Brandon said after he and Dana exchanged another glance and she nodded her encouragement to him, "The FBI, didn't give us anything we didn't already know. These fingerprints don't resemble anything we've seen before."

"Let me guess," Dixie said, her voice sounded as if she were about to lose her patience, "they're human, but not human."

"Yes," Brandon said, he was astounded.

"Okay," Dixie said, taking a cleansing breath. "I'm going to ask the two of you to go out on a limb and tell me what you think about these findings."

"We don't know what to make of these results," Brandon said.

"One thing," Dana cut in, "is the fingerprints themselves. They seem to exhibit their own properties. It's hard to explain, it's like they're reversed. There are swirls where there should be ridges, and ridges where there should swirls."

"What?" Dixie was flabbergasted. She shook her head as if to clear it.

"That's the only way I can describe it," Dana said, and Brandon nodded his agreement.

"Would you care if I had someone else take a look at these?" Dixie asked.

"Please do so," Dana said. "We want this guy caught just as badly as you do. He's not doing our city any favors by dropping his murdered victims here."

Dixie nodded reflectively, thanked them both, and left the room. As she walked along the hallway, Dixie tried to find any reasoning to these murders. They were obviously some sort of revenge tactic the killer had worked out in his head, but revenge against whom or what. Revenge against Springfield? That seemed thin. Revenge against women? That seemed more feasible. All women? The killer so far had taken a sort of cross section of women from different parts of the country, from different backgrounds and careers. Revenge against the country? Dixie could probably work that into a theory along with the revenge against women theory, but something kept nagging her that another element was missing. She thought it best to keep searching and to keep her eyes open.

Dixie roused herself out of her semi-trance and made herself ready to talk to the technician working the videotapes available to them. Most of the larger trucking companies in the Springfield area had surveillance cameras that would record most of the activities that took place on their property. The trucking companies that Jack had chosen to leave his victims with had eagerly submitted videotapes from the offending crime dates, and Dixie was on her way to see if they had caught him on tape. One of the first things the investigative team had done was to check available videotape of the crime scenes, but nothing was found or revealed to be out of the ordinary. So a second, more extensive and intensive search of the videotapes was ordered. It was hard for Dixie to believe that so much physical evidence of this case simply didn't exist.

"Hi, Matt," Dixie said to the back of the video technician's head as she entered the room and saw him looking into a video monitor.

"Hi, Dixie," Matt said, turning his head to see her and give her a smile. They had worked together earlier on this same case, and after finding nothing on the videotapes worth mentioning about the case, she had asked him to review the tapes more closely. Dixie had left him alone for about a week, but now she needed answers and hoped he had some for her.

"I hate to put pressure on you, Matt, but I need something to go on," Dixie said as she pulled up a chair to sit next to him.

"Well," Matt said, hesitated, then continued, "I did find something on almost all of the tapes, but you probably won't believe me when I tell you."

"Let me guess," Dixie said, weariness crept into her voice, "it's human, but not human."

"How did you know?" Matt looked at her with a serious expression, then smiled a smile that lit up his whole face, letting her know he was teasing her.

"You," Dixie accused, returning a brief smile.

"This person is sneaky, and smart, and from what I can tell, clairvoyant," Matt sobered. He knew Dixie preferred an air of professionalism, and he knew she had let him slide with the little joke he had just pulled.

"Okay," Dixie said, drawing out the word, and sounding doubtful.

"The first time through the tapes, I was looking for solid physical evidence. When nothing showed up, my first thought was that the tapes had been tampered with," Matt said, then took a breath, it was obvious that he was nervous. "When you asked me to review the same tapes, I did, unsuccessfully at first, but, last night, I came across something on one, and looked for something similar on the rest of them. I rechecked everything this morning after getting some sleep to make sure I was seeing what I thought I was seeing. It's not much, and it's really thin, but it's all I came up with."

"It's all right, Matt," Dixie said trying to give him a comforting look. "It's likely that you can't tell me anything more farfetched than what I've heard today."

"Okay, number one, this guy does not want to be videotaped for obvious reasons. Number two, this guy somehow knew which way the cameras were facing and sweeping on every parking lot he visited. That's hard to do. I could believe he could have had inside help getting around the surveillance cameras at one trucking company, maybe two, but not half a dozen."

"How could a person get by with not being videotaped by a surveillance camera?" Dixie asked.

"A person could have inside help to turn the cameras off, or to change or erase the recorded videotapes," Matt said. "That would be the most obvious, I would think. A person could time how long a camera takes to complete a sweeping circuit, but that person couldn't be sure if there were hidden cameras. I think it would be very unlikely that a person could get away with that successfully. A person could stay out of camera range, and with a well-placed bullet, take out a camera, but there again is the possibly of hidden cameras.

"What I have found are accidents. On one tape, a trucking company's automatic sprinklers had been on, and on their normal sweep, had gotten part of the main drive's pavement wet. The videotape didn't record the killer leaving, but it recorded the wet tracks his vehicle made after he drove through the water."

"Are you sure about this?" Dixie's interest was awake; this was the closest thing she had heard to a real clue all day.

"There were six cameras that swept across that same driveway within seconds of each other, all from different angles, not a one captured a vehicle, but they all six recorded the same wet tracks," Matt was adamant.

"What type of tracks?" Dixie asked. "Single or double?"

"Single track," Matt answered, he had a pretty good idea what Dixie was asking. "With the popularity of four-wheel drive vehicles, the same tire manufacturer can now make tires to fit pickups, SUVs, and eighteen wheelers with the almost same tread pattern. The track I have on tape gives me no clue as to how big the tire was that made it."

"What else?" Dixie pressed, she was eager, but trying to remain calm.

"The same type of situation at another trucking company," Matt went on. "A smoke plume. The cameras didn't record a vehicle, but they did record the evidence that one had been there."

"What type of vehicle are we looking for?" Dixie asked.

"It's hard to say," Matt said.

"Why?" Dixie asked. "Can't you take measurements of the tracks, how high the smoke plume was, make an educated guess?"

"I could," Matt confessed, "but I wouldn't want to give you false hope, or be responsible for giving you a false lead."

"Isn't there anything you can give me?" Dixie asked, she wasn't far from pleading.

"Tell you what," Matt said, "the tire tracks I can work on and maybe come up with something. The smoke plume was pretty much dissipated by the time the camera picked it up, and it being recorded at night will make it even harder to do anything with."

"Okay," Dixie said, her newfound hope was starting to dwindle. "Is there anything else?"

"Yes, there is one other thing," Matt said, hesitated, "there's the bodies themselves."

"What about them?" Dixie's interest was peaked again.

"With most of the area trucking companies, they employ three types of camera surveillance. One type is the sweeping method, where a camera sweeps a particular area, and then another sweeps a different area, but overlaps the first camera's range," Matt said, and looked at Dixie with a quizzical expression to see if she was following his lead. Dixie nodded for him to continue. "Next is a popular method, what you might call a flashing method. This is where several cameras flash a scene onto one monitor in a prescribed sequence. For example, camera one might record the entrance driveway for five seconds. Camera two might record the employee parking area for five seconds. Camera three might record the truck driver's entrance to the dispatch office for five seconds, and so on, I think you get the gist. This type of method is usually used on the interior of a building and not the exterior, but there are exceptions. Third, there is the motion detector method. This type acts much like motion lighting used in home security.

When a sensor is tripped or activated, a corresponding camera powers on and sweeps that area. One camera might be activated by several sensors placed in strategic positions.

"The killer somehow knew which trucking companies employed which surveillance method, and somehow knew the timing sweep of the cameras or what sequence the cameras ran, or how to avoid the sensors. This killer somehow knew how to fly under the radar, so to speak."

"You said something about the bodies themselves," Dixie prompted.

"I'm getting to that," Matt said, there was no hint of impatience or irritation in his voice. "I just wanted you to understand how slick this killer is. He was able to get onto the trucking company parking lots, place the bodies onto their front steps, and get off of the parking lots without being recorded. In every instance, no matter what camera method was used, one moment the bodies aren't there, and the next moment they are there."

"Matt, do you have any idea what we're dealing with here?" Dixie asked, she sounded defeated.

"I wish I knew," Matt said. "It's almost as if this killer can manipulate the laws of physics as we know them."

"It's like he's human, but not human," Dixie sounded deflated.

"As much as I hate to say it," Matt sounded defeated, "yes."

"Thank you for trying, Matt," Dixie said. "Can you get me something on the tire tracks and possibly the smoke plume?"

"I'll do what I can," Matt said, but didn't sound hopeful.

Dixie stood from the chair, placed it back where she had found it, and walked toward the door leading into the hallway.

"I'm not giving up," Matt said to her. "I just don't want to give you false hope."

"Okay, thanks," Dixie said, nodded her farewell, and left the room. She held in her tears and walked down the hallway. She had another stop to make, and that was to talk to the forensic doctor in charge of the autopsies of the victims.

"Dixie!" Dr. Kenneth Barstow exclaimed as he got to his feet to meet Dixie when she walked through the doorway into his office.

"Hi, Doc," Dixie said, she had been in steady contact with Dr. Barstow from the very beginning of her involvement in this case.

"Please have a seat," Dr. Barstow said, motioning to a high-backed, plush, padded chair that faced his desk. Dr. Barstow was in his mid-fifties and always seemed genuinely glad to see Dixie whenever she came to see him.

"I need something to go on, Doc," Dixie said.

"I wish I had something concrete to give you," Dr. Barstow said. "The fact is this killer is vicious. The only victim that was different from the rest was Rachel. She must have said or done something to really set him off for him to stab her that many times."

"Are there any similarities that you've found since we last talked?" Dixie asked.

"I'm afraid not," Dr. Barstow said, shaking his head. "We haven't found anything other than what I've already told you, but we are expanding our search to include anything out of the ordinary that might link the victims together. I've asked other forensic doctors to look at the evidence we've gathered, and even asked them to give me their input on any test or investigative procedure I might have missed."

"Okay," Dixie said, she felt as if she were being drained. "Keep me posted?"

"Of course," Dr. Barstow said. "Keep your chin up, we'll get him."

Dixie was on the move again; her next stop was to check with the local investigative team. The local team consisted of police officers representing the Springfield Police Department, the Greene County Sheriff's Department, and the Missouri Highway State Patrol. The team had recently been organized to help sort through such things as eyewitness accounts of the neighborhood watch program known as Crime Stoppers, and incoming phone calls claiming to have seen Jack. Most of these leads were dead ends, they didn't match the timeframe established by the videotapes to which Matt had access.

"Hello," Dixie said as she entered the room. There were three representatives from each law enforcement agency, and between them they had made up their own schedule of which ones would work which shift. There were some who preferred to work the day shift, some who preferred the evening, and some who preferred the late night-early morning. Dixie had requested the support group on a volunteer basis only, and the only requirements she stipulated were that she wanted an even number of representatives from each agency, representatives of each gender, and as many representatives as possible of race, religion, and culture. She had gotten what she asked for. The team consisted of three Springfield Police Officers, two male officers, one white, one of Oriental background, and one Afro-American female; three members of the Greene County Sheriff's Department, two white males, one Hispanic female; three members of the Missouri Highway State Patrol, one white male, one African American male, and one Native American female.

The three-member team returned Dixie's greeting as she sat down onto a chair at the end of the table in the room. The table held several telephones with multiple telephone lines on each one. At the far end of the table sat two fax machines, and each officer had his or her own computer station.

"I don't want to take up much of your time, but I would like some kind of a progress report," Dixie said, trying to sound businesslike without sounding stuffy.

"There's not much to report at this time," said Jessie, the Native American woman with the Missouri Highway Patrol. Jessie could see the weariness in Dixie's face, and hear it in her voice. "We have established contact with the local law enforcement agencies from where each victim was located, and they are keeping us abreast of any new information that becomes available to them about the victims. The Tennessee State Police is keeping especially close contact with us. They've even offered to send their own representatives to assist us, but we told them they could do us the most good by remaining there and keeping us informed of any new findings."

"Are they cooperating?" Dixie asked.

"They are not only cooperating but giving us detailed information about their own investigation," Jessie said.

"Like what?" Dixie asked.

"Well, evidently, Officer Brewer had a video camera mounted on the dash of her police cruiser," Jessie said. "There was some sort of a malfunction with the camera, and it didn't start recording until after Officer Brewer stopped behind the vehicle she pursued down the mountain."

"Did her camera record a license plate number?" Dixie was trying hard to keep her excitement reigned in.

"Not what you'd expect," Jessie said.

"What?" Dixie said, shaking her head one time, closing her eyes, then snapping them open again, all in one motion.

"Let me explain," Jessie said, holding up a hand, palm toward Dixie, "when Officer Brewer parked behind the vehicle she was pursuing—"

"What type of vehicle?" Dixie cut in, her excitement starting to rear and prance, much like a spirited horse.

"No one can tell by the video, but they think it's either an eighteen wheeler trailer, or a heavy truck," Jessie answered. "When Officer Brewer parked behind the vehicle she had been pursuing, for some reason she parked at an angle facing toward the interstate, and that's when the video camera started to record."

"Did the camera record anything at all worth recording?" Dixie asked, her excitement wanting to buck and snort now, but she was keeping a tight reign.

"It recorded Officer Brewer walking in front of her cruiser, and she disappeared from the picture," Jessie said, then explained. "A lot of law enforcement agencies that deal with traffic stops are doing this now, walking to the passenger side of the vehicle, keeping the vehicle between themselves and the traffic."

"Okay, go on," Dixie said, her excitement still wanting to buck.

"Well, there's not much else on the tape," Jessie said. "When the vehicle in front of Officer Brewer's cruiser pulls away, it pulls far enough forward so the camera doesn't record any more of it than it already has."

"Shit," Dixie said to herself, she wasn't one to cuss, but she did so now. For now she had control of this bucking bronc she called excitement. "You said something about the Tennessee State Police sharing the results of a detailed investigation?"

"Yes!" Jessie's eyes lit up. Dixie thought maybe Jessie was trying to control her own excited mount.

"It's really ingenious," Jessie continued. "The Tennessee State Police took the videotape to their lab. They slowed it down, and watched the passing traffic on the tape. Then, they stopped the tape whenever they saw a visible license plate number, enhanced it, wrote down the license plate number, and are running them through the Tennessee DMV."

"Hot damn!" Dixie said, she had cussed more in the last few moments than she had all month, but the bronc called excitement was starting to kick its heels up again. Dixie wanted to pull Jessie out of her chair and dance circles with her like a couple of school girls, but then she reminded herself of the air of professionalism she tried to maintain for herself.

"Are they having any luck?" Dixie asked, the bronc called excitement was under control again.

"Some," Jessie said, she too looked more calm. "Some of the license plates are from Georgia, Kentucky, and Alabama. They've asked those states for their cooperation, and so far they've gotten a very good response from all three."

"What about the results they've gotten so far?" Dixie asked. The bronc called excitement was behaving now.

"They've only gotten about three responses so far, and all three give three different descriptions of the vehicle stopped there that day," Jessie said. "I'm surprised at the number of people that don't pay attention to what's goin' on around them."

"All right, keep me posted," Dixie said and headed toward the door.

"Okay, will do," Jessie said as Dixie walked through the doorway and into the hallway. She knew she was getting close, she just needed a break. So far nothing she or the support team the Springfield area supplied her had worked. They had set up surveillance in the areas of the trucking companies every night, but with no positive results. The bodies were found on Monday mornings, and no one had seen the killer coming or going. Dixie needed to catch a break, and for her, it couldn't happen soon enough.

Chapter 13

Jack was sitting in his truck on a street in the industrial area of Des Plains, Illinois, a small town just north of Chicago. It was late, around eleven o'clock at night. He was updating his logbook after being unloaded at a warehouse there when he heard and felt the demon whisper into his ear.

"Want to have some fun?" Sultry whispered. Jack looked up to see a young African American woman. She was running hard along the sidewalk on the opposite side of the street, headed in his direction. She was still about a block and a half away and kept glancing over her shoulder. She wore a simple white dress that was hemmed above the knee.

"Sure," Jack muttered, "but what's the deal?"

"You've heard the trucker legend about the trucker who stops to help a woman in distress," Sultry stated. "This, as in the legend, is a situation that is not what it appears to be. I have sent them here for your pleasure."

Jack felt the demon settle into him to await the coming festivities. The legend that Sultry had spoken of was a piece of trucker lore that Jack had heard before. He didn't know if the story was true or not, but he had heard it told more ways than one, and by several different people from all over the country. The story was of a trucker who was driving down a stretch of deserted two-lane highway on a particular day when he saw a woman motorist stranded on the side of the road. The woman was standing beside a car with the hood up. The trucker stopped to offer her some sort of assistance, and as he approached the woman, two men jumped out of the ditch, and started beating the trucker with baseball bats. The two men beat the trucker severely, robbed him, stole whatever they could from the cab of the truck, and left the trucker for dead, lying along the side of the roadway. The whole damsel in distress scenario was a ruse. After the attack and robbery were over, the two men, along with the woman, closed the hood on the car and drove away. After the trucker regained consciousness, he was able to drive to the next town where he obtained medical aid and told his story to the police. The two men and the woman were later caught and brought to justice.

The young, African American woman was about a half a block away when she acted as though she had seen Jack for the first time. She left the sidewalk and ran into the street toward Jack's truck.

"Please, help me!" she pleaded in a breathless scream, reaching her arms toward Jack. Jack finally saw her pursuers. There were three of them, two African American males and one white male.

"Please! Please, help me!" she cried. Jack noticed the convincing tears that streaked down the young woman's face.

She was about halfway across the street when Jack opened the driver's side door of his truck and stepped out onto the running board. He stepped down to the pavement and held the door open for the young woman. He saw that she was barefoot and that the simple cotton, white dress she wore was torn in one place from hem to waist, and one shoulder strap was torn away. She had a pretty face, with wide set eyes that added to her attractiveness and a full-lipped mouth. Her hair hung to just below her shoulders in about four dozen slim braids. There was a colorful, ornate bead at the end of each braid that weighted them down. She was slim and athletic. Jack could hear the beads clack together as the young woman got closer to him.

"Want some help?" Sultry whispered from inside Jack's head.

"Just keep her in the truck once she's in there," Jack answered.

The young woman slowed as she got closer to Jack. Jack suspected this was to allow her "pursuers" to close the gap on her.

"Oh! Thank you!" The young woman cried as she scrambled past Jack, stepped up onto the running boards of the truck, and sat on the driver's seat. Jack felt Sultry leave him and knew the demon had followed her inside the truck.

Jack slammed the door behind her. He knew he wouldn't have had time to climb into the truck behind her before her pursuers closed on him. He knew there would be no need to lock her in, that Sultry would "suggest" she stay put. The young woman's three pursuers formed a half circle around Jack just as she had scrambled into the truck. There would have been no way he could have escaped into the truck by the time the woman had gotten in.

The woman's three pursuers stood before him. The two African American guys flanked him on either side, leaving the white guy in front of him.

"Nice night for a run, huh?" Jack stated. He let himself relax and anticipated the coming rush of adrenaline of battle. He felt the presence of Sultry again, and knew she would be implanting thoughts of deception into the heads of these three.

"Hey, mutha-fuckah, you got somethin' that belongs to us!" the black guy to Jack's left said. The guy gestured wildly and flamboyantly with his arms and hands as he spoke. He wore baggy, loose-fitting, blue denim shorts that hung off his hips, revealing the waistband of his underwear. The shorts were hemmed at the knee, where, incidentally, also hung the crotch. He wore a tight, white tank top, which showed off his muscular arms and shoulders. On his bald head, he wore a tight, black leather head wrap, tied snuggly at the back.

"Leave right now, and you'll have no regrets in the morning," Jack kept his voice calm and even, hiding the anticipation that was building inside him.

"This white boy's funny, Tyrone," commented the black guy to Jack's right. He looked at Jack with half-closed eyes, and his body posture was relaxed but coiled. This guy wore a pair of yellow balloon pants. The shirt he wore was more like a vest, which like the other black guy showed off his muscular body. On his head, he wore a ball cap, advertising one of the Chicago sports teams, the cap's bill was pulled about forty-five degrees off center. Jack couldn't tell which team was being displayed and didn't care. This guy, along with the other black guy, thought Jack looked like the bald, tattooed character Edward Norton played in the movie, American History X.

"I don't think he's funny. I think he's stupid, Raymond," the white guy in front of Jack spoke with a cruel grin. He wore black denim jeans, and like one of his partners, they hung low off his hips, showing off the waistband of red nylon boxers. The tank top he wore was red, showing off a body that wasn't quite as muscular as his buddies'. He wore a visor on his head that was turned backwards with the bill pointing behind him and upside down. Jack figured this was more of a headband to keep his long hair out of his face. Like his partners, he wore an expensive pair of running shoes. This guy thought Jack resembled the character Robert Duvall played in the movie Lonesome Dove, thinking he looked old and easy to handle.

"I don't give a damn what you three losers think. Just blow away and each other," Jack maintained his even tone. He slightly turned, as if to reach for the truck door handle. He had guessed right about the response his last comment evoked, as all three of the guys tensed then moved.

The attack wasn't at all like what happens in the movies, where one person attacks and the rest stand by until it's their turn to attack. All three of the guys attacked at once, and Jack used that.

Jack lifted his right foot, and kicked the white guy in the groin. His back was slightly turned towards the black guy to his right, Raymond, so he turned ever so slightly more, and brought his left elbow up in a swinging, arching blow that landed squarely on Raymond's nose. Then he lunged forward with a devastating right fist that landed a smashing blow on Tyrone's mouth. Jack then drove a pile driving punch onto the top of the kneeling, white guy's head, forcing the white guy face down onto the pavement.

By now, Raymond had recovered, and gotten the tears that had come with the smashed nose, wiped out of his eyes. He whipped out a switchblade and flipped it open. Raymond had a concealed automatic handgun, but Sultry convinced him it would be so much better to cut this white boy. Raymond made a couple of practice, playful jabs at Jack, who parried each half-hearted jab, while checking the other two guys to make sure neither would attack him from the rear. Raymond made one more jab, and Jack attacked. Jack slapped Raymond's right hand holding the knife with his own left hand. At the same time, Jack brought up his own right hand and gripped Raymond's right in it. Jack then twisted Raymond's wrist to the right, exposing Raymond's elbow. Jack placed his own left hand on Raymond's right elbow, and applied hard pressure, forcing Raymond to bend over, and forcing a cry of pain from his mouth. Jack got another scream of pain from Raymond when he kicked Raymond on the side of the right knee, and forced him onto his knees. Jack snatched the knife from Raymond's hand, and in one quick movement, cut Raymond's throat wide open. Jack then twisted the bill of Raymond's cap around, forcing him to look into Jack's red pulsing eyes. Jack grinned evilly as he sunk the blade of the knife to the handle through Raymond's heart. Jack let go of Raymond, and Raymond fell over onto his left side with a shocked look on his face.

"Well, let's go girls, I'm just getting warmed up," Jack said to the other two guys, who had recovered in time to see their buddy killed.

"Raymond?" Tyrone called. He couldn't believe Raymond was dead. Tyrone then said to the white guy. "Yo, Thomas, let's bounce."

"And leave Sharona here with this asshole?" Thomas was indignant.

"You two morons aren't goin' anywhere," Jack said, his eyes had that red tint again. "You girls wanted to fight, now we're gonna fight." Jack advanced on Tyrone, who took a step back. Tyrone regained a little of his composure and reached for his concealed handgun. As the gun came out, Jack kicked Tyrone in the groin and grabbed Tyrone's gun hand. Jack twisted Tyrone's gun hand until the palm faced the sky. Jack put a thumb between the second and third knuckles of Tyrone's gun hand and squeezed as he pulled up on the same arm, which forced Tyrone to release the handgun and to go to his knees in pain. Jack let the handgun fall harmlessly between his feet.

"Down!" Jack snapped as he twisted Tyrone's arm more. Tyrone complied and went face first, flat onto the pavement. Jack kicked Tyrone in the ribs with the toe of his boot, and felt the give as two of the ribs broke. Tyrone let out a cry of pain that sounded more like a sob. Jack picked up the same foot he had used to kick Tyrone in the ribs with, and stomped down onto Tyrone's shoulder blade, at the same time he yanked up on the arm he was holding. Jack felt the arm dislocate from the shoulder, and Tyrone confirmed it by letting out a high-pitched scream. Jack kicked Tyrone in the mouth with his other foot.

"Please don't hurt me no mo'," Tyrone sobbed. He looked up at Jack with pleading eyes. Tyrone spit blood out of his mouth with each sob.

"Yeah, sure," Jack said with no compassion in his voice. "Just like you would have had compassion on me." Jack applied more pressure onto Tyrone's wrist, twisted hard, and felt as well as heard the bones break. Tyrone let loose with another bloodcurdling scream. Jack pulled Tyrone's arm toward himself with his own left hand, and delivered a palm strike with his right hand to Tyrone's exposed elbow. The elbow broke with a sick crack, Jack instantly released Tyrone's arm to let it fall, and turned his attention to Thomas. Tyrone fell unconscious and went limp.

Thomas was bent over Raymond's body, going through Raymond's pockets searching for his concealed handgun when Jack stepped up behind him. Thomas stood up with the handgun and swung it in Jack's direction. Jack blocked the swinging arm and gripped Thomas's gun hand with both of his. Jack applied pressure onto the back of Thomas's hand by pressing both of his thumbs between the second and third knuckles of Thomas's gun hand. He wrapped his fingers around Thomas's wrist and squeezed. Thomas's wrist bent back, palm toward the inside of the forearm. Jack shoved forward with his arms, and at the same time stepped back one step. The sudden change in momentum almost ripped Thomas's arm out of its socket. As Thomas was pulled off balance, Jack twisted at the waist, to add to his momentum, and slung Thomas onto his back. Jack placed the handgun he had taken from Thomas onto the ground between his own feet.

"Come and get it," Jack teased in a calm voice.

Thomas got to his feet, and flicked open a switchblade of his own. He let loose with a war cry and charged at Jack. Jack parried the hand holding the knife and sidestepped the charge of Thomas. Jack grabbed the upside down, turned around backwards visor, and yanked down hard. The visor slid down over Thomas's face, and settled around his neck. Jack jerked hard on the visor, the elastic strap dug into Thomas's throat, forcing Thomas to step backwards toward Jack. Jack already had his next punch chambered. As Thomas stepped back, Jack pulled hard on the visor with his left hand, and delivered a shattering, fisted blow to the base of the back of Thomas's skull. The force of the blow broke the elastic band around Thomas's throat, and he went to his knees. His brain tried to decide which pain was worse, the back of his head or his bruised throat. As Thomas's brain deliberated, Jack stepped up behind him, wrenched his head back, and delivered a nose breaking blow to Thomas's face. Thomas's nose exploded in a shower of blood. Before Thomas could react to his nose being obliterated, Jack twisted one of his arms, forced him face down onto the pavement, and stood on the arm he had wrenched back. Jack stood on the arm, just above the elbow, and repeatedly stomped hard on the outstretched hand of Thomas. The bones in Thomas's hand broke and were crushed. Jack didn't let up. He gripped Thomas by the hair on the back of his head and scraped his face back and forth on the pavement. Next, Jack yanked Thomas to his feet and slammed his face into the side of the truck, then slung him face first back onto the pavement of the street.

"Get up," Jack said, he kept his tone low and even. "We aren't done yet. Get up."

"Please," Thomas's tears mixed with the blood that was running down his face. "I-I can't, please."

"Get up!" Jack raised his voice.

"Please," Thomas pleaded, his tears intensified. He held his good hand toward Jack as if to ward him off.

"Get…up!" Jack raised his voice more and punctuated each word.

"Please, Mr.," Thomas was sobbing uncontrollably. "I'm hurt bad. I-I don't think I can use my hand anymore."

"Get…up!" Jack yelled, and kicked Thomas in the ribs. "What were the three of you boys gonna do to me?"

"Please, don't hurt me again," Thomas tried to crawl away.

"What were you three cock-suckers gonna do to me?" Jack was insistent, and kicked Thomas in the ribs again.

"Please, please," Thomas blubbered.

"Answer me!" Jack screamed and kicked Thomas again.

"The girl, Sharona, was supposed to be the bait," Thomas said between quick, hitching breaths. "Then the three of us was supposed to jack you."

"Didn't work out that way, did it?" Jack asked as he delivered another kick to Thomas's ribs.

Thomas's only answer was to sob uncontrollably and spit blood.

"Well, at least two of you cock-suckers can live and learn from this as you watch me and Sharona drive away," Jack said as he headed for the truck.

"Before you go, mutha-fuckah," Tyrone had recovered, and was pointing his handgun at Jack's head. "I'm gonna stick this gun all up in your face."

"Fuckin' nigger," Jack said loud enough for Tyrone to hear him clearly.

Tyrone let loose with a war cry of his own as his finger around the trigger of the handgun went white with the pressure of squeezing. Jack took a half a step to the side, did a 360 spin, and squatted simultaneously. This movement brought Jack to stand beside Tyrone. Jack grabbed Tyrone's gun hand in a one-handed grip by the wrist, and pulled it sharply toward him, locking Tyrone's elbow against Jack's chest. Jack next swung his own free arm in an arch toward Tyrone's head. As Jack's arm got closer, he bent his arm at the elbow and wrist, placing the back of his own wrist against his own chest. This movement exposed the hard striking area of the elbow just above the forearm. Jack yanked hard with the arm that held Tyrone's wrist as Jack's elbow of his other arm smacked onto Tyrone's temple. Jack swung his elbow past Tyrone's head, this was known as hitting beyond the target, and chambered the same elbow for the next blow. Still holding Tyrone's wrist, Jack once again yanked on the wrist he had captured in his grip, and brought his free elbow back into a devastating blow onto Tyrone's exposed nose.

The gush of blood from Tyrone's nose was geyser-like. Tyrone's eyes watered involuntarily, blinding him. The pain from his smashed nose was immense and evoked a choked sob from him. Fear combated pain for control in his brain, as the smell of blood, his spilled blood, filled his nostrils. Tyrone tried to speak, tried to tell his attacker that he had had enough, and to plead for an end to this torture, but nothing came out but gurgles.

"What's the matter?" Jack rasped into Tyrone's ear. "I always thought you couldn't hurt a nigger by hitting him in the nose. Maybe you're a special kind of pussy nigger."

Tyrone only whimpered. The fear and pain were slowly being replaced by anger, and Tyrone realized that this was dangerous. Every time so far that he had let his anger and hatred of this white boy take over, this white boy had turned it around on him. This white boy was by far a better fighter than not only himself, but the three of them put together. A thought suddenly came to him, and Tyrone relaxed, and stopped resisting his attacker.

"Please," Tyrone pleaded with a whisper.

"You bet," Jack replied, and delivered one last fisted blow to Tyrone's already ruined nose.

Tyrone moaned loudly as he knelt onto his weak knees and clasped his demolished nose with both of his hands. The flow of blood was so great now that it was starting to run down his throat. Tyrone swallowed, then spit the blood, and his eyes let loose with another flood.

Jack stepped away from Tyrone and turned his attention toward Thomas who still lay where Jack had left him. Thomas didn't move, but stayed lying on the ground, watching Jack. Thomas's ribs screamed from the pain, and it hurt to breathe.

Jack looked at himself now for the first time since this little exercise had begun. His shirt and pants were splattered with blood, and not a drop of it was his. He pulled off his shirt, and let it drop to the ground. Tyrone had recovered somewhat by now, and he and Thomas watched Jack do his little striptease act. Jack sat on the running board of his truck, removed his boots, stood, and removed his pants. Jack never hurried, or showed any sign that he was nervous. He opened the driver's side door of his truck, and placed his removed clothes on the floorboard in front of the driver's seat. Jack raised his eyebrows in a look that challenged both Tyrone and Thomas, but neither rose to the occasion.

"When you two wimps talk to the police," Jack spoke in an even tone to them. "Be sure to tell them that this was the handiwork of Jack." Then Jack softly sang a verse of the song, "My Sharona", by The Knack.

Both Tyrone and Thomas jerked as if Jack had struck them again at the mention of his name. Jack smiled at them as he saw their reaction. He climbed into the truck and closed and locked the driver's side door behind him. He gave Tyrone and Thomas another glance, then donned a clean pair of pants and shirt. Jack dropped into the driver's seat, looked at Tyrone and Thomas one last time, depressed the clutch and levered the gear shifter into gear, pushed in the button to release the air brakes to his truck, and slowly pulled away, never once showing a sign of being rushed.

Sharona had watched the entire fight from inside the truck. The thought that she should stay inside the truck had been a strong one, and she had been fascinated by the battle and how short it had actually lasted. When Jack had climbed inside the truck, Sultry had eased up on her power of suggestion on her, and fear replaced fascination as she had watched Jack pull on a pair of jeans and a shirt. She had cringed in the furthest corner of the sleeper from him, drew her knees up to her chest, and encircled them with her arms. When she felt the movement of the truck, she sprang to the far side of the sleeper, pulled back the covering of the sleeper window, and looked out. There, she saw Tyrone and Thomas, they were still where Jack had left them on the ground. They both saw Sharona at the same time as she saw them. Both Tyrone and Thomas reached for Sharona in a useless gesture. Sharona was slapping at the window and weeping tears that ran down her cheeks, that was the last time that Tyrone and Thomas saw her alive. When Tyrone and Thomas did talk to the police, the only thing they could agree on was the name Jack. Neither could agree on Jack's description or his truck.

Chapter 14

Jason rolled over in bed and wasn't surprised to not find Diane there. He flung the covers back and climbed out of the bed. He headed to the bathroom, relieved his bladder, and climbed into the shower. After the shower, Jason got dressed, and headed downstairs where he heard voices. Diane and Christine were standing in the kitchen laughing when Jason walked in there.

"What'd I miss?" Jason asked, kissed Diane on the cheek, and took the cup of coffee she offered him.

"I told mom that I want a man just like you," Christine said.

"Well, I'm flattered," Jason said, putting an arm around Diane's waist.

"That's not what I meant," Christine said, exasperated, then she got a mischievous look in her eyes. "All I meant is you make decent money, hand most of it over to mom, and you're hardly ever here."

Jason joined their laughter this time. The telephone rang, and Christine, being the closest one of the three to it, looked at the name that appeared on the caller ID screen.

"Oh, it's Keith," Christine announced. She picked up the cordless handset, pressed the talk button, held the handset to her ear, and said, "Hello."

"Hey," Jason and Diane could hear Keith as well. "This is a real treat. I don't get to talk to a good-looking, single girl very often."

"Don't worry, Keith, I won't tell your wife you just said that," Christine winked at Jason and Diane.

"Wow, I must have a really big mouth or really little feet," Keith was laughing. "I seem to be able to put both of my feet in my mouth quite a bit."

"Well I don't have personal experience, but I've always heard that men with big feet have…" Christine trailed off and just let it hang there.

"Oh! Ouch!" Keith laughed even harder. "Is the Fox Monster there?"

"Yes, he is," Christine said. Jason and Diane shared a laugh as Diane shot her daughter a quizzical look.

"Can—I mean, may I talk to him?" Keith caught on to the game Christine was playing with him.

"Sure, hang on," Christine handed the telephone to Jason.

"Hello," Jason greeted his friend.

"Man, what'd I do to deserve that treatment?" Keith blurted out, laughing.

"You're lucky," Jason said. "I live with that."

Christine stuck her tongue out at Jason.

"Tease," Jason said to her. Diane slapped him playfully on the shoulder.

"Is she displaying her oral muscle organ again?" Keith used his trucker accent.

"Four," Jason answered, using the same accent.

"Give her a 'Damn It Girl' for me," Keith solicited.

"Keith says 'Damn It Girl,'" Jason related to Christine.

Jason and Diane saw Christine make her eyes go wide and round at the same time that she made her mouth go small and round.

"Is there another reason you called, besides lusting after my step-daughter?" Jason winked at Christine.

"I'll tell ya, just as soon as I pull my big feet, make sure you tell Christine I have big feet, out of my big mouth," Keith was laughing again.

"Keith says to tell you he has big feet," Jason told Christine.

"He has to prove that myth to me," Christine said loud enough for Keith to hear.

It was Diane's turn to make her eyes go wide and round while making her mouth go small and round, in a mocking gesture toward her daughter who blushed and smiled back at her mother.

"Hey, man, I just called to tell ya that our loads are ready," Keith sobered.

"Where are you?" Jason asked.

"I'm still at home, but I asked my dispatcher yesterday to call me when our loads were ready," Keith explained.

"When are you wantin' to leave out," Jason asked. He pulled Diane closer to him, buried his face in her hair, and inhaled , enjoying the soft giggle he got from her and the hand she place on his chest.

"How about noon?" Keith offered.

Jason checked his watch and said, "That's sounds like a plan to me."

"Okey-dokey, see you then, bye," Keith bid his farewell.

"Bye," Jason said, and they both disconnected.

"Well, I better get ready for work," Christine announced, and disappeared to her room. She reappeared a few moments later and halted her exit long enough to kiss Diane on the cheek.

"Bye, you guys, I love you," Christine called over her shoulder as she resumed her progress toward the door.

"Love you, too," Diane and Jason chorused.

"Have a good day," Diane added.

"Be careful," Jason furthered.

"Well, now what do you want to do?" Diane teased Jason by flashing her blue eyes at him.

"You have to ask?" Jason pulled her closer in a firm embrace.

"We only have three hours before you leave," Diane was still teasing. "Do you think you can do me any good?"

"I'll try," Jason admitted.

"You'll do better than that," Diane informed him and led him toward the bedroom.

They started slow, taking their time, enjoying the exchanged kisses and caresses. They undressed each other and reveled in the sensation of the skin on skin contact. Their eyes met as often as their lips, and to them, one was just as exciting as the other.

After about an hour of lovemaking, they fell asleep in the comfort of each other's arms. Diane woke first and woke Jason soon afterwards.

"Well, hell, I guess I better get ready to leave," Jason groaned, rubbing the sleep from his eyes.

"I know," Diane faked a pout. "I miss you already."

Jason kissed her quickly and slipped out of bed. Jason headed for the shower for the second time that morning. After his shower, he redressed and gathered the items he usually took with him on the truck.

"You make sure you come back to me," Diane told Jason. She was standing on the step just below the threshold of the driver's side door of the Peterbilt.

"I'll do what I can," Jason looked her in the eyes.

"I don't think you understand, Mr. Fox," Jason could tell Diane was teasing him. "I will need you to pleasure me many, many more times just like you did earlier today."

"You should know you don't have to ask me to do that," Jason was grinning.

"I'm trying to make you feel special and needed," Diane was still in her teasing mode.

Jason's only response was to pull Diane close and kiss her full on the mouth.

"Wow, you sure do that pretty good," Diane breathed when their lips parted.

"Bye," Jason said, patting her on the rump.

Diane climbed down as Jason started the truck. They waved to each other after Jason put the Peterbilt in gear and released the brakes. That feeling of impending doom haunted Jason again as he eased out on the clutch and drove toward the end of the driveway.

About twenty-four hours after leaving Strafford, Missouri, Jason and Keith were approaching Flagstaff, Arizona. This was one of those rare occasions when Keith was in front of Jason, or as truckers call it, running the front door. They had left Strafford in plenty of time for both of them to make their deliveries Friday morning, Jason to a grocer warehouse in City of Industry, California, and Keith to a grocer warehouse in Mira Loma, California. They knew their reloads were waiting on them at a trucking company in Downey, California. Their reloads would take them right back to Springfield, Missouri.

Sometimes when two or more truckers are running together, they will monitor another channel besides channel nineteen on the CB, so as not to interfere or be interfered with by other truckers. Some truckers think it rude to hold personal conversations on channel nineteen, as channel nineteen is sort of the official, unwritten channel of Smokey Bear reports, road hazard reports, accident reports, and the like.

Jason and Keith were monitoring channel forty of the CB, and their conversation primarily dealt with the new hours of service that the federal government would be implementing as of January 4, 2004. Roughly stated, the new hours of service would raise truckers' drive time from ten hours of driving to eleven hours, while also raising the mandatory break time from eight hours to ten hours. Many truckers were unsupportive of the change. Jason and Keith were instead discussing how to make the new changes work in their favor.

As they were driving along, talking back and forth on the CB, Jason noticed a dead fox lying on the shoulder of the interstate.

"Damn," Jason said into his keyed CB microphone. "Someone ran over my ass."

"I wondered if you would see that," Keith laughed into his keyed microphone.

"I should have stopped and picked my ass up," Jason replied.

"You could have hung the tail from your CB antenna," Keith suggested with humor.

"Oh, sure," Jason responded. "I would be the only man in history to be thrown in jail for stopping and picking up his own ass."

"Fox, you are nuts," Keith said into his keyed microphone, calling Jason by his CB handle.

"I hear that quite a bit, so it must be true," Jason said into his keyed microphone.

"I heard you had a pretty rough week, last week," Keith changed the topic of conversation.

"Someone's been telling on me again," Keith heard Jason say over his CB speaker.

"Yes," Keith said. "Diane told me about it, and the only reason she did was because she's worried about you."

"Well it was pretty rough," Jason admitted into his keyed microphone. "When I got home at the end of that week, I kissed the dog and patted Diane on the head."

Keith's only response was to laugh.

"I went to the building supply store the other day," Jason said, continuing their CB conversation.

"Yeah?" Keith countered. "What kind of trouble did you stir up there?"

"There I was," Jason related the story, "walking up and down the aisles of the building supply store, minding my own business, when all of a sudden, stuff from this particular part of a shelf just flew off the shelf, hit me, and stuck to me. I got scared and started running up and down the aisles, yelling and waving my arms. Pretty soon, this little building supply guy starts chasing me, yelling at me to stop where I am. I yell back that I'm scared. Another building supply guy jumped out in front of me and tackled me to get me stopped."

"You weren't stealing the stuff?" Keith clarified.

"No, the stuff attacked me," Jason was still having fun telling this story.

"Okay," Keith said into his keyed microphone, "I'll bite. What was the stuff stuck to you?"

"Stud finders," Jason replied.

"Okay, my turn," Keith said into his keyed microphone. "I wear the pants in my house, it's just my wife tells me which ones to wear."

Jason's only answer was to laugh.

"And I run things at my house," Keith continued. "I run the washing machine, the dishwasher…"

A car passed Jason and eased back in front of him. Jason saw the driver look into his rearview mirror, say something to the passengers, and motion toward Jason's truck. The passengers all turned to look at Jason's truck in unison, and Jason knew they were checking out the stuffed Wile E. Coyote mounted on the grill.

"Better not look down into this next four wheeler, WolfKat, the gal drivin' it made me homesick," Jason said into the keyed mic of his CB

"Home sick, I reckon," Jason heard Keith's voice agree over his CB speaker.

They shared a laugh over this. The rest of their trip was like that. They stopped for the night at a truck stop in Barstow, California, using the fifteen-hour rule, although it didn't take them fifteen hours to drive from Santa Rosa, New Mexico to Barstow. The next morning was Friday morning, and they were on the road at midnight. They headed south on I-15, and when they got to the I-10 intersection, Keith went east toward the Mira Loma exits, and Jason went west toward the City of Industry exits.

"God bless, see ya later," Keith said to Jason over the CB

"Keep yer powder dry. Meetcha at Downey," Jason replied.

They were both unloaded by 7:00 A.M. Pacific Time, and both were backed up to the loading docks at the warehouse in Downey, California by 8:00 A.M. After visiting for a few minutes, they both climbed into their respective sleepers for a few hours' sleep.

They were awakened a few minutes apart by the dock workers who had loaded them. It was 12:00 noon, and they were loaded. All they had to do now was sign and collect the bills of lading, get a seal for the trailer doors, and check out with the guard at the gate. Both of them took a couple of minutes to bring their logbooks up to date, then they pulled forward from the docks a few feet and closed their trailer doors.

About five hours later, they were sitting at a truck stop in Kingman, Arizona. They planned to spend the night here, leave at midnight, and possibly be home by Sunday morning. They ate supper together and took their showers separately. Jason called Diane, and they talked and laughed for a few minutes. Later Jason and Keith walked to their trucks together and said their goodnights.

Jason was sound asleep when someone started beating frantically on the side of his truck. Jason scrambled off the sleeper bunk, shoved his legs into the legs of his jeans, and climbed onto the driver's seat of his truck. He had looked at the stereo clock on his way out of the sleeper, and saw that it was 11:45. He saw that the person doing the pounding on the side of the sleeper was Keith, and not only did he have his cell phone out, it was activated. Jason opened the driver's side door.

"What's wrong?" Jason asked, still half asleep.

"I don't know," Keith shoved the phone at Jason. "Take this. It's Diane. She's crying and doesn't want to talk to me. This can't be good. I'm going to go get ready to run."

"Hello!" Jason said the word even before he had the phone to his ear. Keith was right, this probably was bad.

"Oh, Jason!" Jason heard Diane say between sobs.

"What's wrong, honey?" Jason was wide awake now.

"It was him! It was him!" Diane's voice said to him over Keith's cell phone.

"Diane? Who?" Jason was trying hard to understand.

"Jason?" Jason recognized the voice of Selena.

"Sal? What in the hell's goin' on there?" Jason was baffled.

"Diane's had a pretty bad scare," Selena said, trying to stay calm herself. "I've got her, so don't worry about her, okay?"

"All right," Jason started to calm down.

"I've got her at our house, mine and Billy's," Selena explained. "Billy's here, Dewey's here, Christine's here, and Diane's parents are here. Don't worry about Diane, she'll be fine, you just concentrate on getting home, okay?"

"All right, Sal," Jason said. "What happened?"

"Some guy calling himself Jack tried to drag Diane off the Blanket Transportation parking lot tonight," Selena said. "I got her away from him, and we both knocked him around a little. Diane's still a little shaken up. She wanted to call you. I want you to be careful coming home."

"I will, Sal, thanks," Jason said. "Does she want to talk to me again?"

"She probably does," Selena said, "but the paramedics gave her something to help her sleep, and it's taking effect."

"All right," Jason said. "Me and Keith are on our way."

"Please be careful," Selena said to him. "I don't think she could stand the thought of losing you. Besides she's safe, there'll be someone with her all the time."

"Okay, Sal, thanks a bunch. Bye," Jason said to Selena.

"Bye, Jason," Selena said, and they both disconnected.

"What's up?" Keith said. He was standing beside Jason's truck again.

"That killer, Jack, tried to drag Diane off tonight," Jason said, as he handed Keith back his phone.

"Do you want to keep this?" Keith asked, and offered the phone back to Jason.

"No," Jason raised a hand. "You keep it. Selena said the paramedics gave Diane something to help her sleep."

"Selena?" Keith looked confused.

"Come on, get in," Jason got up off the driver's seat. "I'll fill you in while I get dressed."

Fifteen minutes later, Jason and Keith were headed east on I-40. It's roughly a little over thirteen hundred miles from Kingman, Arizona to Strafford, Missouri. The both of them knew they could legally be home by Monday morning, and they both agreed they would try for early Sunday morning, if not by late Saturday night.

Eighteen hours later, eighteen hours total of hard trucking, they dropped their trailers on Blanket Transportation's main terminal parking lot. They had stopped once in Casa Blanca, New Mexico to fuel, and again in Oklahoma City to top off their fuel tanks. The only other times they stopped were to go to the restroom, truckers call this squirting the dirt, and to get something to drink.

Jason called Billy and Selena's house to find that Diane was still there, and he told Keith that was where he was headed.

"All right, Fox," Keith said and embraced his friend. "If you need anything, call me."

If Jason had known what would happen the following week, he would have held his friend a bit longer—hindsight is always twenty-twenty.

Chapter 15

At about the same time that Jason and Keith had been bedding down in Kingman, Arizona on their return trip, Diane had parked her car in front of Blanket Transportation's dispatch office. It was late on Friday night, around eleven o'clock. Diane got out of her car, went around to the passenger side, and picked up two styrofoam containers of food from the passenger side seat. She carried the containers into the dispatch office, and after setting them down onto a table, waved at Selena, who was on the telephone. Selena waved back and tried to cut her phone conversation short. Diane made another trip to her car. She reached through the rolled down passenger side window and brought out two styrofoam cups. As she headed for the door to the dispatch office again, Diane froze. Was that a man standing in the shadows beside the door leading into the dispatch office? If so, who was he? That was strange, most of the drivers for Blanket Transportation were friendly enough not to try to hide in shadows. She couldn't remember doing anything to anyone who would want to harm her. Maybe this stranger was after Selena.

Diane was standing in front of her car. She knew she couldn't make it to the door to the dispatch office without this figure catching her, if he chose to do so—and what was that slung over his shoulder? She couldn't tell because the lighting was so poor, and this person was making sure to stay in the shadows. Diane also felt certain that she wouldn't be able to get back inside her car before this figure could catch her.

Diane moved toward the driver's side door of her car and hoped that what she thought she saw was just an illusion. As she set one of the cups on the roof of her car, she saw that the figure was not an illusion. The figure dropped what it was carrying and lunged toward her. Diane screamed, threw the cup she was holding at the figure, then reloaded, and threw the one that had been on top of the car. Both missed. Diane screamed again as the figure grabbed her from behind, pinned her arms to her sides, and pulled her away from the car.

After Jack had completely finished with Sharona, and she had been washed and wrapped by him, Sultry informed him that her body was to be dropped on the parking lot of Blanket Transportation. Not only that, but there would be someone special there with whom Jack could have extra special fun.

Jack had gotten onto the Blanket Transportation property unobserved. It was a busy place, as most of the trucking terminals in the Springfield were. Trucks were always coming and going all hours of the day and night. With the aid of satellite communications, loads could be dispatched virtually all over the country from one base terminal. The only holdback was bills of lading, drivers still had to have one-on-one contact with a dispatcher, but that was minor.

Jack had Sharona's plastic-wrapped corpse slung over his shoulder and was on his way to the front steps of the trucking terminal when a blue mid-nineties Thunderbird drove up and parked. Jack immediately ducked into the nearest shadows he could find and stood perfectly still. He watched her make her first trip into the dispatch office, and before he had a chance to move, she had come outside once more. Before he knew exactly how he was going to escape, and Sultry wasn't helping much either, he thought she had spotted him. When she changed her body posture and interrupted her pace, he knew she had spotted him. As she went for the driver's side car door, he dropped Sharona's body and rushed toward the woman.

Diane struggled against her attacker. He had one arm wrapped around her waist, and had her arms pinned to her body. As he tried to cover her nose and mouth with his other hand, Diane caught a glance of her captor. She turned her head as far as she could, and strained her eyes to try to look at this man. The man she saw holding her could not possibly be standing there holding her.

"Hello, Diane," Jack rasped into her ear. To Diane the voice sounded coarse and rough, like the devil voice that came out of the character Linda Blair played in the movie, The Exorcist. "We're going to have so much fun, and maybe Selena will join us." Diane could feel his erection.

One of Diane's favorite movies was Michael Mann's The Last of the Mohicans, which also starred one of the scariest charters she had ever seen. The character, Magua, played by Wes Studi, was one of the most revolting she had seen. The Last of the Mohicans wasn't the only movie Diane had seen Wes Studi in, she had also seen his performance in Larry McMurtry's Streets of Laredo. When she thought about that, the character Magua changed. The next man she saw holding her confused Diane. She did a slight double take as she thought she saw Keith holding her. Diane knew that wasn't possible because Keith was in California with Jason. That was when she started to fight back by twisting, turning, kicking, and trying to bite the hand covering her mouth.

Jack was having trouble keeping a firm hold on Diane. In the past, Sultry would bombard Jack's victims with images of scary characters from movies until a sharp reaction was received. This time, however, the victim had done something that had never been done before, she thought about the person behind the character, and that had broken the spell. Then Sultry, out of desperation, tried to project someone Diane trusted. Jason would have been too obvious, so Keith was chosen, but Diane had reasoned through that.

Selena stood to stretch her back and saw a man grab Diane from behind and try to pull her toward the side of the building. Selena slammed the telephone handset back onto its cradle, hanging up on the person she had been talking to, and sprinted toward the side door that would take her outside. She stepped out onto a small landing just outside the door that was atop a half dozen steps.

"Hey! Let her go!" Selena shouted as she bounded down the steps. As she approached them, Selena couldn't make herself believe what she saw. Holding Diane was the character Jamie Sheridan played in the movie, The Stand, but like Diane, Selena saw through the illusion. Although she worked nights, Billy taped the television show "Law and Order" for her, and she thought about Jamie Sheridan's character in that series. Selena blinked her eyes, shook her head once, and kept advancing. The next person she saw holding Diane against her will was Jason. As much as Selena liked Jason, if he ever hinted at doing Diane harm, she would be the first one in line to kick his ass. The illusion of Jason faded away, and Selena hit Jack a knee buckling blow to the jaw. Jack let go of Diane, spun around, staggered, and went down onto one knee. Selena swept Diane behind her with one of her arms.

"Are you okay?" Selena asked Diane.

"Yea, I'm all right," Diane said, "but who's that?"

Before Selena could answer, Jack was on his feet again. Selena pushed Diane behind her an arm's length away and prepared to defend them both. Selena set her feet in a defensive back stance, knees bent, and got her hands up in front of her. She made fists with her hands, one she kept at chest level just under her chin and close in tight to her body, knuckles pointed toward the ground. The other one, Selena held about shoulder height, elbow bent, knuckles pointed toward the sky.

Jack jabbed at Selena's face with a fist of his own. Selena stepped back half a step, out of range of the jab, and set her feet again. Jack threw another jab with the same hand just to see what would happen. He found out. Selena slapped Jack's jab down with the hand held at shoulder height, she took a half a step forward toward Jack, and threw a jab of her own with the same hand.

"Keep your fist tight!" The voice of her Tae Kwon Do instructor filled Selena's head. "Strike primarily with the first two knuckles of your fist! Keep the bone structure of your fist, wrist, elbow, and shoulder aligned as mush as possible! This will lessen the likelihood of you having broken bones and sprained joints."

Selena's jab landed squarely on the end of Jack's nose, and rocked his head back. Jack took an involuntary step back before he caught his balance. Selena stepped a full step forward, and brought her trailing leg up in a front kick that she put her weight behind. The kick caught Jack in his abdominal section. The force of the kick bent Jack over and forced him back a step. As Selena set her foot back on the ground, she had her next blow chambered, it was a cross that glanced off his temple and sent him sprawling to the pavement face first.

Jack was no sooner on his stomach on the pavement then he was moving again. Selena had planned to put him into a submission hold, but he had moved too quickly, and she backed off a couple of steps. Jack looked at her from a half kneeling position, he was on one knee, with the other foot planted beneath him. Jack's eyes flashed red for an instant, and Selena didn't know if she had just seen what she thought she had just seen. She was still debating this in her head when Jack made his second attack.

Jack circled. He was being cautious this time, no head-on attack. This dark-haired tart was a bit crafty. He had encountered women like this, women who fought back with little or no fear, in his younger days, and it excited him. Sultry had often whispered in his ear that when women said no, they more often meant yes, they were just playing a game of hard to get. Sultry might want Jack to do his thing with the blonde, Diane, and that was fine, Jack had no problem with that, but this dark-haired one, Selena, was going to get the same treatment.

"Sally, are you okay?" Diane asked of her friend and sister-in-law. Diane was behind Selena, trying to stay out of the way and trying to keep her nerves under control, she was scared almost out of her mind. Diane's eyes kept going to the bundle that had been dropped in the shadows by her attacker. She was afraid she knew what it was and tried hard not to think about it. Diane put a hand on the back of Selena's shoulder.

"Yes, I'm fine," Selena answered Diane, but kept her attention on their attacker.

"I think he dropped a dead girl's body wrapped in plastic over there by the side of the building," Diane tried to keep from crying. She moved closer to Selena, turning with Selena to always face their attacker.

"Diane," Selena said, "I need you to get in your car, and get out of here."

"No!" Diane snapped. "I won't leave you. I'll go inside and call the police."

"No," Selena said. "If he gets by me, I can't protect you."

"Then whatever happens to you will happen to me because I'm not leaving you," Diane was defiant. Selena gently pushed Diane away and braced herself for the attack she was certain was about to happen.

Jack sneered and attacked for the second time. He did a sort of skipping step toward Selena and turned his body so he was side on to her, making himself a harder target to hit. Jack picked up his lead foot, the right one, and faked a low round kick, then readjusted his hip, leg, and foot, and followed through with a kick directed at Selena's head.

Selena moved only slightly away from the low round kick, and didn't commit to a full block of the kick. That's what saved her from having her head taken completely off by the second follow-up kick directed at her head. The kick connected to the side of her head, but with less force than if she had not been ducking, spinning, and moving away from it. Selena's instructor was very good at drilling his students on the importance and defense of combination kicks. The low round kick-high round kick was one of many combinations that Selena's class had practiced, and defended against. When her attacker had started with the low round kick, Selena's training made her suspicious that some sort of combination would follow. She had guessed right, and it had saved both her and Diane.

Selena felt the pain of the kick as her head was snapped around to the right. She spun away from the kick and tasted blood, her own from having the inside of her cheek smashed against her teeth. She thought her teeth hadn't been loosened from the kick and considered herself lucky. As she straightened from the ducking and spinning of her evasive move, her attacker landed a solid left jab to her left eye, and Selena saw stars.

Selena went down hard onto her rump and shook her head, trying to clear it. The stars she saw were getting brighter, as the darkness of unconsciousness threatened to close in around her. She was still with it enough to see the foot streaking toward her head. Selena got both arms up in a double arm block to block the kick, then she trapped her attacker's leg against her body by wrapping one of her arms around it and squeezing hard. Selena leaned back and pulled the man off balance just enough. As she leaned back, Selena chambered her other arm for her next blow.

Just as the man skipped on the leg Selena wasn't holding, she brought her sitting weight forward, and delivered a hard punch to the inside of the thigh of the leg she was holding, the meaty, tender part on the inside of the thigh, just below the groin.

At the same time Selena was delivering her punch to the inside of his thigh, Diane was implementing her own little end around attack. As Selena's punch found its mark, Diane kicked the attacker's other leg out from under him, and clothes-lined him at the same time.

Jack grunted his pain as Selena's punch created a dull, sick, numbing pain on the inside of the leg she had captured. That pain was short lived as Diane kicked the leg he was standing on out from under him, and clothes-lined him at the same time. The pain he felt when he went down hard on his ass was greater than any he had felt in a long time. The inside of his thigh hurt, his neck hurt from being clothes-lined, his other ankle hurt from the kick that sat him down so hard, and the force of landing on his ass so hard jarred him from his tail bone to the top of his skull.

"Sultry, you son-of-a-bitch, I could use some help here," Jack muttered under his breath.

"Neither one of them will respond to any of my suggestions," Sultry sounded anxious.

"Shit," Jack muttered again and felt Selena move.

Selena got quickly to her feet, still holding her attacker's leg tightly against her side with her arm. She allowed her grip to slide down to the man's ankle, he wore western-style boots, but she thought she could apply enough pressure through them. Selena hooked the toe of the man's boot behind her arm, between her elbow and armpit. She wrapped her arm around the man's ankle, and with her forearm, applied pressure to the tendon on the back of the man's leg, between the heel and the ankle, and applied more pressure by wrapping her free hand around the wrist of the arm applying the pressure. The man let out a cry of shock and pain, and tried to kick

Selena with his free leg. Selena stepped on the flailing leg, and by curling her toes up and turning her foot to the inside, exposing the hard bone on the outside of her foot, she put pressure on the nerve just above the ankle on the inside of the man's leg.

Jack howled his pain. He had to get out of this before Selena decided to plant her other foot in the middle of his crotch, or Diane tried to practice kicking field goals with his head. Jack twisted his body, kicked with both feet, then alternated his kicks enough to throw Selena off balance. The instant Selena stepped off his trapped ankle, Jack pulled hard with the leg she still had trapped, and pulled her closer. When Selena was within range, Jack planted his free foot in the middle of her stomach and pushed hard with both feet.

Selena let go of the submission hold she had on the man and almost fell to the ground again. She caught herself, regained her balance, and again assumed a defensive stance.

"I'm Jack, and I've had enough of you two bitches!" Jack roared as he leapt to his feet.

"Then leave!" Diane shot back, the name Jack wouldn't register with her until later.

Jack, instead of following Diane's advice, attacked a third time. Selena side-stepped his attack, and planted a round kick of her own into Jack's mid-section. As Jack clutched his gut and bent over with a whoosh of escaping air, Selena pulled her kicking foot and leg back, and delivered a side kick to Jack's exposed ribs. Jack went down again, and when he instantly jumped back up, he was running away.

Selena felt her bleeding lip with cautious fingers. The cut started on the inside and ran to the corner of her mouth. When she pulled her fingers away and looked at them, she saw blood and knew her mouth would be sore the next few days, and she would probably have a bruise and a fat lip. Next, Selena tentatively felt her eye, it would turn black, she had no doubt about that. Selena looked at Diane who gave her a blank stare.

"Diane, are you all right?" Selena asked as she approached Diane slowly. "It's over. He's gone. Are you hurt?"

"It was him," Diane responded, her words slow and deliberate. "He said he was Jack. Oh my God, Selena, are you okay."

"I'll heal," Selena said and embraced Diane. "Come on, let's go call the police."

Dixie was sitting at another long table, this time looking over and re-reading the letters that Jack had left with the bodies he had dumped. In addition to the letters left with the bodies, others had been sent to the Springfield Police Department. All were in their own clear, plastic evidence bags, and Dixie, along with Matt, was trying to rule out the possibility that some might be hoaxes.

Dixie, along with the FBI, the Springfield Police Department, the Greene County Sheriff's Office, and the Missouri Highway State Patrol, had collectively decided what would be released to the press and what would not. The letters had been leaked to the press, and now there were hundreds of letters to sort through. Some were fakes, but there were others that mentioned times, places, dates, names, and family names of the victims. The fakes were easy to spot; they weren't on the same type of strange paper that Jack used. Those were the ones that had Dixie's concentration. In any investigation, all leads and clues should be considered and followed up on, and Dixie was doing this, but there were certain letters that Dixie thought had a particular feel to them.

Tom had been right, not all of the FBI agents stationed in Springfield were happy about her being there. Most of them cooperated with her without complaint, but she had learned early on which ones were better left alone. Speaking of the devil, Dixie looked toward the doorway just as Tom stuck his head through it.

"Let's go Agent Crenshaw," Dixie saw Tom was excited. Whenever there was someone else around, Tom always addressed her as Agent Crenshaw, but when it was just the two of them, he called her Dixie. "We might have just caught a break. We got a call from one of two women that say they just kicked the shit out of some loser calling himself Jack."

Dixie never flinched, she dropped the letter encased in the evidence bag, and was on her feet in an instant. As she headed for the doorway, Dixie grabbed the jacket she had hung on the back of a chair.

"Who are the two victims?" Dixie asked as she fell in step with Tom, and the two of them walked briskly down a hallway that would lead them outside.

"All I have are first names," Tom said as he held the door leading outside open for Dixie, "Selena and Diane. Selena is a nighttime dispatcher for a trucking company called Blanket Transportation in Strafford, and Diane showed up there for a late night supper and visit."

"Are they friends? Coworkers? Lovers? Sisters?" Dixie asked as she and

Tom looked at each other over the top of the car they were about to get into.

"Don't know," Tom answered as he got behind the steering wheel and started the engine. "The person that took the call said the lady that called it in, Selena, mentioned that the guy called himself Jack, and that person contacted me."

"Where is Strafford?" Dixie asked as Tom turned on the warning flashing lights, and drove them out of the parking lot and onto the streets of Springfield.

"Just a few miles up the road," Tom said, heading for the interstate. "We'll be there in a couple of minutes."

"Who else will be there?" Dixie wanted to know.

"The lady that called it in, Selena, said the other lady, Diane, was about to go into shock," Tom said, merging into the flow of traffic that would take them to the interstate. "Our people sent an ambulance. Local Strafford Police, any Greene County Sheriffs, and Missouri Highway State Patrol in the area were asked to respond and seal off the area."

"Good," Dixie responded as they merged onto the interstate, and Tom accelerated rapidly to the point of burying the speedometer needle past its limit.

"Responding law enforcement knows you are en route, and that you will take charge once on the scene," Tom said taking the Strafford exit; he never took his eyes off the road.

"Tom, would you interview Selena while I interview Diane?" Dixie asked, as Tom brought the car to a screeching halt and flung the transmission into park. "I know you know the drill on this, I just figure if Diane is on the verge of going into shock, she might be more comfortable talking to a woman first."

"No problem," Tom answered. The part of the parking lot where the fight had taken place was surrounded by yellow crime tape. Lights from the police cars and the ambulance flashed, alternating blue and red across the scenes of police officers and paramedics. Tom and Dixie crossed the yellow police tape after showing their badges to the police guard there. Tom said with a motion of his hand, "I say we check at the ambulance first."

Tom and Dixie approached the ambulance where they found the paramedics treating two women. One of the women was refusing any medical attention but was hovering close to the second woman who was sitting on the rear bumper of the ambulance wrapped in a blanket. The woman wrapped in the blanket was slightly shivering and had a dim look in her eyes.

"Excuse me," Dixie said, "are you Selena and Diane?"

"I'm Selena," Selena said, facing Dixie.

"I'm FBI Special Agent Dixie Crenshaw, and this is my partner FBI Special Agent Thomas Bradford. We would like to ask you a few questions if you feel up to it," Dixie said, showing Selena, Diane, and the paramedics her badge.

"I feel up to a few questions, but I don't know about Diane," Selena said, playing the part of nursemaid to her friend.

"I'm fine, Sally," Diane said, her eyes showing a bit more focus.

"Ma'am, would you please go with Agent Bradford?" Dixie asked Selena.

"Sure," Selena said, after Diane gave her a reassuring nod. Selena started to take a step away, then suddenly changed her mind, showed Dixie the back of her hand, and asked, "Would you like to get a swab of my knuckles?"

One of the paramedics stepped forward with several single-tipped cotton swabs, took a sample of each of Selena's scraped knuckles, then dropped each swab into its own container, and sealed it.

"Thank you," Dixie acknowledged the paramedic. "One of us will collect those from you before we leave." The paramedic nodded, and retreated.

"Please step over this way, ma'am," Tom said to Selena.

After Tom and Selena stepped away, Dixie sat next to Diane on the bumper, hoping that if she sat next to Diane she would seem less threatening. Dixie turned to look at Diane and tried to give Diane her best comforting smile.

"May I get your last name?" Dixie asked, taking out an ink pen and a small, palm-sized writing tablet.

"Fox, Diane Fox," Diane croaked.

"Thank you, Mrs. Fox," Dixie said. "What were you doing here tonight?"

"I came up to have supper with Sally," Diane said, her voice improving.

"Sally?" Dixie let it hang there.

"I'm sorry," Diane said, blushing a little. "I call Selena Sally."

"Okay," Dixie said writing in her tablet. "Can you give me a description of your attacker?"

"No," Diane paused, "it was like his face kept changing."

"I'm sorry," Dixie said, it was more of a question than a statement.

"It's hard to explain," Diane said, she was blushing again. She let her eyes leave Dixie's face, and she looked at the ground, as if she were ashamed.

"Mrs. Fox," Dixie started, "may I call you Diane?"

Diane simply nodded, without looking at Dixie.

"Diane, I'm here to help, not to pass judgment," Dixie said, setting her writing tablet aside.

"I can't explain what I saw," Diane said, paused. "Like I said, it was like his face kept changing."

"Would you recognize any of those faces if you saw them again?" Dixie asked, she kept her voice soft and gentle. Dixie put what she had just heard from Diane together with what the lab personnel had revealed to her, and decided she had better consider every possibility on this case.

Diane took in a quick breath, keeping her gaze trained on the ground. Diane's shoulders shook as the tears started to run down her cheeks. Dixie put her ink pen and tablet away, moved closer to Diane, and wrapped an arm around her shaking shoulders. Diane leaned against Dixie, and sobbed openly, crying tears of anguish, fear, and frustration. Dixie wrapped both arms around Diane, pulled her closer, and tried to comfort her. This went against her training as an agent for the Bureau.

"I'm sorry," Diane said and pulled away a little. Dixie let her go but stayed close. Diane wiped at her eyes and nose with the ends of the blanket that was draped around her shoulders.

"Are you all right?" Dixie asked after a moment's pause.

"Yes. Thank you. I'm fine," Diane nodded, and finally looked at Dixie. "I saw him standing over there in the shadows," Diane pointed to the spot. "I didn't know if there was someone there or not. When I did decide that there was someone there, I tried to get back into my car, but he grabbed me from behind and tried to pull me toward the shadows. That's when I got my first look at him. He looked like someone in that movie The Last of the Mohicans. Did you see that movie?" Dixie nodded.

"Well anyway," Diane went on slowly, "my husband has all these movies at the house, and when I saw that character, I remembered seeing that actor in another movie that my husband has, and it was like the guy holding me, his face changed."

"Changed to what or who?" Dixie asked when Diane seemed to stop.

"His face changed to my husband's best friend, Keith," Diane said, and the tears started to come again, but she turned them off, "but I know Keith is in California with my husband, Jason."

"Please, keep going," Dixie said, she had her ink pen and tablet out again.

"That's when Sally came running out of the dispatch office, and the fight started," Diane said.

"I heard the two of you beat him up and ran him off," Dixie prompted.

"I didn't do much," Diane said, under a slight grin.

"I'm sure you did more than you think you did," Dixie said and got to her feet. She took a business card from a pocket and scribbled on the back of it with her ink pen.

"I need to talk to some more people here. If you think of anything else, or just need to talk, please don't hesitate to call me. On the back is my personal cell phone number." With that said, Dixie handed Diane the business card.

"When can I go home?" Diane asked, a little timid.

"I'll see if Agent Bradford has any questions for you," Dixie gave Diane a comforting smile. "I'll send him over. If he doesn't have any questions, I don't see any reason why you can't go home. Would you like me to call someone for you?"

"No, I'll be fine. Thank you," Diane said and also stood.

Dixie stood by herself, waiting for Tom to finish his interview with Selena. She absently kicked at a few pieces of gravel that lay at her feet. She looked skyward at the stars as she pondered every piece of evidence and information that was available to her concerning this case.

"The things I heard tonight are pretty farfetched," Tom said to Dixie as they drove back toward Springfield.

"I know," Dixie said. "I've been hearing the same kind of thing from the lab personnel."

"Both women seemed sincere," Tom said. "Except for who they say they saw, their stories matched on the key points."

"We're dealing with something unnatural here, Tom," Dixie said. "Whatever this is we're dealing with seems to have the ability to make its victims see what it wants them to see."

"The dead girl wrapped in the plastic seemed to have been killed differently than the others," Tom speculated.

"We should get the autopsy results later this morning," Dixie said. "I hope we can stop this thing before more women have to die."

The next morning, Dixie and Tom were in a briefing with Dr. Barstow, along with other key personnel connected with the case. Representatives from the Springfield Police Department, the Greene County Sheriff's Department, and the Missouri State Patrol, along with FBI agents were present. The autopsy had been performed, and Dr. Barstow had called for this briefing to announce his findings. Dixie would have normally stood in on the autopsy, but she had opted for some sleep, thinking this day would be another long one.

"The victim shared the same trademark wounds as the other victims," Dr. Barstow said. The briefing was held in a room with a long table. The lights were dimmed, and Dr. Barstow had a projection screen set up, and a slide projector hummed at the end of the table where he was seated. On the screen was the autopsy photograph of the victim known as Sharona. Dr. Barstow continued, "As you can see, there is the same laceration across the throat, and the pelvic hair and skin have been removed in what the assailant refers to as 'scalping'."

Dr. Barstow pressed the button on his handheld remote and advanced the projector to show several photographs of the wounds. He stopped at a photograph that showed the inside of the victim's thighs. There were long strips of skin and flesh missing from the thighs. "As you can see, the killer took these parts, referring to the act as taking 'tender cuts'. From what I can tell, the killer did this while the victim was still alive."

Dixie closed her eyes and bowed her head. She was imagining the pain and torture the victim Sharona must endured. She hoped that mercifully Sharona had passed out from the pain.

"And finally there is the note," Dr. Barstow pressed the button on the remote to advance the next frame.

Dear Boss,

You're not smart enough to catch me. I've been doing what I want, when I want right under your noses. Why bother? I'm ridding the population of some of the dregs of society. I'll be sending you another dreg, along with another informative note next week. My collection of scalps is growing. I have them stretched and tanning. I run my fingers through their hair every day. You'll never catch me. You would do better to concentrate on catching real criminals, and stop wasting your time trying to catch me. I really enjoyed eating the tender cuts I took from this one.

Sincerely,

Jack

Catch me if you can.

"Thank you, Dr. Barstow," Dixie said, after she raised her head and opened her eyes. Tom got up from his chair and turned up the lights. Dixie continued, addressing everyone in the room. "Two things: One, the viciousness of the murders is escalating. The note makes a cannibalistic reference. I think most of you will agree that our unsub is a white male. And, two, he's crossed the racial line. Most serial rapists and serial killers stay within the boundaries of their own race. There are exceptions to the rule, George Russell, a black man, killed three white women, for example. We've tried all conventional methods of capturing him, and now I'm open to suggestions."

"We could set a trap for this Jack," suggested an agent Dixie had never seen or met before.

"All of our efforts to do that very thing in this area have failed," Dixie said, she tried very hard not sound condescending.

"I'm not talking about here," the other agent stated, not showing any signs of resentment.

"I'm afraid I don't know you," Dixie said, looking directly at the agent. "Will you please tell us who you are?"

"I'm, sorry, my name is Lucas Daniels, and I'm with the SOI unit of the FBI," the agent said, introducing himself and displaying his badge. Lucas was thirty-five years old, just short of six feet tall, trim, and clean cut.

"SOI?" Dixie asked, then said. "I don't recall ever hearing of such a unit."

"Special Ops Investigation. The Bureau thought I might be of some help," Lucas said. "I'm here strictly to observe and offer suggestions as I see fit. I'm not here to infringe or take over, Agent Crenshaw."

"Okay," Dixie remained calm. "In most cases like this, it is customary for the assisting officer, that would be you, to announce himself to the facilitating officer, that would be me, or Officer Bradford here." Dixie motioned toward Tom.

"Of course," Lucas smiled and blushed. "I apologize for any impropriety. As I stated before, I'm here to strictly observe, and this was the best way to observe unobserved, as it were. Again, I apologize, Agent Crenshaw, I meant no harm."

Dixie nodded her acceptance of the apology.

"What have you been working on lately?" Tom asked.

"I've been working in conjunction with the Border Patrol, the Texas Rangers, the DEA, and the ATF in southern Texas, New Mexico, Arizona, and California," Lucas responded.

"How do you think you can help us?" Dixie asked.

"I've read the reports that you've sent to Quantico," Lucas said. "Let me say that your work is exemplary. I've read about the failed surveillance tapes and the seemingly failed attempts at the local populace spotting the perp. What I'm suggesting is to take the offensive and go looking for this unsub."

"How do you suggest we do that?" Dixie was trying hard to not be indignant.

"What do you know about this killer?" Lucas prodded, he knew he was on thin ice with Dixie and was trying to stay close to the edges. "I mean besides the most obvious, he likes to kill women?"

"All right, Hot Shot, if you have something to say, say it!" Dixie felt a restraining hand on her arm from Tom.

"I'm sorry, Agent Crenshaw," Lucas held up his hands in a surrendering posture. "I'm really only trying to help. Do you know how the killer transports the victims? Why has he picked this city over all the rest? Is there a pattern to the cities from where he picks his victims? Were all the victims treated about the same? Is the time of the abductions to the time of the body drop-offs the same?"

"Do you think just because I come from a small town in Tennessee, that I'm stupid?" Dixie was off her chair and on her feet, her eyes blazing.

"Again, I'm sorry, Agent Crenshaw," Lucas was also on his feet, and heading for the door.

"Wait!" Tom stood beside Dixie, pleading to her with his eyes.

Lucas turned, and looked first at Tom, then at Dixie, then back to Tom.

"What was that last thing you said?" Tom was curious.

"About the time frame from abduction to the dropping of the body?" Lucas offered.

Tom prodded.

"Is the killer an opportunity killer, or are the abductions planned?" Lucas proffered.

"There doesn't seem to be a clear pattern on that," Tom answered, looking at Dixie.

"Am I correct in stating that the victims are no sooner reported missing, than they turn up here dead?" Lucas asked.

Tom was still looking at Dixie. He raised his eyebrows, set his mouth, and nodded at her.

"Would everyone please excuse us?" Dixie asked of the personnel seated in the room, as she and Tom, with Lucas left the room. They walked down the hall, to a room that Tom and Dixie shared as work space away from the Federal Building.

"Tell us what you suspect, and we'll see if we're on the same wavelength," Dixie said as she shut the door.

"This killer is obviously abducting his victims as he's leaving the area," Lucas said, choosing his words carefully. "The abduction of the Tennessee state trooper was obviously an opportunistic incident for the killer. Has anyone asked the state of Tennessee what's the highest percentage of vehicles stopped on the eastern slope of Monteagle?"

"Eighteen wheelers?" Dixie said. It was more of a challenge than an answer.

"Now, maybe, her abduction and murder were done by a copycat, that's entirely possible, but what if it wasn't?" Lucas was watching Dixie.

"We thought about a trucker as the killer," Tom said, "but it seemed very unlikely that a trucker could dodge being videotaped on so many different trucking company parking lots. Vehicles that big seem to stand out and are hard to miss."

"And besides, the killer would have a hard time matching up his logbook," Dixie offered.

"How well do you know truck drivers?" Lucas asked, he was trying not to smile.

"I admit, next to nothing," Dixie looked at Tom, who shrugged at her.

"Well, most of the more experienced ones, the old timers, think they can write their own rules," Lucas said. "Working with the law enforcement of Texas, I've seen very convincing forged logbooks."

"When a logbook page is signed by a truck driver, doesn't it become a legal, binding document with the federal government?" Dixie's knowledge of such matters was limited.

"Yes, you're correct," Lucas now smiled at her. "Most of the more experienced truckers run what's called a loose leaf logbook, meaning they can add or replace logbook pages at will, making it look as though the original sequential order hasn't been disturbed."

"Even though they know they are breaking the law, they still do this?" Dixie was confused.

"You said the key phrase, Agent Crenshaw," Lucas said. "When a logbook page is signed. A lot of truckers wait to sign their log pages at the end of the week, in case they have to make a correction."

"You think Jack is a trucker?" Tom asked.

"I think the person who abducted, raped, and killed the Tennessee state trooper is a trucker," Lucas said. "If the forensics match to the other victims, then I think that's a starting point."

"What do you propose?" Dixie asked.

"The only communication you've received are the notes found with the body?" Lucas asked, looking at both Dixie and Tom. They both nodded.

"Most killers like this hang around to watch the discovery of the body, the initial investigation, and maybe even try to get involved with the investigation. This killer is different," Lucas said.

"We have videotaped what small crowds that do appear at and around the crime scenes," Tom admitted, "and we haven't had anyone appear on those tapes that we couldn't account for."

"I think that's because the killer isn't hanging around," Lucas said. "Now, if we could establish a pattern to where the victims came from, maybe we could predict where the next one might come from."

"We've done that," Dixie said. "We weren't able to come up with any viable pattern."

"It might be really subtle," Lucas said, hoping he wasn't pushing too much, "an alternating pattern of east and west."

"We weren't able to secure any such pattern," Dixie informed Lucas.

"What's the longest distance that a victim has been transported?" Lucas asked, as if trying to lead them down a certain path.

"Ontario, California," Dixie said after an exchanged look from Tom.

"And the shortest?" Lucas pressed on.

"Oklahoma City," Tom said, not really knowing where Lucas was going with this line of questioning. "What about this idea you had about going after the killer?"

"It would be easier if we had a pretty good idea of where the killer might be next," Lucas said. "You've done the right thing by sitting here trying to catch the killer, but that same killer has somehow eluded not only you, but also the local law enforcement, along with the citizen's neighborhood watch programs. I think it's time to try to understand this killer who seems to travel quite a bit. I need to make some calls. I'll be in touch." With that said, Lucas exited the room, and was gone.

Chapter 16

Jack was furious. Very seldom had he ever lost a fight. Never, had he ever lost a fight to a woman. He was like a caged wild animal. Sultry had let him down. He left the Blanket Transportation terminal parking lot and drove to another trucking company terminal in Springfield.

As Jack climbed down out of the truck cab, he took a deep breath, and got his emotions under control. He walked toward the terminal, counting all of the bumps, bruises, and hurts levied on him by Selena and Diane.

"You'll need to hide these," Jack mumbled under his breath to Sultry.

"Done," came the whispery response.

Jack felt the need for a release. He had just gotten his ass kicked by two women that he felt he should have been able to take without the help of a demon. He felt like any other man that had been beaten up, he wanted to be held by a woman.

"Hi," Jack said as he walked up to the glass that separated him from the person on the other side.

"Hello," Marcia returned, her tone sounded edgy.

"Something wrong?" Jack asked, injecting a note of incomprehension into his voice. He wanted to keep Marcia happy. If any law enforcement agency was to check phone records, they would find that she had called his cell phone number several times.

"Did you have a good trip?" Marcia asked, she looked at him and smiled.

"Yea, pretty much boring and routine like all the others," Jack chuckled and half shrugged.

Marcia looked at him again and smiled once more before returning to her work.

"What time do you break for supper?" Jack asked, glancing at his wrist watch.

"In about fifteen minutes," Marcia answered, a bit absentmindedly. She and Jack had gone out together several times, and she had the nagging thought that he wanted to take the relationship to next level. She was apprehensive, to say the least, and had her doubts about his sincerity. It was just that her experience with sex and men was limited, and she had been hurt emotionally in the past and was determined to be careful this time around. Besides, she felt there was something excitingly sinister about Jack, he had that bad boy aura about him, but she also felt there was a gentle side to him, as if there was a conflict boiling within him just below the surface.

On the nights that they had gone out, she would pick him up in her car at the terminal where he would leave his truck. At the end of the dates, he would always kiss her goodbye. On several occasions, he had held her tightly against him, and she had felt his passion in his kisses as well as the hardness behind the zipper of his jeans. Jack had often asked her to spend the night with him, offering to take her to a motel, rather than spend the night in his truck, but she had always declined. Marcia knew this was a major source of irritation to Jack, although he hid it well. On the nights that she turned him down, he would ask if she would feel more comfortable at her place. She would tell him no, and hope he would move past it, but it seemed to her that he always pressed the issue.

It wasn't the lack of passion she felt for him, but she felt like something just wasn't right. Marcia had prayed for someone who could and would sweep her off her feet. She had turned to God for this, asking for his help, and had explored a little on her own, but always stayed within the limits she felt God would approve. She had tried several singles lines in the Springfield area and had met some very nice men, but none that made her blood cook with passion. Next, she had returned to church where she still attended when she could. There again, she met several nice men, but as before, none that stirred her passion. She wondered if she was asking for too much—or the impossible. She didn't think she was. What she basically wanted was a man who could love her unconditionally, no matter what, like Joseph did Mary, or Abraham did Sarah. A man who could show her passion and make her feel wanted much like Esther and Ruth were. She also wanted steamy passion like Sampson had for Delilah, and David had for Bathsheba, she also didn't want to push her luck with God, but she felt confident that He knew what she meant. Jack certainly had showed her signs of being able to fill the bill on all of those things, but there was a small voice in the back of her mind that held her back, and that made her cautious.

"Have you made arrangements for supper?" Jack raised his eyebrows at her as he asked.

"I brought mine from home," Marcia said. The phone on her desk rang, and she answered it on the second ring. As she spoke to the driver on the other end of the telephone, Marcia realized that in the past, Jack had dropped slight hints, inquiring as to where she lived. This made her uncomfortable, but yet there was that bad boy complex about him that was attractive to her.

"How about I order something by phone and join you?" Jack asked as Marcia hung up the phone. Jack, of course, knew exactly where she lived; he had followed her home and had watched her place several times.

"Okay," Marcia answered. Her uneasiness eased a bit as Jack picked up a phonebook which lay beside the telephone provided for drivers in the lobby. Jack thumbed through the phonebook, found what he wanted, picked up the telephone handset, and dialed the number. He gave Marcia a smile and a wink as he waited for an answer on the other end of the telephone line.

Jack was thinking his own thoughts about Marcia. Sultry had told him that she would be the perfect cover if things ever progressed to the point where Jack would need an alibi. Sultry had related to Jack the source of her prayers and had given Jack the information needed to keep her interested in him. What Sultry hadn't told Jack was that this was getting more difficult to do. As Marcia prayed more for guidance, Sultry found it more difficult to bombard her with suggestions. This was why Jack was unable to get her into bed with him, her power of resistance was getting stronger. If she proved to be impenetrable much longer, Sultry was going to demand that Jack add her pubic scalp to his collection. If that happened, the law enforcement investigators would maybe be thrown off course. None of the victims so far had been local women, and that could possibly make them back up a step and slow them down. Or they might think it a copy cat killing. Either way, Sultry thought it to be to their advantage.

"My pizza will be here in about twenty minutes," Jack informed Marcia as he placed the telephone receiver back onto its cradle.

"Good," Marcia nodded, her uneasiness returned, but it seemed as though outside influences were trying to change and ease her cautious attitude toward Jack.

"What shall we do until then?" Jack grinned at her.

"Keep it up," Sultry whispered into Jack's ear. "We need to try to keep her off balance."

"What do you want to do?" Marcia asked Jack. She looked at him, her gaze almost expressionless.

Jack sat looking back at Marcia, but didn't quite know what to say. Her gaze troubled him; it was as if she knew what he had been doing. She blinked at him, cocked her head to one side, and raised her eyebrows, a slight smile turned up the corners of her lips. This proved to unnerve him even more. Jack opened his mouth to speak, but it felt as though his nerves had closed off his throat. That's when the telephone on Marcia's desk rang, and Jack breathed a sign of relief, saved by the bell.

Jack seized this opportunity, sprang to his feet, looked around, and stepped into the men's restroom.

"What in the hell is going on?" Jack snarled at Sultry as he closed the door behind him.

"I don't know," Sultry said again. "I know the suggestions are getting to her, but it's like she's swatting them away."

"Has anyone else ever done this?" Jack asked.

"Oh, sure," Sultry admitted, then asked. "What do you want to do?"

"If she's not gonna submit to our charms, then we need to get outta here," Jack said. He flushed the toilet and turned the faucet on in the sink. He took a deep breath, turned the faucet off, and opened the restroom door. He hoped the pizza would get here soon.

When he stepped back into the lounge area, Marcia was still on the telephone, she looked at him and smiled. Jack decided to take this time to step outside and busy himself with something about his truck. It didn't matter what, just kill some time, and try to regroup.

"What should I do?" Jack inquired of the demon.

"The impression I get from her is that she thinks she is unattractive, especially her freckles," Sultry tittered. "When you spoke of them before, that seemed to excite her in some way, but take your time about it. Do what you intended to do out here with your truck, wait for your food to arrive, and gradually ease the conversation in that direction."

Jack pushed his bottom lip up under his top one in an expression of comprehension and vaguely nodded. As instructed, Jack took his time outside, he pulled the hood of the truck open, and busied himself checking the fluids.

A car with an illuminated pyramid, advertising a local pizza restaurant on its roof, parked next to Jack's truck. Jack stopped what he was doing, wiped his hands free of dirt and grease on the rag he had for that purpose, and dug out his wallet.

"It's twelve ninety-five," the boy said, as he set the insulated carrying bag on the hood of his own car, opened it, and pulled out a single pizza box large enough to hold a medium-sized pizza.

Jack nodded, opened his wallet, and pulled out a single bill. He looked at the bill in his hand, a twenty, and handed it to the boy, who didn't look to be much older than sixteen years old.

"Keep it," Jack rasped as he saw the boy start to reach for his money bag to make change.

"Thank you, sir," the boy's face split in a wide grin, showing off metal braces on his teeth, as he comprehended the size of the tip.

Jack nodded to the boy and sat the pizza box atop the steer tire on the driver's side of his truck. He walked around to the front of the truck and pushed the hood closed. The wheel wells of the hood fit over the steer tires perfectly and missed touching the pizza box completely, just like Jack, and any other experienced truck driver knew it would. He walked around to the driver's side, reached up under the fender well, and retrieved the pizza box. He hoped the advice Sultry had given him would work. Aside from wanting Marcia as an alibi, he also wanted to sleep with her and sample any and all secret delights her body might have to offer. This thought changed his attitude and helped to motivate him to that end. Besides, it would make it all the sweeter if she was willing and wanted him. A sly smile creased his lips as an old adage surfaced in his memory: Red on the head, fire in the hole. He pushed the thought aside as he reentered the building.

"Oh good," Marcia said as she retrieved a steaming plastic bowl from the microwave oven that sat atop a table behind her desk. "We will get to eat together after all."

"I need to leave for awhile," Sultry whispered into Jack's ear. "I have other interests I need to check on, and something I need to retrieve for you. Just remember what I told you about her, and you'll be fine."

Jack felt uneasy about being left alone with Marcia. It wasn't that he was scared of her, or was he? He didn't think so, but if Sultry couldn't get past her defenses, then how was he supposed to? Freckles, he reminded himself, tease her about her freckles.

"Did you come from a big family?" Jack asked Marcia.

"What?" She seemed surprised at the question.

"Did you come from a big family?" Jack repeated, "I just realized I know very little about you, and I would like to know more."

"Oh," Marcia said, she sounded a bit startled. "Well, not a real big family, I have two younger sisters, and an older brother."

"Are your two sisters pretty redheads like you, freckles and all?" Jack grinned at her.

"Well, yes and no," Marcia said, she was stirring the contents of the bowl in front of her with her fork. "One is a blonde with freckles, and the other has light brown hair with freckles."

"I see," Jack said, he looked as though he was reflecting on something.

"Are you still leaving out tonight?" Marcia asked him.

"Yeah," Jack sighed. "I went by Blanket Transportation earlier to pick up my trailer, but the cops were all over the place there. They weren't letting anyone on or off the place."

"Really," Marcia sounded intrigued. "What was goin' on there?"

"Don't know," Jack said between bites. "All they would tell me was to leave."

"I wonder..." Marcia thought out loud. Movement from Jack brought her attention back to him. "What's that?" she asked.

"A new washable marker," Jack displayed it for her in his hands.

Marcia looked at Jack and his marker with washable ink for a moment, she looked as though she didn't comprehend its meaning, then her face reddened with embarrassment. Their eyes met for a brief instant, and she looked away. At that instant they both were thrown into their own sort of daydream.

In her mind, Marcia was transported back in time to the summer when she was ten years old. She had been raised in a farming community northeast of Springfield, and every summer her family put up hay for the livestock for the following winter. Her father had a brother and a sister that lived nearby, and every year they all got together and helped each other. At that time nearly everyone that baled hay put it in small square bales, or small round bales, the large round and square bales were unheard of at that time. Between the three families, they would put up an average of eight to nine thousand bales each year. The children were expected to help when they were old enough.

On that particular summer, Marcia, her brother, and four of her cousins were helping in the hay field. It was late in the evening, and the last of the hay had been put up, and as a treat, the parents had bought a couple of watermelons. As the day ended the children were gathered under a huge, sprawling post oak, eating their watermelon.

One of Marcia's male cousins, Gary, a rather devious little shit, told Marcia that if she rubbed her face with the juice and rind of a watermelon, it would get rid of her freckles. Later that night, Marcia's brother along with her cousins, caught her behind one of the barns, scrubbing her face with the juicy remains of a watermelon rind.

Catching her wasn't enough for Gary, the ring leader, the teasing and ridiculing drove Marcia to tears and painful embarrassment. Years later, Marcia was able to laugh with the rest of them whenever the story was told, but at the time it happened, she wanted to crawl away and hide. Whenever someone made a comment about her freckles, this memory usually surfaced in Marcia's mind.

Jack's daydream was very different. Jack imagined what it would be like to have Marcia in bed. He let his imagination run wild. He imagined his bare skin on her bare skin, her moving with him and against him, meeting his thrusts. In his mind, he could hear her deep breaths, her sighs, her moans, and her whispers. He imagined his hands on her breasts, and her ass, squeezing and caressing. He imagined his mouth on hers, their tongues chasing each other, his mouth on her neck and breasts, kissing and sucking.

In his mind, he felt her pelvis grinding against his. He felt her body arching against his. He felt her bare legs raised around him and her bare feet on the back of his calves. He felt her hands on his bare back as if she were trying to pull him closer. He even imagined them climaxing together. For now though, the only thing they did at the same time was end their daydreams.

Marcia looked to be on the verge of tears, Jack looked apprehensive and breathless. They sat gazing at each other for a few moments, each unaware of the other's daydream. Jack wanted Marcia more than ever now. Marcia wanted more distance, Jack's fascination with her freckles had triggered her painful memory.

"I'm sorry," Marcia said. She stood up from her chair, tears filled her eyes, as she headed for the women's restroom.

Jack sat dumbfounded for a few moments and was still there when Marcia returned soon after.

"I'm sorry that I upset you," Jack apologized to Marcia as he stood in front of her again, the glass separated them. He didn't know what else to say.

As she listened to him, it occurred to Marcia who she thought Jack resembled. The character Rutger Hauer had played in the movie Blade Runner came to her mind. Marcia was looking at Jack, when she thought she saw a shimmer go over his face. She involuntarily gasped, and stepped back a step.

"What's wrong?" Jack asked, perplexed.

"Your face," Marcia breathed, her words were quiet. Her eyes were wide, and her hands came up to her mouth, then she waved them in front of her own face, trying to demonstrate a shimmer. "Your face shimmered."

"What?" Jack drew out the word, trying to make her sound crazy.

"Look, I haven't been sleeping or eating right lately," Marcia said. She sat back down on the chair, and returned her attention to the computer screen.

"It's okay, Marcia," Jack's tone was soothing. "People tell me all the time that I look like someone else they know or have seen, and very seldom are two of them alike. I guess I have that kind of face."

"I guess so," Marcia agreed, but didn't look at him. She just wanted him gone. "Are you still gonna take the load you were assigned?"

"Yes," Jack said. He didn't want to leave, but Sultry returned and announced that she needed Jack's help.

"Okay," she tapped a few keys on the computer's keyboard, then said. "I'm sorry Jack, I just had a bad memory."

"That's all right, don't worry about it," Jack said, he was in a hurry to leave now. He closed and picked up his pizza box. "I'll see you later." Jack headed for the door.

"What's the deal?" Jack asked Sultry as he headed for the truck.

"One of my other contacts needs some help, and you're just the person for the job," Sultry tittered.

"Where are we going?" Jack asked as he climbed behind the steering wheel of his truck, and fired up the engine.

"You'll meet him in Cheyenne, Wyoming," Sultry's whispery voice said in Jack's head.

"What's the problem?" Jack asked.

"He's involved in a project somewhat like yours, involving gay men," Sultry rasped. "The authorities are getting too close for comfort, I need you to run interference, and create a diversion. In return, you'll receive the same aid if ever you need it."

"When?" Jack was intrigued.

"As soon as we can get there," Sultry's whispery voice laughed.

Jack was ready for this. The situation with Marcia had deteriorated rapidly, and he needed a release. He drove back to Blanket Transportation and was allowed access to his assigned trailer. He backed the tractor under the trailer and coupled it to the tractor. Jack climbed back into the driver's seat of the tractor, pulled out his logbook, and updated it. After that, he completed his walk-around inspection, climbed back into the cab of the truck, and pulled away.

The load he was under was scheduled to deliver in Clearwater, Utah in two days. The route he chose would take him right through Cheyenne. He didn't know what was expected of him, or how he would accomplish the task, but he knew Sultry would provide the answers when the time came.

A few hours later, Jack exited off of I-29 in Iowa at exit ten, where Iowa State Highway 2 crosses I-29. There is a cluster of truck stops at that intersection, and it is also the short route to I-80 West via Lincoln, Nebraska. Jack pulled off the highway and onto the parking lot of one of those truck stops. He had been on the road for about five hours and needed a short break. It was well after midnight, and not many people were about.

"A diversion to take your mind off of your troubles with Marcia awaits you in the men's restroom," Sultry whispered in Jack's head.

Jack had a pretty good idea what this meant. Sultry obviously had some poor unsuspecting victim on the hook waiting for Jack. Jack walked slowly toward the restroom, and when he entered it, closed and locked the main door to it behind him. It was like a million other public restrooms. Two sinks hung on one wall, with mirrors hung directly above them. Two urinals hung on the same wall just beyond the sinks, separated by a partition to offer privacy for their users. Along the same wall were two stalls containing toilets, both of the stall doors were closed. Jack heard someone urinating into the water or one of the toilets.

"When he's finished, go into that stall, he's committed one of the atrocities you hate so much," Sultry whispered into Jack's mind, "but, beware, he has a friend in the other stall."

Jack gave a very slight nod of acknowledgment. Most of the time, he never worried about the outcome of any physical conflict with anyone, as long as Sultry was backing him. When he prepared for such a fracas, it was as if his knuckles, elbows, knees, and any such striking point the chose became as granite. He still felt pain from blows he inflicted, as well as those few that were landed by antagonists. He also bled, and bruised from scrapes, and blows, but through Sultry, he somehow seemed to heal faster, and the pain subsided at a quicker rate. He had no doubt this encounter would end any differently.

Soon the stall door that Sultry had spoken of opened, and a huge Hispanic man emerged from the stall. Huge comes in many shapes and sizes, the Hispanic man that faced Jack stood around the six foot four inch line, and Jack guessed this man would make any set of bathroom scales groan toward the two hundred and fifty pound mark. Jack stood his ground in front of the main door to the restroom. The Hispanic man gave Jack a dismissive glance, leaned over one of the sinks, and began washing his hands, while eyeing Jack in the mirror.

Jack stepped into the recently vacated stall and looked at the toilet seat. His blood began to heat, then to boil. Sultry had been right, this was forgivable by only one way. The toilet seat had been left down, and the Hispanic man had urinated on it. Jack stepped back to the spot he had previously occupied, in front of the main door to the restroom and in direct view of the Hispanic man when he looked into the mirror again. The Hispanic man shut off the water and pulled several paper towels from a dispenser that was fastened to the wall near the sink. As the Hispanic man dried his hands, he turned to face Jack, and leaned his buttocks against the sink he had just used to wash his hands in, a slight, almost challenging smile started to curve his lips at the edges.

"You forgot to do something in there, Julio," Jack said to the Hispanic man in an even tone. What was Sultry about to get him into, Jack wondered.

"No habla Englase," the Hispanic man's eyes sparkled with a touch of humor, he thought the man that stood in front of the door reminded him of a Pee Wee Herman type person.

"I bet you'll understand enough English when I call your mama a whore," Jack's humor matched that of the man he had named Julio.

Julio stood straight throwing the paper towels to the floor, all appearances of humor fled from his face, to be replaced with red hot anger.

"I knew it!" Jack exclaimed, laughing, slapping his knee. "Not only is your mama a whore, she raised a lying, mother fucking Mexican!"

"Little man," the Hispanic man hissed through clinched teeth, Jack did notice the man had a Hispanic accent. "I will give you one chance to take back your unkind words about my mother."

"Tell you what," Jack said in a conversationally tone. "If you'll go back in that stall, and lick up the piss you just squirted all over the toilet seat, I won't stomp the dog shit out of your cock sucking ass."

"You will kick my ass?" the Hispanic man laughed.

"You will lick your piss off that toilet seat," Jack stated, all humor gone from his face and tone. The Hispanic man noticed a slight red glow in Jack's eyes. "If you do it on your own, then I won't hurt you, but if I have to drag your useless, cock sucking, mother fucking ass in that stall, I will beat your ass 'til you can't walk."

"Big words for such a little man," the Hispanic grinned again.

"Problemo, Hector?" came a voice from the other stall.

"No," Hector answered the voice from the stall, but kept his eyes on Jack.

"Your mama will know how big I am when I'm finished with her," Jack's grin invited Hector.

Hector leaped forward with surprising speed for such a big man. Both hands were clinched into fists and swung dangerously at the end of trunk-like arms. Jack feigned to the right, then moved left, as he pivoted on the ball of his left foot. He ducked under Hector's flailing arms, rose to his full height, and maintained his pivoting motion, as he brought around a devastating left hook. The hook punch had all of Jack's weight and momentum behind it as it connected with a loud smack to the base of Hector's skull just below the ear in that soft spot where the neck meets the skull.

Hector had no chance of stopping his forward momentum, and along with the tremendous force of the hook punch from Jack, he slammed his forehead into the solid door that Jack had been standing in front of just a moment before. Hector bounced off the door and sat down hard on his ass which jarred his already swimming head.

"Olay, mother fucker!" Hector heard Jack laugh.

Hector shook his head and tried to clear his vision. His head hurt from the blow from Jack, which felt like he had been hit with a fist-sized stone, and it also hurt from smacking it into the door. Hector relived it all again in what seemed like slow motion, the blow to the back of the head had weakened him to the point that his arms went limp and gave his poor head no cushion when he went head first into the door. His spine protested from the shock of all of his weight being slammed down onto one point on his ass. For all intents and purposes, Hector's fight was over, but Jack wasn't about to stop there.

When Hector hit the floor on his ass, Jack stepped around behind him and wrenched the big man's head back with a fist full of hair. Jack could see Hector's eyes were still glazed and cloudy from the hard knocks he had just taken. Jack punched straight down onto Hector's nose with his other fist. Jack felt Hector's nose crunch beneath the blow, and blood gushed down the front of Hector's shirt front, as Hector let out a blood-curdling scream.

Jack released his grip on Hector's hair and grabbed him by the nape of the neck. Jack shoved Hector ahead of him into the recently-vacated stall. As Hector supported himself on his hands and knees, Jack planted a hard kick between Hector's buttocks, driving the big Hispanic man into the stall to the point where Hector's already injured forehead struck the toilet.

"You lick every drop of piss off that toilet seat, you overgrown sack of snake shit," Jack hissed at Hector, as he straddled the back of Hector's neck. Jack reclaimed his hold on Hector's hair, this time with both hands, and rubbed Hector's face along the toilet seat, as the barely-conscious man licked up his own urine, leaving bloody streaks from his destroyed nose.

A noise behind Jack brought him around to face Hector's partner that had occupied the other stall. This man was also Hispanic but not as large as Hector. The look on this man's face was of pure surprise and horror.

"I didn't hear that toilet flush," Jack's icy tone, along with the red eyes galvanized the man to take a step back to stand ramrod still against the wall behind him. "You had better not left anything in that toilet that you don't want to eat." With that, Jack released his hold on Hector, and leaped toward the other man.

The man screamed and darted for the main door, but his nervous hands and fingers couldn't unlock it.

"Please," the man cried and sobbed, "please, don't hurt me."

Jack, quick as a striking snake, had the man by the throat and started to squeeze. The man wasn't sure who his attacker looked like, but it sure wasn't Pee Wee Herman.

"You forgot to flush," Jack growled at him.

"I'm sorry, I'll do that right now," the man breathed, he made no attempt to hide his fear.

"Damn right you will!" Jack hissed and slung the man back toward the stall he had just vacated. The force which Jack used to throw the man was so great, that he slammed back first into the concrete wall that formed a corner at that stall. As the man bounced off the wall, Jack planted a hard, solid kick to the man's groin, but before the man could crumple from the pain, Jack hit him with a merciless right cross that sent his limp head back into the concrete wall. Jack picked him up by the nape of the neck, and the seat of the pants, and draped him over the toilet. Jack let the man's head droop into the toilet bowl which was, as Jack suspected, unflushed with shit.

Jack returned to Hector, who was just as Jack had left him, only unconscious. Jack lightly slapped Hector's cheeks.

"Wake up, you son of a whore," Jack chided. Hector's eyes opened and were filled with fear when they focused on Jack.

"Relax," Jack said, keeping his tone quiet and even. "Our conflict is over. The question is: Did you learn anything?"

Hector's gaze was filled with pain and fear.

"Do you want me to tell you what you've learned?" Jack asked, still leaning over the big man. Hector's only answer was a painful moan.

"You learned to raise the toilet lid when you take a piss in any toilet from now on," Jack rasped in Hector's ear. "You learned that this country is the United States of America, and we speak English here. If you want to speak that shit you speak, then take your sorry ass back across the Rio Grande. And lastly you learned that when I say jump, you'll drop whatever your doin' and come runnin' because if you don't, I will tie you down, and make you listen to the screams of pain I will inflict on your mother, your sisters, and your daughter. Am I making myself perfectly clear?"

Hector's eyes cleared enough to be filled with understanding. Then his eyes filled with fear, as he realized that this man was serious.

"Ah, yes," Jack chided. "I know where your mother lives, and that you have one sister still living with her, while the other two share an apartment, and I know when you have visitation of your daughter, and where she lives."

"How—" Hector started.

"Never mind," Jack ordered, he had Hector's head pinned against the toilet, one side of the big man's face pressed against the toilet seat. Jack jammed one of his thumbs into the hollow spot behind Hector's jaw, and sunk it to the first knuckle, to emphasize his next point. "You just remember that when I call, you come running. I'll let you know the time and place. Understand?"

Hector's eyes were wide with pain and fear. His mouth opened and closed, much like a fish out of water. Through the fear being instilled into him, and the pain being inflicted upon him, Hector managed a slight nod of comprehension.

"Good," Jack said, stood to his full height, and unzipped his jeans. "This is so you won't forget anything that happened tonight." Jack urinated on the back of Hector's head.

Chapter 17

Jason was dreaming, he knew he was dreaming, and he couldn't wake himself. He was in his usual domain, a truck, his truck. It was late at night or early in the morning, shortly after midnight. He was on a highway with very little traffic, it could have been the four-lane section Highway Thirty in Ohio, or I-64 east of Mount Vernon, Illinois, but the most startling thing about this dream was the fact that Diane was strapped to the hood of the truck. She was on her back, wearing a pair of blue jean shorts and a T-shirt. She was crying and looking at Jason with imploring eyes to help her.

She was tied to the hood of the truck on her back, with her head and shoulders resting on the windshield, and her feet toward the nose of the hood. Jason was thankful at least for that. At least this way Diane's blood wouldn't rush to her head, and she could see where she was going. If she had been tied with her head toward the nose of the hood, Jason imagined it would have been even more nerve wracking for Diane to not be able to see where she was going.

Jason couldn't help but look at her. Diane was a beautiful woman, anyone could see that, and many of Jason's acquaintances had said as much. He looked at her, from the top of her head to her bare feet. She lay on her back, arms splayed wide, and secured somehow to the hood of the truck. Her legs had been coupled together, Jason was also thankful for this, and then bound somehow to the hood. How Diane had been secured to the hood, Jason couldn't see, nor did he care, his main concern was how he would get her off.

Jason couldn't stop or help Diane at the moment because Jack was standing on the running board of the passenger side of the truck, this was a dream after all. Jack's eyes were glowing a fiery red, and his smile was of genuine humor.

"Here's the deal, Jason," Jack explained, he was shouting at Jason through the open window of the truck door. To Jason, Jack bore a striking resemblance to the character Gary Sinise played in the movie Reindeer Games. "If you stop to help sweet Diane now, I can get to her before you can. If you keep going, and cover the next hundred miles in an hour and fifteen minutes, then she's yours for the taking."

Jason did some quick calculations in his head. He knew to cover that distance in that length of time would require a speed of about eighty miles per hour. Jason looked at Diane and saw the pleading and fear in her eyes as she craned her head around to look back at him. He wanted to stop, but knew he couldn't. He tried to wake himself, but couldn't. Jason looked at Jack, who was still smiling, the smile turned into a chuckle, then a laugh.

"The catch is, Jason," Jack said, "that sweet Diane won't know about our little deal until it's all over, and you can't tell her until then. So what you have to ask yourself is: Do you take the chance that I can get to her first if you stop now, and by the way, I will, but I won't kill her, oh no. Or, do you run the miles in the time allotted and be her hero. On one hand save her from what I'll do to her, or take a chance that you can get to her faster than me."

"How do I know I can trust you to keep your end of the bargain?" Jason asked, he considered Diane's position, she was on her back on the hood of the truck. He knew that driving at that speed for that length of time would heat the hood to an uncomfortable temperature. He also knew Jack was correct, if he stopped now, there was no way he could get to Diane before Jack could. Jason made his decision and hoped Diane would understand.

"What do you want me to do, swear on this Bible?" Jack asked, as he reached through the open door window of the truck, and placed his right hand on the Bible that appeared in the passenger seat, this was a dream after all.

Jason reacted at once. When Jack had reached through the open window, he of course, reduced his grip on the truck by half. Jason turned the steering wheel to the right, then the left. The swerving motion caused Jack to loose his footing, then his grip, and he disappeared from the open window. Jason wasted no time, he took his foot off of the accelerator pedal, stepped on the brake pedal, and eased the truck to a stop. He barely had the driver's side door open before he jumped from the driver's seat.

"Honey, I'm comin'," Jason called to Diane. He heaved himself up onto the truck hood, and saw Jack sitting next to Diane's head. Diane was crying, her teary eyes met Jason's.

"I warned ya," Jack said to Jason, his eyes were glowing red hot. Jack raised a large, strong-bladed knife and brought it down toward Diane. Jason lunged for the knife and the arm welding it. As Jason and Jack locked up, they toppled away from Diane and off the side of the truck.

Jason jerked awake before he hit the ground. Diane was asleep next to him, and Jason squeezed her with the arm that was around her. Good thing, he thought, because weren't people supposed to die if they dreamed they were falling and hit the ground before they woke up? Jason didn't know if that was an old wives' tale or not, he was just glad the nightmare was over.

Diane was also dreaming. In Diane's dream, she was lying naked someplace in the dark. She knew she was naked because she could feel whatever she was lying against touching her bare skin. She explored the space she was in by feeling around with her hands, fingers, feet, and toes. Just as she suspected, she was in some sort of human-sized box. A coffin? That thought raised her blood pressure. She didn't think so, she could feel cool air from several vents caressing her bare skin.

She heard something. The noise was familiar to her, it sounded like the flushing of a toilet in a camper. Next, she heard a scream like from a woman, then she heard a thump. She could not make herself believe what she heard and felt next. The space she was in started to rock, not side to side, but longitudinally or long ways. She heard what sounded like grunts from boar pigs when they breed sows. She also heard the sounds of weeping, screams of agony, and pleadings to stop. Whatever, or whoever was making that noise directly on top of her was definitely two different people. Diane put her hands on the wall directly in front of her and felt vibrations there, more like thumps.

Diane heard a louder, extended grunt, then a loud, wet, slobbery sigh. Mixed with those sounds was the sound of all out anguished weeping. Those sounds of the weeping broke Diane's heart. Whoever that was, Diane got the feeling that person did not want to be there or doing whatever they had just done, and Diane's heart went out to her.

The next sounds she heard, she couldn't quite make out. She thought she heard a gurgling sound. Then there was the noise of what sounded like plastic sheeting being rattled, and the sound duct tape makes coming off the roll. All of the sounds were muffled and hard to make out, and Diane wasn't sure of any of them.

The next sound she heard, she also felt through the vibrations of whatever she was lying in. There was a click, a sound of something being raised on gas cylinders, then another click as the top of her darkened space was lifted away. Light, bright light to her, invaded Diane's previously darkened space, forcing her to cover her eyes with one of her hands. Her other hand tried to cover her naked breasts.

"I will probably have to help you cover those," said a smooth voice. "Come on out of there, and we'll chat about it." Diane took the hand offered to her with the hand that was serving visor duty. The voice that had spoken to her sounded familiar, but she couldn't quite place it. She had a lot of questions she wanted answered.

"Who are you? Where am I? Why am I naked? Do I know you?" These questions fought to be the first out of Diane's mouth. Had she actually spoken?

"Patience, Diane," the smooth voice said. "All will become clear to you, but, right now, I need you to step down here beside me."

Diane did as she was asked and tentatively stepped down beside the owner of the voice. Her eyes hadn't quite adjusted to the light yet, and she was still very much aware that she was naked. As her eyes adjusted, she tried to see who had just helped her, but her attention was drawn to something else. Someone was behind her, and that really made her nervous.

As she spun in that direction, she realized she was in the cab of a truck. Her gaze landed on the plastic wrapped body of a dead woman sitting on the passenger seat. Anyway, Diane thought the woman was dead, wrapped in plastic as she was, tape sealed both ends. Both the woman's eyes and mouth were open, giving her face the look of shocked pain.

Diane let out a sharp, surprised squeal, and involuntarily jumped back a step, bumping into the owner of the voice that had spoken to her. Diane felt two strong hands firmly grab her, stroke her, caress her, then strong arms encircled her. Diane knew who this man was now. This was the man that had attacked her and Selena.

"Please don't," Diane whispered, and tried to pull away.

"Diane, look here," Jack said, and Diane's eyes followed Jack's pointing finger. Hanging on the wall directly above where Jack had helped her out of where she had been were about half a dozen triangular shaped patches of skin covered in curly hair. Diane instinctively knew what she was looking at, was repulsed by it, and tried to pull away. Jack gripped her more tightly and pointed again. Diane looked to the side of the scalps where Jack was pointing and lost her breath. On the wall next to the scalps were spaces allotted with names above them. Diane silently read the names as tears rolled down her cheeks, Christine, Megan, Selena, and Dixie.

"Why?" Diane wept and turned away.

"This fate is not for you," Jack said to her, his face looked more like

Keith's now. "I will take you and sustain myself on you, but you have to come with me willingly."

"And if I don't?" Diane composed herself.

"I think those four spaces speak for themselves," Jack smiled at her. His face changed again, and Diane saw Jason standing there. His smile vanished as he sobered, and his face morphed back to his own. He said, "Oh, and you will see their faces, and they will see yours as I fuck each one of them, then add her scalp to my trophy wall."

Diane woke with a start and a loud gasp. She didn't know where she was at first. She felt arms around her and started to fight. She was lying in a bed, and that added to her anxiety. She wore only a thin, short nylon nightshirt with nothing on underneath, and that quickened her heart rate and breathing even more. It seemed as though it was daytime outside, but the room she was in had the curtains pulled over the windows, letting in only dim light.

"Diane, honey, it's me. I've got you. You're all right." Diane recognized the voice of Jason. She relaxed a bit, then struggled against him again as a thought struck her. If her attacker could make himself look like someone else, maybe he could make himself sound like someone else. When she chanced a look back, she saw her attacker, Jack, reaching for her from across the bed. She screamed and jumped.

"Diane, sweetie, I love you." Diane heard Jason's voice again and felt his arms let her go. She scrambled to the edge of the bed where she sat still. It had been another nightmare. She hung her head and took a deep breath. She turned her head and looked at Jason. It was the 'I love you' that had stopped her, and it really was Jason this time. He made no move toward her.

"I'm sorry," Diane offered him a slight smile.

"You don't need to apologize to me," Jason said, he was still lying on the bed, he hadn't moved. "I'm the one who owes you the apology for not being here to protect you."

"You would think that, wouldn't you?" Diane asked. She raised her feet off the floor, rolled, spinning on her rump, and stretched out alongside her husband again, who instantly encircled her in his arms once more.

"When did you get home, and how did I get here?" Diane seemed confused. "The last thing I remembered, I was at Billy and Sally's house."

"I got home about seven o'clock last night, dropped the trailer at the yard, came home and got the pickup, and went after you," Jason explained.

"How'd I get here?" Diane asked, then flashed her blue eyes at him, as she indicated the nightshirt, "And dressed in this?"

"Billy and Sal helped me get you into the pickup and over here, and Sal helped me get you out of your clothes and into this," Jason said, rubbing a portion of the nightshirt between one of his thumbs and forefingers. Diane seemed to accept this and snuggled closer to him.

"Are you all right?" Jason asked, squeezing her in his arms.

"I would be better if the nightmares would stop," Diane said, she caressed Jason's chest with one of her hands.

"I know that feeling," Jason said, his voice husky. He liked the feel of her hands on him.

"What?" Diane broke Jason's grasp on her, propped herself up on one elbow, and looked at him intently.

"Remember the rough week I had that you told Keith about?" Jason asked.

"Yes," Diane looked worried now.

"I had nightmares all that week of what happened to the two of you the other night," Jason confessed. "Every time I laid down that week to catch a nap, the nightmares would start."

"Oh, honey, how horrible that must have been for you," Diane said. "Why didn't you tell me? How did you get through the week without any sleep?"

"Oh, I slept that week, it just wasn't as much," Jason smiled at her. "Besides, when we got married, I promised to try to lighten your load, not add to it. I didn't want to sound like a whiner."

"You have lightened my load," Diane stretched out next to him again and snuggled in once more. "Before you came along, I had to work, now I do by choice. You've done a lot for me, and I appreciate every bit of it."

"Are you scheduled to work today?" Jason asked, giving her another squeeze.

"Yes, the evening shift," Diane said, she snuggled against him again.

"Well, I'll call your boss and tell him you won't be there," Jason started to get out of the bed.

"He won't like it, me not having a doctor's excuse," Diane warned Jason.

"He probably won't like the idea of me telling him to kiss my ass if he gives me any shit about it, either," Jason said as he got out of bed and pulled on his jeans.

"Thank you," Diane said and got out of bed herself.

"Where are you goin'?" Jason asked.

"I have to pee," Diane said, darting toward the bathroom.

Jason went to the kitchen, picked up the cordless telephone, and punched in Diane's work number. As the phone rang, Jason said a silent prayer of thanks to God, thanking Him for protecting Diane.

"Hello," said a female voice.

"Hello," Jason said. "I need to speak to Stewart, please."

The phone went silent, and Jason knew he had been put on hold.

"This is Stewart," said a voice on the other end of the telephone line that Jason recognized as Stewart's. "How may I help you?"

"Hi, Stewart, this is Jason, Diane's husband."

"Hey, Jason, how's it goin'?"

"I'm all right. The reason I'm calling is for Diane."

"Diane? Is she all right?"

"You heard?"

"Heard what?"

"About the guy that attacked her the other night?"

"Oh, shit! That was Diane?" Stewart exclaimed. Jason knew Stewart had a thing for Diane, but neither one of them spoke of it. "Is she all right? Who was the other woman?"

"Her sister-in-law, Selena. Like I said, the reason I'm calling is for Diane, I think she would be better off staying at home a couple of days."

"You wouldn't happen to have a doctor's note to back that up would you?"

"No, I don't," Jason said, he was prepared to go off on Stewart if he gave him any static over this.

"Well, you know, Jason, I can't show her any favoritism at all. I made the rule about doctor's notes to be fair to everyone, and I'm just trying to be fair."

"I see," Jason bit his anger back. "Well, you'll either make an exception in this case, or you can replace Diane. That's my rule."

"How much time do you think she'll need?"

"Just a couple of days."

"All right, have her call me in a couple of days."

"Okay, one of us will."

"I would prefer her to call me."

"One of us will," Jason repeated.

Jason heard Stewart give a sigh of defeat. "Okay," he said. "Tell her we're thinking about her."

"All right, I will. Thanks, Stewart. Bye." Jason said and disconnected. He stood there for a moment and thought he had better call the weekend dispatcher. He punched in the number, held the phone to his ear, and listened.

"Blanket Transportation, this is Richard, may I help you?" Jason recognized the voice of his assigned dispatcher.

"Well, hell, I had no idea you were on duty this weekend," Jason said into the telephone.

"Yep, it's my turn to hold the fort down," Richard said.

"I just called to see if you had anything really pressing that you needed me on," Jason said.

"No," Richard said. "Selena told me what happened the other night. Take a couple of days and be with your wife, we'll get by." Jason knew Selena wasn't one of Richard's favorite people, so for them to even speak was a surprise to Jason. On the other hand, Jason knew Selena would try to bargain with the devil on Diane's behalf.

"All right, thanks," Jason said, just as Diane screamed.

"Jason!" Diane screamed.

"Gotta go," Jason said into the phone, dropped it, and ran.

Jason ran down the hallway. It sounded to Jason as if Diane's scream had come from the bathroom. As he approached, he saw the door to the bathroom was closed. He tried the knob. It turned. Jason pushed on the door, and it opened.

Diane was crouching on the floor in the further most corner away from the door. She screamed again as Jason fell on his knees in front of her. Diane's eyes focused on Jason, she threw her arms around his neck and started to sob.

"Are you all right?" Jason softened his voice. He felt Diane nod against his shoulder.

"I thought I saw him in this room with me," Diane sobbed.

"There's no one here but us," Jason kept his voice low and soft.

"I'm sorry," Diane sniffed and dried her eyes with one of her hands. "I don't mean to be such a baby."

"You're my baby," Jason said. He tore a length of toilet paper off the roll hanging on the wall and handed it to Diane.

"Thank you," she smiled through her tears.

"My pleasure," Jason smiled back at her and wrapped his arms around her. "Come on, let's get you up off the floor."

Diane clung to Jason as he helped her to her feet.

"I'd like to get cleaned up," Diane said, she looked embarrassed.

"Do you want a bath or a shower?" Jason asked, trying to sound sincere, and not add to her embarrassment.

"A bath," Diane almost whispered.

"Do you want me to draw it for you, or do you want to do it?" Jason asked.

"I can do it," Diane said. "I want to leave the door open."

"Okay, sweetie," Jason turned to leave the room to give Diane her privacy. "Let me know if you need anything."

"Jason," Diane gripped his arm, and he turned to face her. "Thank you."

"You are welcome," Jason said, kissed her on the forehead, and left the room.

After her bath, and Jason felt secure in the fact that Diane would be okay, he called Dewey, his brother-in-law, Diane's brother, and asked him to pick up a few things for him. When Dewey arrived with the items, he questioned Jason about them. Jason explained, and Dewey helped him assemble the fifty-five-gallon plastic drum, the chains, and rope into a homemade punching bag. Whenever Jason was home, he would spend at least an hour, if not more, punching and kicking the thing. That with the push-ups and sit-ups he did, he eventually got into shape again.

Later that night, as Jason sat on the sofa and Diane slept with her head on Jason's lap, Selena called.

"How's the patient?" Selena asked over the phone.

"She's sleeping now, but this morning was rough for her," Jason kept his voice low. "Are you all right?"

"I'm fine, just a little sore, and my knuckles hurt," Selena said.

"Sal, are you having any illusions or dreams about the attacker?" Jason asked.

"No," Selena answered, her tone was cautious. "Why do you ask?"

"Diane thought he was in the house with us a couple of times today," Jason confided.

"How horrible," Selena breathed, "for her and you."

"I wonder why you aren't affected by this guy the way Diane is," Jason said, keeping his voice low.

"I don't know," Selena said. "The only thing I can figure is she had more direct contact with him, and he chose to have contact with her, but he didn't choose to have contact with me."

"That makes sense, I guess," Jason said.

"Well, I won't keep you, I just wanted to check on her," Selena said.

"Thanks for calling," Jason said.

"Let me know if you need anything," Selena offered.

"Okay, thanks," Jason said.

"Bye," Selena said.

"Bye-bye," Jason disconnected.

Later Jason awoke, still seated on the sofa, and found Diane gone. He leaped to his feet, and called out, "Diane?"

"I'm up here, honey," Diane called from the upper level.

"You all right?" Jason asked as he started that way.

"I'm fine," Diane answered. "The telephone woke me up."

"I'm sorry," Jason said, as he approached her, she was in their bedroom, getting dressed.

"Keith called to check on me and to say that he's gonna pick up his next load in Jefferson City in the morning, going to Sparks, Nevada for Tuesday morning," Diane said as she buttoned her blouse. "Then Christine called to check on me. She said she was sorry for not being here with me, but when I told her you were still here, she felt better. She said she was going to stay with one of the girls from work that lives alone and hasn't lived here very long."

"I'm sorry the phone woke you," Jason leaned against the door jamb.

"It's all right," Diane flashed her blue eyes and a smile at him. "I hadn't talked to Keith and Kat in a while, it was nice, and I was worried about Christine."

"You hungry?" Jason asked.

"I was gonna cook you some supper," Diane said.

"I can take care of that," Jason protested.

"I know you can," Diane smiled again, "but I would like to get back into a regular routine."

"As you wish," Jason said, putting one foot about two feet in front of the other, bent at the waist, and swung an arm low in a mock bow.

"Come on, D'Artagnan," Diane looped one of her arms through one of Jason's, and led him down the hallway toward the kitchen.

That night, Diane and Jason slept in each other's arms. Their love making had stopped. It's not that they didn't want to, but Jason felt more compelled to do his part to make Diane feel loved and cherished, as he had promised to do in their wedding vows. Jason also didn't want to be in the act of making love, and Diane have another one of her attacks. He was also afraid that sex would make Diane want to pull away from him. So Jason instead decided to try to show Diane how much he loved her by showing her patience, understanding, and empathy. It worked. Diane emotionally moved closer to Jason where she felt protected, valued, and loved beyond anything she had ever felt before in her life. It seemed as though the closer Diane and Jason were, the better chance they had of keeping the nightmares at bay.

The next morning, Jason and Diane were in the kitchen together. Jason was making a batch of his famous pancakes, while Diane scrambled some eggs and sipped a cup of coffee. Diane seemed more comfortable and relaxed, more like herself. They were listening to a station on the stereo that they could both agree on. Diane liked a station there in Springfield that played the Oldies, while Jason was more of a classic rock fan. They compromised on a light rock station that advertised it played the "hits of yesterday and today." A song, "Doin' It All for My Baby", by Huey Lewis and the News, came on the stereo. Jason stopped what he was doing, took her into his arms, led her into a slow dance, and softly sang along with words of the song. When the part of the song came for the guitar solo, Jason spun Diane around and held her tight against him, her backside against his front side. Diane was giggling as Jason took her right arm by the wrist in his right hand, and extended it to its full length. Jason wrapped his left arm around Diane's middle, and imitated holding a guitar pick in his left hand. As the guitar solo started, Jason imitated playing the guitar with his left hand on Diane's stomach, while imitating pressing the guitar strings against the frets of the guitar's neck with his right hand. Diane's giggles turned to full, all-out laughter, as Jason swayed his body against hers as he used her body for his imaginary guitar.

When the guitar solo ended, Diane broke Jason's grip on her and turned to face him. She placed herself in his embrace and wrapped her arms around him. She looked into his eyes and smiled at the concern she saw lingering there. Diane placed her lips against Jason's, daring and teasing him to kiss her. Jason resisted until he reminded himself that Diane had initiated the kiss, and then he let his passion run wild.

"Don't think I haven't noticed how patient you've been with me these last couple of days," Diane said to Jason when the kiss ended.

"I've been patient with you?" Jason teased.

"I'm ready," Diane confided. With that she took Jason by the hand and led him to the bedroom, breakfast forgotten. Jason made a mental note to send Huey Lewis and The News a thank you note.

One hour later the phone rang, and Jason begrudgingly answered it.

"Hello," Jason snapped. The telephone in the bedroom wasn't equipped with a caller ID, so he had no way of knowing who was calling, but he was also thankful that whoever was calling hadn't called any earlier.

"Jason?" Jason recognized the voice of Richard his dispatcher.

"Yeah, it's me, Richard. What's up?" Jason said as he swung his feet out of bed, and sat up.

"I hated to call," Richard said, "but I've got a couple of short runs that need to go, and I thought of you. They aren't more than three hundred miles away, they would pay the bills on the truck, and they would keep you close to home."

"Hang on a second, Richard," Jason said, took the phone handset away from his ear, covered the mouth piece with his other hand, looked at Diane, and opened his mouth to speak.

"Go on," Diane said, her voice was even and calm. "I'll be all right. In fact I was thinking of calling Stu to see if he would let me come in tonight."

"Are you sure?" Jason asked. He knew what Richard had said was true, and he needed to run some miles for the week to at least pay the expenses of the lease agreement. "You say the word, sweetie, and I'll stay with you longer."

"No," Diane said and touched his cheek with one of her hands. She was looking at Jason with that look that she knew turned him on. "I'll be all right, I think the worst is over."

"Give me a run down," Jason said into the telephone mouthpiece.

After he rang off with Richard, Jason once again wrapped Diane in his arms. She responded by pulling him closer, down next to her, and eventually on top of her.

Chapter 18

Keith sat on a barstool in a casino in a truck stop in Reno, Nevada. He was killing time. His reload information hadn't come through yet, and he had gotten tired of sitting in his truck. He had bought ten dollars' worth of quarters and was idly plugging them into a slot machine. He had called his dispatcher about an hour ago, and his dispatcher had told him that he would probably be reloaded out of North Las Vegas, Nevada, but that he needed to stay put in case something else came up, and besides, the load in North Las Vegas hadn't been confirmed yet. So Keith sat on the barstool in front of the slot machine, plugged in his quarters, and sipped his diet soda. His winnings weren't much, but he was winning more than he was losing.

When Keith looked outside, he was surprised to see it had grown dark. How long had he been playing slots? Keith had told his dispatcher to call him on his cell phone if a reload materialized, but his cell phone hadn't rung all day, and that surprised him. Normally, in a situation like this, Keith's dispatcher would have called, if for nothing else than to let him know that dispatch hadn't forgotten about him.

Keith gathered his winnings and cashed out. He stepped outside and took in a lungful of fresh air. He blew it out slowly and looked around. The sodium lights started to come on automatically.

Some of the bigger truck stops had fuel islands for big trucks, and separate fuel islands for RVs. Such was the case at this particular truck stop, and the fuel islands for the RVs were full. Keith had to pass near those fuel islands to get to the parking lot where he had left his truck parked. He decided he would check his satellite communication system before he called dispatch, just in case someone had forgotten to call him on his cell phone.

As he crossed the RV fuel island, three people approached him, a young Oriental woman and an older Oriental couple. This was becoming commonplace more and more, people approaching truckers, usually to beg for money, and Keith braced himself for their pitch.

"Sir, could you please help us?" The younger Oriental woman asked, her accent was heavily Oriental.

Keith considered a moment, then asked, "Like what?"

"My name is Ahna," said the young woman, and bowed slightly. She then motioned to the older couple, and said, "This is Mr. and Mrs. Hsiu, and they can't find their daughter. Have you by chance seen a young Chinese woman?"

"No, I haven't," Keith said, shocked at Ahna's words. "How old is she?"

"She's sixteen," Ahna answered.

"Where was the last place they saw her?" Keith asked, indicating the Hsius.

Ahna conversed with the Hsius for a few moments, "They say she was in the RV, and then she was gone."

"Have you called the police and let the management of the truck stop know about the disappearance?" Keith asked, trying to stay calm, more for the Hsiu's benefit than his own.

"Yes," Ahna nodded. "The police say they are on their way, and management said to remain with the RV in case she comes back."

"I'm on my way to my truck," Keith told Ahna. "I will keep my eyes open for her."

"Keep your eyes open?" Ahna shook her head, not comprehending.

"I will watch for her," Keith restated.

Ahna turned toward the Hsius and translated. Mrs. Hsiu was wiping at the tears that were spilling down her cheeks. Mr. Hsiu bowed toward Keith and said something in Chinese. Keith looked at Ahna for the translation.

"He says, 'Thank you,'" Ahna smiled at Keith.

"Tell them, they are welcome, that I'm sorry for their loss, and that I hope they find their daughter soon," Keith bowed slightly, turned, and walked toward his truck.

When Keith reached his truck and climbed into the cab, he found that no message waited for him on the satellite communication system. He pulled out his cell phone, and punched in dispatch's phone number. While the cell phone electronically dialed the number, Keith watched the activity around the RV fuel islands. Other RVers approached the RV operated by the Hsius, obviously inquiring why they hadn't moved their RV from the island so other RVers could fuel. Keith watched the exaggerated reactions of the RVers when they were told the reason the Hsius hadn't moved their RV, it was like watching an elaborate game of charades.

"Blanket Transportation, this is Selena, may I help you?" Keith heard Selena's voice from his cell phone.

"You damn sure can," Keith teased, and heard her giggle in response.

"Hello, Keith," Selena said. "What's up with you?"

"Well, my illustrious dispatcher was supposed to get back to me if he came up with a load, but he never called me back or sent me a message telling me one way or the other," Keith explained. He could hear Selena tapping the keyboard of her computer.

"It looks like they have you on a pick up in North Las Vegas, Nevada for tomorrow afternoon," Selena told Keith, he could tell she was reading the information to him. "That load delivers to Shawnee, Oklahoma Thursday morning, and from there we'll probably load you out of Oklahoma City to come back here. Or there is a Woodland, California load that loads tomorrow afternoon that goes to Saint Louis, Missouri for Friday morning, and from there your guess is as good as mine."

"Do I get my choice?" Keith asked.

"Let me double check to make sure these loads aren't assigned to someone else," Selena's voice said into Keith's ear, and he heard her tapping her keyboard again.

"I'll be so glad when they put us on your board," Keith said by way of making conversation while he waited.

"I just hope it doesn't create hard feelings here in the office and out on the road," Selena's voice confided to him.

"I'm so sick of listening to the cry babies in the office and on the road that I don't care anymore if this move does make them cry louder," Keith said. "I just don't want them to take it out on you."

"I think I can take care of myself," Selena's voice sounded confident in his ear.

"From the way Diane told me you handled that asshole Jack the other night, there's no doubt in my mind that you can take care of yourself," Keith praised her.

"We were lucky," Selena's voice in his ear had the hard edge of truth to it. "My knuckles are still swollen and still hurt. I still have a puffy lip and a black eye."

"I still say you two girls kicked his ass," Keith said.

"I still say we were lucky," Selena's voice took on the tone of persistence, then she said. "Here we go, you can have either load, it's your choice. There is another Blanket Transportation driver unloading right now where you unloaded this morning, and he will get whichever load you pass on."

"I'll take the North Las Vegas," Keith said.

"Anything else?" Selena's voice sounded normal again.

"No, I'll get ready to leave here pretty quick," Keith said. "Thanks, Selena, bye."

Keith clicked off after he heard Selena tell him goodbye. Keith started his truck and pulled out his logbook. He was in the process of bringing it up to date, when a Reno police officer knocked on Keith's driver's side door.

"Good evening," Keith said after he rolled down his window.

"Hello, sir," the police officer said. "Are you the gentleman that the Chinese woman spoke to about the missing girl?"

"Yes, I am," Keith confirmed.

"Are you preparing to leave?" the police officer asked.

"Yep, just as soon as I can," Keith said.

"Would you mind to step out of the truck while I take a quick look inside, please, sir?" the police officer asked.

Keith started to protest, then saw the young woman named Ahna and the Hsius watching them. He put himself in their place and relented.

"Sure," Keith said, opened the driver's side door, and climbed down, letting the police officer have access to his truck. As Keith stood there he thought about his appearance, the long hair pulled back in a ponytail, the tattoos that covered both of his arms from wrists to shoulders, and the piercing, three in one ear, two in the other, and, of course, the tongue. Looking at him, most people would consider him a suspect for something like this. Most people, except Jason, whose favorite line was, "WolfKat, you're the perfect example as to why folks shouldn't judge a book by its cover." Keith grinned at the memory. There were very few people he would lay his life down for, and Jason was very near the top of it.

The police officer climbed into the cab of the truck and ducked into the sleeper. Keith could hear the police officer moving around inside the truck, and soon he was standing on the ground beside Keith again.

"Thank you for your cooperation, sir," the police officer said. "You're free to go."

"Thank you," Keith said and climbed back into the driver's seat. He released the air brakes, eased his truck out of the parking space, pulled off the truck stop property, and merged onto I-80 eastbound.

Keith once more pulled out his cell phone, set it on its holder, and connected the headset to it. He checked the time and saw that his wife Kat wasn't off work yet, so Keith knew he had time to talk to Jason. He put on the headset and punched in Jason and Diane's number. Jason answered on the second ring.

"Howdy," Jason's voice sounded in Keith's ear.

"What's goin' on?" Keith asked.

"Not much. Where ya at?" Jason asked, using his trucker accent.

"I'm leaving Reno, headed for Sin City," Keith answered, using Las Vegas's universal nick name.

"Aha! Stay away from those ranches down along 95," Jason teased. Prostitution was legal in the state of Nevada, and houses of prostitution had several nicknames, such as cathouses, whorehouses, houses of ill repute, and so on. In Nevada, those houses were called, in some variation, ranches.

"Why? What goes on at those ranches? Is that the voice of experience talkin' there, Fox?" Keith feigned ignorance, teasing. They both laughed. Then Keith sobered. "How's Diane?"

"She's doin' better," Jason said. "I'm gonna keep her home the next couple of days."

"I bet good ole Stu liked that," Keith prompted.

"I don't much care what Stu likes," Jason answered. "Especially when it comes to Diane."

"Is she there where I can talk to her?" Keith asked.

"Sure, hang on," Jason said. Keith heard Diane ask who it was, and heard Jason tell her that it was Keith.

"Hi," Keith heard Diane's voice say over the phone. To Keith, she didn't sound like herself.

"Hey, girl, what's goin' on?" Keith greeted, using his trucker accent.

"Not much," Diane answered. "Just hanging out, letting Jason pamper me."

"You take all of that you can get," Keith advised, in his normal tone, then switched back to his trucker accent. "Well, look, darlin', I just wanted to give you a shout, and check on ya. I know you're in good hands, so I won't keep ya. Take care, God bless, bye-bye."

"Bye," Keith heard Diane say, and they both disconnected.

At exit 46, Keith left the interstate and merged onto U.S. Alternate 50 eastbound, and followed that to Fallon, Nevada, where he turned south onto U.S. 95. A little over two hours and about 135 miles later, Keith came to the intersection of U.S. 95 and U.S. 6. There had once been a small truck stop there, but it had long since closed down. There was still plenty of room to park several trucks there, and many trucks stopped there in the middle of the night.

Keith pulled over and parked, to take a short nap. There were three other trucks already there, and Keith parked where he wouldn't crowd any of them. He pulled off his shirt, jeans, and boots in the sleeper, stretched out on the sleeper bunk, and went to sleep.

About three hours later, Keith was awakened by someone knocking on the side of his truck. Keith sat up, looked at the stereo/clock, and read the time to be three a.m. He slid off the bunk and pulled on his jeans, shirt, and boots. He stepped into the cab area and looked out the driver's side window of his truck. What he saw startled him.

A man of about medium height and weight, dressed much the same way he was dressed, was holding a naked Oriental girl in front of him. Keith did a double take, the man holding the girl was Jason. Keith couldn't make himself believe it, he had just spoken to Jason a few hours ago, and Jason was at home in Missouri. Keith shut his eyes hard, then snapped them open again, and shook his head, as if to clear it. The illusion of Jason's face dissolved into a face Keith had never seen before.

Keith could tell the girl had been crying. Tears were still running down her cheeks, as she pulled and strained against her captor. Keith powered down the driver's side window.

"Hey, man," the man holding the Oriental girl said. "Can you help me out? I'm trying to fuck this sweet young thing, but she won't hold still. Would you hold her down for me?"

"I'll do better than that," Keith said, picked up his cell phone, and pressed the power button. The cell phone's screen and numbers lit up, and it beeped, but the reception bars were nonexistent.

"I already tried that, but I couldn't get much of a signal. That's why I came to ask you to help me," the intended rapist grinned at Keith.

Keith opened the driver's side door and climbed down, he kept his eyes on the man holding the weeping girl. He left the truck door open.

"I'll hold her for you, if you'll hold her for me," the man said.

"Do you have a name?" Keith asked him.

"It's Jack, but I think you already knew that," Jack said.

"Why don't you let me have the girl?" Keith asked, and reached a hand toward her.

"You can have her, too, after I have her, we can both have her," Jack grinned and winked at Keith.

"What's your name, sweetie?" Keith asked the girl, but Jack confirmed what he already suspected.

"She no speaky English," Jack teased using a pseudo-Oriental accent, then sobered and said. "I bet if you called her momma a whore she would understand English." Jack laughed. "Come on, Keith, let's have some fun with this little virgin slut. No one will ever know, I won't tell, and besides who's gonna care about this little slant-eyed Chink?"

"Why don't you give me the girl and walk away," Keith said, hoping against hope this tactic would work. Then a thought struck him. "How do you know my name?"

"I know quite a bit about you, Keith," Jack said. The girl didn't struggle anymore; her eyes were filled with terror as she looked at Keith. Jack had her in a firm submission hold. Jack's eyes flashed red momentarily and grinned at the reaction he got from Keith. "I know about twenty years ago, you would have gone along with this."

"That was then," Keith said. "I've left that life behind."

"Oh, it's still there," Jack still teased.

"Just let me have the girl, and you can walk away, no questions asked," Keith tried to keep his voice from sounding like he was pleading.

"I saw two of your 'friends' the other night," Jack chided Keith. "Wow, I bet Diane and Selena are a couple of hot pieces. Whew, how do you stand being around two hot women like that, and not being able to touch?"

Keith's anger started to build, and he knew that was dangerous.

"I didn't get to feel Selena very well, but what Diane has in her bra is more than a handful," Jack's eyes shone a consistent red. "I bet if you got the two of them together, and got them sexed up, they would have your dick so sore, you couldn't stand to hold it when you took a piss."

Keith made fists with his hands, took in a deep breath, and took an aggressive step toward Jack and the girl. Jack grinned, and shoved the girl at Keith. Keith caught her around the bare waste, to help keep her from falling. She immediately put her hands on Keith's chest, and pushed away as far as she could. Keith still had a hold on her, to support her and keep her from falling, when she raked both sides of his cheeks with her fingernails, and drew blood. Keith let her go, he stayed calm, and took off his shirt. He wiped at the blood on his cheeks, and held out the shirt for the girl, she looked puzzled, then took it from him, and put it on.

"Get in the truck," Keith said, he kept his voice soft, and motioned toward the open door of his truck.

The girl said something in Chinese, it almost sounded apologetic to him, and reached out a hand as if to touch Keith's bleeding face.

Suddenly, Jack grabbed the girl by her hair, and pulled her from between himself and Keith. Keith was still touching his injured face with fingers, when Jack kicked him in the crotch. Jack then slung the girl around by her hair, with her screaming the whole time, and hurled her face first onto the ground, and into the dirt. Jack advanced on her and kicked her hard in the ribs.

Keith went down on one knee, clutched his crotch, tried to catch his breath, and at the same time fought the building sick feeling. He swallowed hard and fast between breaths, and tried successfully to hold down his gorge.

"Damn, I bet that hurt," Jack said, he stood a few feet away, facing Keith, his hands on his knees, grinning. Keith looked up at him, and thought he bore a striking resemblance to the character Sam Elliot played in the movie Roadhouse.

Keith coughed once, reached around to the knife case that hung on his belt, on the side facing away from Jack and unsnapped it. He pulled out the lock-bladed knife and got ready to lunge. He put his thumb on the blade stop, got ready to apply pressure, and flip the blade open. Keith heard Jack laughing, and when Keith looked at him, Jack's eyes were still glowing a faint red.

Keith lunged, brought the knife up, and flipped the blade open as he reached for Jack.

"Run!" Keith yelled at the girl, and pointed toward the open door of his truck.

Jack casually leaned away from Keith, and pulled out a knife of his own. Jack leaped back out of Keith's reach, and brought his own knife around in a sweeping arch. Jack's knife nicked the flesh of Keith's knife arm on the underside, just above the elbow.

Keith spun around to face Jack, touched the wound that Jack had just given him, and saw it had drawn blood but was superficial. The pain from the kick to his crotch and the knife wound were superseded by the building rage of his anger. Keith checked his anger and mentally turned it into energy.

"Do you feel it?" Jack teased in a light voice. "Do you feel the anticipation of the kill?"

Keith ignored him, and lowered himself into an attack stance, knees bent, back straight, but leaning forward a little, and arms held loose and wide. Jack did the same, grinning the whole time, and the two men circled, facing and mirroring each other. Jack feigned a lunge a couple of times, but Keith kept his cool and didn't make any moves that would telegraph a defense against a real attack by Jack.

When Keith circled close to the girl, he bent lower, extended a hand to her, but never took his eyes off Jack. The girl took Keith's hand, and he helped her to her feet. Keith then gently motioned and pushed her to stay behind him. The girl somehow understood Keith and followed his lead.

"How nice," Jack continued to tease. "Chivalry must be a universal language."

Jack attacked as he finished speaking. Keith fought the urge to dodge to one side or the other, knowing that if he did so would expose the girl to Jack's knife, as she stood directly behind him. Keith, instead, stepped toward Jack, closing the attack space, and throwing off Jack's attack momentum.

When Keith closed the distance between himself and Jack, Jack had no time to readjust the angle or speed of his swinging arm that held the knife. Keith stepped to the inside of Jack's arcing arm and slashed with his own knife. Keith's knife found its mark, and sliced a vertical cut between the wrist and elbow of Jack's knife arm. Keith ducked under the swinging arm of Jack like a boxer, and came up on the outside of the attacking arm. As Keith came up, he turned the blade of the knife so that it bit flesh again, this time the underside of Jack's knife arm between the elbow and shoulder.

Jack never slowed down, it was as if he didn't feel the pain, he came around with a backhand swing with the same arm. Keith, surprised by the backhand attack, stepped back a step, and let the attacking arm of Jack whistle by him. Keith took back the step he had just given up and swung his own arm in a low inside move. Jack recovered quickly and blocked Keith's knife with his own knife. There were a few sparks as the knife blades met, and both men grappled for a superior hold over the other with their free hands. Jack won the grappling contest, and gripped Keith's free wrist with his own free hand. The grip was tight and painful to Keith, but he knew he didn't have time to dwell on it, instead, he yanked his trapped arm down hard, and simultaneously head-butted Jack hard across the bridge of his nose.

Jack, involuntarily, stepped back and reached his free hand to his injured nose, as he let out a grunt of pain. Keith took another step toward Jack, and planted a well aimed kick of his own to Jack's groin. Jack's knees buckled as he went down on them hard, and vomited.

"Damn, I know that hurt," Keith stated to Jack.

Keith turned to the girl, and once more motioned to his truck. She still looked as if she didn't trust him. Keith put himself in her position and understood what she must be going through. He had been stationed many places around the world when he was in the Navy, where English wasn't the primary language, and whenever he and a couple of his buddies would venture out on leave, the differences of language could be a barrier. There were times when he was convinced that some of those people chose not to speak English, but he didn't think this was the case here. This girl was faced with a life-threatening situation, and he thought she knew it. He didn't think language was a barrier here, he thought this girl honestly couldn't speak English. Keith racked his brain for a way to communicate with her, then in an instance of inspiration, he spoke the one word he knew she would understand.

"Hsiu?" Keith asked her, adding a hopeful nod.

The girl gave Keith a look of joyful surprise, then once more looked as if she didn't fully trust him, and slowly nodded. Keith nodded with her, and motioned toward his truck, then held his hands up, palms toward her, and hoped this would convey to her that he meant her no harm. The girl slowly walked toward Keith's truck, glancing at him a few times, and giving Jack a wide berth. She was on the bottom step of the running board, and about to step onto the next one, when they both heard Jack roar behind them.

Keith turned to meet Jack's attack almost too late. Their knives met, and sparks flew once more from their edges. As Keith parried Jack's knife with his own, Jack hit Keith with his free fist with a blow to the face. The blow was enough to weaken Keith's defense enough to give Jack the upper hand.

"I've fucked around with you enough!" Jack screamed at Keith, then added in a low rasp. "I could kill you right now and cut off your balls for a trophy, but I won't. I have something else in mind for you that will probably be worse than death."

Jack hit Keith again, Keith dropped his knife, and fell to his knees. Unconsciousness threatened to invade, and take over, but Keith fought against it.

"Enjoy your freedom while you can," Jack laughed at Keith, as he hit him with a fist to the jaw that sprawled Keith into the dirt. Keith watched as Jack picked up his knife and stuck it into a back pocket of his jeans.

"You'll find your knife down around Springfield," Jack grinned at Keith, then pulled the girl out of Keith's truck, "along with her. Oh, one more thing," Jack said as an after thought, "here's a preview of things to come."

As Keith watched, Jack's face changed from his own to that of someone he had known in the Seals, a friend named Cal. Before Keith could register the face change, Jack's face changed from Cal's to the face of Jerry, another friend from the Seals. Just as Keith registered the face change, Jack changed his face once more, this time to the face of Jason.

"You figure it out," Jack winked at Keith, as he resumed his own face, and ushered the girl to his truck.

Keith tried to get to his feet, but every effort he made was slowed by the threatening unconsciousness. He reached a hand toward the girl, who seemed to finally understand that he had meant to help her and reached back toward him. Keith could only watch, helplessly, as Jack shoved the girl into his truck, and then drove off southward.

When Keith saw Jack drive off, he screamed in frustration, and doubled his efforts to get to his feet, especially when he saw that Jack was pulling a Blanket Transportation trailer. Keith finally climbed behind the steering wheel of his truck, and checked his cell phone; it was still showing a weak signal. Keith depressed the clutch, put the shifter into fifth gear, and eased out on the clutch.

"How 'boutcha WolfKat? You gotta copy?" Keith heard Jack's voice over his CB speaker. "I know you're back there, and that you'll be comin' after us. Well bring it on, good buddy. That's what you are, ain't it, a good buddy? That's the rumor around your terminal, that you and that cock sucker Jason are queer for each other."

Keith was gaining speed as he geared up his truck. He finally reached thirteenth gear, and pushed the accelerator pedal to the floor. He figured he was reaching the one hundred mile an hour mark when he reached for his CB microphone.

"Break One-Nine for a Smokey Bear," Keith said into his keyed mic. Smokey Bear was the nickname truckers used for state patrolmen or state policemen. Nothing but static came from the CB's speaker.

"Break One-Nine for a Smokey Bear," Keith repeated into his keyed mic.

"There's no one out here, but you and me," Keith heard Jack's voice from his CB speaker. "All of the Smokey Bears, along with all the people in the little towns between here and Las Vegas suddenly had the urge to go home and go to bed."

Keith cursed to himself.

"Come on WolfKat, don't give up on me," Keith heard Jack's voice over his CB speaker. "My truck is much like the one your step dad had when you was a kid. Remember that? Remember how fast that truck was? Remember goin' with him on runs? Do you remember those days?"

Keith remembered those days, and he remembered they weren't good ol' days either. His step dad was a good man, Keith guessed, he just had no business having kids around him when he had been drinking, which was more often than not. In Keith's mind, there was no such thing as a good drunk.

"This little girl is asking about you." Keith heard Jack's voice over his CB speaker. "Did I forget to mention that I speak a little Chinese?"

Keith saw the lights of the trailer that Jack was pulling.

"There you are," Keith heard Jack's voice over his CB speaker. "Well, tell us goodbye. This ol' truck will do about a hundred and forty. Maybe we'll see each other again. Who knows, maybe next time we can fight over Diane or Selena." Keith heard Jack laugh. "Oh, by the way, May-Ling says she wished she could have gone with you, but like I told her, it's too late for that now."

Keith bit back his anger, he knew there was nothing he could do or say that would get Jack to pull over and stop.

"Well, it's time for us to go," Keith heard Jack's voice over his CB speaker, "so toodle-loo, happy trails. Keep your powder dry. Sianara. Adios. Aloha. Chow. Goodbye." With that, Keith watched Jack's truck slowly pull away and outdistance him. Before long, the lights of the trailer that Jack was pulling were swallowed by the darkness.

Keith tried to raise Jack on the radio with no success. Next, he tried his cell phone, but it still showed a low signal. He raced over the Nevada desert throughout the night, and finally came to a small roadside service station that had a public telephone mounted on pole beside the building. Keith braked to a stop, set the air brakes, leaped from the truck, and ran to the telephone. As he picked up the receiver, a small sheet of paper was released from its holding place on the cradle and floated to the ground. Keith held the receiver to his ear but heard no dial tone. Keith clicked the cradle arm several times but still heard no dial tone.

Keith replaced the receiver to the cradle and stooped to pick up the paper. There was writing on one side of it that read:

Dear good-buddy,

Better luck next time. You better worry about your own hide rather than this little piece of ass in here with me. I'll leave you a small surprise in Springfield. Ha! Ha! Ha!

Sincerely,

Jack

As your old seals' motto went: catch me if you can.

p.s. remember that girl in that little town just north of Kuwait City?

In his mind, Keith was transported to a small town just north of Kuwait City, Saudi Arabia on a very hot afternoon. Keith had been the leader of a small eight-man team called the Misfits. Their primary job was to search and rescue, but on occasions, they were used for reconnaissance. Such had been the case that day. They had been deployed on a mission to seek out the enemy and report the location, but to only engage if fired upon first. This was their third time out without a rest, and Keith couldn't help feel that he and his men were being picked on.

Keith had ordered a short break, and he, with his men, had spread out along a seemingly-deserted street, but they all knew danger could very well be hiding just below the presumed calm surface. The abandoned street was narrow and dirty. The buildings that lined the street were vacant, and their dark doors and windows shone like empty eye sockets. Several burnt out vehicles littered and lined the street which made Keith and his men wary of any possible hiding enemy.

Keith and two of his men, who also happened to be close friends, sat near the bumpered ends of two of these derelict vehicles. The rest of the men in the small, tight group automatically spread out, some pairing off, but all keeping a watchful eye for anything out of place or anything that moved. Keith and his two friends were speaking in low tones, mainly about the women the each of them had had last night and sipping bottled water.

Each man was expected to carry his own heavy pack of supplies on his back, which consisted of rain gear, food, water, medical supplies, and so on. Some of the men had slung these burdensome packs to the ground to catch a small break from the weight. Each man carried an M-16 A-2 Assault Rifle, each with five fifty-round clips. Keith's M-16 A-2 also had a five-shot grenade launcher. Each man carried a 9mm automatic side arm with two extra seven-shot clips. The only man in the small group that carried anything extra was the radio man.

237

Keith sat between his two friends on the curb of the street. Jerry sat to Keith's left, and Calvin, everyone called him Cal, sat on Keith's right.

"I need to find a place to take a leak," Jerry murmured to his companions, shifted his weight, and prepared to rise to his feet. He had just gotten his legs under him and was about to stand when the commotion started. A young girl, Keith guessed her to be around fifteen or sixteen years old, burst from one of the darkened doorways in which one of his men had taken his break and ran screaming into the street.

The man under Keith's command that had been standing in the doorway let out a small cry of shock and alarm and instinctively grabbed for her. He missed her, but got her clothing, which ripped, exposing a bare shoulder. The girl's eyes were wide and wild. She swung a fist, struck him on the forearm, just above the elbow, hit the nerve there, and made him relinquish his hold on her.

"What the—" Jerry started as he stood and looked that way.

"No!" Keith shouted at Jerry, reached for his friend, and tried to pull him back down to his sitting position.

The first bullet hit Jerry just above his left eye and took most of the top of his head off. The second bullet hit Jerry on the right side of his neck and nearly took off the rest of his head.

"Shit!" Cal spat, trying to backpedal away from what was left of Jerry.

"Stay down!" Keith ordered Cal, but it sounded more like a plea.

The man that had grabbed the girl caught half a dozen rounds in the legs and head. He was slammed back against the wall and was dead before he hit the ground.

Keith recognized the expression on Cal's face as shock and disbelief. Keith was still trying to get Cal to take cover when the large caliber bullet struck Cal on the left side of his torso, front to back. The large caliber round blasted its way through Cal's ribcage and exploded out his back, taking most of the left lung and part of the heart with it. Cal was hurled back against the wall, bounced off of it, hit face first against the burned out car that sat at the curb there, and fell onto his back on the sidewalk at Keith's feet. Cal's expression had turned from shock and disbelief to one of fear and surprise.

"Keith?" Cal said, he blinked, and with the single word, blood gushed from his mouth. Several of the men were shouting at Keith, the radioman didn't wait, he got on the horn, and relayed coordinates and the information he had at that time.

238

"Return fire! Engage!" Keith screamed above the cacophony. Keith bent to Cal. The wound was massive, and Cal was loosing a lot of blood fast.

"Keith?" Cal pleaded.

"Right here, buddy," Keith tried to hold back his tears.

"Tell my parents that I love them," Cal's expression implored. Keith could tell the shock was starting to wear off, and Cal was feeling a lot of pain. Keith got out the two vials of morphine each of them were required to carry from Cal's pack, and gave him both doses. Keith knew he couldn't save his friend, but he could make his passing much more painless. Keith saw Cal's expression relax and knew his friend wasn't feeling much pain.

"Thank you for being my friend," Cal chocked and coughed.

"It was my pleasure," Keith couldn't hold his tears any longer as they rolled down his cheeks. Keith took one of Cal's hands in one of his own, felt Cal give a slight squeeze. Keith saw Cal's gaze glaze over as his grip relaxed at the same time. Cal took one more ragged breath, let it out with a shudder, and breathed no more.

Keith wiped his eyes, grabbed his M-16 A-2 Assault Rifle, flipped the switch for the three-shot bursts, and picked his first target. Bullets zinged around his head, making snapping sounds, and the air was full of the sound of gunfire and the smell of cordite. Keith felt satisfaction as his first target grabbed his chest, screamed, and fell dead. Keith's men were picking their targets and thinning them out.

The girl lay curled up on the sidewalk against a building on the far side of the street. She made herself as small as possible and covered her head with her arms and hands to protect it as well as block out the sound. Her gaze caught Keith's, he could tell she was scared out of her mind.

"What's her story?" Keith shouted at one of his remaining men.

"Don't know, Chief," the man replied. "She ran across the street, was almost hit several times by enemy fire, and collapsed where she is now. Every time she tries to move, one of those bastards that are shooting at us takes a shot at her."

"Has she been hit?" Keith asked.

"I don't think so," the other man replied.

"Is she with them?" Keith asked.

"I don't think so, Chief," the man answered.

Keith slammed a fresh clip into his rifle, racked the slide, and sprinted from behind his cover toward the girl.

"Chief?!" Several of Keith's men shouted at once.

Keith sprinted across the street as bullets whizzed around him. He ran hard across the street, kept the M-16 A-2 tight against his shoulder, and continued to fire the automatic three round bursts. As he reached the midway point across the street, Keith activated the grenade launcher, and pumped three of its projectiles into the building from where the enemy fire was coming.

Keith lowered a shoulder, as he continued to run, and braced himself for the shock waves from the exploding grenades. The repercussion knocked Keith off his feet in mid-stride, he landed hard on his side and rolled. He tried to keep his forward momentum, as he came out of his roll, bounced onto his back, and skidded to a stop just short of the curb a few feet from where the girl still lay. Keith looked into her frightened eyes, he tried to stay low and use the curb as cover. His men continued to provide cover fire for Keith, the three grenades had lessened the enemy fire, but Keith still found himself pinned down in the gutter of the street.

"Are you all right?" Keith shouted at the girl.

The girl only looked at him.

"Have you been hit?" Keith tried again.

His only answer was a look of fear and confusion from the girl.

"Can you hear me?" Keith shouted.

The girl yelled something at Keith, but he didn't understand the language she spoke. Keith saw the fear in her eyes and heard the panic in her voice. He understood that she was in a hostile environment and was faced with strange men who spoke a strange language and fired loud weapons. He fleetingly thought that he would probably react the same way if he had had no prior training.

More bullets zinged around Keith, some bit into the curb, and spat concrete shards and chips into his face. Keith rolled out of the gutter and onto the sidewalk, as his men returned fire. Keith sprang to his feet, turned to face the girl, and planned to help her to her feet.

To his surprise, the girl was standing but not on her own. A man stood behind her and held her in place, an arm wrapped around her neck, squeezing her throat. Her eyes were filled with fear and pleading for help. The face behind the girl was grinning and evil. Keith took a step toward her, but the thing that held her leveled a pistol at him and fired. Keith spun out of the line of fire and caught his last glimpse of the girl and her captor. Keith's last look at her was of her imploring eyes and arms that reached for him. Keith saw the eyes that were in the vile face behind the girl faintly glowed red, just before the man holding her pulled her into the shadows of the building.

Keith's men charged across the street to join him, and together they entered the building but found nothing. No girl, no man with red eyes, no one that had been shooting at them, no dead or wounded, no spent casings.

Keith reread the note. All of the anger, frustration, and pain built to a frenzy inside Keith. He straightened his arms to his sides, arched his back, tilted his head back, and screamed at the night sky.

After his mad minute had passed, he remembered what Jack had said about leaving a surprise for him in Springfield. Keith returned to the driver's seat of his truck and formulated a plan. He would continue on to North Las Vegas. It was a drop and hook at the warehouse there, he would switch the trailers, and he would try to beat Jack to Springfield. Going to Shawnee, Oklahoma would have to wait. He might also want to consider contacting the task force in Springfield about his encounter tonight. Keith fired up the diesel engine of his truck and made the black smoke roll out of its stacks as he continued south toward Las Vegas.

Keith thought about the friends he had seen die on that fateful day in the small town near Kuwait City. The pain of that memory seized his heart, and the tears started to come. That had been the beginning of the end for him in the Navy Seals. Upon their return to the base camp, his commanding officer had commanded him and his men to return for another mission. Keith had refused, his team had just returned from their third mission without a suitable rest, and he was not going to endanger the lives of his remaining team. His CO had brought him up on court martial charges for insubordination. The hearing had ended with Keith being able to leave the Seals on his own accord without court martial charges being brought against him.

Keith then thought about the friends he had now, Jason, and Diane. He thought about his wife, Katrina, whom he loved so much. With her, there was the promise of a new, fresh life. He counted all of the friends he had met since moving to Missouri, he even counted Selena as a friend. He had met her through Jason and Diane, of course, before she had gone to work for Blanket Transportation, and also counted Billy, her husband and Diane's brother, as a friend. Keith knew he had a lot to live for, and he knew he wasn't ready to lose it all.

Keith thought about the face changes Jack had showed him: Cal to Jerry to Jason. What could that mean? Jack's words, "You figure it out," bothered him. With the excitement of the fight with Jack, the surprise of the girl, and the shock of the memory of Cal and Jerry's deaths, Keith knew he probably wasn't thinking too clearly. Keith had always felt responsible for Cal and Jerry's deaths, even to the point of writing letters of condolences to their families. He thought about those three faces again and Jack's ominous words.

"Oh shit!" Keith exclaimed, his mind cleared, and the proverbial light went off in his head. Keith somehow knew that Jack meant to kill Jason. Why? It didn't matter, Keith just knew he had the chance to keep Jason from being killed.

Tears streamed down his cheeks as he thought about the girl, May-Ling, was that what Jack had called her? He hated the thought of anyone doing harm to a child. The girl that day so long ago had been little more than a child, about the same age as the girl tonight. Keith drew in a deep breath which helped to give him focus. He made his decision, and with a little luck, he planned to be in Springfield the following night.

One other thing bothered Keith as he gazed at the note. A phrase at the end of the note, "Catch me if you can," that was also his team's slogan in the Seals. Keith knew he had to keep moving, he knew that one phrase could be enough to throw suspicion onto him if anybody dug deep enough. He figured that the FBI would dig deep enough. He wiped the tears from his face, asked a prayer of protection from God, and started on his way.

Chapter 19

Dixie was dreaming. It was a kind of review of her life that started with the funeral of her mother. She was standing in the rain, holding hands with her father, beside her mother's grave. Her father held an opened umbrella over the two of them with his other hand. Dixie heard the rain hitting the umbrella; it was a sound that would forevermore be etched into her memory with one of the saddest days of her life. Dixie was crying tears of sorrow, not only for the loss of her mother, but also for the sadness she felt coming from her father. She looked up into his face and saw the tears running down his cheeks. It seemed to Dixie that's all he had done for the last three days, and all she knew to comfort him was to hold his hand. He tried a smile and wink on her, but the tears overpowered the gesture. Dixie tried a smile and wink of her own on him, and although hers was less coordinated, it brought a genuine smile to her father's face which in turn made her smile briefly also.

There were people standing with them and around them: Family and friends—a lot of friends. Dixie knew her mother had been very popular with the people in the small town in which they had lived. As Dixie looked around the crowd, she recognized most of the relatives gathered there, but there were so many people there that she didn't know. She recognized the mayor of Dandridge, his wife, and their children, one of which she went to school with. There was also the sheriff, his wife, and children, and the police chief, with his family. Wow, Dixie thought, her mom must have been really popular.

Directly across the grave stood a man who looked to Dixie to be in his early twenties. He stood in between a half a dozen armed deputies. He wore an orange coverall, his hands were handcuffed, his feet were shackled, and chains ran from the handcuffs and shackles to a wide belt around his waist. This particular man kept his face covered as much as possible. To all outward appearances, he was sobbing great tears of sorrow and regret. When Dixie had asked her father earlier who the man was, her father's only answer was that he was the man that had hit her mother head on in the car crash that had resulted in her death.

"Is he a bad man, Daddy?" Dixie had asked her father.

"I don't think so, honey," her father had told her. "It's just sometimes people do things they wish they hadn't, and sometimes they're in the wrong place at the wrong time. I think both of those things happened to him."

"Why is he here?" Dixie wanted to know.

"The judge wanted him to see how much pain and sorrow he had caused and made it part of his punishment to be here today," Dixie's father told her, this was a dream after all, and some dreams just didn't make sense. When Dixie grew older, she realized her father had been the most patient, forgiving man she had ever known. He had lost his temper with her only a few times as she grew up, but everyone has a rebellious streak during adolescence.

Dixie watched the man crying, keeping his face covered as much as possible. Every so often, Dixie thought she caught a red glint in the man's eyes, and a cruel grin on his lips whenever he looked at her. Dixie would have to ask her father about that later, to see if he saw those things too.

"Our Father in heaven," the minister was praying, "we ask that you show your great mercy on all the living gathered here today. Although we will miss her in this life, we can be comforted in the knowledge that our dear departed sister is residing with your angles right now. Dear Lord, we would ask that you send your angels of comfort to this gathering and pour out your divine mercy and comfort to us all. And Lord we would ask that you touch every soul here, so that one day we can all be greeted in the streets of heaven by this wonderful woman. Amen."

Several "Amens" resounded throughout the gathering. As Dixie opened her teary eyes and raised her head, the man in the restraints looked at her. His eyes were teary also, but glowing red, and that evil grin was back on his face.

"Bye for now, Dixie," he said to her, and it seemed that she was the only one there that saw and heard this. "We will meet again." With that said, the deputies led him away. Dixie never saw him again. No one ever saw him again. Somehow, from the cemetery to the jail, he had successfully made his escape and was never seen again.

Several people approached Dixie and her father, touching them, consoling them, and saying things like, "If you need anything, don't hesitate to call" or "Sorry for your loss" or "Take care of each other." Dixie's father was a rock through it all and graciously accepted every condolence. Some of these people were women that Dixie would see throughout their chang-

244

ing lives. Dixie would learn a few years later that some of these women had provided physical comfort to her father, even one of her aunts, a younger sister of her deceased mother, but none filled the emotional hole left by the passing of her mother. Dixie realized many years later that her father had done that for himself as much as for her. No woman replaced her mother, no woman became her stepmother, although she found out later that some had wanted that role. Her father had not allowed any woman to replace Dixie's mother in marriage. Dixie knew he had had his flings, but she suspected that when they grew just a little serious, he ended them.

As they walked away from the gravesite and toward their car, the rain stopped, and the sun came out. Dixie's father folded the umbrella, handed it to her, squatted down, and motioned for her to climb onto his back. Dixie climbed on and rode her father piggyback style to their car. All thoughts of the strange man in the restraints at the gravesite left her mind completely, and she never thought about him until now, in this dream.

Dixie's dream fast forwarded a few years to the time of her first period. Although her father was quite capable of teaching her the proper hygiene methods, he asked the aunt he had had the fling with to step in and take over. Dixie had had a class and film in school on the changes the female body goes through once puberty strikes, but the hygiene part was not covered. Her aunt was very patient and explained to Dixie what she needed to know. The same aunt would help again once Dixie started dating, and her father wanted a woman to have the sex talk with her.

The first major argument Dixie and her father had was over a dress for her junior homecoming dance. Dixie wanted a black, sleeveless, slit up the side, strapless, see-through-the-back dress. While her father wanted her to have the powder blue, puffy-sleeved, knee-length, padded shouldered, high-collared, zip-up-the-back gown. The argument lasted two days with Dixie crying tears of frustration and sorrow. She had always been able to talk to her father about anything. He had made everything they did together fun.

Whether it be working on cars, he wanted Dixie to know the basics, from changing the motor oil, to changing a flat tire, to telling if a car she was thinking about buying had a lot of body putty or side tracked down the road. He wanted her to have some knowledge in case she had to have one worked on by a mechanic. They planted a vegetable garden every year, and Dixie learned responsibility and discipline through the hard work of maintaining a well-groomed garden. They even managed to raise a few calves. Dixie's father guided her through the process of borrowing the money to purchase the calves, managing her leftover loan money to buy feed and hay for the calves. Then the selling of the calves, the repaying of the loan, the calculation of her profit, and the decision of the purchase of more calves. Everything Dixie and her father did together, he taught her lessons and made them fun.

When he found her crying over the dress, his heart sank.

"Dixie, honey," he tried to comfort her, "I don't want your date thinking he can have his way with you by the way you're dressed."

"Daddy," Dixie said through her tears. "I don't want the dress to make him feel good, I want it to make me feel good about myself."

"Fine, but it shows so much of you," he countered.

"Yes, it does," Dixie admitted, then added, "but the parts it covers will stay covered and private until I decide to share them with someone else."

"I didn't have to hear that," he was shocked.

"Then hear this," Dixie had his attention now. "The time when I do share my body with someone else will not be during or directly after this dance."

Dixie's father bought her the dress she wanted. She went to the dance and came home at the hour her father had requested the same way she had left, a virgin. The loss of her virginity would occur a few years later, while she was with the marines, and with a man she cared for very deeply, and who still called her to this day, but that wasn't part of this dream.

Dixie's father had been sick for a while, but he never complained to her. He tried to hide it as much as he could, but in the end, the pain of the cancer was too much. Dixie spent the last few months of her senior year in high school caring for him. When he could no longer work, the community pitched in with whatever they could do. He had cashed in a fifty thousand dollar life insurance policy he had kept on himself that had finally matured. He paid off the remaining balance of the house mortgage and made his own funeral arrangements.

"Is there anything I can do for you, Daddy?" Dixie asked when the cancer wouldn't allow him to do much more than breathe.

"Oh, Dixie, my sweet Dixie," he whispered, patting her cheek with his hand. "You're beautiful just like your mother was, and I'm proud to be the one you call Daddy."

"I'll do anything you ask, Daddy," she said through her tears.

"John Wayne," he said. "Would you to watch John Wayne movies with me?"

Dixie went out and rented every John Wayne movie she could find. When the managers at these movie rental places found out why she was doing this, they put an unlimited rental on every one of them. When her father had said John Wayne movies, Dixie knew he meant the westerns, and she got everything from Stagecoach to The Shootist and even a few that predated Stagecoach. The only exception she made to the westerns was the movie, The Quiet Man.

During the days when Dixie was in school, volunteers would stay with her father until she got home, and they all understood that no John Wayne movie that had not been viewed by father and daughter together was to be watched in her absence.

"What are you gonna do after you graduate high school?" her father asked Dixie one night as she ate her supper.

"I've been thinking about joining the marines," Dixie told him. "I talked to the recruiter when the school had a military day, and I've already taken their entrance exam."

"What field do you want to pursue?" he was genuinely interested.

"Law enforcement," Dixie never hesitated when she answered him.

"You can do this?" her father asked between his labored breaths.

"The test scores say I can," Dixie answered. She knew it hurt him to talk, but she also knew it would do her no good to try to stop him. Dixie knew he was trying to satisfy himself that she would be okay after he was gone, and she felt she could at least grant him this one wish. Besides, it might make his passing a little easier on both of them, especially him if he knew she could fend for herself.

"Good girl, Dixie," he smiled at her and patted her hand.

"Are you ready for the Duke?" Dixie asked, imitating the speech cadence that people associated with the way John Wayne had spoken. He smiled his answer to her.

Dixie's father held on to life long enough to see her graduate high school, he died two days later. He had prearranged his funeral, taken care of any outstanding debts—there weren't many—and left a clear and binding will, Dixie would get everything. It hadn't been much, but she was grateful for all he had left her, especially the last week of watching John Wayne movies together.

Her father's funeral was modest, he hadn't wanted to spend any more money on it than was absolutely necessary. Dixie knew he had wanted to leave her as much as possible. He was laid to rest next to her mother, and one of the things she had done was purchase one headstone for them both. The people that had gathered for his funeral couldn't say enough good things about him, and all admired the way Dixie had held up during his last few months on this Earth and after his death.

Two weeks after her father's funeral, Dixie left for the U.S. Marine Corps.

Dixie woke from her dream. Her pillow was wet from tears, and her throat felt sore. The memory of the dream was vivid in her mind. She felt sad, and she missed her father. As she lay there in bed, her loneliness consumed her, and she felt all alone in the world.

She checked the time on the alarm clock on the bedside dresser and decided the time was close enough to get up. She went through her routine, showering, the brushing of the teeth, the application of deodorant and perfume. She put up her hair and applied what little makeup she wore.

On her way to work, Dixie stopped at a convenience store for a bagel and a cup of coffee. The morning was cool and clear. The harsh heat and humidity of August had given way to the more comfortable temperatures of September. Soon, Dixie thought, the leaves would be turning. Her thoughts returned to her father, and when this case was wrapped up, she decided she was going to visit his grave.

That put her in a little better mood until she pulled onto the parking lot of the Federal Building. Several reporters were positioned beside the door she went through every morning.

Dixie had been very good about releasing statements to the press each week. She herself didn't give the statements to the press, but encouraged representatives from the different branches of local law enforcement to issue the statements. At first, they had been resistant to this, in times past, the FBI had played the You-give-me-all-the-information-you-have-and-I'll-use-it-to-make-myself-look-better-and-shut-you-out game. Dixie told them that this was their town, their county, their state, and she wanted to lead this investigation from the shadows. It took some time, but she convinced them. As a group, they decided who would give the press the statements each week, and what information would be released. Dixie also encouraged them to go as a group, using the same people so they would become familiar to the public, but alternating their spokesman each week. So far this had worked, but now with little to no results in the investigation, no leads, no suspects, no arrests, the press was getting impatient. They were getting tired of reporting each week that no progress was being made.

Dixie sucked in a three count of air and let out a cleansing breath. She parked the car, opened the door, and got out. When the reporters saw her, they swarmed toward her, and just when she had resigned to the fact that she was going to have to face them, the door she needed to go through swung open.

Several members of the Springfield Police Department, the Greene County Sheriff's Department, and several members of the contingent of FBI agents that were assigned to the Springfield area came through the door, made a protective circle around Dixie, and with military precision, ushered her into the building, closed the doors behind them, and shut the press out.

"Wow," Dixie said to all of them, as she looked at each one. She was out of breath and flushed. "Thank you."

"No problem," one of the deputies told her. "We'll make sure that door stays clear from now on."

"Thank you," Dixie repeated.

"I tell you what," Tom's voice came from behind Dixie. "Now I know how to get these guys to do something after you're gone, just put on a pretty face."

"You old smoothie," Dixie turned to face him. She felt her cheeks fill with the color of embarrassment.

"I was on my way out to escort you in myself when your own personal bodyguards blew past me," Tom told her.

"You?" Dixie emphasized the word by raising an eyebrow at him. "You let a bunch of what you would call snot-nosed brats get past you?"

"I was showing my sensitive side, Agent Crenshaw," Tom said in a mock tone of aristocratic indifference as he straightened and stuck his nose in the air.

Dixie laughed, threw caution to the wind, looped her arm through Tom's, and led him down the hallway to the offices they shared.

When they entered the office, Dixie froze when she saw what was lying on her desk. She had seen photos of the object. It was rectangular and a beige color, and Dixie knew what it was in an instant.

"What's wrong?" Tom asked her when he felt her go still and sensed the abrupt change in her mood.

"The envelope on my desk," Dixie said, she still hadn't moved, "do you see it?"

"Yes," his answer was almost a question.

"Do you know what it is?" Dixie asked, she kept her voice soft and controlled.

"Just an envelope," Tom shrugged. "Dixie what's wrong?"

"It's from him," Dixie murmured, her eyes never left the envelope. "It's from Jack."

"How do you—" Tom stopped, realization dawned in his mind. "It wasn't here when I unlocked the office this morning. The reporters—he used them as a diversion to get in."

"You round up the reporters," Dixie said, she tried not to sound bossy. "I'll get the techs working on this for prints and see if our surveillance cameras picked him up."

"You got it, boss," Tom reluctantly disengaged his arm from Dixie's and ran down the hall toward the door Dixie had been escorted through just a few moments before.

Nothing—nothing that could be useful. The prints matched the prints that had been lifted from the other victims and their effects. Every reporter gave a different description, no two matched, but they all agreed that someone had contacted them in person to tell them that the FBI and the police knew more than they were telling. The video surveillance tapes only recorded his retreating shadows.

Dixie sat at her desk with the note that had come in the envelope in a clear plastic evidence bag. It read:

Dear Dixie,

I've been watching you, and I like very much what I see. You can end all of this by meeting me on my terms. Although you are not my type, I still want to have you very much. I have my cap set for someone else, but before I take her, I want you. I can see you when you're sleeping, and I know when you're awake. If you meet me, the killings will stop, and I will go away after I take the woman of my choice. I'm willing to do whatever it takes to get what I want, the question is, are you? I'll be in touch.

Hope to have you soon,

Jack

Catch me if you can.

Dixie reread the note and hung her head. The two questions that kept running through mind was: Did she have what it took to make the sacrifice

Jack was obviously asking of her—lay down her life so that others could live? The other was: Could he be trusted? She didn't think he could be trusted to stop killing and disappear, these types usually didn't. She could count on one hand the number of people she would be willing to die for, and two of them were already dead, but she felt it unfair to count her parents in that group. That lessened the number by two, and none of them were strangers. She hadn't known any of the victims. Brenda Brewster, the Tennessee State Trooper, was the closest victim that had hit home for Dixie, so far.

Dixie's thoughts turned to the note and envelope. They were very old, over one hundred and fifteen years old. The paper the note had been written on shared the same watermark as did some of the notes that Jack the Ripper had written to Scotland Yard. This sent chills down Dixie's spine. Had Jack the Ripper been reincarnated? She didn't know, but she did know that her fascination with Jack the Ripper was over.

The recent rapes and murders had shaken her. The note today, the one she held in her hands, scared the hell out of her. She had been on her own for over six years now, and she missed her dad, she wanted him here now to comfort her. Her eyes started to tear up when Tom came through the door.

"We may have something," Tom said. Then when he saw her asked, "Are you all right, Dixie?"

"Yes, I'm fine," Dixie said, she rose to her feet, and wiped her eyes with her fingertips.

"We can wait a few moments if you need to," Tom offered. He took a step toward her, but stopped.

"I'm fine," Dixie repeated, and smiled at him. "What do we have?"

"An eyewitness that says he saw a truck and cop car on the shoulder of the road on I-24 at the bottom of the westbound slope of Monteagle the day Officer Brewster disappeared," Tom told her.

"Is he legit?" Dixie asked. "How do we know this isn't another trick by our friend Jack to throw us off track?"

"He's a known offender to the State of Tennessee," Tom filled her in. "He was stopped here in Springfield for a traffic violation, speeding I think. Anyway, when the arresting officer ran his name, the computer kicked out an outstanding warrant from Tennessee."

"What does Tennessee want with him?" Dixie was refocused now.

"Drug trafficking," Tom talked as they left the room and walked toward the interrogation rooms. "It seems, he was arraigned on drug trafficking, released on bail, and never showed for his day in court."

"Tennessee wants him back?" Dixie felt she already knew the answer to that question.

"You bet," Tom confirmed. "They're on their way to get him."

"Are they allowing us any room to maneuver?" Dixie asked.

"I'm sure they will, they want Jack worse than this—" Tom didn't finish the sentence, he preferred Dixie to fill in the blank. She smiled her appreciation at him.

"What's his name?" Dixie asked. She and Tom had driven from the Federal Building to the Greene County Lock Up where the prisoner was being held.

"Lewis Chambers, age twenty-two, high school graduate. Two prior convictions, one drug trafficking, the other assault, both unrelated. He did community service on the trafficking charge and served one year for the assault charge. I guess he figured this was his third strike, so he ran," Tom read from a piece of paper in an opened file folder.

"Have you talked to him yet?" Dixie asked him. She and Tom were watching Lewis through a one-way glass, he was sitting on a chair pulled up to a table.

"Nope," Tom said. "I was waiting to see how you wanted to handle this."

"I'm sure he will want to plea bargain," Dixie thought out loud. "As much as I want to catch this Jack, I don't want to let this guy walk."

"Let's play it by ear," Tom suggested. "See what he has to say, see where it leads."

"Okay," Dixie nodded. "Good cop, bad cop?"

"Can I be the bad cop this time?" Tom asked, Dixie recognized the telltale stern humor in his tone.

"You are bad," Dixie played along.

"And don't you forget it, little missy," Tom leaned toward her, and gave her a leering grin.

"Come on," Dixie stifled a grin and started toward the door to the interrogation room. She paused with her hand on the door. "Tom, let me handle this at first. If he seems unresponsive to anything I have to say, I'll give you a look, at that point, I want you to scare the pants off of him."

"You sure about that?" Tom asked, he looked Dixie in the eye.

"We need answers, something to link with Diane and Selena's account,"

Dixie said.

"You got it," Tom assured her.

The young man known as Lewis looked up from the table at which he had been sitting as Dixie and Tom came through the opened door which Tom closed behind him. Lewis looked at Dixie as if he was undressing her with his eyes. Dixie knew they had made the right choice about who would play the good cop, and who would play the bad cop.

Lewis sat leaning back as far as he could in the chair. He had shoulder length, light brown hair which looked like it needed to be washed. Acne was running its course on his young face and would leave its telltale pock-marked scars. He was dressed in jeans, the current style was called wide legs, and Dixie knew if Lewis stood to his feet, the crotch of his jeans would hang down to his knees. He wore a T-shirt that looked to be two sizes too big for him, a denim jacket, and expensive running shoes. He also wore a baseball cap with the bill pointed down his back and the elastic band pulled down to just above his eyebrows.

"Hello, Mr. Chambers," Dixie opened her badge case to show him her shield. "I'm FBI Special Agent Dixie Crenshaw, and this is my partner FBI Special Agent Tom Bradford. We would like to ask you a few questions about what you saw at the bottom of Monteagle," Dixie sat on the chair across the table from Lewis.

"FBI?" Lewis looked puzzled. "What do the Feds want with me?"

"We believe you may have information concerning a crime we are investigating," Dixie stated, as she folded her hands in front of her on the table and looked directly at Lewis.

"Crime?" Lewis shifted his gaze to Tom, who was leaning against a wall across the room, then back to Dixie. "What are you talking about?"

"The statement you made to the arresting officer about seeing a Tennessee State Trooper car that had a semi-truck pulled over at the bottom of Monteagle," Dixie said, she kept her tone and gaze flat.

"Yeah," Lewis's expression turned to that of a fox about to invade the hen house. "I might have some information about that, but not for free, like I told that cop that busted me."

"Not for free, Mr. Chambers?" Dixie played the part of being perplexed.

"I mean, I'll tell you what I saw, but I want a lesser sentence in return," Lewis never batted an eye. The chair he sat in was on casters and had a swivel base. He adopted a posture of relaxed indifference and swiveled himself in half circles back and forth.

"I can't make any promises, Mr. Chambers," Dixie made her eyes go wide in an expression of shocked bewilderment.

"Then neither can I," Lewis found something interesting to look at on his fingernails.

"Mr. Chambers, I'll do what I can, but with your past record, it would be wrong of me to tell you that I can affect the outcome of your hearing," Dixie tried again.

"Let me know when you're ready to deal, and I'll tell you what I know," Lewis said dismissively.

"Surely even you know that the jumping bail and fleeing across state lines won't look good for you," Dixie said, looking right at him. Lewis remained silent. "We are asking for your help. Several women are already dead, and I fear more will follow if we don't stop this guy. You can help us do that."

"And what do I get in return?" was Lewis's only concern.

"What if one of these women was your mother, or a sister, wife, or girl-friend?" Tom spoke for the first time.

"Well, they're not," Lewis shot back. "What's the big deal about this truck at the bottom of the mountain, anyway?"

"We believe it may hold some answers to some questions we have about the killer," Dixie said.

"Well, if the killer is a truck driver, it wouldn't surprise me," Lewis said, he relished the idea of being the center of Dixie's attention for the moment. "I mean all they ever do is stink up wherever they go, they drive slow and make way too much noise, and they're always in the way."

"Thanks for clearing that up for us," Tom said in a sarcastic tone.

"Can you give us a description of the truck?" Dixie asked, she shot a questioning look at Tom.

"I want some guarantee from you that you'll help me before I answer that," Lewis insisted.

"I can't give you that with your past record," Dixie stood her ground. "Now what about this truck you saw?"

"Not until you give me something," Lewis raised his voice.

"I can't promise you anything," Dixie kept her voice calm. "What did the truck look like."

"I want to see a lawyer," Lewis said.

"What color was the truck?" Dixie didn't let up.

"A lawyer," Lewis reiterated.

"What name appeared on the side of the truck?" Dixie kept pushing.

"It was just a fucking truck! All right?" Lewis slammed his hands down on the table top as he screamed at Dixie.

Dixie took a deep breath, let it out, and shook her head slowly. She looked at Lewis with pity in her eyes. She looked at her wrist watch, pushed herself back from the table, and rose to her feet.

"I need to make a phone call," Dixie said as she approached Tom. Tom nodded his understanding and took a step away from the wall.

"Wait," Lewis said to Dixie as he watched Tom. "Where are you goin'?"

"I'm not leaving," Dixie said to him over her shoulder. "I'm just going to call about a sick friend. I'm just going to move over here and ask you two gentlemen to hold the noise down." She took out her cell phone and absently punched in the number for time and temperature.

"Oh, I get it," Lewis showed Tom a sly look. "Good cop, bad cop tag team."

"I don't know about any of that," Tom said in a calm tone. He calmly approached the one-way glass and lowered the louvered blinds. Next, he twisted the rod to close the blinds. When he had accomplished this, Tom stood in front of Lewis on the opposite side of the table. "But I do know that play time is over."

Just as Lewis realized what Tom had said and before he could react, Tom reached across his body to the left with his right hand. He stooped slightly, and gripped the end of the table with his right hand. Tom exploded with movement. He stood erect and, with his right arm and the twisting of his body, lifted the table off the floor and sent it crashing into the wall across the room from Dixie. Next, Tom took one large step toward Lewis, who, out of fear, leaned back in the chair to the point that he almost tipped it over. Tom planted his left foot on the chair seat between Lewis's legs and gave a forceful kick that sent Lewis rocketing backwards in the chair. Lewis screamed his fear, waved his arms in the air, and kicked his feet until the back of his chair collided with the wall behind him.

Lewis's head smacked the same wall just a second after the chair did, and he instinctively covered the injured part of his head with his hands. The instant his hands made contact with his head, Tom gripped Lewis by the throat, forced his head back, and trapped Lewis's hands behind his head, against the wall. Tom's face was inches away from Lewis's. His grip cut off Lewis's air, but Tom knew his own limits and was still in control.

"Now you listen to me, you little shit," Tom said in a low menacing growl, making his eyes mere slits. "I'm only gonna waste my breath on your sorry ass one time. I was a Viet Nam POW, tortured every day. If you don't tell me what I want to know, I'll show you in great detail what Charlie did to me, and you'll be begging me to turn you over to the State of Tennessee. Do you fucking understand me?"

Lewis's only answer was a wince, a blink of his terrified eyes, and a moan. Tom released Lewis and backed away from him. As Lewis continued to rub the back of his aching head with one hand and massage his throat with the other, Tom retrieved the table he had slung across the room and put it back in place.

"Okay, bye," Dixie said into her unresponsive cell phone and closed it.

"Did you see what that maniac did to me?" Lewis accused Tom as Dixie turned to face them.

"See what? Who?" Dixie asked, then said. "I was on the phone, and thank you both for being quiet while I was on the phone."

"You didn't see—" Lewis started, then stopped, somehow knowing his pleas would get him nowhere.

"Now, Mr. Chambers," Dixie said as she put away her phone and reseated herself in the chair across the table from Lewis, continuing as if nothing had transpired. "Can I get your cooperation, or do I need to make another phone call and this time leave the room."

"No! No." Lewis said as he gave Tom a frightful look. "I'll try to remember what I saw. Where is that other agent that said he would help me?"

"Other agent?" Dixie didn't have to act confused.

"Yeah, he said that if I played your game, that in the end you would help me," Lewis said, his tone sounded desperate.

"What was this agent's name?" Dixie really had no idea what was going on now.

"Lucas," Lewis said, paused, giving the impression of deep concentration, "Daniels. Lucas Daniels."

Afterwards, as Lewis was being prepped to be transported to Tennessee, Tom and Dixie were strolling outside the building. The sky was clear, and the air crisp. The transition from summer to fall in the Ozarks can be as different as night and day. Sometimes summer and fall can kind of cooperate, summer giving way to fall in a seemingly gentle ushering gesture. Other times, fall seems to kick the door down and barge right on in with winter tight on its heels. This was not the case this year, the sun was out and it was pleasant, a gentle breeze caressed the leaves of the trees and made them sound as if they too enjoyed the weather by sighing their pleasure.

"Tom, I didn't know you were a Viet Nam POW," Dixie said to him.

"Well—" Tom let it hang there as he made a seesaw motion with one of his hands.

"You weren't a Viet Nam POW?" Dixie's tone was accusing, but filled with humor.

"That statement was half right," Tom stopped walking, and looked at Dixie as she stood and looked at him. "I was there—in Viet Nam, but never a POW."

"Was it bad?" Dixie asked, her voice was quiet and inquisitive.

"You know, most Viet Nam Vets don't like to talk about their experiences with people who weren't there, because if you weren't there being faced with what Charlie was throwing at us, and having to make the kind of decisions we had to make, then there's no way you can possibly understand why we did what we were forced to do," Tom's voice was rigid, as his whole body went stiff. Then, he seemed to relax. "I'm sorry, Dixie, I didn't mean to get gruff."

"It's all right, Tom," Dixie put a comforting hand on his arm. Tom looked at Dixie's hand on his arm, then looked into her eyes.

"I enlisted and went over there thinking I was doing my duty for my country, taking a page from JFK, asking not what my country could do for me, but what I could do for my country," Tom started, a far off look in his eyes as he tilted his head back slightly. "I kept my nose out of trouble, did what was asked of me. Went on patrol when it was my turn, even volunteered for a few extra when it was slow and quiet. Saw the usual action for over there. Got shot at more times than I could count. Saw guys next to me shot down. Saw friends blown to bits by mines. We would just be walking along, and all of a sudden, a loud boom, and we would be in the middle of a fire fight. Bullets flying all around us, making snapping sounds in our ears whenever they would go right by our heads. Some of the younger draftees crying for their mothers, pissing their pants, scared out of their minds.

"We would search villages, looking for Charlie. Search for weapons, these people had nothing, dirt poor, just trying to survive. Just when you would start to feel sorry for them, a kid would run up to you out of nowhere with a shoe shine box that was wired with a grenade. Or we would be out on patrol, and one minute we would see women and children working in the rice paddies, and the next minute those same women and children would be shooting at us with enemy weapons. It got to the point that we didn't know who the enemy was. The attitude among most of us was to kill them all, and let God sort them out.

"People who weren't there don't realize that the NVA and the Viet Cong issued bounties on all GIs, especially officers. The NVA, and the Viet Cong more or less told these people that the more American solders they killed, the more of their family members would be spared. About the only Vietnamese we trusted were the Montenyards."

"Montenyards?" Dixie asked, the word feeling funny as it rolled off her tongue.

"Yea, Montenyards, a fierce tribe of people that lived in the mountains. They could be mean, and never ran from a fight. We used them as guides, but they would also engaged the enemy. They still used bow and arrows, and spears, sometimes crossbows," Tom explained, then continued.

"The North Vietnamese Army, the NVA, was made up of tenacious fighters. The Viet Cong were tough guerrilla fighters who knew the terrain and had very imaginative hiding places. Sometimes it was like fighting ghosts. Sometimes they would force civilians to do what they wanted them to do by harming or killing their relatives or friends.

"I did some things over there that I'm not very proud of, Dixie. Things that I had to do in order to survive. Things that took years of therapy to deal with the memories afterwards.

"Then, after I did my tours, I came home to a country that was in turmoil. I started to doubt my justification in Viet Nam, but I soon learned that I wasn't alone, there were others just like me. We were confused, hurt, and sometimes ashamed. At one time, I wanted to die. Then I met the woman who would become my wife, and that started my healing process.

"She told me I should take the lemons life had given me and make lemonade. So I did, I went to college on the GI Bill, took the FBI exam, and went back to work for my country. We got married, I got assigned to the Springfield area, and this is where we settled.

"One of the bright spots in my life was taken from me four years ago when she was raped and stabbed to death. The guy was never caught.

"You ask me if it was bad. Yes, it was bad over there, but not nearly as bad as living through all of that, coming home to find someone like her who could love someone like me, only to lose her to someone like him.

"Dixie, you won't have to ask me to back you up, I'll be there. I'll do anything to help catch this guy, even lie to little pissants like Lewis."

Dixie patted Tom's arm again, she knew it had taken a lot for him to tell her all of that, and she had a greater respect for him. She had known other Viet Nam vets, but none had been as open with her as Tom had just been. She released his arm and looked away as he wiped a couple of runaway tears from his cheeks. She heard him sniffle and let out a deep sigh.

"I'm sorry," Tom muttered, he kept his voice low, trying to hide the tremor there.

"For what?" Dixie almost sounded indignant, then her tone eased. "I lost my mother to a drunk driver when I was very young, and my father when I was a senior in high school to a different kind of killer, cancer, and I never once saw him use tobacco. I know about the injustice of losing people you love, and don't you apologize to me for being human about it."

"Thank you, Dixie," Tom said quietly. She nodded, and offered him an understanding smile.

"Tom, have you ever heard of a branch of the Bureau called the SOI?" Dixie asked him.

"No, I haven't, but that doesn't mean it doesn't exist," Tom reflected.

"And Lucas Daniels?" Dixie pondered.

"Your guess is as good as mine, probably better than mine," Tom winked at her.

"I think it's time I made an unscheduled phone call to the deputy director," Dixie said.

"You go, Dixie," Tom said in a mock cheer, "and don't take any shit off him."

A little over one hour later, Dixie once again found herself puzzling over the note that Jack had somehow gotten to her. It didn't seem possible, but here it was. How, she wondered, could have someone gotten paper this old and slipped passed every security device in the building? It seemed unnatural, almost supernatural. She let her thoughts stop there, not wanting to believe.

"Well?" Tom said, he was leaned against the door jamb. The sound of his voice made Dixie jump ever so slightly.

"What?" Dixie sounded as if she had been sleeping.

"What did the deputy director have to say?" Tom came into the room, and sat close to Dixie.

"He denied any knowledge of the existence of a branch of the FBI known as the SOI," Dixie sounded as if she was quoting. "He went on to say that there is no agent currently with the Bureau named Lucas Daniels."

"Okay," Tom said. "Tell me this, how did this guy get inside this building, and participate in a closed meeting?"

"I wish I knew," Dixie said. "We should probably consider the fact that he was our killer."

"If he was our boy, then I give him credit for having balls," Tom said.

"Do you think it's possible that the killer is a truck driver?" Dixie asked.

"What do you know about truck drivers?" Tom answered with his own question.

"There were a couple of truck stops around Dandridge where I grew up. I know what they look like," Dixie said.

"When the eastbound and westbound scale houses were open in Strafford, there were a few times the Bureau was asked to participate in cases dealing with kidnapping, gunrunning, things along that line. Some of those guys had some pretty imaginative places to hide things—and people," Tom said.

"I wonder why we never considered truck drivers before?" Dixie wondered aloud.

"It's hard to say, especially with all the weird crap goin' on with this case," Tom said.

"I think I'll make some phone calls to a couple of the trucking companies here in town, maybe they can help us out," Dixie said.

"I might have something too," Tom said.

"Oh?" Was Dixie's only response as she cocked an eyebrow at him.

"A lady dispatcher for a local trucking company on the west side of town called the task force a couple of nights ago, said one of their drivers pulled some kind of magic trick with his face the other night. I didn't think much of it until now," Tom said. "I think I'll call the trucking company, see when she works again, and swing by to see her."

Chapter 20

Diane was waiting tables again. She wore her waitress uniform which consisted of a pink dress with the hem at mid-thigh. The uniform dress had white lace around the ends of the arm sleeves and the collar. The uniform dresses of all the waitresses were made to fit their bodies snugly, and Diane's fit really tightly around her large breasts. She wore a dark pink apron over the uniform dress that covered her from neck to waist, tying in the back. She also wore tan pantyhose and white walking shoes.

After she and Jason had finished making love, he had taken a shower and gotten ready to leave. As he packed, Diane had taken a hot bath to also get ready for work. Jason didn't want to leave. She knew that he, in fact, always hated to leave home. The question everyone always asked was: Then why do it? The answer Jason always gave was, "I'm good at it, I can pretty much pick my own hours and loads, and nothing else pays like it does."

It was her third night back to work, Diane comforted herself with the knowledge that Jason hated leaving her. Neither of them had ever had this type of relationship, each hating being apart, but loving the reunions that took place afterwards. Besides, this was a bad time of the year to be taking time off.

Primarily, the trucking industry gets a bit of a boost between the months of October and December because of the Christmas holidays. Chain stores that have regional warehouses purchase huge amounts of toys, clothes, and items that can be intended for Christmas gifts, such as power tools, or hunting and fishing equipment. Diane knew that Blanket Transportation had done her a huge favor by letting Jason take the time off he had taken for her benefit this close to that season. Also, this was the time of the year when the money for the license and permits pertaining to the truck would be collected. Usually Blanket Transportation would automatically withhold these funds at about one hundred dollars per week. The cost of the license and permits for the Peterbilt that Jason drove usually ran about sixteen hundred dollars per year.

Diane busied herself with her work, thinking happy thoughts about the last few days she and Jason had just spent together. Never had any man taken the time that Jason had taken to be at her beck and call. Diane didn't know how she could love him more, but she found herself wanting to, especially in light of the events that led up to them spending those days together. He had risked his life to get home to her, had risked his future employment with Blanket Transportation by staying home with her, had been very gentle with her and indulged her every whim, and had asked nothing in return. He had never once asked what was in it for him, but had stayed by her side as long as she had needed or wanted him there.

Diane thought about these things as she stood at her work station wrapping dining utensils in napkins. The small television there was on low volume, and the weatherman was giving his summary on the small screen.

The other people Diane worked with had been very gracious to her upon her return. The other waitresses had welcomed her back to work with warm greetings and hugs. The male cooks also did so awkwardly, offering her shy smiles and blushes. Even Stu was amiable and didn't make a big deal about how he had let her take the time off.

Diane looked out the huge windows that separated the dining room from the parking lot. Night had fallen, and the parking lot lights were lit. It had recently stopped raining, and everything Diane could see though the windows seemed shiny. The air had been chilly before the rain, and now it was even more so. It seemed that whenever it rained like this, the business in the truck stop restaurant improved. That had been the case this time, and the rush had come and gone.

"Diane," Stu was standing in front of her.

"Yes," Diane shook herself out of her reverie. "Hi."

"You all right?" Stu asked, looking into her eyes.

"I'm fine. Did you need something?" Diane broke off the gaze with Stu. She suspected the way he felt about her and didn't want to give him any encouragement.

"I need you to stick the tanks," Stu said.

"Stick the tanks?" Diane said as if not comprehending. She knew what it meant, had done it many times before, she just didn't particularly want to do it now, after dark, and in the cold. This meant she would have to go outside and go to the shed at the rear of the main building. The shed was located between the rear wall of the main building and another shed, making a sort of alleyway. She would have to fumble around in the dark unlocking the padlock on the door there because there was no light out there, get the long stick out of the shed, lock the door back because Stu was afraid someone might steal something out of the shed, measure the amount of fuel in each underground tank, record the reading, and replace the stick in the shed, all while trying to keep warm. Not what she really wanted to do, especially after her encounter with Jack not so long ago.

"You want me to stick the tanks?" Diane asked again.

"Yeah," Stu said, "the day crew didn't get it done today."

"Can't one of the guys do it?" Diane tried not to sound like she was pleading.

"No, one of the guys can't do it," Stu sounded as if he was mocking her. "They're all busy, everyone in here is busy, and besides, everyone else has been carrying your load while you were off, so I need you to do this."

"All right," Diane said in a sheepish tone. She didn't want to, but she would. She left what she was doing and retrieved the jacket she had worn to work. She got the key ring that held the key to the padlock to the shed door and a flashlight from behind the fuel desk, and walked outside. The air was crisp, cool, and damp, as Diane took in a couple of deep cleansing breaths.

Diane found the key to the padlock on the key ring and held it tightly in her hand. She pushed the button on the flashlight and checked to make sure the flashlight worked. Then, she stepped around the corner to the shed. It was dark, as she had known it would be, and wished Jason was here now to hold her. She put the key in the lock, turned it, and the lock popped open, Diane jumped at the small clicking sound it made. She took the padlock off, swung the hasp open, and hung the unlocked padlock through the eye-hole. She then pulled the handle to the shed door, the shed actually was an old trailer container, it swung up, and Diane pulled it toward her, and then swung it away. She pulled the door open on creaky hinges, which did nothing to calm her already edgy nerves.

Diane illuminated the dark interior of the shed/container with the beam of her flashlight until she found the measuring stick. The fuel must be really low for Stu to be this worried about how much was in the tanks, Diane thought. In a way she thought Stu was right, no one there had not said a bad word to her about the time off she had taken. She reasoned it wasn't for him that she was doing this but for her coworkers.

The areas where Diane had to stick the tanks were well lit. One was on the truck diesel fuel islands and the other was near the gasoline pumps. After each reading, she would record the result with an ink pen and order pad she kept in her apron. With this chore done, Diane returned the measuring stick to the shed/container, and closed the door.

Diane thought she heard someone behind her just as she swung the door handle into place, but when she whirled around and directed her light in the darkness, a slight mist from the moisture in the air was all she saw. She returned to her task, flipped the hasp into place, put the padlock through the eyehole, and clicked it shut without jumping this time. When she turned to leave, Stu stood there in her path, not more than two inches away from her.

Diane sucked in a huge amount of air with an audible sound and dropped the flashlight. She staggered backwards against the door of the shed/container, and concentrated on getting her breathing and heart rate under control.

"Are you okay?" Stu asked, taking a step toward her.

"What do you think?" Diane was indignant. "You scared the bejeesus out of me."

"I didn't mean to," Stu offered as a way of apology.

"What are you doing out here?" Diane's tone was suspicious, and she had a pretty good idea what Stu's answer would be.

"I came to check on you," Stu said, "to make sure you are okay."

"I was fine until you showed up and nearly scared me to death," Diane accused.

"I—" Stu started, stopped, then tried again. "I think you know how I feel about you."

"Oh, please," Diane almost scoffed and tried to brush passed him in the small space.

"I mean it," Stu stopped her by barring her way with one of his arms.

"I'm happily married to a man I love," Diane's fear suddenly changed to anger, as she turned to face him. "Besides I'm fifteen years older than you, I've already raised my kids."

"I would never do anything to hurt you, Diane," Stu said, lightly caressing her hair with the hand he had used to bar her way. When Diane made to push passed him, Stu grabbed her by her upper arms and pushed her against the rear exterior wall of the main building.

The force Stu used to push her against the wall momentarily forced the air out of Diane's lungs, he pressed his chest against hers. She stood with the wall pressing against her back, and Stu pressing his body against her front. She gasped for breath as Stu placed his mouth over hers, slipped his tongue into her mouth, flicked the end of hers with his, then retracted it before Diane could bite down on it. If that wasn't enough of a shock, she felt him shift his weight and body, then pull the zipper down at the back of her uniform dress and force her legs apart with one of his knees. Diane had the briefest thought that he had done this, or something like this, before. She somehow twisted out of the lip lock he had on her, just as she felt him start to grind his pelvis against hers, letting her feel his erection. The next thing she felt was him unhooking her bra with the deft movements of the fingers of one hand. She finally remembered her arms were free and tried to use them. First, she tried to push against him, then she tried to hit him with her hands and fists, then eventually she tried to scratch him with her fingernails, but he was pressed so tightly against her that she couldn't get good leverage to push him away, and he had his face buried between her shoulder and face. She could only hit his back, and the only bare skin he gave her access to was the back of his neck, and besides, he had his chest pressed so hard against her sternum again that it was hard for her to breathe, and her muscles felt tired and stiff from the lack of air. He kept his hair cut short, too short for her to pull with her hands, and he kept his face buried close to her neck. Diane felt shock and revulsion run through her body as she realized that Stu was sucking on the side of her neck, trying to give her a hickey.

"I want to see, feel, touch you all over," Stu breathed in Diane's ear, then he started to suck in a new spot on her neck.

"Please, stop," Diane gasped, tears streaked her cheeks, and she found she couldn't move when she tried.

"I want you," Stu whispered. Diane could hear the passion in his voice, and that scared her even more. As if he had read her mind, Stu covered her mouth with one of his hands to prevent her from screaming, while he fumbled with the belt, button, and zipper to his pants, and found another spot to suck on the side of her neck. Diane wondered how many of her co-workers Stu had done this very thing to, and she started to cry.

Diane had never been raped before, didn't want to be now, and wondered how she would cope with it afterwards. She knew Stu's life wouldn't be worth a plug nickel when Jason found out what had happened. Jason, she thought, would he even want her after this?

Diane doubled her efforts to get away. It was hard for her to move, Stu had her legs spread wide, which made it hard for her to get any leverage, and they were barely touching the ground. One of his hands was clamped tight over her mouth and was pressing the back of her head against the concrete block wall, which hurt, and her head was pressed back at such an angle that she couldn't see what was going on, which added to her anxiety. Stu's other hand was now ripping at her panties. Somehow, he had ripped open her pantyhose, and now he was ripping at the last barrier between her and his bare, stiff penis.

"No! Let me go!" Diane shouted when Stu took his hand away from her mouth. It seemed he had given up on ripping her panties, and was content to hold her panties aside.

"I think the lady said no," Diane heard a voice say. She recognized the voice, but couldn't place it. Stu had heard it too, flinched, and Diane and Stu both turned toward the voice at the same time.

Diane found it hard to believe who she saw standing in the opening of the small alleyway created by the exterior main wall of the main building and the other shed/container.

"I like the way you've arranged these," the man gestured with one of his hands at the alleyway. He started to walk toward them.

"You're not allowed to be here," Stu said to the man while keeping Diane pressed against the wall. Diane pleaded for help from the man with her eyes.

"I'm here now, and you're gonna let her go," the man said in a calm voice. When he stepped forward into the glow thrown off by the dropped flashlight, recognition came over Diane. The man was a dead ringer for the character Eric Schweig had played in the movie, The Missing.

Diane's anxiety didn't ease up. Although this man was possibly her savior, how would she react if this man tried to touch her? She drew inward on herself and tried to close out the world. Diane closed her eyes, tried to shut this reality, she thought of her daughters, then she thought of Jason.

Diane heard Jason's voice in her head as he had told her once before, "Rape isn't really about sex, but about control. Rape is usually motivated mainly by anger, never love or sex. There are exceptions to the rule, date rape, for one. Men that commit date rape are typically control freaks, not wanting to take no" for an answer." While she thought about Jason, she thought about every aspect of him, and that's when she thought about how he was such a movie nut. That thought led her into the next one, a barely remembered fact that Jason had told her about the actor Eric Schweig, that he had played the part of one of her all time favorite movie characters, that of Uncas in Michael Mann's production of The Last of the Mohicans.

Diane snapped her eyes open, and there before her stood someone who looked very much like the character Uncas that Eric Schweig had portrayed so well. Diane didn't know whether to be relieved or scared even more. She got a grip on reality, as much as she could anyway, and made herself realize that the man that stood there was not Uncas, or even Eric Schweig playing Uncas, but Jack.

"I wasn't asking then, and I'm not asking now, Stu, let her go," Jack said, his voice sounded like a deep rumble.

"How do you know my na—" Stu started, stopped, looked more intently at Jack, then as some form of recognition hit Stu, he released Diane, and stepped away from her. Stu started to blubber, his chin quivered, and his bottom lip flapped in and out as his eyes filled with tears. He stood in a half crouch, grabbed at his sagging pants, stumbled, and slammed his back into the shed/container opposite of the wall that he had just had Diane pinned against.

"No!" Stu screamed, but Diane doubted if anyone else heard it. Diane also reasoned that if Jack could project a certain image of himself at her, then he could probably do the same thing to Stu, although she doubted that Stu saw the same image she saw.

"How did you find me?" Stu asked. He couldn't seem to make his fingers do the necessary movements to get his pants where they needed to be in order to fasten them.

"My, my," Jack chuckled, his eyes glowed a slight red. "You remember me. That's good. I thought the last time we met, I fixed it so it would be hard for you to beat off, let alone attempt something like this, but I guess Viagra does work wonders."

Both Stu and Diane involuntarily looked at Stu's still erect penis, both with shocked expressions, but for different reasons. Diane was shocked, that even after the sudden emotional change that Stu had just went through, his erection was still at full mast, if that was what full mast looked like on him. Stu was terrified out of his mind that Jack would find some way to use it against him.

"I'm here to save you," Jack said to Diane, as he took another step forward, raised a hand, and offered it to her.

"No you're not. The last time we met you were no better than him," Diane said as she motioned toward Stu. She took another step backward, stepped on the flashlight, lost her balance when it tried to roll away, and sat down hard on her rump with a splash in the middle of a low spot in the pavement that had filled with water from the recent rain.

Stu took the opportunity of Jack directing all of his attention toward Diane to try to escape. Stu took two steps when Jack grabbed him by his shirt front, and yanked him around to face Jack. Stu let out a pain and shock filled grunt.

"Please," Stu sobbed, the memory of the last beating he had taken from this man was still very vivid in his memory.

Diane started to cry, not particularly for Stu, but for the situation they were in right now. She still sat in the water, she felt it on her bottom, and knew her panties, pantyhose, and dress were soaking it up. She put her hands on the ground and into the water, and tried to scoot further away from the violence that she was afraid was about to erupt in front of her. She continued to weep as she scooted away. The violence she was afraid of happened and was over before she could comprehend.

Jack took one step forward and shoved Stu into the container that was at his back. Then as Stu bounced off the container wall, Jack still had a firm grip on Stu's shirt, Jack took one large step backward, and yanked Stu forward with all of his might, and at the same time kneed Stu in the crotch. Stu screamed again, and grabbed at his aching groin as Jack yanked Stu forward again, then released his grip on him, and sidestepped out of Stu's path. Stu ran face first, full speed, and with no attempt on his part to stop himself, into the concrete block wall against which only a few moments ago he had had Diane pinned. As Stu bounced off this wall, blood spouted from his nose and mouth. Jack grabbed him by the scruff of the neck and spun him around to face Diane who was still sitting in the cold water. Jack kicked Stu on the back of the leg, right behind the knee, and forced him down onto his knees.

"You better make this apology really heartfelt," Jack rasped at Stu. "You better make me believe you're sorry."

"Diane, I'm really sorry," Stu blubbered through his bloody lips, and then his voice took on a more urgent tone. "Please forgive me."

Diane's only response was to nod; she too was shocked and terrified to speak.

"Get up," Jack said to Stu, pulling him to his feet by his ears. Jack turned Stu toward the opening of the little alleyway, and delivered a hard, forceful kick to Stu's rump. Stu stumbled forward and fell face first into another low spot filled with water from the recent rain.

"If you even dream about this woman, I will end your useless existence," Jack hissed to Stu, his eyes were almost completely red.

Stu got to his feet slowly, walked away, and never once looked back toward Diane.

"Let me help you to your feet," Jack said to Diane as he extended a hand toward her.

"Please, just leave me alone," Diane said to the image of Eric Schweig in the character of Uncas, as she cried more tears.

"I'm the only way out of here," Jack tried again, smiling at Diane as he extended his hand toward her once more.

Diane reluctantly took the proffered hand, and Jack gently helped her to her feet. He placed his other hand on the small of her back, and felt her bare skin there, as she jumped from the touch of his hand on her bare skin.

"I'm sorry," Jack pulled his hand away. "Let me help you." Jack zipped up the back of Diane's uniform dress. Diane stepped toward the opening of the small alleyway, and tried to still herself from running.

"I'll be around if you need me, Diane," Jack called to her lightly.

"I'll be fine, just please leave me and my family alone," Diane mustered the courage to say.

"Yes, you are fine," Diane heard Jack say, and she knew his words carried a double meaning. When she turned to look at him, he was gone, and that spooked her even more. There was only one way out of there, she stood in it, yet Jack had pulled a Houdini right in front of her. This time she did run and didn't stop until she was inside the restaurant.

When the other two women Diane worked with saw her coming, both of them did double takes at her. They saw the mixed expression on her face of bewilderment, shock, and shame, along with the tears that streamed from her eyes. They saw the disarray of her clothes, the uniform dress that didn't fit just right, the bra that had evidently quit working, the sagging pantyhose, and the disheveled hair, and they both feared the worst. Both of the two waitresses immediately stopped what they were doing, and rushed to Diane's side, each fearing that she might collapse in the middle of the dinning area. They each took an arm and ushered Diane to a small alcove behind the kitchen that they used as a break area. When they had her seated, one of the waitresses returned to the kitchen for a glass of water, while the other dug a cell phone out of her purse.

"We need to call the police," Erin, the waitress that had retrieved the cell phone said.

By that time, Sandy, the other waitress returned with the glass of water and handed it to Diane. Diane thankfully accepted the offered glass and took a sip. She nodded, then shook her head side to side.

"No," Diane said. "Sandy would you please hand me my purse?"

Sandy did as she was asked and handed Diane her purse. Diane unzipped it, and pulled out her wallet, unsnapped it, and pulled out a business card.

"May I use your phone?" Diane asked Erin who immediately handed it to her.

Tom entered the dispatch office and stopped for a moment to take in his surroundings, he guessed he was in the driver's lounge. He had entered through the door Marcia had requested. Against one wall, stood several vending machines of all types, one for sandwiches, one for sodas, one offered juices and sports drinks, another presented chips, cookies, and candy through its clear glass front, and one for hot drinks, coffee, hot chocolate, soup. Arranged in the middle of the room were two plush sofas facing each other, on either side of a coffee table. There was a dining room-sized table with matching chairs between the sofas and vending machines. On the wall opposite the vending machines was mounted a twenty-five inch color television, which was tuned to a local station, the volume on low.

Across the room from the door through which Tom had just entered, there was a row of six large double-paned glass panels. On the other side of these glass panels, Tom could see a countertop that was built right up next to the glass panels and separated on each side by partitions made of the same countertop material. The partitions gave the countertop the appearance of desks that faced the glass panels. On each one of these desks was a telephone, a computer monitor with keyboard, writing implements, and personal effects, such as photographs of spouses and children or grandchildren.

Behind one of these sat a large, overweight man, talking on the telephone. The big man seemed to be in an argument with the party on the other end of the phone line. His face was red, and he looked to Tom as thought he was about to go into a cardiac arrest. Tom turned away and tried to suppress a smile that threatened to break across his face.

"I swear, I wish truck drivers hadn't changed with the times," the large man said to Tom as he placed the handset to the telephone back into its cradle with a severe motion.

"Problem?" Tom inquired. This man looked to be about Tom's age and had an attitude of no nonsense about him that Tom liked immediately.

"Used to be you could give a truck driver a load and forget about it. The load would get there on time, and everybody concerned was happy," the big man said with a flourish of his hands. "Now days, some of this new generation that call themselves truck drivers want to hang out in casinos, trash around in truck stops, and the like."

"Just the new generation does this?" Tom asked, but already knew the answer.

"Hell, no," the big man said. "In this day and age, some of the old timers are just as guilty. With divorce more common among truck drivers today, some of the drivers don't have much to look forward to when they get home, so they find diversions elsewhere, and that sometimes affects their work and schedules."

"The driver on the phone?" Tom nodded toward the telephone the other man had just hung up.

"Yep, found the company of a lady truck driver, and they holed up in a motel for two days. Now he wants me to try to reschedule his unloading appointment for a day later," the big man chuckled, and shook his head. "That poor kid deserves a break, his ex-wife cleaned him out when he was away on a run, sold his pickup, and ran off with someone she felt she got a better offer from. I'll reschedule his appointment time, that's not that big of a deal, but I have to lean on him a little, so this doesn't become a habit with him."

"I see," Tom smiled and nodded.

"I'm sorry," the big man said. "I'm rattling on, what can I do for you?"

"I'm Special Agent Thomas Bradford with the FBI," Tom said as he took his ID case from an inside pocket of his suit jacket and opened it to show the big man his badge, "and I'm her to speak to Marcia Crockett."

"Of course," the big man picked up the telephone handset again. "I'll let her know you're here." He paused then said into the handset, "Thomas Bradford here to see you." Then to Tom as he placed the handset back into its cradle. "She'll be right out."

"Thank you," Tom said.

A door opened in the wall next to the vending machines, and Tom caught his breath. The woman he saw standing in the doorway was by far the prettiest redhead he had ever seen. She wore blue denim jeans that looked more painted on than pulled on, high heeled cowboy boots, and a green button-up shirt that snuggly fit the contours of her waist and breasts. Her red hair spilled over her shoulders in loose, gentle curls. Tom's mouth went dry, and his palms started to sweat. When he had finally made contact with her via telephone, Tom had no idea that Marcia was such a knockout. He shook his head slightly, what was he, in junior high again?

"Won't you come this way, Agent Bradford?" Marcia invited, smiling at him. She had noticed Tom's reaction. She was attracted to Tom when she first saw him, just as he was to her, but she hid it much better.

"Sure," Tom said absently, then to the big man behind the glass, "See you later."

"I'm Marcia Crockett," Marcia said as she extended a hand to Tom, who touched it briefly in a soft handshake gesture.

Marcia led Tom through a spacious room, and then down a short hallway. Tom found himself watching the sway of her hips and butt as she walked in front of him, and he had to mentally slap himself to bring his mind back to why he was here. Marcia opened a door and stepped through, and when Tom followed her through it, she closed it behind him.

Tom took in the room at a glance. In the center was a dining room-type table with six matching chairs. Along the far wall was a sink with faucets inlaid in a countertop. On one end of the countertop was a coffeepot with brewed coffee in it. At the same end of the countertop in a niche stood a refrigerator and a soda machine.

"I thought we would be more comfortable here and less likely to be interrupted," Marcia said. "Can I get you something, Agent Bradford, coffee, soda?" She moved across the room to the coffeepot.

"Uh, coffee would be fine, thanks," Tom knew he had requested it more for the opportunity to see her move again rather than for the refreshment. He thought she knew the reason also as she looked over her shoulder at him, smiled, and asked if he wanted cream and sugar.

"Two creams and one sweetener instead of sugar, if you have it," Tom said, finding it hard to take his eyes off her.

"There you go," Marcia said to him as she set a steaming mug of coffee on the table in front of him. Marcia then sat with her own mug of hot coffee on a chair at an adjacent corner of the table. She watched Tom take a sip of his coffee and nod his approval.

"How can I help you, Agent Bradford?" Marcia asked.

"I'm here about the phone call you made to the task force," Tom explained, and pulled his badge case from his jacket pocket. He laid the case open on the table for her to see his badge, and pulled a palm-sized note pad from another jacket pocket, along with an ink pen.

"I'm impressed, I've never met an FBI agent before," Marcia said as she flicked her green eyes from the badge to look into Tom's eyes, smiling when she saw him blush.

"What can you tell me about the man you spoke to the task force about?" Tom asked after he felt he had established control of himself again.

"He calls himself Jack, but that's not his real name," Marcia said.

"How do you know that?" Tom raised an eyebrow at her.

"I pulled the file we have on him," Marcia said.

"Any chance I can see that file?" Tom asked.

"Sorry, not unless you have a warrant in one of your pockets," Marcia grinned at him.

"How well do you know him?" Tom went on, he took another sip of coffee.

"Not as well as he would like me to," Marcia caught Tom's gaze and held it with that response.

"Can you elaborate on that?" Tom asked, as he pulled his gaze away from Marcia's, and started to write again.

"We went out a few times, nothing serious," Marcia said. "He seemed like a nice guy, and not bad looking, he gave me his cell phone number, and I called him a few times. When he was in town, and we were both free, we would go out. I would come here to the terminal or to a place where he could leave his truck for a few hours, and we would go out."

Tom was scribbling on his note pad again. He wanted to ask if she had slept with Jack, but thought better of asking. He told himself that he would concentrate on the task at hand and do his job. As much as he wanted to possibly get to know Marcia better, he also didn't want to disappoint Dixie.

"What does your wife do?" Tom heard Marcia ask him.

"What?" Tom was taken off guard.

"I noticed your wedding ring," Marcia explained. It was hard to miss, especially when he did that twirling thing to the ring with the little finger and thumb of the same hand.

"It's a long story," Tom said, he hated to give Marcia this answer, but he didn't want to get derailed, and he needed to keep control of the interview.

"I'm sorry," Marcia said, it had been her experience in the past that when men gave answers like that, they were usually trying to hide something, such as a bad marriage. "I didn't mean to pry."

"It's all right," Tom said, he laid down his ink pen, sat back in his chair, and sighed. "Sometimes it's hard to talk about her. I met her at a time in my life when I had almost given up on my own life. I lost her about four years ago."

"I'm really sorry," Marcia said.

"Forget about it," Tom said after a moment of silence, and picked up his ink pen once more. "What can you tell me about this guy?"

"Well, aside from not telling us who he really is, he's just an average guy," Marcia said. "He never gave me any indication that he was anything more than a truck driver. He wanted to take our relationship a step further, and I just didn't feel a connection with him, not the way he wanted."

"Did that make him angry?" Tom asked, ink pen poised again.

"Not at all, he was pleasant about it," Marcia said. "That's when I thought I saw his face ripple."

"I see," Tom said. "What can you tell me about that?"

"Not much, it could have been just me," Marcia said. "I haven't been sleeping very well lately, and it could have been my mind playing tricks on me."

"Where can I find this Jack?" Tom asked, he could identify with not sleeping well, lately his dreams had taken him back to Viet Nam, even more than usual.

"I don't know, he's not one of our regular drivers, he's what the old timers refer to as a wildcat," Marcia explained. "He hauls for several different trucking companies, and he's not hauling for us right now. He could be anywhere."

"What about an IC number, a driver ID number, a commercial driver's license number, or a vehicle license number?" Tom asked.

"Nothing matches, but it checks out legal," Marcia said.

"How is that possible?" Tom pressed.

"I don't know," Marcia was confused herself with her answer. "All information we have on file on him matches the truck he drives."

"What kind of truck is that?" Tom felt as though he might be getting somewhere now.

"It's a Peterbilt," Marcia answered.

"Do you know the color, model, year?" Tom lead.

"A black 379," Marcia said without hesitation, "and it has a very large sleeper on it."

"You're sure about that?" Tom asked.

"Yes," Marcia said with a nod, blushed, then added. "He tried to get me inside it more than once."

"Oh?" Tom asked, stopped writing, and looked at her.

"I didn't get inside his truck, Agent Bradford," Marcia looked Tom squarely in the eye, then added. "I never slept with him either."

"I didn't seem to imply—" It was Tom's turn to blush.

"It's all right," Marcia waved one of her hands. "Like I said, he wanted to be intimate, but I didn't."

"What was it about him that made you feel that way?" Tom tried another tactic.

"I want something a little more stable than what he has to offer," Marcia explained. "I know all truckers aren't alike, they're people like anyone else, but maybe I'm just selfish, I don't want someone who is gone more than he's here."

"Then why even start any kind of relationship with him?" Tom asked.

"Do you know what it's like to be lonely, Agent Bradford?" Marcia asked.

"Yes," Tom said after a moment.

"He seemed like a nice guy, and he said he wanted the same thing I did, just someone to talk to now and then, and I agreed," Marcia said with a shrug. She took a sip of her coffee, then added, "Later we started going out some, and then he wanted to get serious, but I just didn't feel the connection."

"Did the two of you have a fight?" Tom asked.

"What?" Marcia was astonished. "I just told you what happened, and all I know about him."

"Please, Miss Crockett, we are after a murderer here, a serial killer. I have to consider all possibilities, and I have to be objective," Tom said, he added a soothing tone to his voice. "What else can you tell me about him?"

"I find it hard to believe that Jack is this killer," Marcia said.

"Why?" Tom really wanted to believe her.

"He's so meek and mild," Marcia said. "He jokes a lot and likes to laugh."

"Kind of like the boy next door?" Tom led her.

"Yea," Marcia said with another shrug.

"Son of Sam, Gasey, Dahmer, Bundy, and possibly Jack the Ripper all had those same traits," Tom informed her. "Are you covering for him?"

"No," Marcia said defiantly, then added after a deep breath. "I'm sorry. I haven't seen him since the last night he was here."

"What about calling his cell phone?" Tom tried another approach.

"I tried calling his number a couple of nights after the last time he was here, and he's changed his number," Marcia said.

"How often does he haul for your company?" Tom didn't give up yet.

"He doesn't haul for us on a regular basis," Marcia said. "He contacts us, we don't contact him."

"All right," Tom said as he pulled a business card from his pocket, and slid it on the table toward Marcia. "If you think of anything else, or he makes contact with you or your company, will you please call me?"

"Of course," Marcia smiled at Tom, as she took the card. Tom rose to his feet, folded his writing pad, and put it, along with the ink pen, into the pocket he had pulled them from.

"Thank you for your time and the coffee," Tom said to her.

"You're welcome," Marcia said, as she rose from her chair. "Let me show you out."

As before, Marcia walked ahead of Tom, who as before, watched the sway of her bottom and hips, then felt guilty for doing so.

Dixie was preparing to leave for her motel room when her cell phone rang.

"Hello," Dixie said into her phone after she pushed the talk button, not recognizing the phone number that appeared in the caller ID screen. She was somewhat glad for the distraction, her feeling of loneliness was almost all consuming.

"Hello, is this Agent Dixie Crenshaw?" asked a voice that Dixie faintly recognized. Not too many people had her private number, so that narrowed the field considerably.

"Yes," Dixie answered, then asked. "Who is this, please?"

"This is Diane Fox," Dixie heard the voice say, and remembered her at once. "Do you remember me?"

"Of course, Mrs. Fox, I remember you," Dixie had a sneaking suspicion that she knew the answer to the next question before she asked it. "Are you all right?"

"Jack paid me another visit," Dixie heard Diane say.

"Where are you?" Dixie asked, and was out the door when she got the answer.

As Dixie drove to the truck stop, thoughts of her father gave her a feeling of melancholy. She used her cell phone once more to call Tom on his and apprise him of the new development. Dixie knew Tom had gone to the west side of Springfield to interview the female dispatcher. Tom said he would meet Dixie at the truck stop.

"Are you all right?" Diane was startled to hear the voice from her past. She was still seated on the stool where Sandy had left her and periodically checked on her. Diane looked up to see the owner of the voice was Gary, the ex-deputy sheriff, ex-boyfriend. Gary now wore the uniform of a private security guard.

"Yes, I'm fine," Diane snapped, sat up straight, and looked around for Sandy or Erin.

"What's wrong?" Gary said, he felt the tension in the air.

"Sandy," Diane called over Gary's shoulder, then said to him. "Lately people don't seem to be who they really are."

"Diane. I'm here," Sandy said as she trotted up behind Gary and shot a glance between the two of them. "Is everything okay? Gary is the closest thing to the first officer on the scene and wanted to see you."

"You see him as Gary?" Diane knew from past experience that Jack could somehow appear as multiple people to different people, but so far he hadn't appeared as the same person to two people simultaneously.

"Yes," Sandy said, she looked at Diane perplexed.

"Agent Crenshaw is on her way," Diane said to Gary, as if to test him.

"Good," Gary said, raised his hands, palms toward Diane. "I'm not your enemy, Diane."

"Okay," Diane breathed a little easier. "I'm sorry."

"Don't worry about it," Gary hooked his thumbs through his belt. "I'm just gonna stay with you until Agent Crenshaw gets here, all right?"

"All right," Diane nodded.

"It shouldn't take her long to get here," Gary said. "Diane are you all right?" Diane had looked past Gary to see Stu approaching, and she took in a sharp breath of fear.

"Stop!" Gary snapped after he spun to face Stu, and put a hand toward him in a halting gesture. "Don't come any closer."

"Gary," Stu whined. "I just want to speak to Diane for a second."

"Not right now, Stu," Gary stood his ground.

"Please, Gary," Stu tried again.

"Just leave, Stu," Gary sounded stern.

"I'm sorry, Diane! I'm sorry!" Stu called passed Gary.

"Leave," Gary growled at Stu.

A trickle of diarrhea ran down the back inside of one Stu's leg, while a stream of urine ran down the front inside of the other as Stu saw Gary's eyes flash red for a brief instant. Gary's face melted into Jack's face in front of Stu's eyes, and Stu felt his knees go weak. Stu was transported in his mind to another truck stop a few hundred miles away where there had been another case of sexual misconduct with another female employee by the name of Rachel.

"Don't make me tell you twice," Jack hissed to Stu, as his face took on the contour of Gary's once more.

Stu shook his head as to say no, but never took his eyes off of Jack/Gary's face. His breaths came in short, sharp gasps, his lower lip was sucked in and blew out with every exhale. He took one step backwards in retreat, turned, stumbled, regained his footing as he was blinded by his own tears, and nearly flattened Erin, who wanted to check on Diane, with his headlong, mindless retreat.

"Would you bring Diane a glass of water?" Jack posing as Gary asked Erin.

"Sure," Erin replied, glad to help.

"Come away with me," Diane heard Gary say to her. When Diane looked up at Gary in confusion, at what he had said to her, she froze in fear. The man that stood before her was Gary, but not Gary, she couldn't put her finger on it, but she had a pretty good idea he was really Jack.

"I can be anyone you like," Jack said to her. It seemed to Diane that Jack altered his face to look like Jason, Keith, Gary, Selena, then Dixie in the blink of an eye. "It won't matter to me, just as long as you decide."

"Sweet Jesus, please help me," Diane gasped in horror, her eyes wide with fright as she looked with disbelief at the creature before her.

"N-N-N-O-O-O!" The voice that screamed was not Jack's, but something much older and deeper. It was a long, agonized scream of rage and fear, and Jack hastened his own retreat.

Chapter 21

"Blanket Transportation, this is Selena, may I help you?" Selena greeted as she answered the ringing telephone.

"Sally," Selena heard Diane's voice from the earpiece of the handset she held to her ear. Selena could tell that Diane was crying by the watery voice and sniffling sounds that came through the earpiece.

"Diane, honey, what's wrong?" Selena was horrified, all work-related tasks put aside. Selena checked the time on the clock that hung on the wall behind her, and confirmed that Diane should still be at work.

"Where's Jason?" Diane asked, Selena could tell that Diane was trying to keep her composure by speaking between halting breaths. "I need him here now."

"Just a second," Selena said, punched a button on the telephone desk set to put Diane on the speaker phone, and free up her own hands. Selena replaced the handset to its cradle, and hit the escape key on the computer key pad to clear the monitor screen. With speed even she didn't know she possessed, Selena typed in the corresponding commands to bring up the screen for the trucks in the Blanket Transportation fleet. She then punched in Jason's truck number, and the reply gave Jason's location to be at Marsh-field, Missouri.

"He's coming through Marshfield now," Selena told Diane. "What's wrong, Diane?"

"Jack was here tonight," Diane's voice sounded calmer to Selena now, maybe because she knew Jason was so close. Then Selena heard Diane's voice take on a sobering, stern tone. "Selena, Jack somehow posed as you, Keith, and Jason tonight, and fooled me every time. Don't tell Jason that, but when he gets here, I need to know it's really him."

Selena, like Dixie, wasn't one to swear, but she did so now, under her breath.

"Sally?" Diane's voice came from the speakerphone sounding like a plea.

"Sure, Diane," Selena said. She typed in a text message to Jason, then hit the send key, held her breath a second, then read the words on the monitor screen that verified that the message had been successfully sent to Jason's truck.

"Thanks, Sally," Diane's voice said between sniffles.

"Anytime," Selena answered her friend, then asked. "Is there anything I can do?"

"Let our family know," Diane's voice simply said from the speaker-phone. "I need to go now, Sally."

"Sure," Selena hit the disconnect button on the telephone. It was all Selena could do to keep from crying herself.

The message light lit up on the incoming message indicator on Jason's satellite communication system, accompanied by a corresponding buzzer. He had had an uneasy feeling boiling in his gut ever since he had left Saint Louis, Missouri. He reached across the cab of his truck and picked up the keyboard/screen unit off the passenger seat. The unit had a motion lock on it, so that only incoming and saved messages could be read, but no messages could be typed or sent from the truck while it was moving. He knew that Selena knew that when he was this close to the terminal, and she sent him a message that needed an answer, she would have to wait until he got to the terminal for that answer.

"Now what?" Jason muttered to himself as he activated the communication system to read the message. He felt he knew Selena well enough to know that if she sent him a message with him this close to home, it must be important. With that in mind, Jason's guts clenched even more, and he steeled himself as he pushed the final button to display the message.

Jason had been right. Selena had known that he wouldn't pull over to the shoulder of the interstate to type in an answer to her. She had typed in a message that would leave him with no questions to ask or ponder, but would motivate him to get to Diane P.D.Q. Jason sucked in and held his breath, and his heart went from thumping to thundering in his chest as he read the message:

JASON, DIANE NEEDS YOU. JACK PAID HER ANOTHER VIS-IT TONIGHT AT WORK. HE REALLY SCARED HER. GET TO HER A.S.A.P. GO IN HOT.

Jason digested the message. He could feel adrenaline being released into his body. Jason mashed the accelerator pedal to the floor with his right foot. He had been cruising at a speed of seventy miles per hour, but with the mashing of the gas, as truckers frequently called it, Jason knew he was approaching the triple digit speed and that black smoke was boiling out of the twin exhaust stacks. He was fortunate that there was very little traffic on the road ahead of him and that none of the traffic was connected with law enforcement.

As he approached the Strafford exit, exit 88, Jason took his foot off the accelerator pedal, and pressed down on the brake pedal with the same foot, turned on his right turn signal indicator, and flipped the Jake brake on full. As the truck slowed its speed, Jason applied easy pressure to the gear shift, took his foot off the brake pedal, and gunned the accelerator pedal with the same foot just enough so he could ease the gear shift into neutral. As the gear shift glided into the neutral position, Jason once more gunned the accelerator pedal with his right foot, enough to bring the engine RPMs up to match the transmission RPMs, and slid the gear shift into the next lower slot, while pushing the button on the side of the shifter forward. He had just dropped four gears. With that done, the Jake brake sounded off its telltale cackle, and Jason repeated the sequence, and this time dropped two gears, then dropped another four gears. The Jake brake sounded like it was going to blow the stacks right off the back of the tractor.

As Jason neared the top of the exit ramp, he checked the traffic to his left, and made a quick right turn at the yield signposted there. About one hundred yards from there was Strafford's only traffic light. Jason's light was red, and that night he decided it didn't pertain to him. He went right through it. Thankfully for him, there was no cross traffic to argue the point.

The truck stop where Diane worked was the first one through the traffic light on the right. There were two main driveways to it, one was the entrance, and the other the exit. The entrance driveway served double duty as cars also used it for their entrance and exit driveway. Most truckers who voiced an opinion felt this was a design flaw, as most people in four-wheelers felt they had the right-of-way whether they did or not, and this had created several near misses and a few fender benders at the entrance driveway.

Jason hit the entrance driveway as he dropped another gear, and listened to the Jake brake sound its protest. Directly off to the right of the driveway were the diesel islands for truck fueling, and to the left were the gasoline pumps and restaurant parking for cars. Jason glanced at the fuel islands, but didn't turn his truck that way. It would be closer and faster to go in through the restaurant doors that faced the car parking lot.

Jason remembered the last line from Selena's message: GO IN HOT. That's what he did. Fortunately, there were no four-wheelers directly in his path. Jason took up three quarters of the restaurant parking spaces when he brought his truck to an abrupt stop directly in front of the huge glass panes that separated the restaurant dining area from the parking lot. He shut off the headlights, placed the gear shift into neutral, and set the parking brake with deft movements.

Jason scrambled out of the truck, shut the driver's side door, and started around the front of the truck. He slowed his pace as he approached the main doors to the restaurant. Gary stood in front of the doors, blocking his path.

"I can't let you go in until I know it's really you," Gary told Jason, he had his hands up, palms toward Jason, patting the air.

"What?" Jason chuckled in an exasperated tone of disbelief.

"Diane's had a bad scare," Gary said, he maintained the warding off posture. "I'm not gonna let you in unless I know it's really you, Jason."

"Like a password," Jason offered, teasing, but knew from Gary's response that he was serious.

"Yeah," Gary nodded as if he and Jason had finally established a rapport.

"Out of my way, you fuckin' One Bullet Barney," Jason growled, and shoved passed Gary who decided that Jason was really Jason.

Jason stopped just inside the door, his searching eyes met Diane's as she spotted him, and for an instant they were lost in each other's gaze. As if from a signal that only the two of them could hear, they rushed toward each other, and embraced each other with both their arms and lips.

"Are you all right?" Jason looked into Diane's pretty blue eyes when their kiss ended, then motioned with his head toward the truck. "Sally told me to come in hot."

"I'm glad you're here," Diane choked back a sob, laid her head against Jason's shoulder, and tightened her embrace on him. Jason couldn't ever remember hearing any words sweeter than those.

"Are you Jason Fox?" a voice said from behind him.

"Yes," Jason said, after he turned his head in the direction of the owner of the voice, and saw it belonged to a Missouri Highway State Patrolman.

"I can appreciate your urgency to get to your wife," the patrolman said, "but I must ask you to remove your truck from this parking lot, it could be contaminating part of a crime scene."

"Will you be okay?" Jason asked Diane, looking around the room. He saw, for the first time, that Christine was there, along with Diane's parents, and her two brothers. They all voiced their greetings to him.

"Yes," Diane whispered to him.

When Dixie approached the truck stop in her rental car, there was a large eighteen wheeler backing out of the main entrance drive. It turned to the right and pulled into the truck parking side of the parking lot. It then pulled through one of the fuel islands and circled around behind the main building of the truck stop and from Dixie's sight. Dixie parked her rental, she took a deep breath and couldn't shake the feeling of being so alone in this world. She got out of the car, closed the door, and went inside.

"Agent Crenshaw," Diane greeted her, when Dixie stepped through the doorway. Dixie noticed the small crowd of people that was huddled around Diane. Dixie was surprised to find herself in Diane's embrace, and she didn't quite know how to react. The Bureau had always maintained a stance of impartiality toward witnesses, victims, and suspects. Dixie hesitated a moment, then returned Diane's hug. Dixie felt there was something about this woman that made her want to be nurtured.

"Are you all right, Mrs. Fox?" Dixie asked when they mutually broke their embrace on each other.

"Yes," Diane said with a sniffle, then smiled at Dixie. Dixie wondered where this sudden familiarity Diane obviously felt for her came from, and more importantly, why did she feel the same way toward Diane? Dixie didn't know for certain, but she estimated Diane's age to be in the mid-forties. Dixie herself was thirty and calculated that Diane was certainly old enough to be her mother, maybe that's where the feeling came from. Dixie did some quick calculations in her head, her father had died about eight years ago, and he had been in his mid-fifties. Dixie figured that Diane would have been in her mid-teens when she, Dixie, had been born, and her father would have been in his thirties. A hundred years ago it would not have been uncommon for girls of Diane's age to marry and bear children with men of her father's age, especially in Missouri or Tennessee. Dixie dismissed this train of thought, her father and Diane had never met or were lovers, but still, there was that nagging feeling of wanting to be nurtured and loved by this woman that Dixie couldn't explain. She had always been a straightforward, shoot from the hip, see everything for its face value kind of girl, but for the life of her, Dixie couldn't explain this feeling.

"I need to ask you some questions," Dixie stated, as she tried to compose herself once more.

"Okay," Diane told her, and Dixie noticed, for the first time that night, how swollen and red Diane's eyes and cheeks were from crying, "but first,

I would like you to meet some of my family."

"What happened here tonight, Mrs…Diane?" Dixie asked. Diane, once again, reminded Dixie that her first name was Diane and asked that Dixie call her that. They were sitting alone in the small alcove the waitresses used as their break area, on a couple of chairs, facing each other. Tom had called a few minutes earlier to tell Dixie that he was headed to the scene of another dead girl that looked to have been dropped off, and that he would inform her later of his findings.

Diane held up fairly well as she related to Dixie all that had befallen her this night. When she got to the part where Stu tried to force her, Diane started to cry. When she got to the part where Jack made his entrance, Diane was sobbing hard.

Dixie, once again, went against her training, she put away the pad of paper and ink pen she had been taking notes with, and held Diane tightly in her arms. Dixie didn't say a word, but held Diane close, and stroked her hair.

"I'm sorry," Diane said and pulled away. She looked Dixie in the eyes briefly, then embarrassed, cast her eyes downward.

"Don't you dare apologize to me for this," Dixie said, her voice stern. "You have held up remarkably well through all of this. I don't know that I could have held up as well as you have."

Diane's only answer was a shy look at Dixie, a brief smile, and a sniffle.

"Now," Dixie said, she pulled several tissues from one of her pockets and began wiping tears and snot from Diane's face. "What do we do from here? Do you want me to arrest Stu? There are several charges I could bring against him."

"No," Diane answered, she looked at Dixie, and offered another brief smile.

"Diane, he shouldn't be allowed to roam free after what he tried to do to you," Dixie insisted.

"No, the person you should probably arrest will be my husband, Jason," Diane said, then continued when Dixie gave her a startled look. "When Jason finds out what Stu has done, he will want to string him up, and not necessarily by the neck."

"Diane, your husband Jason drives a truck, doesn't he?" Dixie spoke slowly, a thought had just come to her.

"Yes," Diane said, she started to regain her equanimity. Dixie had relinquished the tissues to her, and Diane was wiping away the remaining tears.

"You just missed him, he was here a few minutes before you got here?"

"Why did he leave?" Dixie stood to her feet, and began to slowly pace, hand to chin, head bowed.

"A state trooper asked him to move his truck, so Jason decided to drop the trailer at the terminal," Diane explained.

"Diane, is there any way that Jason could be helping this Jack, or even could be Jack?" Dixie knew she had just shimmied out onto a very shaky limb. What she knew Diane didn't know was that not only was the FBI, breathing down her neck, but also the city of Springfield, Greene County, Christian County, Stone County, and Taney County were feeling the crunch of lost tourists dollars. They all blamed the lost revenue on the murders and in turn blamed her, Dixie, for the lack of results, no suspects, and certainly no arrests or convictions. They, the cities' and counties' officials, didn't want these murders to affect the tourist season next year any more than they already had. In short, they were screaming for an end to this, and every one of them had their fingers pointed at Dixie.

"Absolutely not," Diane's voice was calm and hid a hint of laughter.

"How can you be sure?" Dixie watched Diane close for any hint of uncertainty in her expression or answer.

"No matter where he is, or what he's doing, if I need him, Jason will get to me as fast as he can," Diane said without hesitation. "He was on his way in from Saint Louis when this happened tonight. He and his friend Keith were on their way back from California when this Jack showed up the last time. I know it's not him."

"Will you be willing to help me prove that, Diane?" Dixie asked. Something reminded her of what Lucas Daniels had said about some of the old time truck drivers thinking they could write their own rules. Then her cell phone rang.

"Hello," Dixie answered.

"Better get over here," Dixie heard Tom say. "We got another one. It looks the same, but different, you'll have to see it to see what I mean."

"Where are you?" Dixie asked.

"Blanket Transportation in Strafford. We got one witness and maybe a suspect," Dixie thought Tom's voice took on a conspiratorial edge.

"I'm on my way," Dixie said to Tom, pushed the disconnect button on her cell phone, replaced it in her pocket, and turned to Diane. "I have to go now, but I'll be in touch."

"Okay," Diane said and embraced Dixie once more.

Chapter 22

Tom arrived at the Blanket Transportation terminal, shortly after the call from Jesse, the Missouri Highway Patrol member of the task force. He found a place to park and walked toward the members of law enforcement that had formed a loose perimeter around the crime scene. He flashed his badge as he walked past them, more from habit than anything else.

"Agent Bradford," Selena said as way of greeting as she saw him approach.

"Hello, Mrs...." Tom searched his mind for her name.

"Selena," Selena offered.

"Of course, I'm sorry for not remembering," Tom said, his eyes shifted from her to the man that sat next to her.

"This is Keith Doyle," Selena offered, she had a blanket and an arm wrapped around Keith's shoulders. They sat side by side on a park type bench in front of the dispatch office. It looked to Tom as if Keith was on the verge of shock.

"Hello, Mr. Doyle, I'm Special Agent Thomas Bradford with the FBI," Tom said, as he showed Keith his badge. "Do you feel up to answering a few questions?"

"Sure," Keith muttered, then as if an afterthought, asked, "Can Selena stay?"

"I'm sure your wife would like to know you're all right. How about I go call her, and leave you two gentlemen alone?" Selena asked, and with a subtle movement, rose and walked away. she knew it was a lame excuse, that Keith had probably already called his wife, but she also felt pretty sure that Tom wanted a few moments alone with Keith. Besides, she knew that Keith was in good hands with Tom.

"Mr. Doyle, may I call you Keith?" Tom asked, he remained standing in front of Keith.

"Sure," Keith answered and gave Tom a brief glance.

"I can tell this has been a traumatic experience for you, but I need some information," Tom stated as he pulled out his writing pad and ink pen from an inside jacket pocket.

"Dreams," Keith said, barely audible.

"What's that?" Tom asked, he thought he had heard what Keith had said, but he wanted to make sure.

"Dreams and nightmares every time I try to sleep," Keith shot Tom a glance. Since that night at the deserted crossroads in Nevada, Keith dreamed and thought about his fallen comrades more than he ever had. "Do you have any idea what that's like?"

"Yes," Tom said, did he ever, the dreams of Viet Nam were plaguing him now more than they ever had.

"It took me awhile, but I finally figured out where I've seen this Jack before, and it doesn't make any sense," Keith said.

"Oh?" Tom was intrigued.

"In a small town just north of Kuwait City. I was a Navy Seal then, on a routine patrol. He looked different then, but the eyes were the same," Keith's eyes seemed to be focused on a far point, and his voice seemed to echo from there.

"His eyes?" Tom asked, at the mention of this, he forgot all about his pad and pen.

"They flashed red back then, they flashed red the other night in Nevada, and they flashed red here tonight," Keith explained, his eyes still focused, his voice still hollow.

"They flashed? Like twin red flash bulbs, or more of a pulse?" Tom tried to keep his voice calm, but even he heard the quaver there.

"You know, don't you?" Keith asked.

Tom closed his eyes, took in a deep breath through his nose, and breathed it out slowly through his mouth. He sat on the bench beside Keith, hung his head slightly, with his face turned toward Keith, he spoke slowly and deliberately, and related to Keith his story.

"I was part of an elite six man team in Viet Nam, a special group connected with the Studies and Observation Group," Tom took a deep breath.

"You were a SOG? I've heard about you guys," Keith said, he came out of his daze a little. Tom had his full attention.

"Well, sort of," Tom said. "We were connected with the SOGs, but the military denied our existence. Anyway, there were two of us Army Green Berets, two Marine Recons, and two of you Navy Seals. We were on a special fact finding mission, trying to get proof of American POWs. Of course, this was all hush-hush, near the end of the U.S.'s occupation of South Viet Nam.

"The six of us had volunteered for this little incursion, all six of us didn't want to leave any of our boys behind. We had special clearance. All insignias and proof of rank were removed from our uniforms. I guess, I should say, none were added to the special black uniforms we were given.

"Each one of us carried an M-16 with enough clips for two hundred rounds, a .45 automatic pistol, with enough clips for fifty rounds. We each carried our own food and water, enough for three days. One of the seals had a map of where a chopper would pick us up at the end of our mission. One of the marines carried a radio, only to be used in a dire emergency, or if we found some of our boys. I carried a sawed off double barreled twelve gage shot gun, with fifty rounds. And, we all six carried a small first aid kit.

"Our second day out we came upon a camp. To this day, I can't be sure if it was a POW camp or not. I try to convince myself that it wasn't, anyway, in the end, we marked it on the map and turned it over to our superiors.

"I don't know how we got discovered, but soon we were not only in a fire fight, but a fight for our lives. The camp was made up of NVA and Viet Cong both. When the fire fight broke out, we ran. We thought we could shake them, lay low for awhile, then circle around for a second look. It didn't happen that way.

"We were outnumbered, I don't know how bad, but there was a bunch of them. The NVA pretty much stayed in camp, but the Viet Cong gave chase, and we couldn't shake them. We ran from them and fought with them all day and all though the night. Whenever I hear that song 'Run through the Jungle' by C.C.R., I'm right back there.

"Finally, they ran us down, had us cornered. Almost all of us were down to the last few rounds in our last clips of our rifles and pistols. We huddled together, all of us scared, in the middle of the night, and just a couple of kliks from our LZ.

"We decided that this qualified as an emergency, and we would use the radio. We knew we didn't have much time that the Viet Cong would soon be moving in on us. We got out the map, took a reading, found our position, and called it in. The answer we got was that help was on the way, but we were too far west, that we needed to move about one klick to the east.

"Well, what were we gonna do, we damn sure couldn't stay there, and we started to see the tops and outlines of the Viet Cong's Coolie hats as they tightened their circle on us. I got out my shotgun. The barrels were sawed off just shy of the stock, which really made it easy to carry and handle, especially in a situation like this one. I loaded the shot gun. I put two handfuls of shells in each of the front pockets of my pants. I put two shells in my mouth for a quick reload, and put four in between the fingers and thumb of my non-shooting hand.

"I told the other five what I had in mind. I would punch a hole in the Viet Cong's perimeter to the east, then they would go through, and I would bring up the rear. No one else came up with a better idea, so that's what we did.

"When I was about thirty feet from the first poor bastard, I cut him down with both barrels. The blast from the shot gun was deafening in the quiet night, and the flash from the blast leaped from the end of the barrels about three feet, but it looked a lot longer in the dead of night. I didn't hesitate, I broke open the shot gun, reloaded with two of the shells in between my fingers, and blasted the next one to hell. Again, I didn't take time to think, I broke the shot gun open, and reloaded with the two remaining shells in between my fingers, and took out the next one in line. I repeated the reloading of the shot gun and fired again. In between blasts from the shot gun, I saw small flashes of red, like red fire flies. I just thought it was my eyes seeing red spots from the shot gun blasts.

"By this time, the Viet Cong looked like they were scratching their asses, and wondering what was happening to them. We took that as our sign to run. The other five took off running in the direction we needed to go, and I brought up the rear. Every so often, I would stop, turn, and give them another blinding blast from the shot gun.

"I was running through the jungle, following the path my team had taken, the blasts from the shot gun had damn near deafened me, when one of my buddies grabbed me, and pulled me down. 'Choppers,' he said in my ear, and then I could hear them.

"Two Hueys came flying over the treetops, just barely missing tops of the trees, and blasting rock music over their exterior speakers. Our radio man was linked up with the pilots, and when they were almost on top of us, he yelled, 'Now! Now! Now!' Both Hueys opened up with their twin mini-guns. In tandem, each set of mini-guns was capable of six thousand rounds per minute, but of course you know that. Twelve thousand rounds per minute, every seventh round was a tracer round. They lit up the night, and defoliated that section of jungle with their first pass. They circled around for a second pass. We shot at the Viet Cong that had survived that pass who were shooting at the choppers. The Hueys made their second pass and opened up with their mini-guns again.

"One of the pilots told our radio man that one chopper would touch

down in the new clearing they had just created while the other would provide cover fire. He didn't have to tell us twice. When that chopper touched
down, we all scrambled for it.

"I was the last one to board, and as I started to climb aboard, a voice
in my head told me to look down. When I looked down, I saw one of the
chopper's runners had landed across the chest of one of the Viet Cong, and
he was still alive. When I was about to step aboard, this Viet Cong looked
right at me with this evil grin on his face, and his eyes flashed red and
pulsed. The noise from the chopper's rotors was loud, but I still heard this
Viet Cong say to me in perfect English, without a Vietnamese accent, 'We'll
meet again, Tom.' He watched me climb aboard and fly away.

"On the flight back to our camp, I realized what the red flashes were
that I had seen. The red flashes were the eyes of the things that looked like
the Viet Cong. I've never forgotten that. Later, when I asked the other five
in the team if they had seen anything like that, they all denied seeing anything remotely close to that. A couple of them even recommended I see the
company shrink, I didn't though.

"When my wife was murdered, I relived the story I just told you in vivid
detail for a few days afterwards in my dreams. I hadn't had that dream for
about three years, and they started again a couple of weeks ago. It's always
the same, it never differs, and I just want them to end. You're the first person I ever told that story to," Tom wiped a tear from the corner of one eye
with a finger when he was finished.

"It's possible that whatever you saw that night was the same thing I saw
just north of Kuwait City, and then same thing I saw here tonight," Keith
offered. He noticed throughout Tom's narrative, Tom twirled the ring on his
ring finger, first with the little finger and thumb of the same hand, then with
the thumb and fore finger of the other hand.

"It sounds like it," Tom caught himself twirling the ring, he offered Keith
an embarrassed grin as their eyes met, then said. "An old habit I can't seem
to break."

"I hope you catch this guy," Keith said.

"Tell me about Kuwait," Tom said.

"There's not much to tell," Keith said, he felt more comfortable with
Tom now. It was as if the two of them, although from different generations,
had shared the same near death experience at different times. People who
share near death experiences, especially military personnel, tend to draw
close together.

"Anything, no matter how small, could help," Tom said.

"Looking back, I know now that he set a trap for us. He killed two of my best friends, and when I thought I had him, he just vanished like mist or smoke, or…" Keith trailed off, Tom could see the mental gears working.

"Or?" Tom prompted.

"As if he stepped through a doorway, and was gone," Keith breathed.

"A doorway, like in a building?" Tom thought he knew where Keith was going with this, but wanted clarification.

"Reality," Keith almost whispered, then said, "It was as if he stepped out of this reality, and into another. I know it sounds crazy, but we looked everywhere in that building, on that block, and it was as if him and his buddies had never been there. No tracks, no spent cartridges, no signs of anyone ever being there. They were there one instant, and gone the next."

Tom and Keith looked at each other. Keith's gaze pleading for Tom to believe him. Tom's gaze considering the possibilities.

"Is it okay if I come back?" Selena asked as she approached the two men.

"Certainly," Tom smiled at her, and took his cell phone from a jacket pocket. "I need to call Agent Crenshaw anyway. If you will excuse me."

For the second time that night, Dixie was on her way to a crime scene. The time she had spent with Diane seemed to take the edge off her loneliness. Just as she was about to drive her car off of the truck stop parking lot, a truck with no trailer exited off the highway onto the truck stop parking lot, nearly side swiping her car. Dixie muttered an obscenity under her breath and continued on her way, not knowing that the person she had almost had her near miss with was Jason Fox.

Dixie drove to the Blanket Transportation terminal and found a place to park well away from the crime scene itself. Tom approached her when he spotted her walking toward him.

"What do you have?" Dixie asked as Tom fell in step beside her.

"His name is Keith Doyle, truck driver. Selena knows him," Tom informed her. "In fact, Selena is the one who phoned it in. She called the task force and got a hold of Jesse. Jesse knew you were responding to a possible Jack sighting here in Strafford and knew I was conducting an interview in Springfield. Jesse called me."

"Good girl," Dixie said. "So what is Mr. Doyle's story?"

"He says he met up with Jack in the desert between Reno and Las Vegas in the middle of the night," Tom related. "In fact, he says Jack woke him up beating on the side of his truck. He says Jack was holding this girl, and tried to get Keith to help him rape her. He says Jack kept changing his face to look like other people that he knows."

"Like who?" Dixie had been listening intently, but now interrupted.

"Like Jason Fox," Tom said, "but he went on to say that he knew Jason was here in Strafford at that time. Anyway, he says he got out of his truck, and a fight ensued. He says he tried to save the girl, but that she didn't speak English, and by the time he had communicated to her that he was trying to help her, it was too late."

"Do you believe him?" Dixie asked, she and Tom had stopped walking just out of ear shot of everyone else. There were paramedics, crime scene investigators, and members of the Strafford Police Department as well as the Greene County Sheriff's Department there, and Dixie wished to stay out of their hearing range.

"Oddly enough, I do," Tom said. "With everything else we've encountered on this case, his story seems to fit right in. He has some nasty bumps and bruises. From what he told me, he and Jack had a pretty good tussle, and he caught the worst end of it. That's scary, Dixie, Keith Doyle is an ex-Seal."

"He knows Jason Fox?" Dixie asked, a thought had just occurred to her.

"Yea, he says they're best friends, and Selena confirmed that," Tom told her, they walked up to Keith and Selena.

"Mr. Doyle, I'm FBI Special Agent Dixie Crenshaw," Dixie said to Keith as she unfolded her ID case and flashed her badge. Keith and Selena were sitting on a bench a few feet from the door leading to the dispatch office. Keith held an ice pack to one side of his face, while Selena dabbed at a cut above one eye and another at the corner of his mouth. Dixie saw that Keith's eyes were red-rimmed from crying, and that his blank stare looked like shock victims she had encountered in her past. Dixie tried to ignore the smell of body odor that came from Keith, she would have to make it a point to ask about that.

Keith's eyes rolled up to meet Dixie's, and she saw that what she thought was shock was actually sadness and despair. To confirm this, more tears rolled from his eyes.

"Do you feel up to answering a few more questions?" Dixie asked, she tried to make her voice as gentle as possible.

Keith's answer was to shoot a questioning look at Selena.

"It's all right," Selena told him. "This is the agent who helped me and Diane the other night."

"Sure," Keith croaked as he swung his gaze back to Dixie.

"Would you excuse us?" Dixie asked Selena.

Keith grabbed one of Selena's arms in protest, obviously not wanting her to go.

"It's all right," Selena told him as she eased his grip off her arm. "I won't be far away. Would you like a soda or something to drink?"

Keith eased his grip, closed his eyes, and nodded slowly. Selena placed a comforting hand on the top of his head, then dismissed herself from their company.

"Mr. Doyle, may I call you Keith?" Dixie asked, she sat on the bench beside Keith, trying to appear less intimidating.

"Sure," Keith nodded.

"I'm sure this is hard for you, but I need to hear your account of what happened here," Dixie said.

"I already told Agent Bradford everything that happened and everything I know," Keith said, he glanced at Dixie, then looked away.

"I know, he told me what you told him, but I would like to hear it from you," Dixie prompted, she had learned from past experience that the more a person related an account such as this, the more details that person seemed to remember.

"Okay," Keith said after a deep sigh. "I was on my way to North Las Vegas from Reno. I wasn't in any big hurry, I didn't have to be in Vegas until the next morning, so I pulled over at a crossroads to take a nap. I got woke up by this guy who later called himself Jack. At first I thought he looked like my friend Jason, but then he somehow changed his face. He had that girl over there. I climbed out of the truck to try to help her, but she didn't speak English. She was naked, so I threw her my shirt once this Jack threw her down on the ground. I tried to talk to her in between fighting with Jack. It seemed to be all a game to him. In the end I lost. I had pulled a knife on him, but he took it away from me, and said I would find it in the Springfield area. I caught him here tonight as he was dumping her body. We had another fight, and when Selena saw what was going on, she came running out here to help me. Jack took off. That's about all I can tell you."

"Now see, that's more than what you told Agent Bradford," Dixie smiled at him. She had a feeling that Keith was telling her the truth.

"I just hope it helps catch this guy," Keith said.

"Well, this will help," Dixie said, she had her pen and pad out making notes, then asked. "Why do you think he ran when Selena came outside?"

"I don't know," Keith shook his head. "I figure he either knew he was outnumbered, or he's scared of Selena."

"Why would he be scared of Selena?" Dixie asked. From the reports she had received, she knew that Jack didn't back down even if he was outnumbered. The three men he had taken on in the Chicago area was evidence of that.

"Maybe because Selena got the best of him before," Keith offered.

"That makes sense, I guess," Dixie said, then paused as if she was lost in her own thoughts. Then with a motion toward Keith, indicating his appearance, she asked, "How did you get here, like this?"

"I don't know that I should answer that," Keith said a bit reticently and not meeting Dixie's gaze.

"Keith," Dixie soothed. "If you're worried about your logbook, I can assure you that if you showed it to me, I wouldn't have the slightest idea how it worked. Besides, you're helping me."

"I drove straight through," Keith said after a moment's hesitation. "I didn't stop to eat, sleep, or shower, just to fuel when I needed to."

"Why?" Dixie was truly perplexed.

"Jack kept taunting me," Keith said. "He passed me on the interstate several times, it was like a game to him, like I said before. He would pass me, and egg me on, torment me to try to catch him. When he did pass me, he always made it a point for me to see that poor girl, she was still alive then."

"Why didn't you try to call for help?" Dixie asked, this seemed totally unbelievable to her.

"Every time I called nine-one-one, I got a busy signal," Keith said. "That whole trip back I didn't see one Smokey Bear or County Mountie. Every scale house was closed. No one believed me when I would call on the CB for help. The people working the toll booths on the Oklahoma Turnpikes thought I was crazy. Every time I tried to call home or to call here, I got a recording telling me the system was down. Besides, it was like he was egging me on."

"You said that he kept changing his face," Dixie said, she decided to go in another direction. "Is there any one face he used more than any other?"

Keith didn't answer.

"Keith I need to know, this may hold clues to Jack's true identity," Dixie said.

"I didn't believe it when he first used his face, and I didn't believe it tonight when he used it again," Keith said.

"Who?" Dixie asked, but she thought she already knew the answer.

"Jason Fox," Keith answered.

Chapter 23

"How did the interview go with the lady dispatcher?" Dixie asked Tom. They were a few feet away from Keith and Selena and conversed in low tones.

'The description she gave me fits our boy," Tom said. Again he caught himself twirling the ring on his ring finger and gave Dixie an embarrassed glance. She smiled and winked at him. Tom was the closest thing she had to a friend here, Diane was running a close second.

"Could there be a future contact there?" Dixie asked.

"I doubt it," Tom said, cleared his throat, and continued. "She says they went out a few times, and he wanted to kick their relationship up another notch, but she says she didn't feel the same way, and she hasn't heard from him since. I wanted to take a look at the file they have on him, but she said not without a warrant."

"Do you believe her?" Dixie asked.

"Yep," Tom answered almost before Dixie had finished. His eyes suggested he was entertaining a daydream.

"Tom?" Dixie had never seen him like this. "Is there something else?"

"I don't know, Dixie. She said she would find it hard to believe that this guy was the one we were looking for. Yet, there were things I found strange about her story. It wouldn't hurt to interview her again," Tom said.

"Okay, set it up after a couple of days, and go interview her again," Dixie thought the solution was simple.

"I can't," Tom looked sheepishly at her. "I don't think I can be objective, and I don't want to compromise our investigation, and I damn sure don't want to make you look bad."

"Okay, I'll talk to her," Dixie placed a hand on his arm. "Is there something else?"

"I loved my wife. I hated it when she was murdered. I'm not looking to replace her, but there could be something here between me and Marcia, if I read her signs right. Why now? It's just not fair," Tom hung his head.

"I'll talk to her, and if I think she's leveling with me, I'll have her give you a call if she's interested," Dixie offered.

"If the Bureau gets wind—" Tom started.

"It'll be our secret," Dixie said after she made a shushing motion with her hand.

"Thanks," Tom said, his voice barely above a whisper.

Dixie was about to say a comforting word to him, when her cell phone chimed a tone indicating she had a waiting text message. She took her cell phone from a jacket pocket and flipped it open. Her eyes went wide and she was visibly shaken as she almost dropped her phone.

"What is it?" Tom moved closer to her.

Dixie's only answer was to show Tom the screen of her phone. Tom read the message twice to convince himself that it was real. The message on the screen read:

Tell Agent Tom good luck with Marcia, her legs are locked tight at the knees. Maybe I'll detour through Mt., on my way to Ca., & c someone that u know and love Dixie. Otherwise U can probably find me in a small town in Ca., that has the same name as one of your medical staff in Spgfld. No 1 but U will find me, Dixie. Come soon, & maybe save a life.

Catch me if you can,

Jack

"What's goin' on, Dixie?" Tom asked, their previous conversation forgotten.

"How?" Dixie croaked, tears flowed down her cheeks. "How did he know?"

"Dixie?" Tom was concerned, he had never seen her like this. Since he had known her, Dixie had always maintained an air of professionalism. When other people Tom had worked with would have beat their head against a brick wall, Dixie never let him see her sweat.

"I met someone when I was in the marines, we dated off and on, kept it simple," Dixie said, she wiped tears from her face. "I felt we were moving too fast and getting way too serious too quick. I backed off, it was one of the most miserable times of my life. The time we spent apart was when I realized I had fallen in love with him."

"Where is he now?" Tom asked, but somehow felt he already knew the answer.

"He went home to be with his family about a week ago," Dixie said with a sniffle.

"Montana?" Tom guessed.

"Yes, his family owns a ranch somewhere between Butte and Missoula," Dixie said.

"What's his name?" Tom asked, he was fascinated, and curious to know what kind of a man Dixie went for.

"Kyle Michaels," Dixie answered.

"What does he do?" Tom asked.

"We were in the MPs together in the marines, he went to work for the U.S. Marshall Service when we got out of the service," Dixie said.

"I'll call the Bureau and get him some protection," Tom pulled out his cell phone.

"Wait, Tom, he won't take kindly to the FBI babysitting him," Dixie said.

"Are you gonna take kindly to his nuts and scalp hanging on Jack's trophy wall?" Tom looked her squarely in the eyes.

"Fine," Dixie said, there was no defiance in her voice, only resignation. "I'll call him and tell him what's going on and what to expect. Then, I'll call your lady dispatcher."

"No need for that, Dixie, this is more important," Tom said. He dialed the digits on his cell phone and held it to his ear.

Dixie dialed her own cell phone and spoke to her boyfriend Kyle. A plan formed in her head as she and Kyle spoke, a plan to trap Jack. The plan she had would involve a civilian, and she knew the FBI would frown on that, but she was close to her wits' end on this case. Besides Jack had upped the ante, played a trump card, made it personal, and now she more than ever wanted it to come to an end.

"I have a plan," Dixie told Tom when they were both off their cell phones. "For this to work, I'm gonna need a CDL, and Tom, if that lady dispatcher wants a search warrant, that's exactly what I want you to take back to her. I want to know as much about this guy as possible, and right now she's the only one with answers."

"Okay, Dixie, but why the CDL?" Tom was perplexed.

Dixie told him her plan.

That night after Jason and Diane arrived home, he had drawn her a nice hot bath. The hickeys on her neck still bothered him, but he knew now wasn't the time to pursue the matter. He would allow her to take her bath, and maybe she would see them in the mirror before or after her bath and volunteer the information. He concentrated on the important thing, that being that Diane was still alive and all right.

The phone rang as Jason was drawing Diane's bath, and he could hear her talking, but couldn't make out what she was saying. He knew he was being silly, Diane had never given him any reason to believe she would want to have an affair. What she had gone through tonight was a very traumatic situation, and he should be ashamed of himself for thinking the thoughts he had been thinking.

"That was Agent Crenshaw on the phone, you know the lady FBI agent I've told you about?" Diane said. She stood behind the bent form of Jason who was testing the temperature of the bathwater by holding a hand under the faucet and saw him nod.

"She called to say she would like to see us both at the Blanket Transportation Safety Office tomorrow," Diane said casually, then she stepped close to Jason, pulled him erect, wrapped her arms around him, and held him tight, his backside against her front, "and to suggest I explain to you how I got these hickeys on my neck that I didn't know I had."

"Diane," Jason started to say more, and tried to turn to face her, but she held him in his place.

"I love you more than I've ever loved anyone outside my family. I would never intentionally hurt you, I'm not like your ex-wives. The only real man I've ever known is the one I have a hold of right now. I didn't want these hickeys from Stu, in all the crap that went on tonight, I forgot he put them there. I need you now, more than ever, Jason," Diane said and released her hold on him.

Jason turned to face her, didn't say a word, but looked into her eyes. He placed her face gently between his hands. Diane tilted her face upward toward him, closed her eyes, and parted her lips in a sigh of ecstasy.

"I lov—" Diane started to say, but Jason cut her off with a kiss. She wrapped her arms around him and held him tight. Jason kept one hand on the side of her face, wrapped the other arm around her waist, and pulled her closer to him.

"Thank you," Jason breathed when they parted, they leaned their foreheads together.

"For what?" Diane whispered back to him.

"For staying true to me," Jason said, his tone still quiet.

"I do it by choice, not because I feel I have to," Diane responded.

"I'll be outside for a little bit," Jason told her. "You gonna be all right?"

"I'll be fine," Diane said. She knew where he was going, and that he needed to release his pent up anger.

Shortly after her first attack from Jack, Jason had gotten a hard plastic fifty-five gallon drum from Dewey. Jason had drilled holes in one end of it, threaded equal lengths of chain through the holes, tied them together with a length of rope, and hung it about head high from a tree limb in the yard at the side of the house, making himself an inexpensive punching bag. He had spent some time every time he was at home pounding on the thing. That combined with the sit-ups and push-ups he had started were trimming his belly and toning up his body. Diane had watched the transformation, and it excited her. She knew the punching bag would get quite a workout tonight.

"I wasn't worried about you wanting Stu," Jason said to Diane. He lay on his back in bed, an arm wrapped around Diane. With the arm around Diane, Jason traced the contours of Diane's back and hips with light caresses of his fingertips. He grinned to himself whenever he felt her skin develop gooseflesh from his teasing touch. Diane lay on her side, her head rested on Jason's shoulder and chest, one arm over his middle.

"What?" Diane asked, as if startled from a daydream. In fact, she enjoyed the sensation of the gooseflesh as much as Jason did. The daydream she had was actually reliving their lovemaking earlier that night, after her bath. The memory brought gooseflesh of its own. The terror she had lived through this very night had sparked something in her, something that made her want to fight back. She, like Jason, had pent up emotions, and the best way for her to release them was through sex. Sex with Jason. She was the one who had initiated their lovemaking after his workout and subsequent shower. Initiated was not the right word, ambushed was a better word. She wanted Jason, needed Jason, she was determined, and had her way with him, not that he complained. He had been worried that they would be faced with more sleepless nights as she relived this night through more nightmares. When she wouldn't take no for an answer, he knew she would probably be fine.

"I said I wasn't worried about you wanting Stu," Jason repeated.

"Then what?" Diane raised her head, turned, and looked Jason in the eye.

"Jack," Jason said and looked at Diane as if he had guessed her deepest secret.

"You can't be serious," Diane said, she rose onto an elbow and looked at him. "Why would you ever think that?"

"I know how much stock you put in heroes, and from what you told me tonight, he saved you," Jason said. "He was here to save you when I was out on the road."

"Has it ever occurred to you that Jack set this up?" Diane asked. "Even when he was trying to convince me that he could look like anyone, I knew it was still him, still a rapist, still a killer. I don't ever want to see him again."

"I'm sorry," Jason whispered. He was relieved when she curled up next to him again.

"Besides," Diane whispered in his ear, Jason heard her lower her voice to the 1-900 tone he liked so well. Diane smiled to herself when she heard Jason suck in his breath and felt the shudder of anticipation shiver through his body as she caressed her hand down his stomach to a point south of his navel, and north of his thighs, "when I saw you land that truck in front of the restaurant parking lot where trucks aren't permitted, I knew it was you, and that my hero had arrived."

"You saw that?" Jason breathed.

"After the fiasco with Gary, no one would let me come to you," Diane said, her tone still low and silky, she was still teasing him with her fingers, "but you definitely got my attention."

"Impressed?" Jason asked, he squeezed her with the arm he had around her, and kissed her on the top of her head.

"With you, every day," Diane sighed as she turned her face toward Jason's, and felt the solidifying payoff of her teasing hand.

"Selena sent me a message and told me to go in hot," Jason kissed Diane's upturned face, starting at her forehead, working his way down one cheek, around her chin, and back up her other cheek.

"You certainly did," Diane whispered, the result of her teasing achieved, "and I still am."

"I don't need another message from Selena," Jason whispered, and turned on his side to face Diane.

"Good," Diane laughed, reversed Jason's momentum, and rolled on top of him.

The next morning found Jason and Diane sleeping in each other's and love's embrace. Their lovemaking of the previous night had been more than just the mere act, but more of an appreciation of each other. Jason appreciated the fact that Diane was still alive and still loved him. Diane appreciated the fact that it was Jason who was her hero, and wanted to be here with her.

Jason awoke first, slipped out of bed, and did his bathroom routine. Diane met him at the bathroom door and gave him a playful squeeze as they passed each other.

"Diane, I love you," Jason said, he was sitting on the bed. He had dressed while Diane showered. He held up a hand in a stopping gesture when Diane started to speak, and continued, "Just hear me out. I've never put any limits on you, or made any demands, but now I want you to quit. Stay at home for awhile, find another job if you like, or better yet, go on the truck with me. I've tried to make enough money so you wouldn't have to work, but if you want to, that's fine, just not for Stu anymore."

"My hero," Diane said, smiled, and sat beside him on the bed.

"Mom?" Christine called from the far end of the hallway.

"In here," Diane called back, snuggled next to Jason, kissed him on the cheek, and rested her head on his shoulder.

"I just—" Christine started, then stopped when she came through the doorway and saw Diane and Jason.

"Am I interrupting something?" Christine asked, she looked from Diane to Jason several times, blinking.

"Probably," Jason teased with a growl.

"You're just horny," Christine gave him a mock pinched-faced look.

"I know how to deal with you," Jason said with a mock stern tone, stood, and walked toward the door. "I'll get my Best of the Who CDs out, and queue up their song 'Squeeze Box'."

Christine rolled her eyes at him, then grabbed him, and kissed him on the cheek before he exited the bedroom.

"What's up?" Diane asked Christine, then said. "We have an appointment this morning, talk to me while I get dressed."

"Maybe I should ask you that," Christine said, her tone accusing, she shot a look at the doorway to make sure Jason was no longer in earshot.

"What?" Diane asked her daughter with a laugh of disbelief.

"You and Jason doin' all right?" Christine asked, she still sounded suspicious.

"Yes, we're fine," Diane replied as she started to get dressed.

"No problems?" Christine pressed.

"No, none," Diane smiled at her daughter.

"Are you sure?" Christine added a teasing tone to her voice, as if trying to draw her mother into her confidence.

"Yes, I'm sure," Diane said. "What are you trying real hard not to ask me?"

"You know I love Jason, and I would hate it if you did something to mess that up," Christine said sternly.

"What are you getting at Christine?" Diane was just as stern.

"Your friend dropped this off at my work last night, and asked me to give it to you," Christine said, she watched Diane's expression for any hint of guilt of an affair.

"My friend?" Diane stopped dressing, and looked perplexed at Christine, who handed her a folded note.

"Jack," Christine half-whispered in a conspiratorially tone.

Diane gasped, snatched the note from Christine, opened it, and read:

My Dearest Diane,
I can't wait to see you again,
Jack
P.S. You have beautiful daughters.

The scream Diane let out scared Christine and brought Jason on the run.

"What's wrong?" Jason's eyes were wide and full of concern, he looked from Diane to Christine, then back to Diane. He didn't care who answered him, as long as he got one.

"This," Diane sobbed and extended the note to Jason, who took the note in one hand, wrapped his other arm around Diane's shoulders, and pulled her close to him.

"What's going on?" Christine asked, the worry in her voice sounded close to hysteria. "I thought Jack was a friend of yours. He talked about you like he knew you really well."

"He does," Jason said, he looked into Diane's eyes, and saw the pain, despair, and fear there. Diane gave him a barely detectable nod, and offered him a slight, weak smile.

"Jack here," Jason said, indicating the note with a shake of his hand, "Is Jack the rapist, the guy who's been killing those women."

"Oh my God!" Christine cried, her eyes went wide, and she covered her mouth with both of her hands, then calmer said. "I thought he was trying to take mom away from you."

"We aren't gonna let that happen, are we?" Jason asked Diane, who shook her head, wrapped both arms around him, and tried to snuggle closer to him.

"Please make it stop," Diane pleaded and started to sob again.

"Come here," Jason said to Christine, and wrapped his other arm around her shoulders when she stepped toward him. Christine and Diane were face to face, almost kissing, and they wrapped their free arms around each other.

"Don't give me any shit over this, Christine," Jason whispered loud enough for both of them to hear. "I want you to go pack a bag, and go stay with your sister for a few days."

"But I—" Christine started, but was cut short by Jason.

"Just do it!" Jason snarled, "Please, please do this."

"All right," Christine pulled away to go do as she was asked. When she got to the doorway, she turned and looked at her sobbing mother one more time, then went to pack.

Chapter 24

About a half hour later, Christine was on her way to her sister Megan's house in Ozark, Missouri. Jason and Diane decided to drive the Peterbilt to Blanket Transportation, it was due for an oil change and service, and Jason called ahead to the Blanket Transportation shop to make sure they had the time to do it today while he and Diane were talking with Agent Crenshaw of the FBI.

Jason had never dealt with the FBI before, but he thought it strange that this FBI lady wanted to meet them here, and not downtown, like in the movies. Diane seemed to trust her, and that was good enough for Jason.

"Let's stop by the truck stop for a minute," Diane said to Jason.

"All right," Jason said. "What's up?"

"I've been giving your offer about me quitting some thought, and I think I'll take you up on it," Diane said, then smiled at him.

Jason pulled through a diesel fuel island and parked just beyond the canopy, so if another truck wanted to fuel at that same island, Jason's truck wouldn't be blocking it.

"We won't be long, will we?" Jason asked Diane.

"Not unless Stu wants to try to talk me out of this," Diane said, then added a touch of pleading to her tone, "and please, honey, let me handle this. I'll let you know if I need help."

They walked into the truck stop, and Diane walked up to the fuel desk.

"Would you please page Stu?" Diane asked the woman working the fuel desk.

Stu appeared from a hallway that connected to the offices at the rear of the building shortly after his name was paged. To Diane he didn't look so good. Jack had really given him a beating, and that showed on his bruised, swollen face, and the limping steps he took.

"Diane," Stu said with enthusiasm and took two quick steps toward her, then almost stopped in his tracks when he saw Jason. Stu figured by now Jason had heard all about the previous night.

"Hi, Stu," Diane said, she was nervous, and felt herself start to stiffen up, but pressed on, "I just came by to tell you: I quit."

"Now wait," Stu pleaded and reached out to touch Diane, but quickly withdrew his hand when he met Jason's smoldering gaze. "Let's at least sit down, and talk about this, Diane. You're my best waitress, and I've given you a lot more time off than I should have, at least give me another chance."

"No," Diane said, feeling her anger build. "What you did last night was inexcusable. Not only did you try your thing with me, but when Jack showed up, you ran off and left me to face him by myself. I could never trust you enough to work for you again." Everyone in the truck stop within earshot of this conversation stopped what they were doing and what they were saying, and turned their eyes and ears toward Stu, Diane, and Jason.

"Come on, let's go to my office," Stu offered, and reached for Diane's arm. Jason stepped between them, and Stu's outstretched hand brushed against Jason's chest.

"You heard the lady," Jason rasped into Stu's face.

"This doesn't concern you, Jason," Stu found some courage somewhere.

"The second you pinned my wife against the wall, it concerned me," Jason said through clenched teeth. "Some day you'll pull some stunt like this, and you'll get your empty head ripped off, and shoved up your cock sucking ass, but it won't be by me, and it won't be today."

"That sounds like a threat," Stu challenged in a voice loud enough for everyone in the room to hear.

"No threat," Jason paraphrased a John Wayne line form the movie, Chism, he forced himself to calm down, "fact."

"I quit," Diane said to Stu, as she leaned around Jason. She gripped one of Jason's forearms with both of her hands, pulled him slightly, and said, "Come on, honey, let's go."

Jason continued to look at Stu, as he allowed himself to be led away by Diane.

"Thank you," Diane said to Jason as they drove toward Blanket Transportation.

"For what?" Jason asked. "I didn't do what you asked me to do."

"Yes, you did," Diane said. "You were my hero."

Jason and Diane walked hand in hand to the shop. Jason checked in with the shop foreman, and told him where he had parked the truck.

"Any idea what this is all about?" Jason asked Diane as they walked toward the dispatch office entrance. He still held her hand, and she still wanted him to.

"No," Diane answered. "When she called last night, she said we might be able to help her with her investigation."

"Well, let's go see," Jason opened the door to the dispatch office for Diane.

Richard, Jason's dispatcher nodded to them both when they entered the room. Richard sat at his desk behind the glass and was talking on the telephone. Without taking the handset away from his ear or seemingly without losing concentration in his conversation, Richard pointed to a door at the far end of the room. Jason waved his thanks to Richard and held that door open for Diane also. They walked down a hallway, and Selena stepped out of a doorway to meet them.

"We're in here," Selena said, she saw the frightened look on Diane's face, and pulled her into an embrace. Selena's face still showed a couple of yellow bruises from her first fight with Jack, and a couple of fresh ones from the fight she had with him the other night when she tried to help Keith. She gave Jason a brave smile, touched him on the arm, then ushered them into the room.

The room was windowless and sparsely furnished. In the center of the room sat a table big enough to seat eight, with that many chairs. At one end of the room was a refrigerator in a corner, a soda machine next to that, and a counter that ran the length of the room to the next corner with cabinets underneath and a sink. Another door adjacent to that corner led to other rooms and offices. A young attractive woman and an older, distinguished-looking man stood next to that door leaning against the wall, they were both dressed in dark blue suits.

At the head of the table sat Leonard Blanket, owner of Blanket Transportation. Next to him, and on the far side of the table away from Diane and Jason, recently showered, and with a fresh change of clothes, sat Keith. His face was bruised in several places from his recent fight with Jack. Next to him sat his wife Katrina. They both stood when Diane and Jason entered the room and walked around the end of the table. Jason saw that Keith moved slowly and stiffly. The four of them exchanged embraces. Keith kissed Diane on the cheek, as Jason gave Katrina a kiss of his own on her cheek. Keith hugged Jason next, returned to his seat, then, with little more than a warning look to his friend, shot a slight look toward the man sitting in the chair next to his own.

Next to Keith sat Clifford Strokes, Blanket Transportation's safety director, the man Keith had warned Jason about with his eyes. Clifford had a thick file on the table in front of him. Next to Clifford sat a young man dressed in the uniform of an officer from the Missouri DOT. Selena resumed her seat on the near side of the table, next to Leonard, and across from Keith. Jason held the chair next to Selena and across the table from Clifford for Diane to be seated.

"I would prefer you sat there, Jason," Clifford spoke up before Diane sat down.

Jason looked at Keith, who shrugged, and rolled his red rimmed and blood shot eyes, which also had a shocked look about them. Jason thought Keith looked as though he had been crying, and his face looked haggard. When Jason looked at Leonard, Leonard's only answer was to raise his eyebrows at Jason and nod. Jason released that chair, and held the one next to it for Diane who sat down without a word or a look to anyone.

"Well, let's get started," Clifford said when Jason seated himself. Jason felt nervy, something didn't seem right. Clifford motioned to the DOT officer and said, "This is Officer Mike Atwood with the Missouri DOT."

Mike and Jason exchanged looks and nods.

"We need to review your record," Clifford announced and opened the folder.

"For?" Jason asked, it was no secret that he didn't like Clifford very much.

"Because I said so," Clifford said without looking up.

"I didn't know about any of this," Diane said to Jason, and laid an apologetic hand on his arm.

"I'll have to ask that you refrain from talking or participating in this meeting, Mrs. Fox," Clifford snapped, he did look up this time. "If it had been up to me, you or Mrs. Doyle would not be sitting in on this meeting, but that was not my decision. I can live with that, but I will ask that the two of you not participate in the meeting."

Diane lowered her head with a slight nod, after she shot a glance at the young woman standing across the room and an apologetic look at Jason.

"My wife has been through a lot in the last couple weeks," Jason said to Clifford as he looked him in the eyes. "If you're gonna speak to her, keep a civil tongue in your head."

Clifford went back to his folder and began shifting papers.

"I've gotten more than one complaint from our company drivers, complaining of you speeding," Clifford said to Jason, his tone and look were hard. "Maybe we should turn your truck down to below seventy miles per hour. I believe it's in the shop today, we could get that done right away."

"When you do, you'll make the payments on it, pay the insurance premiums, and buy the fuel for it," Jason said, pointing a finger at Clifford.

"You don't own the truck," Clifford shot back at Jason. "You're merely leasing it with the option to buy at the end of five years. Until the five years is up, we will dictate to you the terms of the lease, not the other way around."

"Fine, are you through dictating?" Jason asked, placed his hands on the table, and prepared to rise to his feet.

"No," Leonard said to Jason, then to Clifford, he said, "Move on. We won't be turning Jason's truck down today."

"The satellite system in your truck is equipped with a GPS, as you probably know, and through it we've determined that here lately you've blatantly disregarded the rules of hours of service, running over your daily hours. Also, the logs you've turned in don't match the history that we've printed from the GPS," Clifford accused.

"That was probably because of me," Diane said quietly.

"Mrs. Fox, I believe I asked you to remain quiet," Clifford snapped at her again.

"Don't speak to my wife like that, Cliffy," Jason said. He knew Clifford hated to be called Cliffy.

"Officer Atwood here could write you a ticket right now for that violation," Clifford announced to Jason. Jason and Mike Atwood's eyes met. "Let me assure you, Mr. Fox, the day of the truck driver like yourself who doesn't think these laws apply to him, or thinks he can write his own rules, are over. Truck drivers like you are a dying breed. With those things in mind, we've determined that since you don't keep an accurate logbook, that you could fix it to show you being in one place, but actually you're in another," Clifford said, Jason could tell Clifford was having fun with this.

"And?" Jason asked, he thought he knew where this was headed, but he wanted to hear it from Clifford.

"Truck drivers like you are a dime a dozen," Clifford said slowly, his tone was steady. He looked Jason squarely in the eye and said, "The American truck driver is like the American cowboy, he'll either change with the times or be swept away. I'm guessing you're too stubborn to change. If you're willing to break these laws, what other laws are you willing to break?"

"Like what?" Jason asked, he stayed calm.

"Kidnapping for one," Clifford said, his steady gaze still on Jason. "Murder for another."

"Why don't you just come right out and say what you're trying to?" Jason said, he had heard Diane's sharp intake of breath and placed a hand on her forearm.

"You could very well be Jack—" Clifford was cut off by Diane.

"No!" Diane said and slapped her hands on the table.

"Mrs. Fox, I told you to shut up!" Clifford yelled, leaping to his feet.

Jason was on his feet also and kicked his chair out of his way. He pointed a finger at Clifford.

"If you ever speak to my wife like that again," Jason yelled at Clifford, pointing a finger at him, "I'll stick my foot so far up your cock sucking ass that I'll kick you fucking teeth out!"

The room was silent. Diane, on one side of Jason, had a restraining hand on his arm, and Selena had a restraining hand on his other arm. Keith was on his feet also, looking like he was about to interject himself between Jason and Clifford.

"Please sit down, Jason," Leonard spoke in a quiet tone. Jason sat, but never took his eyes off of Clifford.

"You're lucky you didn't come across the table," Clifford chided, then said. "You're also lucky Keith was here to keep me away from you."

"No, you're lucky I was here. I might've been able to keep him from kicking your dumb ass," Keith said to Clifford. "Now, take some advice, sit down while you're ahead, and shut up."

"I'm in control here, and I'll decide when I'm through," Clifford announced to Keith, but loud enough for the whole room to hear. "You truck drivers are all alike, a dime a dozen, and let me be perfectly clear about this, your days of outlawry, like the James Brothers, are over. If you don't change your ways, you may meet their same fate, dead or in prison."

Jason said, "If I'm like one of the James Boys, then that would make you like one of the Ford brothers."

"You're not in control anymore, and yes, Mr. Strokes, you are through," Dixie said before Clifford could retort to being compared to a back shooter. She approached the table, leaving a laughing Tom leaning against the wall.

"But—" Clifford stammered.

"Mr. Doyle gave you some real good advice, and I suggest you take it," Dixie said as she stood behind Clifford. "As far as ticket writing, you're lucky I can't have Officer Bradford here write you a ticket for being a jerk and stupid."

Clifford was still standing, he clamped his mouth shut, and spun to face Dixie with fire in his eyes, but decided to sit and shut his mouth when he saw Tom come off the wall in an aggressive posture. It was Jason's turn to laugh.

"Mr. Fox, I'm FBI Special Agent Dixie Crenshaw," Dixie positioned herself between Clifford and Keith, laid her opened badge case on the table for all to see, especially Jason.

Jason rose from his chair and gave Dixie a slight nod.

"I've heard a lot about you. It's nice to finally meet you," Jason said.

"May I call you Jason?" Dixie asked.

"Of course," Jason said, he was finally coming down off his adrenaline rush.

"Diane, you can talk now," Dixie winked at Diane. "If Mr. Strokes here says anything to you, I'll be temped to clear the room and let your husband do his thing with his foot."

"I think I'll leave," Clifford said, rose from his chair, gathered up his folder, and prepared to exit the room via the door by which Tom was standing.

"Clifford, wait," Leonard stood from his chair. "Unless there are objections, Officer Atwood and I will join you."

"No objections," Dixie said. "Thanks for coming."

Tom sat in the chair vacated by Leonard, and Dixie sat next to Keith in the chair previously occupied by Clifford. Tom, Keith, Katrina, and Selena conversed and laughed in low tones until Clifford, Leonard, and Mike Atwood were out of the room.

"If you ever speak to my wife like that again, I'll stick my foot so far up your cock sucking ass that I'll kick your fucking teeth out!" Keith was on his feet, laughing, as he mimicked Jason. The haggard look was gone from Keith's face now, and his eyes looked less red and shocked. It was as if that's what he had needed to bring him back to himself. "That's classic. In all the scenarios I pictured in my head, that wasn't one of them. If anyone in this room has any doubts about how much this man loves this woman, that should've settled it."

Jason gave Keith a look of mild irritation and a shy smile, then turned to Diane.

"Are you all right?" Jason asked Diane, putting an arm around her. "I'm sorry, I know you don't like it when I cuss."

"I think I can let it slide this time," Diane told him, and relished being held by him. Then she whispered to him, "My hero."

"I'm sorry too, Diane," Dixie said. "I wanted to tell you what I had in mind. I swore Keith and Selena to secrecy in return for the opportunity to be here this morning. Mr. Blanket and Mr. Strokes were happy to help. I had my reservations about Mr. Strokes, especially when he showed up this morning with Officer Atwood, but Jason I think you handled him better than anyone else would have. Besides everyone expects the FBI to be a bunch of jerks."

"Well, now that I'm here, what can I do for you?" Jason asked Dixie.

"I need your help. The FBI doesn't usually involve civilians in their investigations, but sometimes extreme situations call for extreme measures," Dixie said, she pushed a printout of the text message from her cell phone across the table to Jason.

"What's this?" Jason asked, he and Diane read the printout silently together. When they were finished, Jason looked at Diane who nodded to him. Jason took out the note from Jack that Christine had given Diane from his shirt pocket and slid it across the table to Dixie who read it without touching it. She then took an ink pen from her suit pocket, and using it, slid the note to Tom who shared it with Keith, Katrina, and Selena.

"When? Where?" Dixie looked at them both, a look of horror on her face.

"My youngest daughter, Christine, said someone who called himself Jack dropped it off to her at her work last night. She gave it to me this morning," Diane said, she looked worried and was still snuggled close to Jason.

"Oh my God," Keith blurted out, "is she all right."

"She's fine," Jason said. "She's gonna stay with her sister and brother-in-law for a few days.

"I would really like to speak to her about the man that dropped that off," Dixie said, pointing toward the note.

"I don't want my girls close to this thing or take the chance that Jack can get to them," Diane said, tears started to roll down her cheeks.

"Diane, look at this reasonably," Dixie said and leaned forward on her elbows that were on the table. "If Jack knows about your daughters, there's a good chance he knows where your oldest daughter and her husband live."

"No," Diane protested with a whine.

"Diane," Tom spoke up, "if your husband will agree to help Agent Crenshaw, I will put you and your girls and your son-in-law under my personal protection."

"What do you want me to do?" Jason asked Dixie before Diane could answer Tom.

"It's simple," Dixie said. "Take me with you on a trip in your truck to California."

"Where in California?" Jason asked.

"All I have is the clue Jack gave me in his message to me," Dixie said, "a town in California with the same name as one of the people on my medical team here in Springfield."

"What are their names?" Jason asked. Dixie started naming the members of the medical staff.

"There!" Jason and Keith said simultaneously when Dixie got to Dr. Barstow.

"Barstow, California?" Dixie asked and looked from Keith to Jason. "That's what the field agents in California seemed to think also."

"It's kind of the jump-off point for all of California for people traveling west on I-40," Jason said.

"Barstow it is then," Dixie said. "Mr. Blanket has graciously put Blanket Transportation at my disposal to help in any capacity he can. He has a load standing by ear tagged for us. Selena here has all the details."

"It sounds like you have all the bases covered," Jason said.

"Not exactly," Dixie said, hesitated, then continued. "I don't know how this will work with you and me being alone for nearly a week in a truck."

"I'm sure the FBI has agents that can drive a truck," Jason said.

"I need a professional," Dixie countered.

"Get a woman," Jason offered.

"I would rather have someone close to the case, and Jack seems to want your wife, that may be enough to keep you motivated to catch this guy," Dixie stood her ground.

"Why not bait a trap, and wait for him here?" Jason asked.

"Believe me," Dixie said, "we've tried almost everything, but he seems to stay at least one step ahead of us."

"What do you think?" Jason asked Keith as he looked at him.

"They've shot straight with me," Keith said, indicating Dixie and Tom with nods. Jason looked at Selena.

"They've been there when we've needed them," Selena agreed with

Keith. Jason looked at Diane.

"If not for me, then for the girls," Diane said, pleading with her eyes.

"All right, I'll help you," Jason told Dixie.

"As far as the two of you being alone in the truck, I think I can help with that," Diane said to Dixie. "Why don't you come out to the house and spend the day."

"Go on," Tom said when Dixie gave him a questioning look. "I can take care of anything going on here. Besides, you need a little time off."

"All right," Dixie said to Tom, then to Jason and Diane. "What do I need to bring to your house, and what do I need to bring for the trip in the truck?"

"Just yourself for the house," Diane said.

"Two to three changes of clothes and a shaving kit for the truck," Jason said.

"Shaving kit?" Dixie asked.

"Toothbrush, toothpaste, shampoo, any personal hygiene items you might need," Jason explained.

"I think we're set then," Dixie said, pushed back from the table, and rose to her feet. Everyone else did likewise and stretched as they did so.

"You'll be a little while longer, won't you?" Diane asked Jason, they were outside now.

"Probably a couple of hours," Jason confirmed.

"Maybe if it's all right with Dixie, I can ride to the house with her," Diane said.

"Of course," Dixie said.

As Diane and Dixie drove away, Leonard Blanket walked up to Jason. The two men greeted each other and shook hands.

"I have a favor to ask of you," Jason told Leonard as they walked toward the mechanic shop.

Chapter 25

Upon arriving home, Diane got steaks out of the refrigerator, un-wrapped them from their clear plastic wrapping, and started the precooking seasoning.

"Jason's better at this than I am," Diane said.

"Diane, I don't want you to think that I'm doing this to come between you and Jason," Dixie said.

"What?" Diane was shocked. Dixie saw the disbelief in Diane's eyes and heard it in her voice.

"I've heard about truck driver's reputations," Dixie said.

"Really?" Diane challenged. Dixie got the impression Diane was having fun with her now. Diane asked, "And what reputation would that be?"

"Well, aren't they known for their skirt chasing?" Dixie asked.

"I'm sure Jason did his share of skirt chasing in his single days before he met me, but I would stake my life on the fact that all of that is behind him now," Diane said. Dixie saw the somber expression Diane gave her now, all hints of humor gone.

"You aren't worried?" Dixie asked.

"Not the way you think," Diane said.

"What do you mean?" Dixie asked.

"Jason is not just mad or angry, he's pissed," Diane said, she stopped what she was doing and looked right at Dixie. "He probably feels like you ambushed him, especially with Clifford. You think I'm worried? I am, for you. The trip you take with Jason will be quick. I know the way he runs when he's pissed. Dixie, he'll barely stop long enough for you to pee, let alone long enough to have sex, even if he was inclined to do so."

"I had to do it that way to ensure his cooperation," Dixie defended her decision.

"And you may even be able to explain that to him," Diane said. She got a head of lettuce and other salad-friendly vegetables out of the refrigerator and handed them to Dixie. "Care to make a salad?" Diane asked.

"Sure," Dixie said. She washed her hands, picked a wide-bladed knife from a butcher block holder on the kitchen counter, began slicing and dicing the vegetables, and combining them into a large plastic salad bowl.

"What's he like, really?" Dixie asked after a moment of silence.

"Jason?" Diane clarified. "You're the FBI, I'm sure you ran a background check on him."

"Yes, we did," Dixie confirmed, "but there's only so much you can learn from that. I mean, those background checks don't let you know about a person's personality."

"Well, he's one of the nicest guys you would ever want to meet," Diane started.

"Unless you piss him off?" Dixie tried humor which she saw worked when Diane laughed.

"Yeah," Diane chuckled. "I've never known him to back down when he feels he's in the right or turn his back on a friend."

"What about his friends, does he have many?" Dixie finished combining the ingredients to the salad and began wiping off the counter with a dish towel.

"No, not really, just Keith and a few more," Diane said, she was finished with the seasoning and marinating of the steaks. She placed them on a clean plate, stretched clear plastic wrap over the plate, and put it back into the refrigerator.

"What about Jason and Keith?" Dixie asked. She crossed her arms across her chest and leaned her backside against the edge of the counter.

"What about them?" Diane asked. She placed a saucepan of water on the stove to heat, and took a few tea bags from a crock on the counter.

"Could they act as a team to pull off these murders?" Dixie asked, she was having a hard time making herself believe the killer she was after possessed supernatural powers.

"Could they? Yes. Would they? No," Diane said after a moment.

"Why?" Dixie asked.

"Both of those guys love all kinds of women," Diane said after a moment of reflective thought. She set the coffeepot up to brew a pot. "Jason will probably want some coffee. Want some?"

"Sure. That doesn't make you jealous?" Dixie asked and watched Diane closely for any slight mood or facial change.

"Not at all," Diane looked at Dixie and smiled. "Jason shows my mother the same love and respect he shows his own mother, and he loves his mama. I've seen Keith stand in the cold, blowing rain holding a door open for women—young and old—to enter a restaurant with no thought about his own health."

"You trust him?" Dixie asked.

"Yes," Diane answered with a shrug. She got a bag of potatoes from under the sink.

"Can I do something else?" Dixie asked. She realized that this is what she had wanted all along, quality time alone with Diane. She decided to drop the investigator persona and just get to know this woman with whom she felt an unexplainable attachment.

"I thought about making some potato salad," Diane said. She removed the saucepan of tea from the stove, poured the brewed tea into a plastic tea pitcher, quickly washed and rinsed the saucepan, splashed some more water into it, and replaced it on the same coil of the cook stove, all in what seemed to be a few seconds.

"What do you need me to do?" Dixie asked.

"There's some more saucepans under the counter, if you wouldn't mind to get one out and boil three or four eggs," Diane said, she was in the process of peeling potatoes with a potato peeler and dropping them into a colander.

"Of course I wouldn't mind," Dixie said. They laughed as they inadvertently touched when Dixie ran water from the kitchen faucet into the pan. "I feel terrible coming into your home and asking you hard questions about your husband."

"I understand," Diane nodded. "People who don't know or understand truck drivers usually treat them like second-class citizens."

"Is that what I've done?" Dixie stopped in mid-turn from the refrigerator with two eggs in each hand, "treated him like a second-class citizen?"

"You'll see when you're out there," Diane looked at Dixie now. "Signs like 'No trucks allowed', 'No trucks in left lane', 'Truck speed limit fifty-five'. And that's not to mention the number of lawyers that have television ads that target truck drivers, saying, 'If you've been in an accident with a big truck'."

"Really?" Dixie was flabbergasted.

"Hollywood hasn't helped truck drivers here lately either," Diane said. "In the seventies, truck drivers were likeable with movies like Smoky and the Bandit and Convoy, and White Line Fever, and television series' like B.J. and the Bear and Movin' On Somewhere in the early nineties, Hollywood started making truck drivers the bad guys, with movies like Breakdown and Joyride, and if you really want to see Jason pissed, ask him about The Fast and the Furious."

"Really?" Dixie was astonished.

"Yep, did you see that movie?" Diane asked, then continued when Dixie nodded. "Jason hates the shots of the cars speeding around that truck, whipping around it, going underneath the trailer. He really hates the part where one of the guys shoots a harpoon through the windshield of the truck, then climbs across the cable from the car to the truck. Jason says he would have waited until the idiot was about halfway across the cable, then showed the guy how stupid he was by stepping on the brake, pulling the cable free, letting the moron fall in front of the truck, then run his dumb ass over. His words, not mine."

"Wow, I guess I never really thought about trucks or the people who drive them," Dixie said.

"You'll see," Diane said. They heard the sound of a snort from a diesel motor.

"Jason?" Dixie asked.

"And your home away from home for the next week," Diane smiled at Dixie. "Just between you and me, if Jason mistreats you in any way, we'll tell him we'll tell his mama."

"Really?" Dixie laughed.

"He says she has just enough Crow Indian blood to make her mean when she's angry, and something like that would make her angry enough to be mean," Diane confided to Dixie with a wink. "Let's go meet him," Diane said when they heard the setting of the air brakes. She handed Dixie a cup of coffee.

"Hi," Jason said to the both of them as he walked toward them across the lawn. He had parked the Peterbilt in a spot that he and Diane had specially added onto the driveway for that purpose. Jason kissed Diane, and when he looked at Dixie he saw a faraway look in her eyes. He and Diane followed her gaze and saw that she was looking at the GOD BLESS JOHN WAYNE stickers on the sleeper windows. A tear ran down Dixie's cheek.

"Dixie?" Diane asked in a low, soft voice.

"I'm sorry," Dixie sniffed and wiped away the tear. She bowed her head in an attempt to hide her embarrassment.

"Everything all right?" Diane left Jason's side, went to stand beside Dixie, and put an arm around her.

"You mean besides an FBI agent crying like a baby?" Dixie choked out a sobbing laugh and looked at Diane with tear filled eyes. "I'm sorry," she whispered.

"Someone told me once not to apologize for being human," Diane smiled at Dixie, who involuntarily let out another choking, sobbing laugh. Dixie wrapped her arms around Diane, and laid her head on Diane's shoulder. Diane pulled Dixie into a tight embrace. After a moment, Dixie pulled away, wiped her eyes with her fingertips, looked at both Diane and Jason, and spoke. "When I was a senior in high school, my father died of cancer. One of the last requests he made of me was to watch John Wayne westerns with him," Dixie said between sniffs that were becoming fewer. "We lost my mother when I was very young, and my daddy raised me the best he could. I figured it was the least I could do for a man that made countless sacrifices for me."

"I'm sorry," Diane said and wrapped Dixie into another embrace. Jason joined them this time.

"I'm sorry, too," Jason said.

"You see, he's a nice guy," Diane said to Dixie.

"Aren't you worried about your daughters?" Dixie asked. Diane, Jason, and she were sitting in lawn chairs outside on the carport. The barbeque grill stood a few feet away, smoking, and giving off a pleasant odor as it slowly cooked the steaks Diane had prepared for the occasion.

"Of course, I'm worried," Diane said, a hint of irritation in her voice, "but your Agent Bradford says he has it covered."

"Yes, Tom, uh, I mean, Agent Bradford does take his job, and this case especially, very seriously," Dixie said, she tried to hide her embarrassment of the slip of her tongue by taking a sip of coffee.

"Are the two of you close?" Jason asked. Diane had excused herself, gone inside the house, then to the Peterbilt carrying a curtain rod and curtains.

"Yes," Dixie answered with a smile, "but not the way you think. He's like the big brother I never had."

"What is his plan to keep Diane and her daughters safe?" Jason asked.

"I'm not sure," Dixie said. "I know him well enough to trust him with my own life, and from what I know of him, I wouldn't be a bit surprised if he hid them in plain sight."

"And if Jack finds them anyway?" Jason prompted.

"Tom will go to his death defending them," Dixie said without a moment's hesitation.

"Done," Diane announced after exiting the Peterbilt and rejoining Jason and Dixie on the carport.

"What did you do to my truck?" Jason asked, a mock tone of irritation in his voice.

"I hung curtains in the sleeper so Dixie would have a little privacy," Diane answered defiantly.

"And just where did you hang these curtains?" Jason still teased.

"On the outer edge of the top bunk. When you fold it up, the curtains raise out of the way, and when you fold the bunk down, the curtains hang in place," Diane said. She placed her hands on her hips and gave Jason a mock challenging stare. "And if you give me any static about it, I'll add plywood and a locking door to keep you out of that bunk when I'm in it, before I go with you on the truck again."

"Thank you, but I don't want to be any more trouble than I already have been," Dixie said, trying to stifle the giggle building in her throat.

"It's no trouble at all," Diane winked at Dixie. "I'm sorry, but I don't have any soundproof curtains to save you the misery of listening to Jason snore."

"Oh!" Dixie's eyes went wide, and she covered her mouth with both of her hands, but was unsuccessful containing the giggle that escaped.

"What time do we need to leave in the morning?" Dixie asked. She, Diane, and Jason were standing on the carport. They had eaten supper, and Diane's plan to get Dixie and Jason more acquainted had worked, they seemed more at ease with each other.

"Let's leave around midnight," Jason said.

"Okay," Dixie said with a nod.

"You don't have to go, you can stay, we have plenty of room," Diane offered.

"Thank you," Dixie said, and without knowing why, she had Diane in her arms. "I really need to check in with Tom and tie up some loose ends here."

"You are welcome here anytime," Diane said as she tightened her embrace on Dixie.

"I love—" Dixie started, then stopped herself, tried to pull away, but Diane held her in place.

"I love you, too, Dixie," Diane half whispered into Dixie's ear and felt Dixie tighten her own embrace. "I have two daughters of my own, but I have enough love in my heart for one more, and since you know who won't give me another one, I could adopt you, if you like."

"I like," Dixie whispered back, and Diane could tell Dixie was crying.

"You will behave yourself, won't you?" Diane asked Jason later as they lay in bed together, side by side.

"There's only one girl for me, you know that" Jason replied.

"Who is she?" Diane asked with a giggle.

"Actions speak louder than words, I'll show you," Jason said and pulled Diane against him.

"My, Mr. Fox what a big—" Diane started, but Jason cut her off with a kiss.

Chapter 26

Jason, Diane, Dixie, Tom, Christine, Megan, Diane's oldest daughter, and Joe, Megan's husband, met in a private, darkened corner of the Blanket Transportation parking lot. Jason hugged and kissed Christine and Megan and shook hands with Joe and Tom. Dixie and Diane gave each other a farewell hug.

"Please catch this guy," Diane said to Dixie in a low tone.

"I'll do what I can," Dixie promised.

"You remember what I said about behaving," Diane whispered to Jason as they held each other.

"Oh, all right," Jason said in a tone of mock disgruntlement and scraped a boot on the pavement in the same manner, then winked at Diane.

"Be careful," Diane said, and Jason had no trouble discerning her double meaning.

"Let's saddle up," Jason said, turning toward the truck.

Dixie hefted a rectangular canvas duffle bag from the back of Tom's SUV, opened the truck door on the passenger side, and shoved her bag up onto the seat. When Dixie climbed up into the cab of the truck, she was first amazed at how much room there was. She walked between the driver's seat and the passenger's seat, and placed her duffle bag in a corner of the bottom bunk. She ran fingers lightly along the bottom edge of the curtains and smiled. It was such a simple gesture that Diane had made hanging these curtains, but one that Dixie didn't take for granted or lightly. She felt the cab of the truck rock as Jason climbed into the driver's seat.

"Ready?" Jason asked.

"Yes," Dixie said. She tried very hard to hide her excitement, this was all new to her and a bit of an adventure.

"Let's go find our trailer," Jason said, put the transmission into gear, released the air brakes, and eased out on the clutch. He waved as Tom drove by, exiting the parking lot.

"He'll defend them to the death," Dixie told Jason, she had seen the look on his face as she seated herself in the passenger seat. Jason's only answer was to nod.

Jason found the trailer that Blanket Transportation had assigned to them for this trip. Selena was still on duty when Jason and Diane arrived at the terminal. Selena had told Jason that the loaded trailer they were taking to Barstow was loaded for City of Industry, California. Jason and Dixie would meet another Blanket Transportation driver in Barstow. The other driver would have already delivered his load, reloaded, and would swap trailers. The other driver would go back to the San Bernardino-Los Angles area, and Jason and Dixie could do what they needed to from there. Jason found the trailer they were to take to Barstow, lined up with it, and backed up to it. Jason flipped a switch on the console of the truck, and Dixie heard air hissing.

"This is all new to me," Dixie said to Jason. "If you wouldn't mind, would you walk me through what you're doing?"

"Of course. I'm sorry, I take for granted that this is all common knowledge," Jason said. "Before we back under the trailer, I let the air out of the air bags for the air ride suspension on the frame of the tractor. This will put less stress on the tractor when we back under the trailer."

"Tractor?" Dixie asked.

"Technically, that's what these trucks are called," Jason said, he eased out on the clutch, and backed under the trailer, until he heard the fifth wheel clamp around the king pin of the trailer.

"Why?" Dixie asked.

"A truck is what you haul stuff on, a tractor is what you pull stuff with," Jason said, and with deft movements, flipped the switch on the console to inflate the air bags for the air ride suspension. He shifted to granny low, eased out on the clutch, and pulled twice against the trailer to ensure it was hooked to the tractor. When he did his walk around inspection, he would duck under the trailer and visually inspect the fifth wheel to make sure it was hooked properly.

"Do you know how to do an inspection?" Jason asked. He opened his door, then turned to look at Dixie.

"I took a crash course CDL test the other day," Dixie answered.

"Licensed to drive one of these?" Jason asked.

"The FBI helped to push it through," Dixie said.

"Good. Come on, you can tell me what I do wrong," Jason said. He, pulled out the knob to set the tractor brakes, then pulled out the button to activate the emergency flashers, and climbed out of the tractor. Dixie was reluctant, but she climbed down also.

Jason hooked the air lines from the tractor to the trailer, red to red, blue to blue. Jason climbed halfway back into the cab of the Peterbilt and pushed in the knob to allow air to flow from the tractor to the trailer, some of the air would inflate the air ride suspension of the trailer, Jason would listen for air leaks as it did this, and some would release the trailer's brakes. Jason then plugged in the electrical line from the tractor to the trailer, and the trailer lights lit up. Next, Jason locked in the crank handle to retract the landing gear of the trailer and cranked up the landing gear. Jason folded and hung the crank handle on its hanger on the frame of the trailer. Jason got out the claw hammer he kept by his seat and thumped all of the tires on the tractor and trailer as he walked around the rig, looking for burned out lights, blinking lights that were supposed to blink, leaking wheel seals, bad tread on tires, or thinning brake pads.

Jason and Dixie climbed back into the cab of the tractor, Jason in the driver's seat, and Dixie in the passenger seat. Jason pulled out his logbook and started to bring it up to date. He had logged his days off earlier in the evening at home, after a few hours sleep.

"Jason, I need you to explain to me how a logbook works," Dixie said, she had pulled out her own logbook.

"What?" Jason asked and looked at Dixie.

"I need to maintain a low profile and not draw any undue attention to myself. I don't really want to drive, but I will if needed. I would like to pose as your daughter, but I need to know how a logbook works," Dixie explained. Jason noticed that Dixie's Tennessee accent tried to surface when she was nervous, and she was nervous now.

"Okay," Jason said with a sigh. "Basically, I show fifteen minutes on line four, on duty not driving for the inspection we just did, then I'll draw a connecting line from line four to line three, driving. Clifford Strokes and Blanket Transportation like us drivers to log everything within an hour of when they actually happen, and so far the DOT hasn't had much of a problem with that.

"I can log no more than ten hours driving without an eight hour break, either off duty, or in the sleeper, or any combination of the two that add up to eight hours. After eight hours, I can drive for another ten hours."

"I'm impressed," Dixie smiled at him. "That sounded professional and official. Now, what if we were a driving team?"

"The term is running teams," Jason told her, "and that works something like this. If I'm driving, you would log either off duty or sleeper berth. The only line we wouldn't log on together would be driving, line three. We could log off duty together, line one, or sleeper berth together, line two, or even on duty not driving, line four, although that wouldn't be very practical, and would defeat the purpose of running teams, but it could happen in rare cases. "

"All right," Dixie nodded as she took in all the information. Jason could see the excitement in her eyes and could tell she was eager to learn.

"Now, over here where it says 'co-driver', you would write in my name, Jason Fox, and I would write in your name on mine," Jason said. "You would never write in my logbook, and I would never write in yours. No one, not even a DOT officer is allowed to write in or make marks on your logbook pages. You wouldn't show a DOT officer my logbook, or me yours."

"Got it," Dixie said, then asked. "What are we hauling?"

"Groceries," Jason said and looked at the bill of lading. "It says the tare weight is forty-two thousand pounds. It says there are fifty-two wood pallets, so we estimate the weight of those, and I would say we are hauling close to forty-three thousand pounds. We better weigh this wagon."

"Weigh this wagon?" Dixie asked.

"Trucker term," Jason explained and drove to one of the truck stops in Strafford where there was a public truck scale. "Means to weigh the tractor and trailer, to get a gross weight. A lot of truckers use the term to describe open weight stations, 'They're open weighin' yer wagon.'"

Jason pulled onto the scale, rolled down the driver's side window, and pushed the call button provided there. He gave the clerk the information she asked for, pulled off the scale, and found a place to park. Dixie went with him into the truck stop.

"What does this mean?" Dixie asked him after he paid for the weight ticket and handed it to her.

"Well, it's pretty simple," Jason said as they walked back toward the truck, he held no condemnation in his voice. "This truck is licensed for eighty thousand pounds, gross weight. If you divide that weight into two weights of thirty-four thousand pounds, and one weight of twelve thousand pounds, you get—" Jason added a slight lift to his voice to prompt Dixie.

"Eighty thousand pounds," Dixie half whispered and smiled at Jason. "You're right, it is simple."

"Is our weight all right?" Jason asked her.

"Eleven thousand, seven hundred pounds on the steer axle, thirty-three thousand, three hundred pounds on the drive axles, and thirty-two thousand, five hundred pounds on the trailer axles," Dixie read from the weight ticket.

"Are we legal?" Jason asked.

"I think so," Dixie ventured. "Does the weight have to be evenly distributed?"

"No," Jason said. "The only thing is we are goin' to Shakey, and they are sticklers about the bridge law, so in my opinion it's better to set the trailer now and be done with it."

"Shakey? Bridge law?" Dixie's sounded overwhelmed. "I'm afraid I don't understand."

"I'm sorry," Jason said and laughed. "Shakey is the nickname truckers call California. The bridge law is basically forty feet from the king pen of the trailer to the center of the rear wheels of the trailer tandems." Jason pointed to where the king pen of the trailer connected to the fifth wheel of the tractor, then pointed to the arrow painted on the side of the trailer that pointed downward as he explained.

"I always wondered what those arrows were there for," Dixie said. "So if we line up the arrow with the center of the back wheels of the trailer we'll be Shakey legal?"

"Yep," Jason said, he noticed the twinkle in Dixie's eyes as she experimented with the trucker lingo. "Come on, I'll show you how to slide the trailer tandems."

A few minutes later, Jason merged his rig into traffic on I-44 westbound. Dixie watched him run through the gears as they reached cruising speed. Jason felt her looking at him.

"Something wrong?" Jason asked.

"How do you do that?" Dixie asked.

"Do what?" Jason was perplexed.

"Shift like that without grinding the gears," Dixie snapped, irritated. "Don't play games with me or make fun of me."

"I'm not making fun of you," Jason said. "I'm sorry, I took for granted that you knew how."

"Well, I don't," Dixie said. "The Bureau has an agent in Springfield that can drive one of these, and he showed me all he could in the afternoon I spent with him."

"A whole afternoon?" Jason tried to keep from laughing.

"Okay, so I was wrong in thinking that driving one of these would be like driving my daddy's old farm truck," Dixie said, she tried to keep from laughing, gave up, and laughed with Jason.

"How 'bout it westbound, how's it looking over yer shoulder?" a voice asked over the CB speaker.

"You're clear back to the 208, where I jumped on at. Haven't seen a thing to bother ya," said another voice over the same speaker.

"Ten-four. Glad to hear it. It's been quiet goin' westbound. Joplin is all locked up, nobody home. Be careful, have a good night," said the first voice over the CB speaker.

"All righty, right back atcha eastbound, catch ya later," said the second voice over the speaker.

"Joplin's all locked up? What does that mean?" Dixie asked Jason.

"He was talking about the chicken coops west of Joplin, just before the Oklahoma State Line," Jason said, then when he saw the perplexed look on Dixie's face added. "Scale house, truck drivers call scale houses chicken coops."

"Watch out, westbound, you have two in the middle just before the eighty-two exit," said a voice over the CB speaker.

"Two cops in the median," Jason translated for Dixie. They both looked at the two Missouri Highway State Patrol cars that were parked driver side door to driver side door in the crossover between the eastbound lanes, and the westbound lanes.

"Are these two bears still up here, westbound?" asked another voice over the speaker.

"Ten-four," Jason said into the keyed mic of his CB. "They're still sixty-ninin' in the middle."

"They're doin' what?" Dixie closed her eyes, snapped them open, and looked at Jason as she asked with a hint of a laugh.

"Trucker lingo," Jason explained, then looked at her out of the corner of his eye, and grinned.

"I guess I have a lot to learn," Dixie said, then she pointed to the CB radio. "Don't you have to have a special name to talk on one of those?"

"A handle," Jason said. "Yes, you need a handle to talk on one of those."

"I want one," Dixie said. "Do I get to pick one, or does someone give me one?"

"Either way. If you pick one, try to pick one that describes your personality, a trait, or an interest in one or two words," Jason told her, looked at her as she yawned, and asked. "Did you get any sleep last night?"

"No," Dixie said with a shake of her head.

"Try to get some sleep, it's a bit of a hike to Santa Rosa," Jason said.

"New Mexico," Dixie said, showing some confidence as she unbuckled her seatbelt, and walked to the sleeper. She ran her hands lightly over the curtains Diane had hung just for her again, and smiled at the thought of Diane. She no sooner lay down than she was fast asleep.

When Dixie woke, she lay very still for a few moments, not remembering where she was. Then, it started to come back to her. She sat up and re-arranged the clothes she had slept in. She slid the curtains open and peeked out, the sun was up, and she could see they were entering a city.

"Where are we?" Dixie asked, as she climbed out of the sleeper and into the passenger seat, and buckled her seatbelt.

"Tucumcari, New Mexico," Jason answered slowly, he tried very hard to hide his reaction to seeing her like this. She had let down her hair which cascaded down around her face, over her shoulders, and almost to her waist in dark, swooping waves. "How'd you sleep?"

"Like a rock," Dixie said and looked around.

"Yep," Jason said. "I bet you could use a restroom."

"That would be nice," Dixie gave him a smile. "How about a shower?"

"We'll stop up here at a truck stop for the restroom," Jason said. "Can you wait another hour for the shower? I can redeem showers for us on my points card at one of the truck stops in Santa Rosa, and it will look better on my logbook."

"A points card?" Dixie asked.

"The larger truck stop chains offer points cards to truck drivers, and when you fuel there, they usually put a point a gallon on the point card, and then you can buy meals or merchandise at those truck stops," Jason explained. "Along with the points, most offer free showers for fifty gallons of fuel purchased that drivers can use then or redeem usually within seven days."

"You have one of those cards?" Dixie asked.

"I have several, one for each different truck stop chain," Jason said.

"We won't have to use the same shower, will we?" Dixie asked. Jason thought she sounded anxious.

"Only if they are really backed up," Jason grinned at her, saw the worried look on her face, then winked at her, smiled, and said, "If we have to use the same shower, you go first, then I'll take mine afterwards."

"You're ornery," Dixie said with a small laugh. Jason steered the truck into the left lane to pass a car. Dixie turned to look out her window and turned back to face Jason with her eyes and her mouth wide open.

"What's wrong?" Jason asked, but he had a suspicion he knew.

"You can see right down inside those cars!" Dixie exclaimed, "And you can see everything going on inside them!"

"Yes, you can," Jason was nonchalant.

"So what all have you seen?" Dixie asked slyly.

"Well," Jason said, his tone cautious, and speech slow, "I've seen women driving, putting on makeup; people driving, reading a paper or book, working on a laptop, having sex, women showing their hooters. The most irritating is talking on a cell phone."

"That's irritating?" Dixie asked. "Do you always look inside four wheelers?"

"Not so much talking on the phone, but most people in four wheelers who talk on the phone while driving, their IQ drops the second the phone touches their ears," Jason said. "They seem to forget all about where they are or what they're doin', and most of them want to get right in front of a truck and slow down. That's what's irritating.

"One night a few years ago, I was headed south on Interstate 65 out of Gary, Indiana, toward Indianapolis, and all traffic started to slow down. Truck drivers ahead of me were talking on the CB about some guy in a convertible Cadillac shooting at trucks with a handgun as they passed him."

"Oh my gosh," Dixie said in a hushed tone.

"Diane used to get irritated with me for looking inside four wheelers until I told her that story," Jason glanced at Dixie.

"What happened?" Dixie asked.

"One of the truck drivers got a hold of a bear, and they got the guy stopped," Jason said.

"Did anyone get shot or hurt?" Dixie wanted to know.

"Luckily, no," Jason said as he dropped a gear and hit the exit ramp that would take them to the truck stop.

Upon arriving at Santa Rosa, their wait wasn't long, and after their showers were taken, they ate breakfast in the truck stop restaurant. Jason, again, found it hard not to think of how pretty she was. After her shower, Dixie pulled her hair into a ponytail, and applied very little makeup. Jason thought she didn't need much, if any.

"From what I understand, after the first of the year, the government is gonna change our hours of service, and all time logged on lines one, three, and four will count against our daily time," Jason said as they sat in the restaurant booth.

"Whose idea was that?" Dixie asked.

"It certainly wasn't any of ours," Jason answered.

"Now about something really important," Dixie sobered. "What did you decide for my CB handle?"

"Did you think of anything?" Jason answered her question with one of his own.

"No, nothing that doesn't sound silly," Dixie said.

"Well how about…AC/DC?" Jason offered.

"The rock group?" Dixie wrinkled her brow, and shot him a look.

"You don't like them?" Jason asked, and raised an eyebrow at her.

"It's not that, they just aren't my favorite," Dixie said.

"No, the AC/DC I mean has to do with your initials, Agent Crenshaw-Dixie Crenshaw, an acronym, if you will," Jason explained.

"Oh, I get it," Dixie laughed. "I like it."

"When smart ass men truck drivers ask you what that means, and they will," Jason told her, "you can tell them that you can go either way."

"What?" Dixie asked with a laugh and a look of disbelief.

"You can tell them that if you can't shock them one way, you can shock them another," Jason said.

"How's that?" Dixie asked.

"If Diane hadn't told me you were an FBI Agent, I never would have believed it," Jason said.

"And what would you have thought?" Dixie asked.

"Now, I believe that's entrapment," Jason said with a grin.

"Seriously, what would you have thought?" Dixie prompted.

"Model, actress, but certainly not FBI" Jason confided.

"What about Diane?" Dixie asked.

"What about Diane?" Jason asked back.

"You really love her, don't you?" Dixie said.

"Yes, more than anything," Jason said.

"Even though she may be a little big?" Dixie asked, being ornery herself.

"Size doesn't matter," Jason grinned at Dixie. "Isn't that what you women have always told us men?"

"I guess I deserved that," Dixie laughed.

"I need to get some sleep," Jason picked up the check. "Did Diane give you her truck key?"

"Yes," Dixie answered.

"You don't have to come back to the truck with me," Jason told her. "They have a drivers' lounge here, I'm sure you could find something better to do than listen to me snore."

"I'll be fine," Dixie confirmed. "Have a good nap, see you later."

"AC/DC?" Jason heard a man's voice over the CB speaker say.

"Yea," he heard Dixie respond into the keyed microphone of the CB, "I can go either way."

"Hear that? She says her door swings either way," Jason heard another male voice say over the CB speaker.

"That's not what I said," Dixie said into the keyed mic. "If you're not gonna do the listening part of the conversation, then don't attempt the talking part."

"I think you just got zapped," said the first voice over the CB speaker.

"Yeah," said the second voice. "Which side do you think she used, the AC side, or the DC side? Which one would hurt worse?"

"That would depend on where she stuck the connectors on you," laughed the first voice.

"She could stick her connectors anywhere she wants on me," said the second voice. "Can you see her from where you're sittin'?"

"No," said the first voice. "What'd she look like?"

"Hot damn she's a baby-doll," said the second voice.

"Maybe she might want some company tonight," said the first voice. "How 'bout it, AC/DC, want me to keep you company tonight?"

"My daddy used to have a saying that went like this," Dixie said into the keyed mic of the CB, "It is better to keep your mouth shut and appear stupid, than to open it, and remove all doubt."

"Is that a 'no'?" asked the first voice.

"I think so," said the second voice.

"Heart breaker," Jason accused when he slid off the top bunk, then asked, "Having fun?"

"Just killing time," Dixie looked over her shoulder at him. "One of the ways to catch a killer is to understand him, try to get a feel for how he thinks."

"Learning anything?" Jason asked, as he pulled on his boots, he had slept in his clothes.

"Where'd you go, AC/DC?" asked the first voice.

"I'm still right here," Dixie said into the keyed mic. "We're still right here."

"We?" asked the other voice, he sounded deflated.

"Sorry boys," Dixie said into the keyed mic and grinned at Jason.

"Heart breaker," Jason said to her again, with a grin of his own.

"I'm sorry if I woke you," Dixie said. "You were snoring pretty good."

"I'm fine," Jason said as he climbed into the driver's seat. "Do you need to use the restroom? I know I do."

"I'm fine, I used it before I came out, thank you though," Dixie said. "So you're a John Wayne fan too?"

"Yeah," Jason said, then added in his best John Wayne voice. "God broke the mold when he made the Duke."

"That was pretty good," Dixie laughed. "You and my father would have gotten along well together. What's you favorite John Wayne movie?"

"McLintock, without a doubt," Jason said without hesitation.

"Interesting choice," Dixie commented. "Why?"

"Nobody dies in it," Jason said. "Besides, he had some of his favorite people working with him, Maureen O'Hara, Bruce Cabot, his sons Michael and Patrick, his daughter Aissa."

When they stopped for fuel, Jason activated the fuel pump by inserting his fuel card in the card reader. The screen of the card reader called for information that Jason entered on the keypad provided there. Jason then stood back and let Dixie handle the rest of it, telling her to fill both tanks, and explaining to her about the fuel pump on the other side of the truck called the satellite pump.

After fueling, Jason instructed Dixie to pull the rig forward out of the fuel island. He explained that it was good manners to pull out of the way so the next truck in line could fuel. Jason then explained to her how to log the fuel stop, as she followed him inside, and watched as Jason signed the fuel ticket and retained his copies.

"I miss talking to Diane," Jason said, as he pulled the tractor and trailer onto the interstate and ran through the gears.

"She and her daughters are in good hands," Dixie said, her voice was soft but firm. "It's better not to contact them right now. I'm not sure what we're dealing with here, and somehow Jack has been a step or two ahead of us all along."

"How did you get involved in this?" Jason asked after a moment.

"Before my father died, I made up my mind that I wanted to be in law enforcement. A recruiter for the marines was at my high school on a day set aside for military recruiters to talk to the seniors of the student body. I tested, told them what I wanted, and we came to an agreement," Dixie said as she divided her attention between the scenery out her window and Jason. "The marines and the FBI train at the same base in Quantico, Virginia. I went to college on the GI Bill and applied to the Bureau. I was accepted, and the rest, as they say, was history."

"That's quite a story," Jason said, "but, I mean, how did you end up on this case?"

"Well, I had always been fascinated with Jack the Ripper and the murders he committed in London's East End, or Whitechappel, and when the FBI was called in on this case, they sent me," Dixie said.

"This the first time you've handled a case like this?" Jason asked.

"Yes and no," Dixie smiled at him. "This is not my first kidnapping or murder case or even the first case I've facilitated, but it is the first case I've handled that I've had to deal with a serial killer."

"And how do you go about something like that?" Jason asked.

"I do a lot of listening," Dixie said. "Agent Bradford is a wealth of information. The local law enforcement in Springfield, and Greene County, and the State of Missouri have a lot of knowledgeable investigators that I've listened to.

"In the past, the FBI has had a nasty reputation of what you might call double standard investigating, wanting local, and state law enforcement to give up all the information they have on a case to the Bureau, but not getting much, if anything in return—the Bureau, in a sense, shutting out local law enforcement or keeping them out of the loop. I've tried very hard in this case not to do that. Every time we got new, fresh evidence or statements from our field agents from where these women were taken or from people who knew these women, I personally passed it on to the heads of all state and local agencies. I've tried to keep all agencies involved current on what I know."

"What about leaks?" Jason asked. "With that many people and agencies involved, it must have created a nightmare for you with the press."

"My, my," Dixie raised her eyebrows at him.

"What?" Jason said. "Just because I'm a truck driver, doesn't mean I'm stupid or ignorant."

"I guess not," Dixie said. "Well, I decided from the beginning that I wanted to instill trust into local law enforcement. I had to overcome a lot of resentment, not only from local law enforcement, but also the FBI Field Agents assigned to the Springfield area. I instituted some ideas that I can't talk about, and so far they've worked well."

"What about when you're out here with me?" Jason was fascinated.

"Like I said, I showed them I wouldn't shut them out," Dixie beamed. "I really can't talk about the investigation."

"All right," Jason said, resigned.

"Don't be angry with me," Dixie half pleaded.

"I'm not," Jason said. "What would've you done if I hadn't been so willing to help you?"

"I'm ashamed to say that I would have used Keith against you," Dixie shot Jason a glance. "There were things about the last victim that pointed to him."

"Why didn't you?" Jason didn't hide the shock in his voice.

"Again, I can't talk about the investigation," Dixie said. "I hate to say that to you, but what I will say is we believe what Keith told us."

"Any idea who the killer is?" Jason asked.

"No," Dixie said after a moment.

"You said earlier that you didn't know what you're dealing with," Jason said.

"Yes, I did," Dixie said. "Why?"

"Most trucking companies in the Springfield area have security cameras that at least monitor the entrance and exit driveways of their parking lots," Jason gave Dixie a sidelong look.

"I can't—" Dixie started, then caught Jason's look.

"You didn't get even one photo or frame of film on this guy or his truck?" Jason pressed.

"Not even when Keith faced him again at Blanket Transportation," Dixie relented, "but there aren't any cameras on that side of the building. The closest thing we've gotten is a wet tire track and a smoke plume. Really, that's all I'm willing to talk about, I've said too much already. What makes you think he's a truck driver?"

"If he's not, then what are you doin' here?" Jason asked and looked at her. "Keith is the best friend I've ever had, and he tells me most everything. I know about both of his fights with this Jack, what was said before them, and what was said about Diane and Selena.

Chapter 27

Jason woke with a start. Dixie was standing next to him, one hand lightly shaking him while she softly called his name. Jason blinked a few times, then looked at her. He saw her whole body give a sigh of relief.

"Thank goodness," Dixie breathed.

"What's wrong?" Jason asked and sat up, not bothering to cover himself.

"You stopped snoring about ten miles back, and I thought you were awake," Dixie said. "I called your name several times, but you didn't answer, and I got worried."

"Where are we?" Jason asked. He pulled the blanket across his lap, more from embarrassment than modesty.

"At a truck stop in Seligman, Arizona," Dixie said, then turned to go out of the sleeper. "While you get dressed, I'm gonna go use the restroom."

Jason grunted his acknowledgment. He watched her leave the sleeper, then slid off the top bunk, and got dressed. When he looked at the clock on the stereo, he saw it was almost seven o'clock in the evening. Jason dug out his toothbrush, squeezed some toothpaste onto it, and headed for the men's restroom.

When Jason returned to the truck, Dixie was sitting in the passenger side seat updating her logbook.

"That could turn into a bad habit," Jason said to her as he climbed into the driver's seat and pulled out his own logbook. He put on a pair of reading glasses he kept in a holder that was strapped to the sun visor. Then added as she showed him a questioning smile, "Keeping your logbook current."

"You don't?" Dixie's questioning smile turned into a teasing smile.

"Do as I say, not as I do," Jason said and gave her a teasing smile of his own, as he looked at her out of the corner of his eye and over the top of his reading glasses.

Her smile turned into a brilliant chorus of musical laughter that sounded good to Jason. When he paused to think about how pretty Dixie was, how her laughter sounded like music to him, and how much he enjoyed her company, he made himself think of Diane. Before Jason knew what was happening or could stop it, Dixie had gotten out of her seat and crossed the cab to him. She took the log from him and sat across his lap. She took his glasses off and lowered her face toward his. When Dixie's lips touched his, Jason sat up with a huge intake of air. Far back in his mind he heard a deep, soft laugh that faded away. The laughter in his head was as bad as the dream, they both seemed real.

"Jason?" Dixie's voice was low and soft. Jason's eyes were wide and wild as he turned to face her, and scooted across the bunk away from her. "Are you all right?"

"Diane," Jason blurted, "I love Diane!"

"All right. Good," Dixie said slowly, and backed off a step. "I'm gonna use the restroom."

"Okay," Jason ran a hand over his face, then through his hair.

"Are you okay?" Dixie asked, she had turned to leave the sleeper, but turned back to him.

"Yeah," Jason rearranged his blanket. "I'm sorry, Dixie, I was havin' a dream."

Dixie nodded, Jason saw understanding in her eyes. She turned to leave the sleeper, then turned back to Jason, and said, "My dreams are usually about my dad." She then turned and left the sleeper.

Jason slid off the top bunk and got dressed when he felt the cab rock and heard the door shut when Dixie exited the truck. A sense of déjà vu came over Jason as he squeezed toothpaste onto his toothbrush.

The memory of the previous day came back to him, they had taken their time driving across New Mexico and Arizona. Dixie had a little trouble adjusting to riding such long distances at one time, and Jason understood that, taking frequent breaks to allow her to stretch her legs.

"I've never been to California this way," Dixie said from the passenger seat. They were on the road again with Jason, once more, driving.

"You've been to California though?" Jason asked. The dream was still on his mind, but he knew the dream wasn't of his choosing. His dreams up to now had been about Diane. The dream about Dixie was unusual, and the sound of laughing was frightening.

"Yes," Dixie said, yawning, "I was stationed in Twenty-Nine Palms for a short while."

"Tired?" Jason asked.

"I could use a nap, but I want to see some of this country too, I'll sleep later when you do," Dixie said as she gave Jason a glance to catch his reaction.

Jason gave her a quick, questioning, almost frightening glance, which she caught.

"Your dream was about me, wasn't it? I mean, you and me?" Dixie asked, still watching him.

Jason closed his eyes briefly, swallowed, and nodded. "I'm sorry Dixie," he said with a whisper, and chose not to tell her about the evil-sounding laughter that had retracted in the back of his mind when he woke. Thinking about it now, he thought it sounded a bit farfetched, and unbelievable.

"Is that something you want to pursue?" Dixie asked bluntly and again watched him for a reaction. Deep down she thought she already knew the answer, but she couldn't resist the chance to watch him squirm.

"I love Diane, and I've come a long way to have what I've got with her, and I'm not willing to mess that up," Jason said, dividing his attention between Dixie and the road.

"Good answer," Dixie said, suppressing a laugh. She decided to let him off the hook and change the subject. She gave a short sigh and said, "Diane told me that you know quite a bit about America's interstate system."

"Well," Jason said, he was caught off guard and let out a short laugh.

"Well?" Dixie turned his answer into a challenging question. She looked at him, tucked her chin to her shoulder, and arched an eyebrow.

"Okay," Jason said with a nod and a chuckle. "Get the atlas from behind my seat."

Dixie looked, saw the atlas, and pulled it from the box from behind Jason's seat. She then gave Jason a questioning look.

"All right," Jason nodded again. "Open the atlas toward the front, to the pages of the United States." Dixie flipped through the pages, found the map, looked at it, and then gave Jason another quizzical look.

"See any patterns?" Jason asked her.

Dixie's brow furrowed as she studied the map, then as she saw something, her face lit up with a smile.

"Well?" Jason coaxed.

"All of the even-numbered interstates run east and west, and all of the odd numbered ones run north and south," Dixie beamed.

"Good," Jason said, "and?"

"There's more?" Dixie asked, looked at the map again, but shook her head and said, "I don't see it."

"The even-numbered interstates, the ones running east and west, go higher in number from south to north, and…" Jason let it hang there, trying to lead her.

"The odd numbered ones go higher in number from west to east," Dixie blurted.

"Now, turn to the Illinois map," Jason instructed.

"What am I looking for now?" Dixie asked, she didn't try to hide her excitement.

"Mile markers or exit numbers," Jason said, then added when Dixie shot him another inquiring look, "little black numbers with little black triangles pointing towards little white squares along the interstates."

"Okay, I see them," Dixie said, studying the map.

"See any patterns?" Jason prompted.

"The mile markers get smaller as they go south, and they get smaller as they go west," Dixie didn't try to hide her excitement as she almost shouted.

"Very good, I'm impressed," Jason said. "Now, find Effingham and Mt. Vernon."

"All right, got them," Dixie confirmed.

"Look at where I-57 crosses I-70 in Effingham, and where I-57 crosses I-64 in Mt. Vernon," Jason told her. "When two interstates cross, and run together for a short distance like this, the direction they both run determines which mile markers are used on the map."

"You're right," Dixie said, she was amazed, then asked. "What else?"

"You want more?" Jason asked with false astonishment. He smiled. "Turn to the Kansas City map, and then when I tell you, turn one page to the St. Louis city map."

"All right, got them," Dixie said after ruffling through the pages.

"Three digit interstates, starting with an even number, run around cities, such as I-435. Some are like business loops, such as I-470 in Kansas City. Others change numbers, but go by the same rules, like I-270, and I-255 as you will see when you turn to the St. Louis map," Jason said. He continued when Dixie turned to the St. Louis city map. "Three digit interstates, starting with an odd number, run into a city and end, like a spur, like I-170."

"Wow," Dixie said, then turned an approving eye toward Jason.

"Now you know as much as I do," Jason said.

"That didn't take long," Dixie teased, and they both laughed. She sobered, then asked, "You don't like Clifford Strokes very much, do you."

"I wouldn't say that," Jason said. "Not at all would be more like it."

"He said something about the James Brothers, what did he mean by that?" Dixie asked.

"Strokes is a moron," Jason said. "First of all, true Missourians call them the James Boys. The outlaw reference he made has to do with the reputation that Missourians had after the Civil War. After the war, Missourians had a reputation of being bushwhackers, murderers, and thieves. The fighting, killing, plundering that went on along the Missouri-Kansas border was goin' on about seven years before the war started. Quantrel's Raiders, Bloody Bill Anderson, George Todd, and the Black Flag Brigade all were parts of that. The James Boys, first Frank, then Jesse, were involved in all that. Frank and Jesse learned the lessons of war and carried them over to their outlawry years. Clifford Strokes likes to embellish and exaggerate in situations like this."

"Diane said you were sort of a history nut," Dixie said.

"Is there anything Diane didn't tell you about me?" Jason asked.

"I don't think so. You stole the show yesterday," Dixie said with a laugh.

"It really made me mad when he yelled at Diane like that. There was no sense in him doin' that, and he had no right," Jason said.

"I agree with you, I can't imagine anyone being mean to her," Dixie said.

"What's gonna happen when we get to Barstow?" Jason asked, after he sobered.

"I wish I knew," Dixie said, then much to Jason's surprise added. "This Jack kinda has us over a barrel. He seems to know how to avoid and evade the authorities."

"What about the fights Keith has had with him?" Jason asked, hoping Dixie's mood to talk would continue.

"I think Keith was very lucky," Dixie stated frankly. "I knew a few navy seals when I was in the marines, and they were, for the most part, a pretty rough crowd, but I think Keith is alive only because Jack wants him alive for some reason. The first time they fought in the Nevada desert, Jack took Keith's knife from him and used it to kill the Chinese girl. The next time they fought on the Blanket Transportation parking lot, Jack fought just enough to rough Keith up a bit, then ran when he saw Selena coming."

"Maybe Jack is scared of Selena," Jason thought aloud.

"Maybe," Dixie said, "but it could be that Jack can't control her."

"What?" Jason looked at her.

"The dreams we've been having," Dixie met Jason's gaze. "There's no doubt in my mind that Jack is somehow responsible for those. I dream a lot about my father, and I know he's dead, I buried him."

"Some kind of mental suggestion?" Jason asked. "I can buy that, Diane had nightmares after all of the encounters she had with Jack."

"I just wish we knew what we were dealing with," Dixie pondered. "It's like every time he needs someone to look the other way, he somehow makes that happen. If I didn't know any better, I would say he's able to bend the rules of natural physics."

The roar of the truck engine was the only sound that the both of them heard for a few seconds. The bouncing of the air ride seats, the air ride cab, and the air ride suspension added a soothing motion to the silence.

"How far out of the natural world are you willing to explore?" Jason asked her.

"What do you mean?" Dixie answered with her own question.

"How religious are you?" Jason countered.

"My father took me to church when I was a little girl, sent me when I was older, and let me choose for myself when I became a teenager. Why?" Dixie knew she sounded almost defiant.

"Good," Jason stated, "then you know that there are only two forces at work on this world, good and evil."

"I can buy that," Dixie said. When Jason didn't continue, she added. "If you have a theory, I'm listening. You probably won't shock me anymore than I've already been. I have scientific lab techs giving me test results that defy logic."

"There is a story in the New Testament of the Bible where Jesus cast out a demon, or demons, known as Legion from a young man," Jason said, dividing his time between looking at Dixie and the highway. "It's also recorded that Jesus cast several demons out of Mary Magdalene. The Bible goes on to tell of Jesus sending his disciples out on similar missions."

"What's your point?" Dixie tried not to sound impatient.

"Who's to say that Jack isn't himself possessed or a demon?" Jason asked.

"Like I said, nothing would surprise me at this point. He wouldn't be the first one to claim, 'The Devil made me do it,'" Dixie said, turning to look out the window on her side. "How do we deal with it if Jack is one or the other?"

"I wish I knew," Jason said. Dixie could tell he was worried and scared.

"I need to know how to, and I think I'm saying this right, back up a log-book, and how to run more than one logbook," Dixie informed Jason later that night as they lay in their prospective bunks, she on the bottom one, and he on the top one.

"What makes you think I know anything about that?" Jason countered.

"Diane says you're pretty good at both," Dixie tried to keep the laughter out of her voice. It was probably a good thing that he couldn't see her right now, or she might lose what little composure she had at the moment.

"Great," Jason breathed barely above a whisper. They had driven across New Mexico, stopped for fuel on the west side of Albuquerque, then driven on to Arizona. She found it unbelievable how close four wheelers followed or cut in front of trucks. Jason stopped whenever Dixie asked and allowed her to stretch her legs.

"Well?" Dixie covered her mouth with both hands to stifle the laugh that threatened to escape. Then she tapped the bottom of Jason's bunk with one of her feet for emphasis.

"Why?" Jason sounded defensive.

"I need to know how it works for my investigation," Dixie prodded. She crossed her fingers at this telling of a half fib. She in fact did want to know as a result of something Clifton the safety director had said about how Jason could alter his logbook to make it appear he was in two places at once. Besides, Diane had in fact said that Jason was good at running two logbooks and backing up a logbook, but that she didn't think he did either one very often anymore.

"I tell you what, Dixie," Jason said finally. "I'll tell you what you want to know when you tell me what I want to know."

"Goodnight, Jason," Dixie said, she smiled in the darkness of the truck to herself.

"That's what I thought," Jason said to her, and they both drifted off to sleep.

Jason came awake with a start. He lay very still and listened.

"Just be there!" Dixie said with an intense whisper. "Just be there...Yes... No, that will have to wait until after this is all over...I'll see you later...I love you, too. Bye."

Jason heard a beep, then a click, and knew that Dixie had been on talking to someone on her cell phone.

"How much did you hear?" Dixie asked.

"What makes you think I heard anything?" Jason asked, then cursed himself for not keeping quiet and playing possum.

"When you wake up, you stop snoring," Dixie informed him.

"Who is he?" Jason asked.

"What makes you think it's a he?" Dixie barely kept the laugh silent that threatened to escape her. "His name is Kyle. His family is from Montana, and that's where he is now. We met in the marines. I went into the FBI, and he went into the U.S. Marshall Service. He'll be meeting us in Barstow."

"A cowboy. Can I call him Marshall Dillon or Rooster Cogburn?" Jason teased.

"The two of you are gonna get along fine," Dixie said, and Jason thought he heard her eyes roll in that tone.

Chapter 28

The truck stop parking lot was dark. There were several truck stops in Barstow, and Jason picked the one with the largest parking lot. The last leg of the drive had taken them less time than Jason had anticipated.

"What are we doin'?" Jason whispered to Dixie. They were standing at the rear of the trailer they had swapped with the other Blanket Transportation driver. The other driver, at Dixie's request was already on his way back toward Los Angles.

"We're waiting," Dixie breathed.

Jason had parked the rig in a vacant pull-through parking spot in a more secluded area of the parking lot. Dixie had asked him to do this, in her mind keeping this business away from as many patrons as possible, she already had one civilian involved. They were crouched at the rear of their trailer now. Dixie was very adamant about Jason staying with her, not that she was scared to be alone, but wanted to keep tabs on him. She knew if anything happened to him, she would not be able to face Diane.

"We don't even know if we're at the right truck stop," Jason whispered to her.

"Believe me," Dixie whispered back, "he will find us. He wanted this and thinks he has something to prove." Dixie then pressed one of her hands to one of her ears and cocked her head as a voice sounded over her earpiece.

"Red one is in place," said a female voice through Dixie's earpiece, it was barely loud enough for Jason to hear if he pressed close which he did.

"Copy," Dixie responded with a whisper into a hidden mic nestled in her sleeve.

"Blonde one is in place," said a different female voice through Dixie's earpiece, Jason also heard this voice. These were codenames the two female agents had picked for themselves.

"Copy," Dixie repeated with another whisper.

When they had arrived at this truck stop in Barstow, Dixie had explained to Jason what she had in mind. Two female FBI agents would pose as her, and two male FBI agents would pose as Jason. Dixie told Jason that she hoped this would throw Jack off balance and might give her an edge since she had no idea what Jack had planned.

Jason had seen a transformation in Dixie in the last couple of days. When they had first met, Jason thought she was uptight and all business, but in the last few days he had seen her loosen up a little. One of the things was the way she dressed. She would have drawn attention to herself if she would have worn her loose-fitting, conservative suits out here on the road with him. Now she wore tight-fitting jeans, sneakers, a T-shirt, and a light jacket, and she had her hair pulled back into a ponytail instead of pulled up into a bun.

"Did you hear that?" Dixie whispered to Jason.

"Hear what?" Jason whispered back, he hadn't heard anything.

"Me sneaking up behind you." Jason and Dixie both heard the voice come from behind them.

Jason whirled around, his defenses automatically engaged, but Jack had anticipated this and attacked. It was brief. Jack threw a punch that connected with Jason's jaw, and Jason simply went down and out.

"No," Dixie said in disbelief and took an involuntary step backwards. She had initially gone for her primary handgun, a Sig Sauer, but froze, she could not make herself believe that the person she saw standing there was actually standing there.

"Hello, Dixie," Jack said to her, his voice low, deep, and gravelly, like what a dead person's voice might sound like. "You're not playing by the rules."

"No," Dixie repeated with a shake of her head and tears started to flow. Dixie took another step backwards, tripped and almost fell over something. She turned to see that it was just a piece of dislodged asphalt. When she turned again to face Jack, he and Jason were gone.

"This has not gone as planned. Move in now," Dixie said into the mic up her sleeve.

Jason opened his eyes with a grimace and touched his sore jaw. He had taken some hard blows when he was in Tae Kwon Do, but this hurt like hell. He shook his head slightly a few times to try to loosen the cobwebs and clear his vision. It worked, but his head still hurt. He noticed he was sitting on the ground with his back propped against a trailer tire.

"Good, you're awake, I was starting to worry, buddy" Jason heard someone say, and when he turned toward the direction of the voice, he saw Keith squatting on his heels a few feet away.

"I saw Jack drag you here, and I ran him off," Keith said, he kept up a constant surveillance around them.

Jason, trying to buy some time to recoup a little, said, "How did you do that?"

"I kicked his ass," Keith grinned at him.

"Did you learn some new tricks?" Jason asked, his vision finally cleared, and the double Keiths he had seen moments before now merged into one.

"What?" Keith was caught off guard, and looked right at Jason.

"No offense intended, buddy, but Jack has kicked your ass twice. Did you learn some new tricks?" Jason returned Keith's gaze.

"Don't sugarcoat it, buddy," Keith's grinned widened as he chided Jason, "please, speak your mind."

"You can't be here," Jason made himself believe it. "You're back home with your wife."

"You're right," and Keith stood up, his face masked in shadows, then the voice changed. "He couldn't be here, but I can." Jason heard Stu's voice say.

Jason looked on in disbelief.

"You don't have an inkling of a clue of how lucky you are," Jack posing as Stu said. "Otherwise you wouldn't let that fine piece of ass Diane work around people like me. I plan to take her away from all of that."

"Just like that," Jason mused, he was almost back to himself now, but he still didn't trust himself to stand. "Maybe Diane will have something to say about that."

"Oh, please," Stu/Jack chuckled. "Diane is like every other woman that's ever walked the face of the Earth, only good for one thing, maybe two if you can keep them from yackin' long enough to use their mouth."

"You're wrong," Jason said, he tried to keep from looking at Jack.

"Diane will be mine," Jack used Stu's voice on Jason.

"Not if I can help it," Jason said, he started to get his legs under him.

"That sounds like a challenge," Stu/Jack chided Jason. "Fine, I accept."

"Accept?" Jason asked, he wasn't sure what had just transpired.

"Sure," Stu/Jack continued. "Let's make it simple, whoever gets back to her first, gets first crack at her. I predict that I will get first crack at her," Stu/Jack announced, then before Jason could stand erect, Stu/Jack was gone into the night.

FBI Special Agent Melanie Fisk, Red One, and her partner FBI Special

Agent Teddy Biney held their positions. Both of them had heard voices, then had heard what sounded to them like Agent Crenshaw say the word no twice, the second time louder. Then as they watched the spot where Agent Crenshaw was supposed to be, they saw one figure dart out of that spot with supernatural speed as he dragged another figure. They both remained where they were and looked at each other in disbelief.

"What do we do now?" Melanie whispered to Teddy.

"I say we go in there with guns blazing," Teddy's answer was more of a rasp than a whisper and to Melanie, it didn't sound like anything Teddy would say.

When Melanie turned to look at her partner, she saw it was Teddy but not Teddy. His facial features were in the right place, but there was something about his eyes. Maybe it was that red flash she had just seen, and the lingering red shimmer that remained there.

"Teddy?" Melanie asked, she was perplexed.

"No," Teddy/Jack said, as Jack kicked the limp form of Teddy that lay at his feet.

Melanie's eyes widened, and she went for her primary weapon, but somehow Jack had anticipated this, and caught her wrist in a nearly bone-crushing grip. Jack shoved an ether-laden rag in Melanie's face, her eyes rolled up, and her body went limp.

"How about a little road trip?" was the last thing she heard Jack whisper into her ear before she went unconscious.

FBI Special Agent Aaron Knolls watched the parking lot from the position Agent Crenshaw had assigned him and his partner FBI Special Agent Amanda Vail, Blonde One. He was not happy, he had wanted to be assigned with Melanie. The infatuation he felt for her had grown to a full-blown crush, and tonight after this little exercise was over, he had decided to approach her, put out some feelers to see if his feelings were reciprocated. For now, though, he needed to stay focused and catch this guy so he could approach Melanie.

A movement caught his eye from Melanie and Teddy's position. What were they doing over there, dancing? That's what it looked like to him.

"Amanda," Aaron whispered to his partner and turned to look at her. They were standing back to back between two parked trailers.

"What?" she answered with a whisper.

"There's something going on with Melanie and Teddy, we need to go take a look," Aaron knew his whisper sounded anxious.

"No," Amanda whispered back.

"But—" Aaron whispered his protest.

"She'll be fine," Amanda whispered to him.

"What?" Aaron's whisper increased in volume. "You know?"

"Everybody knows," Amanda whispered to him, then smiled.

"Melanie?" Aaron whispered after he swallowed hard.

"Yes," Amanda confided with a whisper. "She thinks it's sweet."

"Yeah?" Aaron whispered to his partner, then turned to look in the direction of Melanie's position. When Amanda didn't answer him, Aaron turned to face her once more. He saw her eyes, they were wide with fear, and a hand with a rag in it was covering her mouth. Aaron traced the hand holding the rag with his eyes, and followed it up the arm, to the shoulder, then to the face. The face looked cold and dark except for the two red glowing eyes. Aaron went for his primary weapon.

"Yeah," Jack answered the last question Aaron had posed, then knocked him out with a single punch.

Dixie had finally recovered from her scare, her boyfriend U.S. Deputy Marshall Kyle Michaels was with her now. Dixie quickly gave him a run down on what had happened and what she had seen. She was certain of that, it wasn't what she thought she had seen, it was what she had seen. Then she told him about Jason's disappearance.

"We have to find him, if anything bad has happened to him, I'll never forgive myself," Dixie said, new tears threatened to erupt, but she fought the urge down.

"All right," Kyle said. "If you hadn't told me this guy reminds you of your father so much, I would be jealous."

"We've just got to find him," Dixie knew she sounded whiney.

"Okay," Kyle soothed her, then hardened his tone. "We will not be splitting up."

Dixie nodded when he forced her to meet her gaze.

Jason saw them approach warily, he was leaned up against the rear of the trailer where Jack had left him.

"Jason?" Dixie asked in a low tone when they were only a few feet apart.

"Yeah," Jason said with a nod.

"How do we know it's really you?" Dixie posed.

"You better hope it's me, otherwise you'll have a hard time facing Diane if I'm dead," Jason said to Dixie, then winked at her.

"It's him," Dixie told Kyle, breathing a sigh of relief. Then she introduced them.

"Nice to meet you," Jason said to Kyle as they shook hands.

"Likewise, Mr. Fox," Kyle said. "I hope someday that I'm as famous in Dixie's eyes as you are." Both Jason and Kyle grinned when they saw Dixie blush.

"We need to check on the other two teams," Dixie interjected. "Where are your people, honey?"

"I left them to guard the perimeter," Kyle said as he scanned the area with his eyes. He acted as though he ignored her slip of the tongue, and shot Jason an imploring glance, hoping he would do the same.

The three of them, as a group, found Melanie's clothes next to Teddy's unconscious form. Kyle bent to Teddy and brought him around.

"Shit," Teddy said as he rubbed his aching jaw and saw the pile of clothes that he recognized as Melanie's lying next to him. They were piled in a neatly, jacket on the bottom, then pants, weapons, shirt, bra, then panties. A note lay on the top of the pile, it simply read:

Thanks,
I needed a redhead for my collection, now I need to go collect the blonde.
Catch me if you can,
Jack.

"Dammit!" Dixie swore as she handed the note to Kyle.

"Burton, Sanchez, I need you down her right now," Kyle spoke up the sleeve of his jacket, into a mic of his own. Then to the other three with him he said, "Just in case we find another scene like this one."

When the two deputies that Kyle had radioed arrived, Burton stayed with Teddy, while Jason, Dixie, Kyle, and Sanchez headed in the direction of where Amanda and Aaron had been stationed.

They found Aaron unconscious, lying on the ground, next to another pile of clothes that were no doubt Amanda's. The clothes were piled the same way, and in the same order, jacket on the bottom, pants, weapons, shirt, bra, then panties. Along with the clothes was another note:

Thanks for the blonde,

I never pass one of them up, and she's a natural blonde too! This must be my lucky night. First a natural redhead, and now a natural blonde. I'm headed for Springfield.

Catch me if you can!

Jack.

"Shit," Kyle breathed when Dixie handed him the note, and he read it. "These notes look like they were prewritten, and he predicted the order we would find them."

"We need to get you to the airport so you can beat him back to Springfield," Jason said to Dixie.

"No," Dixie said, she kept her voice low, and her tone level. "That won't work. Something will go wrong. I can't explain it, but I just know that if I try to beat Jack back to Springfield any other way than in your truck it won't work, and maybe more innocent people will die in the process, and I'm not willing to take that chance."

"Dixie?" Kyle had never seen her like this.

"All of this is just a game to him. He lured me out here on the pretext that I could catch him. He's having fun showing me that he can yank our chains, and now two of our field agents will pay the price," Dixie said and bowed her head.

"Okay. We better saddle up." Jason said to her, and saw the look of despair and defeat in her face. He shook hands with Kyle, and said, "It was nice to meet you."

"Wait," Kyle said to Jason as he turned to walk toward his truck. " I have about a dozen U.S. Deputy Marshals on the outside perimeter, and about that many San Bernardino County Deputies and Barstow Policemen on the inside perimeter. This Jack won't get passed my people."

"He probably already has," Jason stopped walking long enough to say to Kyle.

"Dixie?" Kyle looked at her.

"He's right," Dixie said to Kyle. "I don't know how I know, but Jack has already left this parking lot in his truck, in full sight of everyone, and no one was suspicious enough, or even compelled to try to stop him."

"I'm sorry," Kyle hung his head, he knew somehow too, he was just having trouble accepting it. "Please be careful."

"I will, thanks for coming and helping me. Right now, Jason and I need to get some sleep, we've been up all day and all night," Dixie turned to follow Jason. She stopped, returned to Kyle, pulled him into her embrace, and in front of everyone present, kissed him hard and long on the mouth.

"Dix—" he started, but she motioned for him to be quiet.

"If there's one thing I've learned these last few weeks, it's that life's too short," Dixie purred to him. "Wrap this mess up here, and get your ass to Springfield as fast as you can."

"Dixie?" Kyle was shocked, he had almost never heard her cuss. "Missouri?"

"Yes, Missouri," Dixie said, she still held him tightly in her embrace. When he started to say something else, she silenced him with another kiss. When their kiss ended, she pulled away from him, and said loud enough for the small group to hear, "I love you."

Kyle stood there dumbfounded as he watched her walk away. Her actions just now were so unlike any he had ever experienced from her. When they were in the marines together and dating, she had always been refined and composed and very rarely showed any public display of emotion toward him. After the marines, she opened up a little, but nothing like what had just happened here. He would cherish those three little words she had just said to him and hoped they wouldn't be the last he ever heard her say.

"I love you, too, Dixie," Kyle choked through a sob barely loud enough for her to hear as he watched her walk away. He knew he had a lot to do before he caught that flight to Springfield.

Chapter 29

Jason ran through the gears. He knew he was making the black smoke roll out of the smoke stacks. The load they had on, a load of toys, weighed about ten thousand pounds. He figured they would make good time across I-40 as long as they didn't get stopped by any Smokey Bears.

"We should've dropped the trailer," Jason said to Dixie. "We could've then at least made good time."

"No!" Dixie snapped, asking for an apology from Jason with her eyes. "It might break the rules in this game Jack is playing in his demented mind."

"Let's face it, he's probably gonna kill those two lady FBI agents anyway," Jason argued.

"Probably," Dixie sniffed, "but so far, he seems to have kept to a certain set of rules. I accepted his challenge, tried to outwit him, and lost that round. I'm not willing to do that again. My head will be on the chopping block with the Bureau after tonight as it is now, and quite frankly, Jason, I'm scared of what Jack might do if he thinks I'm trying to cheat at his little game."

"Well, not to throw gas on the fire, but didn't you do that back there with the decoys?" Jason asked.

"Yes," Dixie sniffed again. "I'm worried about who he might take if I break his rules."

"Who?" Jason was afraid he knew the answer to that.

"We've received only one note from Jack expressing an interest in a family in Springfield," Dixie said, then looked at Jason. "You gave me that note."

"Shit!" Jason breathed. "Diane and her girls."

"I'll do anything you need me to do to get us to Springfield as fast as possible in this truck," Dixie told Jason in a flat tone.

"Right now, just handle any California Bears that want to stop us," Jason said, he really had the Peterbilt cranking now.

"One way or the other," Dixie said and held up her badge and Sig Sauer simultaneously for Jason to see.

They crossed the Colorado River, out of California, and into Arizona in just under two hours. Jason held their speed steady at eighty-five miles per hour. He slowed slightly when they approached the Arizona Port of Entry, and hoped that his scale Pre-Pass would give them the green light to go on, and it did.

"All of a sudden I feel tired," Jason said with a yawn.

"Me too," Dixie said. "Maybe it's because we've both been up for over twenty-four hours."

"I hate to stop, but Jack'll have to sleep sometime too," Jason sounded as if he were trying to convince himself.

"Let's get some sleep, then I'll help you do some of the driving," Dixie offered.

Jason pulled into the rest area just east of the port of entry and parked in one of the spaces for trucks. It would be daylight soon, and Jason figured it would be hot, so he let the motor idle with the air conditioner running. Dixie climbed onto the bottom bunk, and Jason pulled the strap to lower the top bunk. As Dixie positioned her privacy curtains, Jason zipped the leather curtains closed that separated the sleeper from the cockpit. Truck drivers often referred to the driving compartment of a truck as a cockpit, especially male truck drivers.

"Are you gonna be all right?" Jason asked Dixie after he had climbed onto the top bunk, he could hear her softly weeping.

"Yes, I'm sorry, I'll try to be quiet," Dixie sniffed.

"You know," Jason said easily, "it would be stupid on anybody's part to blame you for any of this."

"I went against all my training on this, especially after I met Diane," Dixie continued to sniff.

"Well, she does have that effect on people," Jason tried a joke.

"Yes, she does," Dixie laughed between sniffs, then after a deep breath said, "I'll be lucky if I can find a private security job after the Bureau is through with me."

"Will they be that rough on you?" Jason asked.

"Just think of what your safety guy, Clifford Strokes, would do to you if you were in my position, and he was your boss," Dixie said, her tears and sniffs were few and far between now.

"Shit, you are screwed," Jason tried humor once more, thinking it had helped last time.

"You," Dixie chuckled, and kicked the bottom of the top bunk. Jason smiled to himself.

They both woke within minutes of each other around one in the afternoon, and after their restroom routines, they headed out again. They had slept longer than either had wanted, and both reasoned that Jack had something to do with that. The thought of sleeping together had crossed both of their minds, but without saying a word to one another, they had dismissed the thought, and both knew they had scored a victory against Jack's subliminal suggestion.

With Dixie driving some, and Jason showing her how to cut corners on a logbook, a little under nine and a half hours from the California/Arizona line found Dixie driving and bearing down on Amarillo. Jason showed her how to cut corners, because he did most of the driving, with Dixie driving long enough for him to take two to three hour naps.

"Amarillo?" Jason asked, sitting on the bottom bunk. Dixie insisted he sleep there while she drove. It was dark out, and the clock face on the stereo showed ten-thirty P.M.

Jason smiled to himself as he remembered one time when Diane had been with him when they came through Amarillo. She had been talking on the CB to truck drivers off and on all night, nothing suggestive or full of innuendo. As they had gotten closer to Amarillo, Jason had told her that Amarillo was not a good town for a woman to be on the radio, because prostitutes that hung out at truck stops, lot lizards as truckers called them, used the CB to advertise. Jason told her he didn't care if she talked on the CB in Amarillo, but for her not to be too surprised at what she might hear from both men and women. She had gotten a real education that night.

"Ready to drive?" Dixie asked. "You know I don't like driving through big cities. We idiots that drive four wheelers scare me."

"Yea," Jason said, ran a comb through his thinning hair, and rubbed his face with his hands, "I can take over."

Dixie eased her foot off the accelerator pedal, it was hard to believe how fast she had been driving. The speedometer showed eighty miles per hour, and the needle was past that point, and she guessed her speed to be more like ninety miles per hour. She backed her speed down to sixty-five miles per hour, reached a hand over to the console, and set the cruise control. Next she pressed her left foot down on a small pedal left of the clutch pedal that released the steering wheel, which tilted more toward the dash. She reached a hand under the driver's seat, pulled the lever to allow the seat to slide all the way back. When she stood up, she retained her hold on the steering wheel with her left hand, and stepped to her right, in front of the gear shift and toward the passenger side seat. Jason slipped into the driver's seat, pulled the seat up, pressed his foot on the pedal to release the steering wheel, and pulled it back into place. When Dixie felt the steering wheel tilt, she let it go, and sat down on the passenger seat. Jason had talked her through this procedure the first couple of times, now though she was proficient at it, and it took no more than fifteen seconds for them to change drivers.

"Sleep okay?" Dixie asked him, she got her first good look at him now, and although he had slept a couple of times since leaving the rest area in Arizona, he still looked tired. Dixie thought a big part of his haggard look was due to stress.

"Yeah," Jason gave her a smile, "I should be okay until Oklahoma City."

"Well, hell's bells, I don't believe it," said a voice over the CB speaker. "Is that you, Fox?"

"Yeah," Jason replied. "Who's that?"

"This is Mud Flap, I just jumped on the interstate behind you here," Mud Flap's voice responded over the CB speaker. Jason knew Mud Flap's real name was Larry Knight. "Where ya headed to?"

"I'm on my way to the house," Jason said into his mic, then as a way of explanation, "I've got a family emergency at home I've got to get in for."

"Dang, I hate to hear that," said Mud Flap's voice over the speaker. "Well, if you don't care, I'll just tag along."

"No, I don't care, but it's gonna be a fast trip," Jason said into his mic. Dixie sat patiently on the passenger seat, listening and watching.

"Damn it, girls," Jason heard Mud Flap's voice over the CB speaker again. "Hey Fox, there's two girls in this black 379 Pete comin' up beside you, that'sa hollerin' ana showin' off their hooters! I've gotta have me another look at those!"

"Hooter? Does that mean what I think it does?" Dixie asked Jason, whose face had gone hard and rigid. Her expression changed when she saw Jason's demeanor change. Then her countenance changed to one of understanding as she said, "Jack."

"Could be," Jason said, then reached for the CB mic, but before he could speak, Mud Flap's voice came over the speaker again.

"Honey Hush," Mud Flap's voice said over the speaker. "A blonde and a redhead, they don't get much better than that!"

"No, they sure don't," said a deep, hollow voice over the speaker.

Jason kept an eye on his driver's side rearview mirror and could see the truck in question easing up on them. Soon the truck was beside them, and both Jason and Dixie looked on in disbelief. In the passenger side window of the other truck, Jack had somehow seated Melanie on the passenger seat, with Amanda sitting on her lap, facing her. They both looked out the window. Their arms were above their heads, probably tied there somehow, and their breasts touching.

Jason looked at the scene for an instant, then looked into the frightened faces of the two women. Jason could tell they were, and had been, crying. He looked past the women to Jack. Jason noticed the two women's faces change as though they recognized Dixie, then a look of pleading for help came over their faces.

"Back off, Mud Flap, you don't want any part of this," Jason said into his CB mic.

"Are you kiddin', I'm gonna get me another look, they came by me the first time too fast," Mud Flap's voice said over the speaker.

Jack's truck was in the far left lane. Jason's truck was in the lane next to the left lane. Larry's truck had been right behind Jack's. When Jack's truck slowed down so Jason and Dixie could take a good long look, Larry switched lanes, to the third inside lane, Jason didn't see the move. Larry passed Jason on the right, revealing to all that he too drove for Blanket Transportation.

"Bring them hooters up here again so I can see 'em," Mud Flap's voice said over the speaker. Larry turned on his left turn signal and merged into the lane in front of Jason.

"What's the twenty on the hooters?" asked about half a dozen different voices at different times with seconds of each other, some bleeding over onto each other.

"Mud Flap, back down, this is not what you think," Jason implored into his CB mic, then he had to step on the brake pedal and downshift when he saw the brake lights on Larry's truck light up.

"Bring them hooters on up here," Mud Flap's voice said over the speaker.

"Own my way," said Jack's deep, hollow voice over Jason's speaker. "Ol' Fox there must be queer, he spent more time lookin' at me than he did these tits on display."

"Is that right, Fox?" Mud Flap asked. Jason bit his tongue.

"'Course, he's probably gettin to see and feel all he wants to from that sweet, little thing he's haulin' around with him," came Jack's voice over the speaker.

"You have a woman in there with you? Is Gabby with you?" Mud Flap's voice was energized as it came over the speaker.

"No, she's not his wife," Jack's voice came over the speaker before Jason could key up, "and if he's not banging her, he is queer, but if for some reason he isn't banging her, he knows between Diane, Selena, and Christine, there's some prime pussy waiting on him at home."

"Jason?" Dixie asked when she saw the color of his face change. The anger inside him built to a volcanic pressure. He would not deny that he loved all three of the women Jack had mentioned, and in some way he had grown to care a great deal for Dixie. The love he felt for Diane topped all the scales used for measuring the emotion, friendship, companionship, and sexual. Sexual being mentioned last was certainly not the least, but was definitely an added bonus as both of them enjoyed it with each other. The love he felt for Selena was different and not sexual. The same could be said of Christine and Megan, nothing in their relationships pointed to anything sexual, and the emotion he felt for Dixie was more along the parental love he felt for Christine and Megan. This was a blatant lie conjured up by Jack to illicit the reaction he got from Jason, pure anger and rage.

"Jason?" Dixie asked again, her tone more apprehensive now.

"Hang on to something," Jason growled through clinched teeth. He checked the rearview mirror on the passenger side, turned on his right blinker, and swerved into that lane. He mashed the accelerator pedal flat on the floor, and started to gain on Larry's truck.

"Hey, somethin's not right with those girls," Mud Flap's voice said over the speaker, his and Jack's trucks were running side by side. "Hey, Fox?"

"Yeah, Mud Flap, I know, that's what I've been trying to tell you," Jason said into his keyed mic, his speed was fast approaching seventy-five miles per hour. He and Dixie were still a good truck length behind them, but closing, and the three of them were approaching the I-40, U.S. Highway 287 split: I-40 the left two lanes, and normally U.S. 287 the right two lanes, although the far right lane of the 287 exit was closed due to construction.

"Somebody should help those poor girls—agh!" Mud Flap's voice started to say, then screamed over Jason's CB speaker. At the same time, and without any warning, Larry jerked his steering wheel hard to the right to steer away from the horrible face Jack had just shown him through the window. "Fox, he's the devil himself, those red eyes!"

"Damn it," Jason cussed as, once again he was forced to step on the brake pedal, and steered back into the center lane, luckily, at this time of night, the traffic in this section of the city was light, almost nonexistent.

Larry had recovered from his scare and was gaining speed again. No sooner had Jason started to gain speed again, than two four wheelers morphed out with wide tires and wheels, wide fender flares, spoilers, and fins passed them, one on the left, and one on the right at a very high rate of speed.

Larry was almost on top of the I-40/287 split, his and Jason's speeds were up around seventy-five miles per hour, when he changed lanes, back into the center lane. Both four wheelers turned on their right turn signals, indicating they would exit onto U.S. 287, and instead of doing that, they merged into the far left lane.

"Larry, watch out you have two four wheelers comin' up on your left that will probably try to cut you off," Jason said into his keyed mic, trying to warn his friend.

"I'm goin' after those poor girls," was the last thing Jason heard Larry say over the CB speaker.

The two four wheelers, as Jason had predicted, instead of waiting possibly two seconds and merging in behind Larry, tried to zip around him on I-40 and onto U.S. 287. The two highways are divided by a guardrail and an incline that swoops up and away with I-40 towards Oklahoma City, and slopes down and away with U.S. 287 towards Dallas/Fort Worth.

The first four wheeler cleared Larry's front bumper, the second wasn't so lucky. Larry's bumper clipped the second four wheeler, sending it into a spin down along the U.S 287 side, barely missing the guardrail. The force of the collision uncontrollably jerked the nose of Larry's truck toward the same direction. If Larry had steered more toward the right, he might have been able to ride it out onto U.S. 287, but his mind was consumed with trying to save the two doomed FBI women, and he jerked the steering wheel hard to the left.

The force of the sudden jerk of the steering wheel by Larry caused the load he was hauling to shift to the right, which pulled the tractor that way ever so slightly, and started the drive tires to skid. This brought the nose of Larry's truck onto a collision course with the dividing guardrail. When it hit, the tractor rode up on the guardrail in a shower of sparks, tilted toward the U.S. 287 side, and pushed along by its speed, overturned, and slid along U.S. 287 on its right side in a massive and brilliant shower of sparks.

Jason stomped on the brake pedal, the brakes locked up, as tractor and trailer skidded into a slight jack knife before coming to a complete stop. Jason set the brakes, pulled the lever on the steering wheel to activate the flashers, looked at Dixie, opened his door, and leaped from the cab of the tractor. Dixie had been mesmerized by the chase and was in a slight state of shock. She activated her cell phone, and dialed 911. As it started to ring, the CB crackled.

"Dixie, I know you're still listening," Jack's voice came to her through the speaker. "Come on, girl, after I'm done with these two, I'll be ready for you. I'll be waiting for you in Springfield."

"The police, ambulances, and fire rescue on all on their way!" Dixie called to Jason, as she ran up to the overturned truck. Jason was in the process of kicking out the windshield in an attempt to get Larry out. The smell of diesel fuel filled the air.

The four wheeler that had clipped Larry's bumper had slid all the way across U.S. 287 and had come to rest on the far shoulder. The other four wheeler had stopped and had backed up within a few feet of the first one. Two people got out of each car, two young men and two young women, none of them looked happy or friendly. The two girls had on tight shirts, and short skirts, they looked like a couple of party girls. The two guys wore loose jeans, white tank tops, and white baseball caps turned around backwards, with the elastic bands pulled down to their eyebrows. All four were white with deep tans. As they approached, Dixie noticed their walk was more of a cocky strut.

"Jason, we're gonna have some pissed off company real soon," Dixie warned Jason as she watched the youths stomp across the highway toward them.

"You're gonna have to handle it, Dixie, I'm a little busy here," Jason called to her over his shoulder, "and stay back, I've gotta try to get him out before this thing catches on fire."

"I won't stay back." Dixie was defiant. "If something bad should happen to you, well to use one of your wife's lines, my life wouldn't be worth a plug nickel." Jason could tell from her voice that the pressure of the last two days was about to send her over the edge. Even the FBI probably didn't teach their agents how to deal with Satan or his minions.

"Fine, let's get him outta there" Jason snapped at her. He had finally gotten the windshield to shatter, and got it loose enough around the edges where he could wrap his fingers around the edges and pull it free. With

Dixie's help, it was soon lying on the ground.

"Help," Jason and Dixie heard Larry's faint cry.

"We're comin', Larry," Jason told his friend. "Where are you hurt?"

"All over," Larry said, then coughed, and with that was a sound Jason didn't like.

"Can you undo your seatbelt?" Jason asked him, more to try to keep Larry busy and doing something, rather than needing to know. Jason carried a lock blade much like the one Jack had taken away from Keith, the seatbelt was not a concern of his, he could simply cut right through it.

"Yeah, I can do that," Larry rasped with another cough.

"Okay, wait, here's what I need you to do. Swing your legs and feet toward me, then release your seatbelt," Jason said, he had stepped through the hole previously vacated by the windshield, and half stood, half crouched on the passenger side door and broken out window of the overturned cab of Larry's truck. The smell of diesel fuel was stronger now and was mixed with the smell of hot oil from the motor. Jason knew it would be very likely that if hot oil and/or hot diesel fuel were to leak onto hot manifolds or hot exhaust pipes, the fire would be hot.

"My legs really hurt," Larry said with another gurgling cough. "I think my left arm is broken, and my right arm hurts really bad too." When Larry coughed this time, it was more gurgle than cough, and Jason knew he had internal bleeding, probably from the steering wheel, and that it was bad.

Jason reached up and helped Larry swing his legs toward him, Larry was still held in place by his seatbelt. Jason got a hold of him and nodded to Larry who pushed the button to release the seatbelt. Larry let out a wet cry of pain and fell toward Jason, who, with the help of Dixie who was reaching through the hole where the windshield had been, helped keep Larry on his feet when he landed next to Jason.

Jason guided Larry through the area recently vacated by the windshield, with Dixie on the outside gently pulling him. When they had him out, Larry draped his right arm around Jason's shoulders, and Jason noticed the amount of spit up blood on the front of Larry's shirt. Jason took most of Larry's weight as they moved away from the wrecked truck. Dixie moved off to intercept the advancing four youths.

Jason didn't want to lay Larry flat on his back, but he was fairly certain that Larry couldn't sit up on his own. They were at least sixty feet away from the overturned truck when it went up in whooshing flames, not an explosion, but a really hot fire. Jason looked at Dixie, who looked to be arguing with the four youths and holding her own. The group in her little party all jumped when the truck caught on fire.

When the truck had turned over, what little traffic there was had slowed due to rubbernecking. Now that the truck was on fire, someone must have sold tickets because there were all kinds of traffic driving by. Finally, off in the distance, sirens could be heard.

Jason sat Larry on the ground and propped him against a signpost. Larry was a big man, and Jason was almost worn out from helping him along.

"I don't care how bad he's hurt," said one of the young men as he belligerently approached the spot Jason and Larry occupied. "He fucked up my car, and he's gonna pay for it!"

"You back off right now, or the next thing you'll have fucked up will be your teeth," Jason stepped directly in front of him. The aggressive youth took another step toward Jason.

"Brian! Wait!" His buddy grabbed his arm, he had seen something in Jason's eyes he didn't like.

At that instant, the first police car arrived. Dixie had left the youths and was kneeling down beside Larry whose head rested fully against his chest. When Jason looked down at him, he noticed that the blood stain on Larry's shirt had doubled and that he wasn't breathing. Dixie looked up at him and shook her head. Two paramedics arrived and confirmed it. Larry was dead. Dixie unclipped the cell phone that hung on Larry's belt and held it up to her face. She activated the menu and scrolled down the file of stored phone numbers there.

"This guy hit my car in the ass end," Brian was telling the police officer as Jason and Dixie walked up to where they were standing.

"Where's the driver of this truck?" the police officer voiced his question in Jason and Dixie's direction.

"It's a tractor, not a truck," Dixie informed him, her anger was building to an eruption point. "A truck is what you haul stuff on, a tractor is what you pull things with, like a trailer, but, to answer your question, he's sitting right over there, dead, and this little piece of shit killed him."

"Dixie?" Jason asked, no one was more shocked at her use of language than Jason. The four youths shut up, and were looking at her wide-eyed. The police officer blinked at her and then swallowed.

"Ma'am, those are some strong words," the police officer finally managed to say.

"I suppose they have a different story," Dixie challenged.

"Well, yes, they do," the officer said, Dixie's attitude, and offensive posture was starting to make him nervous.

"That's right, bitch," Brian shouted at Dixie and pointed his fingers at her in some cross-arm motion.

"You kiss your momma with that nasty mouth?" Dixie prodded him. Jason wondered what had happened to the conservative, low-keyed Dixie that had been here just a few moments ago. Then Jason realized what was happening here, the pressure she was under had finally reached a boiling point, and this kid was about to get his money's worth. Jason realized that Dixie harbored a dark streak, she was setting this kid up.

"Hey! Fuck you, bitch!" Brian yelled, stepping toward Dixie.

"Hold it!" the officer said. He stepped between them, stared the guy down, then turned to Dixie. "Did you see what happened?"

"Yes, I sure did, Officer," Dixie said. She pointed to Brian and yelled, "That moron cut that burning truck off and is responsible for the driver's death!"

"You're out of yo' fuckin' mind, bitch! I ain't killed nobody!" Brian yelled back at Dixie. More police officers were on the scene now, filling the night with their flashing red and blue lights. They all were enthralled with the unfolding events.

"Please, sir, calm down, and watch your language," the first officer told him.

"She's lying!" Brian snapped, and gave Dixie a hateful look.

"All right, let's see some ID from everyone here," the first officer said, he was calmer now that he had some back up.

Everyone in the group started to comply, then stopped when Dixie whipped out her FBI badge.

"That's not real," Brian said. Actually, it sounded more like a hopeful request. Three of the police officers stepped forward and gave Dixie's badge a closer look.

"If I was you, kid, I'd be on my knees right now pleading for forgiveness," one of the three officers told him. "It's real."

"I'm FBI Special Agent Dixie Crenshaw on a special assignment, and until a little bit ago, was in pursuit of a wanted felon know only as Jack, who has kidnapped two other FBI agents," Dixie said, the two girls in the group gasped, covered their mouths, and looked at each other with terror, it was obvious that these two girls had at least heard the name. The police officers in the group were furiously writing information down onto their note pads. Dixie motioned toward Jason, "Along with my civilian partner, we had him in our sights and were closing in on him, when this asshole cut that truck off and caused this wreck."

"You should have contacted us, we could have helped," the first officer decided to take a stand.

"Really?" Dixie mocked. "How long did it take you to respond to this accident? Jason here had to rescue the other driver before he burned up. Go on, make a call. Call ahead, and set up a road block, then see how many of your people get killed or hurt, and that's if they even lay eyes on him. And you," Dixie said, her eyes flat, her voice low and menacing, her finger pointing inches from the kid's nose, "no matter when it is, no matter what is going on in my life, no matter what kind of a fancy lawyer you hire, I will drop everything I'm doing, come back here, and do everything in my power to fry your ass for vehicular manslaughter, if not murder."

Tears welled in the kid's eyes, his knees shook, his chin quivered, and his bottom lip trembled.

"What? Nothing to say?" Dixie prodded him. "A few minutes ago you were calling me a bitch. Half an hour ago, you were treating that dead man over there like he was part of your personal road obstacle course. You couldn't wait two seconds for him to get by, and God forbid you slow down and go behind him. Well, you know what? I will personally press the charges against you and your racing buddy here on the murder/manslaughter charges. I will personally file charges against the two of you for obstruction in an ongoing federal investigation. You two girls better find new boyfriends, these two will be worth less than what they are now when I'm through with them."

"I didn't do anything!" the other boy spoke up, his eyes wide with fright as Brian hung his head and tried to conceal his tears. Jason lowered his head and shook it slightly. He thought about a proverb Dixie had told two truck drivers a few days ago about how it would be better to keep your mouth shut and appear stupid, than to open it and remove all doubt.

"You weren't racing on a public interstate highway?" Dixie turned on him. "You weren't driving fast, over the speed limit, weaving in and out of traffic? Let me warn you right now, lying to a federal agent is a really, really bad thing."

Brian was all-out sobbing now and looking from person to person in the small group for a friendly face. Everyone either looked away or looked down at their scuffing feet. No one wanted to be in the path of the steamroller called Dixie.

"What's your parents' home phone number?" Dixie said Brian. "You can use Larry's phone, that's the man's name you killed tonight, to call them and tell them what you've done here. Then you can call your girlfriend's parents and tell them what you've exposed their daughter to tonight. And last, but certainly not least, you can call Larry's wife and kids, and tell them why their husband and daddy won't be coming home and what part you played in that."

The words hit him and his racing partner like stones, they both went to their knees weeping.

"We're sorry!" they took turns saying. Their girlfriends had completely backed away from them but stayed close to Dixie, and they eyed her with wary, respectful eyes.

"Sorry?" Dixie wasn't through yet. "The person who drove that truck was a man who had a family. He had parents, a wife, children, nieces, nephews, brothers, and sisters. You two didn't give a damn about him or his family, all you gave a damn about was saving two seconds. Well, I'm sorry, boys, sorry falls short of everything you just took away from Larry's family."

"Agent Crenshaw?" one of the officers finally got brave enough to speak.

"What?" Dixie spun on him, she still had fuel to burn.

"I think they've had enough," the officer ventured.

"Tell that to Larry's family," Dixie said, she felt the adrenaline start to subside, then looked back at the weeping boys huddled together on the ground. "It will never be enough. Come on Jason, let's give them our statements, then we have to get moving again."

Chapter 30

It took a couple of hours to give their statements and for Dixie to file the reports and charges she wanted to file. She had gotten a phone call from the deputy director and received a rather scathing dressing down. Jason had heard some of the words the deputy director had yelled at her, but through it all, and afterwards, she kept a stiff upper lip and held her head high. Jason decided she had John Wayne character.

It took a couple more hours to clear up the accident. Jason wanted to save any of Larry's possessions from the truck, but it had burned down to the frame, leaving a warped, charred metal skeleton. Jason made the phone call to Blanket Transportation, spoke directly to Leonard Blanket, and related everything to him, omitting Dixie's verbal rampage at Brian. When Leonard offered to call Gloria, Larry's wife, Jason told him that he would do it.

"Oh! My! God!" Gloria's voice sobbed in Jason's ear. Dixie let him use her cell phone to make the call. Jason had thought about using Larry's phone, but thought it too morbid.

"I know it's no consolation, but he died a hero," Jason offered, he had met Gloria a couple of times at company Christmas parties and driver appreciation cookouts that Blanket Transportation sponsored.

"What happened?" Gloria asked, she was calmer now, but still weeping.

"He was trying to save two women from the killer that calls himself Jack, when he got run off the road," Jason told her and heard her quick intake of air at the mention of Jack. Jason continued, "With some help, I managed to get him out of the truck before it caught on fire, and burned."

"Well, thank you for that, Jason," Gloria's voice said quietly from the earpiece of the phone. "I guess now I need to go get my kids out of school and tell them."

"Gloria, if there's anything me or Diane can do, don't hesitate to ask, okay?" Jason offered, he knew it sounded cliché, but he wanted to offer anyway.

"Thank you, Jason. Bye," Gloria's voice mumbled, then Jason heard the line go dead.

The events of the previous night had zapped their strength, and after driving about sixty miles east of Amarillo, they again climbed onto their respective bunks in the sleeper and slept.

Dixie was awakened by her ringing cell phone. She held it up to read the name on the caller ID and saw it was Tom calling her.

"Hello," she said after she pushed talk button.

"Hi, Dixie," Tom greeted her, and she noticed he sounded a little different, but she couldn't put her finger on it. "I've got a couple of new developments I thought you might like to know about. I didn't wake you, did I?"

"That's okay," Dixie said, she leaned through the curtains, quietly unzipped the leather curtains that hung between the cab and the sleeper, and was amazed that it was dusk outside. "We needed to be up anyway."

"Yeah, I heard what happened, sorry," Tom said.

"It's all right, but thanks," Dixie said. Jason snorted, his breathing became irregular, and when Dixie looked at him, she saw he was looking at her. She was standing there in her bra and oversized T-shirt. Jason blinked a couple of times, smiled at her, then motioned for her to climb back onto her bunk so he could climb down. When she did, Jason got dressed, squeezed some toothpaste onto his toothbrush, and exited the cab of the truck.

"Everything all right?" Tom asked her, playing the part of the big brother.

"Yeah, everything's as fine as can be expected," Dixie said, she propped herself up on her pillows, and readjusted her phone. "What's up?"

"I've gotten a couple of phone calls," Tom told her. "The first one was from Marcia Crockett. It seems Jack called her last night and wants to meet her tonight. She was willing to give me his file, but she said when she went to get it, it wasn't there."

"It was gone?" Dixie wanted to clarify.

"No," Tom said, his voice grew lower and softer. "The file was still there, but all the pages were blank."

"What are we dealing with here, Tom?" Dixie asked, her voice hushed.

"I wish I knew," Tom said.

"Well, you call Miss Crockett back, and you tell her to stay away from Jack," Dixie instructed. "You tell her he's dangerous."

"I don't think she was planning on seeing him, at least I hope she hadn't planned…" Tom realized he was babbling and slowly working himself into a corner.

"Tom?" Dixie asked.

"Anyway, moving on," Tom continued. "I got a call from one of the agents from the Akron, Ohio area."

"Oh?" Dixie chimed, Tom had her attention.

"Agent Cynthia Grooves told me she had gone back to Rachel's family just a couple of days ago to do a follow-up interview with friends and family," Tom said. "When she interviewed Rachel's boyfriend, a young guy, he told her that he recently became an ordained minister, that Rachel had been recently baptized, and that she was looking forward to being a preacher's wife. That's something we completely missed with our first interviews with her family."

"Okay?" Dixie wasn't following him.

"Something Diane told me the other night," Tom said. "She said that the only time she was able to run Jack off was to speak Jesus' name in a quick prayer asking for Him to help her. Put those two things together, you may come up with something."

"Like what?" Dixie was still not following.

"We all wondered why Rachel had not been raped, but stabbed so many times, I think maybe she had some divine intervention," Tom said.

"Yeah, but she's dead," Dixie reminded him.

"The preacher/boyfriend said that Rachel may have known she was gonna die, and that she probably prayed for her eternal salvation as a precaution," Tom told her.

"Well, that's something certainly to consider and keep in mind," Dixie agreed.

"Where are you now?" Tom asked.

"We are still in Texas, getting ready to cross into Oklahoma," Dixie said. "Why?"

"That's odd," Tom said. "One of the reasons I called was to see if you were involved in what was happening on the Oklahoma Turnpikes."

"Now what?" Dixie asked, then explained. "We've been asleep all day."

"Two of our agents, one in the Oklahoma City office, the other in the Tulsa office, say there was a rash of accidents and incidents along both turnpikes between Oklahoma City and Joplin, Missouri today," Tom informed. "First there were several accidents on the turnpike between Oklahoma City and Tulsa that the agent in Oklahoma City said they will still be clearing that stretch of interstate for another day, and that's not counting the accident reports, fatalities, what haz-mat will have to clean up, and everything else that goes on after an accident. He said he wouldn't be surprised if the state closed the turnpike for awhile.

"Then the Tulsa agent said there were two tanker trucks, one carrying gasoline, the other diesel fuel, that for no apparent reason decided to open every port on their tanks, drive as close to the concrete divider between the eastbound, and westbound lanes for several miles, then set the whole mess on fire. That shut down the turnpike going both directions. When the drivers were asked why they did it, they said that they didn't remember doing it. Can you believe that? The Tulsa agent said the fire crews are still out there fighting the fires. The turnpike will be closed at least for another day, then they will have to assess the damage.

"Then, there seems to have been an earthquake or something down around Muskogee, Oklahoma because the bridge that goes across the Arkansas River just north of there collapsed. Not only that, but every bridge between Muskogee and Oklahoma City seems to have collapsed."

"Jack?" Dixie ventured.

"Sounds like," Tom said. "I'm sure Jason knows another way home."

"I'm sure he does," Dixie agreed, then said. "Well don't stop with all of your good news at once."

"There is one other thing," Tom hedged.

"Yes?" Dixie drew the word out.

"The deputy director wants me to assume the lead on this case," Tom said, Dixie could tell he didn't want it.

"Tom?" Dixie asked after a moment's silence.

"I told him no, that if you went, I'm gone too," Tom stated.

"Don't get yourself in trouble," Dixie counseled.

"If he wants this case run a certain way, why doesn't he come out here and show us how to do it," Tom said. "Besides, after this case is wrapped up, I may do a little consulting, but that will be about it for me."

"Does a certain dispatcher lady have something to do with that?" Dixie teased.

"I'll let you know," Tom said.

"Speaking of ladies, how are they?" Dixie asked.

"I left them with three of our Springfield agents while I came to town to call you," Tom said. "I don't know how Jack knows the stuff he knows, but I wasn't going to take any chances of him having some triangling devices."

"Well, if we're dealing with what I think we're dealing with, it won't make any difference," Dixie said in a quiet tone. "Please, get back to them as quickly as you can. I would feel better if you were with them and, Tom, let Diane call me tonight."

"All right, boss," Tom said. "You two be careful."

"So which way do we go?" Dixie asked Jason. She had taken the time for her morning grooming session after Jason had returned to the truck and had started updating his logbook. When she returned to the truck, she related her conversation with Tom to him, and they continued east on I-40, toward the Oklahoma State Line.

"The only fast way that I know of is to run 40 over to Fort Smith, and run 540 north to Missouri, but I don't like it. It feels like we're being herded or driven," Jason said.

A few hours later when they reached the Arkansas state line, the enormous pressure Dixie had been under the last couple of months was starting to wear on her, and after apologizing to Jason, she went back to bed.

Interstate-540 runs through some of the roughest mountains in the Ozarks, one of which has a tunnel through it. A few miles north of that tunnel is an Arkansas state scale. Jason reasoned that it being as late as it was, the scale would be closed, it was not. There weren't any Pre-Pass scanners across the highway, so Jason had to pull in. He knew they were far from being overweight, everything had been working when he did his walk around inspection before they left the Texas rest area, he knew his logbook was caught up, and that all of his permits were current. All of these things went through his mind as he downshifted up the exit ramp to the scale house.

It was full dark by now, and the secluded scale house was well-lit all around. Jason turned off his headlights as he rolled to a stop sign in front of the scale platforms. He shifted into fourth gear, eased out on the clutch, and cracked open his driver's side window. He eased the truck onto the scale and listened for instructions from the external speaker hanging on a post beside the stop and go lights. When the light turned red, Jason eased the truck to a stop and waited. Something didn't feel right to Jason. He watched for the green light to flash on or for a verbal signal, telling him it was okay for him to proceed, he was disappointed.

"Please pull around to the rear and bring in all of your paperwork," said a female voice over the external speaker.

Jason complied, he parked around back in a well-lit area. He gathered up his logbook, his permit book, the bill of lading for the load they were hauling, then opened the door to climb out.

"What's wrong?" Dixie asked from the sleeper.

"Nothing," Jason answered, he knew she was worn thin from this Jack business. "Just a DOT inspection, it shouldn't take long, go back to sleep."

After he climbed down and closed the truck door, he went to the trailer, got the trailer permit from its holder, and headed for the driver's entrance of the scale house. There were two of them waiting for him, a man and a woman, both dressed in brown DOT uniforms.

"It took you long enough to come in," commented the man.

"Not over fifteen minutes," Jason defended. Most older truck drivers always held it as a rule that law enforcement would allow fifteen minutes for such business. That rule varied from state to state, but most law enforcement officials allow a reasonable amount of time, and that also will vary from state to state, and from official to official.

"Since you took so long getting in here, you should have everything we ask for," said the woman.

Jason knew the drill, had been through it numerous times, but lived by two rules in this type of situation where the inspectors were like this: one, supply only if asked for, and two, admit nothing. One of the most pleasant inspections he had gone through and one of the nicest inspectors he had ever dealt with was at the scale house on I-90 in Haugan, Montana.

The woman inspector scrutinized every permit in Jason's permit book. Next, she went over the trailer permit with a fine-toothed comb and asked Jason a couple of questions pertinent to the permit. Next she asked for Jason's Class-A operator's license which he supplied. Then she asked for his medical card which he produced. At last, she got to the logbook, and Jason had an idea of what she was up to. She had been taking her time with this, drawing out the inspection, and Jason suspected she was trying to add to his on-duty time. He stayed calm, never rolled his eyes, sighed heavily, shuffled his feet, or acted in any way that he was irritated. He spoke only when spoken to and was polite when he did so.

"Your logbook says you have a co-driver," the woman inspector said.

"That's correct," Jason said, looking her right in the eye, actually looking for any hint of red.

"I'll need to see her logbook, too," she said in a dismissive tone, as she slid everything back across the countertop to Jason.

"She's asleep right now," Jason told her.

"Well, I don't have to see her," the woman said in a condescending tone. "Just bring me her logbook."

"No, ma'am," Jason said, as he put his license and medical card back into his wallet.

"Did you not understand, boy?" the male inspector spoke up.

"I understood perfectly," Jason remained calm and never raised his voice, he too harbored a dark streak, somewhat much like Dixie's. "If you want to see her logbook, I suggest you go ask her for it."

"Is the truck locked?" he drew up to his full height and puffed out his chest.

"No," Jason simply said.

"And what will I encounter when I open that door and climb into that truck?" he asked, drawing out his words in a slow Arkansas accent, put his hand on the door handle, stopped, and looked right at Jason.

"A woman, five foot ten, maybe a hundred and ten pounds, prettiest one for miles around, and her name is Dixie," Jason said, letting his Missouri accent dance around the edges of his words, then he had to bite the inside of his bottom lip to keep from laughing when the inspector showed him a sneering grin, pushed the door open, and sauntered outside.

Dixie heard the door open and felt the truck rock, but never thought another thing about it. She had been on the truck long enough with Jason to know that if he needed her for anything, he would speak up, rather than invade her privacy. That was one thing she had learned early about Jason, he had never tried to catch glimpses of her dressing or undressing, or hinted in any way that was what he wanted. He was a true gentleman.

That's why she was surprised when the curtains Diane had specially made for her were forcibly opened, and even more surprised when a face she did not recognize pushed itself into her space. She knew from the expression on the man's face that his eyes hadn't adjusted to the darkness, obviously he had expected to catch her unaware.

She was slightly amused when she saw his expression change to that of an unseen terror when she cocked the hammer back on her Sig Sauer, and the recognition on his face when he stared down the business end of the gun's barrel. Obviously, it was the last thing he had expected when he stuck his head through those curtains, uninvited.

"Who are you?" Dixie growled.

"I—" was all he got out.

"What do you want?" Dixie pressed on with the same menacing tone.

"I—" he tried again.

"I'm sure I would be well within my rights if I shot you right now for breaking and entering," Dixie thought out loud.

"I—" he seemed to be stuck on that one word.

"Could you step a little more to your right, so your brains won't splatter all over the inside of the truck," Dixie said. "Oh, never mind, as empty as your head is, there won't be much spatter."

"Please," he finally muttered.

"So you're not a sailor after all," Dixie said. "With all of that aye-aye business you were spouting, I thought for sure we were at sea."

"No," he croaked. "I'm a—" he started, but Dixie cut him off.

"I don't care if you're the pope," she said. "You back your dumb ass up a step."

"Let me explain," he begged, his hands up in plain sight.

"No, let me explain something to you," Dixie said, she stopped long enough to pick up her badge case, then advanced on him. "You are gonna climb out of this truck very slowly with me watching you all the time. Then we're gonna go inside and sort this out."

"I just—" he started to say, but Dixie cut off his words when she stuck the barrel of the pistol right between his eyes and rested it on the bridge of his nose.

"Tell me, I mean there is the chance I've forgotten, where in my instructions to you did I say I wanted to hear any shit from you?" Dixie asked, horrified at herself for her use of language, she had never been one to cuss. Then she pressed the gun harder into his face, almost pushed him off balance, and stifled a smirk when she saw a wet circle appear at a point behind his zipper, then spread.

"Jesus, lady," he was almost crying now.

"March," Dixie ordered when they were on the ground. She knew she looked a sight, long night shirt, no makeup, hair uncombed, and bare footed. "Go in the same door you came out."

"What the—" Dixie heard the woman inspector say. Dixie shoved the male inspector forward and acquired the woman as her new target, as the man went face first onto the floor.

"You! Out here where I can see you," Dixie ordered the woman.

"I—" the woman said, raising her hands above her head.

"Move!" Dixie yelled at her. Then after the woman complied, Dixie said, "Now tell me what in the hell is going on here."

"She wanted your logbook, wanted me to get it for them," Jason spoke up. "I told them no, and One Bullet Barney here volunteered to go and get it."

"And you let him?" Dixie accused.

" I damned sure wasn't gonna climb in there and wake you up," Jason said.

"It's illegal for truck drivers to carry guns," the woman got brave.

"You can tell that to the judge when you go before him," Dixie said, she opened her badge case and showed both of them her FBI badge. The man felt confident enough to stand, but was conscientious about peeing his pants, even more so when he tried to cover it with his hands.

"You could have told me that out there," the male inspector accused.

"Do you want to try for two?" Dixie asked as she gave him a sober look. "I'm Dixie Crenshaw, Special Agent with the FBI. Why were we pulled in?"

"Routine inspection," said the woman inspector, she felt confident enough to lower her hands.

"Hands back up," Dixie snapped, motioning with her Sig Sauer. After the woman complied, Dixie asked, "Did he pass?"

"Yes," the woman muttered.

"You didn't find anything wrong with him, so you wanted to involve me," Dixie stated, her anger started to build for the second time in as many days.

"It's our right," the woman informed.

"You just interfered with a federal officer on a special assignment in a federal investigation," Dixie informed right back. "You're lucky I don't call the U.S. Marshals and have your two dumb asses hauled off right now." Jason would remember this night for years to come, because as many times as he would cross this scale in the future, whenever the DOT number was run on his truck at this scale, he never was asked to pull around back again.

"But—" the man started to protest.

"Shut up!" Dixie snapped. "Stupid and incompetent."

"I'm gonna buy you a T-shirt that says 'Day 28'," Jason teased her as they pulled back out onto I-540.

"You're a real comedian, Fox," Dixie said with a fake laugh, then her cell phone rang, she saw it was Tom by the caller ID.

"Dixie, bad news," Tom sounded harried. "Better let Jason talk to Diane, this won't be pretty."

Dixie offered the phone to Jason, who asked her to put it on speaker phone, which she did.

"Diane?" Jason asked.

"It's…him…with…her," Diane said between gasps. She sounded on the verge of hyperventilating. She would say a word, gasp, take in a quick breath, then speak. She sounded much like a small child when they try to talk while crying hard. In his mind, Jason could see Diane's chin quiver, her bottom lip tremble, and her head jerk with each hiccupping breath.

"With who, Diane?" Jason was scared now, he knew he wasn't going to like the answer to that question.

"Jack…has…Chris…tine," Diane's shaky voice panted out the words.

"Shit!" Jason yelled. With the taking of the two female FBI agents from California, and with what Dixie had told him about the killings, his blood boiled.

"Tom," Dixie cut off the external speaker to the cell phone, "I know I don't have to tell you this, but pull out all the stops, find him."

"I will, Dixie," Tom said. "I'm sorry, he blindsided me with Marcia. He kidnapped her, wanted to trade her for Diane. When that didn't work, he made me think he had killed Marcia, and tried to take Diane by force. Her daughters, Christine and Megan stepped in to help their mom. Diane's son-in-law, Joe, parted Jack's hair with an arrow from his compound bow, but Jack still managed to grab Christine and get away. I feel terrible."

"Make up for it, Tom, don't try to go back and change it," Dixie advised. "How's Marcia?"

"She's fine," Tom said. "He put her out with ether. She's still a little groggy, but she'll be all right."

"I have to go now, Tom," Dixie said, she heard the sound of the engine of the Peterbilt change pitch and felt the truck gaining speed. "Get me a line on where Jack is, he's probably headed for Blanket Transportation if I had to wager a guess."

"I'm on it," Tom said, then disconnected.

"Jason?" Dixie asked.

"I asked Leonard Blanket to authorize a full retraction of restrictions on this motor," Jason said by way of answer. "Just sit back and enjoy the flight."

Chapter 31

Jason had them to the Arkansas/Missouri State line in a little over an hour. By then I-540 merges with U.S. Highway 71 and is reduced to a two lane highway until it spreads back out to a limited access highway and stays that way to Kansas City. Jason behaved and kept his speed down around the speed limit until U.S. 71 became a four-lane highway again, then he cranked the truck's speed up once more. It wasn't until they reached I-44 that Jason really laid their ears back.

Jason had to guess at their speed. The speedometer had gone well past the eighty mile-per-hour mark, the last numbers on the speedometer, and was approaching the zero mark again. Jason's best guess put their speed at about one hundred and twenty miles per hour.

"Are you all right?" Dixie asked. She was tense and nervous, but tried not to show it.

"I'm fine, just worried about Christine," Jason commented. They were in the hammer lane, that is the passing lane, passing trucks and four wheelers alike. "I love both of Diane's girls like they were my own. I never once tried to force them to like me and didn't ever try to take their father's place. I just want to get to get to Strafford as fast as I can."

Dixie was silent, took out her cell phone, and dialed the hotline in Springfield. All she heard was a recording saying all circuits were busy. She punched the button for Tom's prerecorded number.

"Hi, Tom," she said. "Just wanted you to know we are quickly approaching Strafford. Our ETA is about forty-five minutes. I also wanted to ask if you could get us a police escort."

"Where are you now?" Tom asked, expecting her to say Mount Vernon or somewhere around there.

"We just left Joplin," Dixie said.

"Shit! I'll see what I can do, but if you're going as fast as what I think you are, I won't have to arrange an escort for you, the highway patrol will find you soon enough," Tom said, even Jason heard him over the roar of the engine. "Kyle made it in yesterday, he's here, but asleep right now."

"Okay, Tom, thanks, see you soon." Dixie pushed the end button on her cell phone.

"Damn it, boy. What's the big rush?" asked a voice over the CB speaker.

"No big rush, I always drive this fast," Dixie said into the keyed mic of Jason's CB, letting her Tennessee accent run wild. She mused to herself that she was the communications officer on this flight.

"Shit!" cried a voice over the CB speaker, a voice that Jason faintly recognized, a voice that belonged to the individual that had turned him in to Blanket Transportation for speeding all those weeks ago. "I guess you didn't learn your lesson the first time."

"What's the matter, sugar? Is that part of what they teach you in those truck driving schools, how not to mind your own business?" Dixie once again spoke into the keyed CB mic, her Tennessee accent running amuck. She decided to go for broke and help Jason all she could. "Just peddle a little faster, and maybe you can keep up."

"Public safety should be everybody's concern! I'll call the highway patrol on my cell phone!" the owner of the voice announced over the CB

"Good!" Dixie shot back. "Tell them not to shoot, that there's a federal agent aboard."

"What? What are you talking about?" the voice over the speaker asked hesitantly.

"I can't get through to them, I've tried already," Dixie answered.

"Well, I—" the voice sounded unsure now.

"What, you aren't gonna show us all how smart you are?" Dixie interrupted. "A minute ago you were gonna blow the whistle on us. Now, it seems you've lost your nerve. Have you called yet? Don't bother, by the time you take your thumb out of your dumb ass, we'll be where we need to be. Listen, next time you want to show everyone in earshot of your radio how stupid you are, remember this little saying my father used to say: It's better to keep your mouth shut and appear stupid, than to open it and remove all doubt."

Jason knitted his brows and looked at Dixie with a questioning grin that touched half of his mouth.

"What?" Dixie feigned innocence. "I'm just trying to help."

"Wow, that was awesome. I want to keep up with you," declared the voice of the man driving a tanker truck that Jason passed.

A truck pulling a flatbed trailer was in the hammer lane passing another tractor trailer combination when Jason ran up behind it. As soon as the flatbed cleared the other truck, its driver flashed his headlights to communicate to the flatbed's driver that he was clear to come back over.

"Say thanks skateboard into the mic," Jason told Dixie.

"Skateboard?" Dixie raised her brows. "Thanks, Skateboard."

"My pleasure darlin'," said a male voice with a Texas accent. "Do you look as good as you sound?"

"No," Dixie cracked. "I'm round and low to the ground."

"You catch on quick," Jason commented with a huff of laughter, the exchange between Dixie and the other truck driver had taken his mind off of Jack's capture of Christine.

Dixie grinned and gave a little false shrug at her smug reference to being short and fat. She hoped she could be this happy again after their encounter with Jack. She remembered being this happy with her father once. Other than the happy times she shared with Kyle, and that certainly wasn't the same as with her father, she hadn't been as happy with another man since her father's death.

"I want to ask you something," Jason said, bringing her out of her reverie.

"Sure," Dixie looked at him.

"Back there in Barstow, when Jack snuck up on us, you didn't see him as Jack, did you?" Jason asked. "You saw him as your father, didn't you?"

"Yes," Dixie said, tears welled in her eyes.

"That's why you couldn't shoot him," Jason said.

"Part of the reason," Dixie sniffed and wiped away her tears.

"What's the other part?" Jason wanted to know.

"I—" Dixie started, stopped, then went on, "I was afraid I might accidentally hit you."

"Dixie?" Jason said.

"Hear me out, this is gonna sound like it's goin' one way, but I'm gonna end goin' another," Dixie explained, her Tennessee accent refusing to go away.

"Okay," Jason nodded.

"I never thought I could love someone again the way I've grown to love you," Dixie said, took a quick breath, then went on. "When this case is all wrapped up, and hopefully we all live through it, I don't want our relationship to end. Although you're a little young to be my father, I've grown to love you like one."

"Well," Jason shot a quick glance her way, "if you're daddy was the kind of man I think he was, he would understand what I'm about to say to you. The old timers have a saying that goes like this: You're welcome at my fire anytime. And I know Diane would second that."

"Thank you," Dixie said, fighting off more tears. She reached across the cab of the truck and gave his arm a squeeze.

"Do something for me?" Jason asked. "Call Keith and ask him where he's at, and how soon he can meet us at the terminal."

"Sure," Dixie punched in the number Jason recited for her.

"He's a few miles ahead of us and will meet us there at the terminal," Dixie told Jason after her short conversation with Keith.

"Are you ready for what we might find there?" Dixie asked him.

"I hope so," Jason swallowed hard.

"I hope so, too," Dixie said. "Who do you see Jack as?"

"I've seen him as Keith and Stu," Jason said, he noticed the engine temperature was slowly approaching the two hundred degree mark, reached over to the console, and flipped on the switch to manually run the radiator fan. He then spoke louder to talk over the noise of the fan. "But most of the time I see him as that character Gary Sinise played in that movie, Reindeer Games. Anyway, that's who I saw him as in Barstow when he first snuck up behind us, again when we saw him in Amarillo, and whenever I see him in my dreams."

"I have a theory, if you would like to hear it," Dixie told him.

"Of course," Jason said, saw that the engine temperature had returned to normal, and he switched the fan off.

"Well, it appears to me…" Dixie told him her theory.

The parking lot was empty and quiet. Overhead lights on tall metal poles provided adequate lighting on the driver's entrance side of Blanket Transportation. The night air was cool, it was close to midnight, and a slight fog had lowered itself into the low-lying areas.

Jason and Dixie saw Keith's truck sitting in front of the dispatch office, facing the exit without a trailer hooked to it. They also saw Selena's car parked in its usual spot, and Tom's car parked next to it.

Jason pulled next to Keith's truck and parked, facing the opposite direction. Dixie and Jason looked at each other with wary questioning eyes, everything about this scene seemed too quiet and wrong.

"I don't like this," Dixie whispered to Jason, who didn't think anything about Dixie whispering and nodded his agreement. His first thought and priority were to find Diane, and he had a fairly good idea where to look. He shut the truck's engine off, and he and Dixie climbed out their respective doors, taking pains to shut them quietly behind them.

As they approached the dispatch office door, it opened, and Keith stepped out. When Jason opened his mouth to speak, Keith motioned for him to be quiet. Keith looked into Jason's eyes for a long moment, grabbed Dixie by the arm when she was about to walk past him. Satisfied that Jason was actually Jason, Keith handed Jason a folded piece of paper. Then Keith pointed to his own eyes with the first two fingers of his right hand, then pointed to both Jason and Dixie, then pointed to the note. Jason and Dixie both nodded to Keith indicating they had picked up on the idea that Keith wanted them both to read it. Then Keith walked to his truck, climbed into it, started it, and drove off into the night. Jason opened the folded paper, and with Dixie leaning close to him, they both read:

My leaving is a ploy. Jack's truck is somewhere on this lot, but I can't find it. He still has Christine. The two FBI ladies' bodies were dumped across town. Tom is inside with Diane, Megan, Joe, and Selena, I'll be back soon.
Godspeed my friends,
Keith

"Thank God," Diane cried and rushed into Jason's arms when he had barely stepped inside the door. She had been watching their meeting with Keith from inside the dispatch office.

"I'll get her back," Jason promised Diane, speaking of Christine, as he took the time to kiss every inch of her face.

"You read Keith's note?" Tom asked Jason as he eased his hold on Diane. Jason stepped back from his wife and nodded his response to Tom, who added, "There's more than just one of them out there."

"What do you mean?" Jason asked, giving Tom his full attention.

"I counted five altogether, counting Jack. They came spilling out of Jack's truck when he stopped right here in front of the dispatch office. Every one of them had those red glowing eyes," Tom told Jason as he slowly pulled Jason out of Diane's earshot and into a secluded corner. Tom silently relived a certain night in Viet Nam when he had seen something similar. Tom continued, "Anyway, he shouted a challenge to me, and I think I'm the only one who heard it. Jack said, 'There's only two ways you can get her back. Either trade her for Diane, or have Jason come get her.'"

"Why me?" Jason asked, shaking his head. He was truly perplexed, then asked, "What about backup?"

"All the phone lines are down, including the computers, and none of our cell phones will work," Tom said. "That was one of the reasons Keith slipped you the note when he left. He'll be back, he went after some back-up. And…"

"What?" Jason was perplexed, he didn't Tom very well, but he had never seen the look of fear on the man's face that was there now.

"Every time I step outside, Viet Cong come out the darkness," Tom averted his eyes from Jason's. Jason thought he saw tears starting to form in the corners of Tom's eyes.

"Why me?" Jason asked again, this time more to himself than to Tom, trying to give Tom to recover.

"I was hoping you could tell me," Tom said, giving Jason a grateful glance, then took a deep cleansing breath.

"Well, he's not getting Diane," Jason stated. "I'll go after Christine. Did you see her?"

"Yes," Tom said and hung his head. "He had her tied up inside one of those sleeper windows."

"No backup, that's just great. Never a cop around when you need one," Jason mused.

"This guy can pretty much predict what people are gonna do," Tom said to Jason. "Be careful. He has baited a trap he probably knows you won't resist."

"Keep Diane here," Jason's voice had become hard, he had made up his mind what he must do. He had always maintained that he would lay down his life for Diane, and/or her daughters, and now he chose to do just that.

When Diane saw Jason walk out the door, she started to run after him. Tom caught her and motioned for Dixie and Selena to help him hold her.

"What's he doing?" Diane asked, feared she knew the answer, and started to sob. She grew weak and leaned against her friends.

"This is the only way he would have it," Tom said to Diane in a low, soft voice. "He's not willing to let Jack have you, and he's willing to die to get your daughter back."

Diane cried more tears, started to slump toward the floor, but Dixie and Selena held her up, and eased her into a chair.

Jason walked along the mechanic's shop, keeping as close to the building as possible and trying to stay in the shadows. If they were, in fact, dealing with a demon, and a person possessed by that demon, then there were only a few places to hide, and in these shadows was not one of them. Jason kept his mind blank and rejected every thought that leaned toward an immoral end. It had been one of the things Dixie had told him on their last leg home this very night, and so far it worked.

He thought he would know Jack's truck when he saw it. From the descriptions he had gathered from Tom and Dixie, he was fairly sure he knew what kind of truck he was looking for. He also had a sneaking suspicion he had seen it before.

He reached the truck parking lot and stopped to scan the area. Blanket Transportation was a medium-sized company with about two hundred and fifty trucks; about half were company trucks, and the other half owner/operator trucks. Most of the company trucks were parked on this lot right now, as were a few of the owner/operator trucks.

Jason took a step forward and froze. Was that Jack's truck parked near the middle of the lot? He stepped to the left one step, and the truck disappeared. He stepped back where he had been when he had seen the truck, and it reappeared. He stepped to the right one step, and the truck disappeared. He stepped back to center, and it reappeared. Jason had no explanation for this and didn't take time to try to find one. He started for the truck, keeping the position in his head.

Jason recognized the truck. It looked to be the same black 379 model Peterbilt that had passed him on the Oklahoma Turnpike a few weeks ago. It looked a lot like Keith's truck, except this one had a sleeper that was the size of a small apartment.

When Jason reached the truck, he walked up to it and tried the driver's side door, it wasn't locked. Jason eased the door open, his nerves and muscles tense for anything. The truck's interior was dark and quiet. Jason climbed in and stepped between the seats. He stopped and listened. He could hear a soft thumping sound and could feel it vibrating through the floor ever so slightly. Then he heard the muffled cry for help.

Jason spun toward the sleeper. He went in slowly, peeking around every corner. He had never been in a sleeper this big. Over against one wall was a small stove and sink, with a few small cabinets above it. On the opposite wall there was a bench seat behind a small dining table. Next to that was a closed door. Jason opened it cautiously to find the bathroom that so many of Jack's victims had used. On the opposite wall, next to the sink, were two more matching doors. Jason opened each with the same degree of caution as he had the first. Behind one, Jason found a small shower stall, and behind the other one, a closet. Along the back wall was the bed, a queen-sized one from the looks of it. It was from under here the cries of help seemed to be emanating.

Hanging on the wall above the bed were several small, hand sized, triangular shaped patches of curly hair. Some of the hair was blonde, some was black, some was brown, and one, maybe two, were red-colored hair. Jason knew what they were, and it turned his stomach.

"Help me! Someone please get me out of here!" Jason recognized Christine's voice.

Jason ran his hand along the underside of the mattress frame and found the release lever to raise the mattress and its frame. The mattress and frame swung up on hinges with the help of gas-filled shocks. The whole assembly raised with the hinges anchored along the back wall, and the opening in front of Jason. He could hear the thumping and cries for help clearer now.

Jason locked the mattress and frame in place and reached for the door that sat in the center of the area below the mattress frame. He grasped the handle and pulled up. The door came open, and Jason swung it up and away in the same direction as the mattress frame.

Christine lay on her side with her back toward Jason. She was curled as much as she could into a fetal position. The confines of the box kept her from curling up all the way. Jason also noticed she didn't have much on in the way of clothes. He saw that she was barefoot, no pants, no panties, or bra, just a simple white button up man's dress shirt. He didn't want to think how she had gotten to be dressed this way, but he was conscious that this could very well not be Christine.

"Christine?" he asked, he kept his voice low and soft. He sat at the edge of the box, not looking at his stepdaughter.

"Yes," she snapped, then as if she recognized his voice asked, "Jason?"

"Are you all right?" Jason asked.

"I don't know, I think so," Christine whimpered, and tried to cover herself more with her arms and hands. "He knocked me out with some stuff on a rag, and when I woke up I was in here, like this." At these words, she started to cry.

"There are some clothes in this closet, I'll see what I can come up with," Jason said. After rummaging for a bit, Jason returned with a pair of skimpy, tight-fitting bike shorts. No shoes though, Jack must like his women barefoot—something Jason liked as well.

"How did you find me?" Christine sounded more composed now, starting to think that maybe this was another trick, and this wasn't really Jason. That thing that Jack could do where he seemed to be able to change his face from one person to another really scared her.

"It wasn't easy," Jason said, then handed her the shorts. "Here, try these."

Christine's mind raced, she needed to find a way to see if this was really Jason. She asked, "Will you look at me when I pull on the shorts?"

"Probably," Jason said, and once more, sat down on the edge of the frame.

That was no good, Christine thought, Jason would probably say that. He, too, probably thought she was not who she appeared to be. She remembered Jason had always been reluctant to tell her that he loved her, but she knew he did. If she were to ask him why he had come looking for her, and he said it was because he loved her, then she would know this was not really him.

"Why did you come looking for me?" Christine held her breath for the answer.

"Well, I heard there was a young, hot babe in here, and imagine my disappointment when it turned out to be you," Jason said, still talking low and soft.

"I love you, too!" Christine sprang out of the box, her earlier inhibitions forgotten for the moment, and threw her arms around Jason's neck.

Jason held her awkwardly for a moment, then when he felt her squeeze tighter, he held her closer. After a moment of silence, he spoke, "Christine?'

"What?" came her muffled response.

"Come on, we've got to get out of here," Jason told her.

"This shirt is pretty thin, and if I let you go, you'll see me," Christine said.

"More than likely," Jason agreed, "but can I tell you a secret?"

"What?" she closed her eyes tight, hoping she hadn't made a mistake. She hoped this really was Jason.

"I saw you, when you jumped out of this box, and into my arms," Jason said in that same low, soft voice, "and even if you weren't as pretty as you are, I would still love you just the same." Christine tightened her grip on him more and buried her head on his shoulder. No doubt about it, she thought, this truly was Jason.

"Will you look at me?" she asked again.

"It will be hard not to," Jason spoke softly in her ear, "but no, Christine, I won't look at you. Are you satisfied that it's really me?" She knew it really was Jason now, and not Jack.

"Yes," she said. "How did you know?"

"I had my doubts about you too, ya know," Jason said, they were still holding each other. He gripped the back of her head with one of his hands and kissed her on the forehead. "Come on, your mama is waiting for us." He released her then, averted his eyes from her, turned his back on her, and stepped back into the cockpit. He had an idea of driving the truck back to the dispatch office, but was disheartened when he saw no key in the ignition. He only took the time to look above the sun visor, in the ashtray, and in a pocket on the inside of the driver's door. By then, Christine was ready to go. The shirt's hem hung to a point about midway down her thighs. Jason didn't know about the shorts, and didn't ask, it was past time they left.

Jason climbed out of the truck first, surveyed the surrounding area, satisfied there was no one near, turned, and helped Christine down from the truck. He wished he had been able to find her some shoes, but at least the ground form there to the dispatch office was paved, but there were still small rocks. Jason tried not to think about how much Christine's bare feet might get torn up between the truck and the office. Then he decided he could carry her if it came down to that. He hadn't risked his life to save her, just to be stopped by something like that.

They held hands as he led Christine on a direct path to the dispatch office, stopping long enough when they would emerge from between two trucks to make sure the coast was still clear. So far, so good, and he was thinking about all of this when one of the biggest Hispanic men he had ever seen stepped into his path.

"Oh, hell," Christine gasped as she gripped one of Jason's arms with both of her hands.

"You have somthin' that does not belong to you, I tink," the big man said, grinned, then winked at Christine and blew her a kiss.

"Oh, hell!" she repeated and gripped Jason's arm tighter.

"Christine, honey, I need you to let go of my arm," Jason said to her, but never took his eyes off of the big man.

"I'm scared," Christine tried to keep the whine out of her voice.

"So am I," Jason admitted to her. "If I go down, you run like hell. The dispatch office is straight ahead." He pointed with the nod of his head past the big man.

"When he goes down in front of you, you will go down under me," the big Hispanic man, Hector, told Christine and blew her another kiss. That's when Jason saw the red tint to the big man's eyes. While he was telling her this, Christine released her hold on Jason's arm. Jason moved, he hoped all the hours he had spent pounding on the hard plastic barrel would now pay off.

Jason half jumped at the man and feigned a punch to his face with his left fist. Hector did as Jason had predicted and threw his head back, and where the head goes, the body follows. The big man's body arched backwards, exposing two primary targets.

Jason's momentum had changed, and now he was coming down. He used his down momentum, along with his body weight, and hit the big man with all of his might in his solar plexus with his own right fist. Jason never slowed. As soon as he had his feet set firmly on the ground again, he lunged toward the second target, with a front kick.

Hector was a long way from recovering from having the wind knocked out of him, and was half crouched, and holding his chest with his arms and hands, when Jason's kick connected with his crotch. What little air that was left in the big man's lungs vacated them with his groan of pain.

Jason wasn't done yet. Hector had gone to his knees, one hand holding his near-jellied nuts and the other still holding the area just below his chest. Jason grabbed a handful of Hector's hair on the back of his head and forcefully tilted his head back.

"Listen real close, because this will be the only warning you get," Jason said to him, then doubled his other hand into a fist. "Don't you ever look at my daughter again." Then Jason hit the big man full in the face, right between the eyes, his goal was to make his hand and fist meet. Hector's eyes rolled toward the back of his head, and he went out like a light.

"Oh…hell," Christine said each word slowly and reverently, her admiration for Jason apparent. "I've never seen anyone move like that."

"Yeah, well, don't let it get around, okay, 'cause then everyone will want to see," Jason gave her a wink of his own. She smiled at him and knew she would never look at him quite the same again. As she slipped her hand into his once more, he said, "Come on."

When they arrived in front of the dispatch office, Jason stopped and held Christine back when they took in the scene. Tom, Dixie, Megan, Joe, and Selena were standing in front of the dispatch office, facing Jack who held

Diane against her will. Three other men stood around Jack, one was the smaller Hispanic man that had encountered Jack in a restroom at a truck stop in Percival, Iowa. The big man that Jason had just put down had been his partner. The other two were the two that had watched Sharona be taken away in Jack's truck near Chicago.

"Come, join us," Jack invited Jason and Christine, then showed them his red, glowing eyes and wide smile.

"Mama!" Christine called, and started toward Diane. Jason caught her by the arm, held her back, and ushered her to Selena's outstretched arms.

Chapter 32

Jack stood behind Diane and held her in place, her back to his front, with his right arm wrapped around her neck, squeezing her throat. Jason knew Jack held a strong, long bladed knife in his other hand, he had seen the glint off the blade, and he also knew Jack was holding it somewhere behind Diane's back. Diane's eyes were wide and full of fear. Tears were running down her cheeks, and Jason knew she was terrified. Anytime Diane tried to move or speak to him, Jason saw her arch her back, and squirm as if Jack was poking her with the knife. Once Diane had raised her hands toward Jason, but Jack had squeezed the arm around her neck tighter, and saw her wiggle and arch her back away from Jack. Jason knew Jack was hurting her, and that made his blood boil.

Tom and Dixie looked at each other in disbelief. Both had their handguns out, but each somehow knew what the other was thinking. Each time Tom pointed his gun at Jack, black clad, crouched Viet-cong merged out of the darkness, and approached him with stealth.

Each time Dixie put Jack in her gun sights, she saw her father holding Diane in place, instead of Jack. Dixie and Tom looked at each other, each seeming to know the personal hell the other was encountering. She couldn't make herself believe that her dead father was there, but the suggestion bombarding her brain was far too strong to ignore. Every time she lowered her gun, Jack's grinning face reappeared to her.

Each time they checked their cell phones, they showed no signal. The land lines inside the trucking terminal were dead as well. It was as if there was a bubble, or giant umbrella covering them. They looked at each other again, and realized that any attempt on their part to take Jack down had been taken out of their hands. This was Jack's dance, and so far he was calling the tunes, all they could do was wait for an opening.

Diane hated to move any more than she had to against Jack, she could feel the result of his excitement pressed against her backside. This made her feel violated and added a sick feeling to her fear and sense of doom. She could feel Jack's breath on her neck, as well as her hear it in her left ear. Every so often, Jack would run the tip of his tongue along the bottom of her left ear lobe. This sent stabbing icicles down her back that were all but painful, and made her involuntarily wiggle against him again, much to her disgust, and to his pleasure, so much so, that he pressed against her even more. Diane's skin crawled, she wanted to cry, she wanted to vomit, she wanted Jason to rescue her.

"Last time, Di," Jack rasped in her ear. "All you have to do is sleep with me one time, and you can go back to your Prince Charming and live happily ever after."

"I wouldn't expect Jason to want me back after being with someone else, especially you," Diane spat out the words as she choked down her fear.

"How about it," Jack raised his voice to Jason. "Let me take Di here one time around the bed?"

"I said no!" Diane found her voice, cranked up the volume and at the same time tried to twist away from Jack. Diane loved Jason, but she would not be treated as though she could be bought, sold, or traded. Besides, she knew Jason well enough that he would offer himself for her to keep her from having to endure the rape and possible murder. She did not want to think about Jason giving that part of himself for her.

"Fine, bitch! Have it your way!" Jack snarled and shoved the knife forward into Diane.

"No!" Jason screamed as he saw the point, then most of the blade come protruding through the right side of Diane's chest.

Jack stabbed the knife hard into Diane and inserted the blade all the way to the handle. As he heard Jason scream, Jack released the choke hold he had on Diane and used that hand to savagely push Diane forward. At the same time, he yanked the knife free of her body with the other hand.

Jason saw Diane's eyes and mouth clamp tightly shut in pain as Jack stabbed her with the knife, then saw her eyes and mouth pop open as he shoved her forward and withdrew the same knife. Jason moved, he saw Diane's knees give way and buckle, and he lunged forward to catch her before she fell to the pavement. Jason caught her around the waist, and instead of trying to pick her up, he decided to break her fall. As he caught her, Jason turned at the waist, and pivoted on his left foot, and simply let himself fall onto his back onto the pavement, and held Diane tightly in his arms drawing her down on top of him.

As soon as Jack shoved Diane forward, Dixie mustered her strength, concentrated, and pointed her gun at Jack. He winked at her, gave her a grin, then gave her a dismissive look as her handgun was ripped from her hands by an unseen force, and flung away.

"Tom!" Dixie called, but Tom had his hands full. She found it hard to believe that pointy hatted, Viet Cong troops were advancing on Tom, but there they were, about two dozen of them. They advanced shoulder to shoulder, rifles held in a two handed grip, bayonets pointed at Tom.

Tom drew his Glock .45 Automatic, racked the slide and started firing at acquired targets. Dixie shot a glance toward Jason, then back toward Tom, and made her decision. When she started toward Jack with her back-up weapon drawn from its ankle holster, Jack's three henchmen moved to intercept her.

Dixie never hesitated, she began firing, not wasting rounds on body shots, but aiming for head shots. Her aim was deadly, as she had spent hours on the target range. Each man took at least two bullets to the head before the red glow faded from their eyes, and they went down. The hammer of her gun clicked empty as the last of Jack's men fell. When she looked at a grinning Jack, his eyes were glowing a hatful red, as he gave her a wicked wink. She felt an unseen barrier holding her back when she took a step toward Jack, she then turned her attention toward Diane.

Jason hit the pavement hard on his back. His martial arts training had taught him two things about taking falls such as this. One was to completely relax, resign yourself to the fact that you were falling, and simply go with it—go with the flow. The other thing was to tuck your head to keep it from taking a hard hit. Jason did both of these things, cradling Diane in his arms, protecting her as best he could. Jason hit the pavement hard and absorbed as much of the shock as he could, keeping his tight embrace on Diane. Jason slowly rolled onto his side and gently lowered Diane to the pavement. He lightly brushed the hair away from Diane's face that had fallen there as a result of the fall.

From somewhere, Jason heard the sound of tires squealing and air brakes being set. Then the sound of two doors of a vehicle being shut hard. Jason caught a flash of metal out of the corner of his eye and realized the flash of metal was Jack's knife coming toward him in a killing arch. He covered Diane as best he could with his own body and waited for the inevitable. Jason saw another movement, then heard a thud and a grunt of pain.

"Remember me, Jackie Boy?" Jason heard Keith say. Keith had kicked Jack on the side of the thigh, the kick had been enough to make Jack abort his attack on Jason.

"There's no backup coming," Keith called to Tom and Dixie, then said, "At the end of this driveway is a void that I couldn't get passed, like a doorway to another dimension. The only person I found was Marcia." Keith turned his attention back to Jack. He didn't let up, he had a score to settle.

Dixie, Christine, Megan, and Selena were there and helped Jason with Diane. Diane's eyes were still closed. Jason checked for, and was relieved to feel, Diane's heartbeat and to hear her breathing. Selena positioned herself in a kneeling position, so that Diane's head rested on her thighs and absently stroked Diane's hair, as if not knowing what else to do. Dixie was working rapidly, she tore open Diane's blouse, and checked the wound. Christine knelt beside Dixie, trying to help in any way she could, trying to stay out of the way, and sobbing through it all. Megan knelt at Diane's feet, tears streaming down her face. Joe had gone back inside the dispatch office to retrieve something.

The wound, as Dixie had suspected, went all the way through Diane's chest. Blood wasn't pulsing out of the wound, so Dixie was hopeful the knife had missed a major artery. The other thing that brought hope to Dixie was the fact that Diane's breathing wasn't labored or had that gurgled sound. It was as if the stab wound had missed Diane's vitals. Dixie ripped the sleeves from her own shirt and bandaged Diane's wounds as best she could. Next Dixie retrieved her cell phone, dialed 911, and hoped that whatever bubble had been over them before was now gone. When she did get through to the 911 operator, Dixie ordered an ambulance and police backup, both of which showed up thirty minutes later. Both the police and the ambulance drivers claimed they had trouble finding the place, but Dixie now knew that darker forces had been employed to delay them.

Jason knelt beside Diane, he held one of her hands in one of his, while he wiped the tears away from his eyes with the other. He cried, as he remembered the short life he had shared with her.

"Diane?" Jason's voice was barely above a whisper. Jason's mind was filled with memories of Diane. He remembered the first time he had seen her. She had been in her car, sitting in the driver's seat, leaning across the console, peering at him as he stood outside the passenger side door as they first talked. It was her eyes that he clearly remembered—her pretty blue eyes that sparkled when she laughed her symphonious laugh. Jason had also noticed her cleavage, he was a man after all, and hers was hard to miss, but it was her eyes that had dominated his attention that day. It's funny how the human mind works, one thought or memory can trigger so many different thoughts or memories. Such was the case here with Jason, a song by Juice Newton, "Break It to Me Gently", played in his head. It seemed to him that things like that happened at such odd times, and this was certainly an odd time.

"Honey, please don't go," Jason sobbed. He remembered their first date. It hadn't been much, a simple dinner date. Again, Jason remembered Diane's eyes looking at him over the top of her coffee cup as she held it in front of her face. He would later tease her that she could make a coffee cup sexy. There had been her cleavage again, discreetly on display, on purpose he assumed this time, but as with their first meeting, her eyes won out again. Vince Gill sounded off in his head now, singing, "Let's send up a prayer for this love that we share, cause it can change in the blink of an eye…" Jason had always assumed that he would be the first to go, that Diane would outlive him.

"Diane, please don't leave me," Jason croaked, his voice catching. He remembered their first kiss. It had been after their declaration of love for each other, after Diane had told her cop ex-boyfriend to get lost. Jason had called her as soon as he had parked his truck at the TA truck stop in Strafford. She had driven to the truck stop to meet him, and before she could say a word after getting out of her car, Jason had gently taken her in his arms and had slowly kissed her. It had been raining that night, and Diane's face was partially protected from the raindrops by the brim of Jason's cowboy hat. Diane hadn't resisted, hadn't voiced a complaint that the time wasn't right, she hadn't done a thing except smile slightly and watch it happen. Their lips had met, he pulled her closer, she stepped closer to him, circled her arms around his neck, and pressed herself tightly against him. She would later tell him that she knew he was happy to see her because she knew for a fact that he didn't carry pickles in his pockets. Jimmy Buffet's voice sang "Come Monday" in Jason's head.

"Honey, please stay with me," Jason found it hard not to sob. He remembered their wedding day, an impromptu ceremony orchestrated mainly by Diane. The months that had proceeded their exchanging of vows had been heart wrenching. Both Jason and Diane had had their doubts. Jason and Christine hadn't always gotten along, but Jason finally showed Christine two things. One was that he wasn't trying to take her mother from her, and the other was that he wasn't trying to replace her father. In fact, Jason and Mark got along very well. In the end, it was the love and the emptiness they both felt when they were apart and not communicating. After they were married and separated by Jason's job, it was the communication via telephone that held them together. When they did talk on the telephone, the 'I love yous', the 'I miss yous', the 'I can't wait to see yous' always won out over the bills that needed to be paid, the vehicle that needed work, and the like. They both knew what was important, each other, and they both strived for that end. Juice Newton made another appearance in Jason's head with a few lines from her song, "The Sweetest Thing".

"Diane, honey, please don't go! Stay here with me! I don't want to be without you!" Jason's voice rose. It sounded to the women kneeling around Diane's form that he was on the edge of his sanity. He remembered the first time Diane and he had made love, and the feeling that she would protect him as much as he would protect her. There were two things Jason remembered very well from the first time they had made love. One was the feeling of finally being complete, he had never experienced that with another woman, and the other was, of course, her eyes. During their lovemaking, he had looked into her eyes, when she had had them open, and to him, they were still as pretty as the first time she had used them to flirt with him. Jason wished she would open them now. The opening guitar riffs of The Hollies song, "The Air That I Breathe", sounded off in his head.

"Please, honey, don't go," Jason started to sob again. He remembered the first time she had gone on the truck with him. He remembered the feeling of seeing everything he took for granted in this job, new again through Diane's pretty, blue eyes. He also remembered the scent of her shampoo and perfume on his pillow for days afterwards. Jason had enjoyed going to sleep in the truck when he was on the road to the scent of her on his pillow. Diane did more than that though, when Jason was at home, she would strip the sheets off the bed of the truck sleeper, along with the pillow cases, and launder them. Then, after she would take her baths, Diane would use the pillow cases as towels to dry her hair, then lightly spray them with her perfume, before putting them back on the pillows in the truck. Barry Manilow made a rare appearance in Jason's head with the chorus of his song, "Weekend in New England".

"Diane," Jason lowered his head, closed his eyes, and felt the flood of tears come. The third verse of the song, "Until the Night", by Billy Joel, the verse just before the saxophone solo, sounded off in Jason's head. When the saxophone solo started in Jason's head, Diane opened her eyes, and looked at Jason's bowed head.

"My hero," Diane's voice was soft, almost a whisper. Everyone around her, Jason, Selena, Dixie, Megan, and Christine choked back sobs of joy.

"Let's get you out of here," Jason said, relieved to have his wife back among the living. He started to gently lift her, then changed his mind when he saw Diane looking over his shoulder at Jack. Jason looked at Dixie, Selena, Christine, and Megan in turn, they in turn, gave him the answer he needed with their eyes, and nods of their heads. He continued, looking back at Diane, "Wait. I need to finish this, if I don't, he will never leave us alone."

At that moment Jason heard a thud, a whoosh of air, and the sound of a body hitting the ground hard, followed by a second round of the same sounds. He was afraid to look, but when Jason did he was relieved. Keith lay on his back, not far from Jason, he was beat up pretty bad, but alive. Jason could tell this by Keith's breathing, and the string of cuss words coming out of his mouth.

Jason, along with everyone else saw Tom down on one knee, and everyone wondered who the redhead was kneeling next to him. On the other side of Tom was a prone form with the handle of a knife sticking out of his chest, he wasn't breathing.

"You all right?" Jason called to Keith and Tom.

"Peachy," Keith said. Tom waved, he was too busy being kissed by the redhead.

"My first priority is you," Jason said to Diane. She looked at him with her pretty blue eyes, and Jason knew that she knew what that did to him, but this time there was pleading in those pretty blue eyes.

"Go kick his ass, then take me home," Diane said, she hid her pain well, as she pointed to Jack with her chin. "It's not just me, if you don't put a stop to this, he'll be after Christine, Megan, Dixie, and Selena—he won't stop."

"All right," Jason decided, "but, after this is over, regardless of the outcome, you're getting out of here." He looked at the other four women kneeling there for confirmation. They, in turn, gave it to him with nods of their heads.

When Tom walked up to Dixie, her eyes instinctively went to the third finger on his left hand as they always did. The ring was gone. She saw that his handgun hung limply in his hand, empty.

"Tom?" Dixie asked with a slight grin, then glanced at the redhead standing beside him.

"I took your advice," Tom said with a small shrug and grin of his own. "I decided to stop wishing I could change the past and decided to make a few changes in my future."

"What about this?" Dixie asked, looking toward Jason and Jack. "Can we stand by, and let this happen?"

"Every time I take a step toward that asshole," Tom growled, nodding toward Jack. "More Viet Cong come out of the darkness, I'd say he's got an endless supply that he can call on, and I'm out of ammo. You?"

"I'm out too, and I still can't get a signal on my cell phone," Dixie said, then added in a defeated tone, "Every time I even look at him, I see my father grinning back at me. I hate this."

"It's obviously what Jack wants, and there ain't a whole hell of a lot that we can do at this point," Tom also sounded defeated.

When Jason stood and turned to face Jack, the song, "The Hair of the Dog", by Nazareth sounded off in his head. He stopped long enough to help Keith to his feet and shot a glance at Tom, who along with the redhead was talking with Dixie. They glanced back at him, giving him bewildered, and frustrated looks, accompanied with shakes of their heads.

"If he gets past me, grab the women and run like hell," Jason told Keith.

"You know, the way I'm beat up I can't run very fast, so don't make me have to run," Keith told Jason.

Jason walked to his truck, opened the driver's side door, and got out the claw hammer that he used to thump tires. He put the striker part of the hammer in his left fist and laid the hammer handle along his left forearm.

When Jason stepped up to Jack and faced him, he felt and heard two things in his head. First, he heard in his head Nazareth singing the part of the song that goes, "Now you're messin' with a son-of-a-bitch." Second, the sound and feel of an unseen door closing behind him. He felt as if he had been locked inside an invisible cage with Jack. Jason knew there would be only one way he could walk away from this.

Jason could feel the adrenaline pumping through his body and knew the dangers of feeling overconfident in a situation like this. A person could get drunk on adrenaline, and like alcohol, it could make you feel ten feet tall and bullet proof. Jason recognized this and tried to calm himself a little, but he would need a certain amount of adrenaline to combat the pain. Jason, like anyone who's been in few fights, knew that no matter how good you are, or how good you think you are, there's always someone a little better, and sooner or later you will end up getting hurt.

Jack smiled and bobbed his head as if he too were listening to the same song, he still held his knife in his right hand. To Jason, he still resembled the Gary Sinise character from the movie, Reindeer Games. Jason thought about that for a moment, then remembered the part Mr. Sinise had played in the movie, The Stand, and Jack's face changed.

Whenever Jack would try to project the face of a movie villain to Jason, Jason would counter by thinking of another role the actor behind the character had played, and the illusion would be broken. After a few seconds of this, Jack gave up and relaxed his face to his own.

Jack shifted his feet slightly, but Jason didn't flinch. Instead he lowered his head, tucked his chin, and looked at Jack with a level, steady gaze.

"You know you can't win this," Jack said to Jason, his voice low, and calm.

"Put your money where your mouth is," Jason said in his own even, mild tone. He knew the dangers of a verbal exchange with an opponent before a fight, and had no intention of opening a dialog with this asshole.

"Is the love of one woman worth all this? Worth dying for?" Jack asked. The grin on his face told Jason that Jack was enjoying this.

"There's more at stake here than that, and even someone as stupid as you should know that," Jason tried a new tactic, to see if he could anger Jack.

"Your feeble attempt at chivalry to save Diane will end with your death," Jack stated. "Your friend Keith was no match for me all three times I kicked his sorry ass, and you're not even close to being in the same class as him. For me to kick your ass will be the same as swatting a fly. "

"Funny, you can't say the same thing about Selena," Jason said, he was getting tired of this.

"All a set up," Jack almost whispered, as if confiding a secret. "I can't wait to see the look in her eyes when she realizes what's happened, and that I've been letting her win."

"That won't happen," Jason said in a low voice.

"Listen," Jack said, still using his conspiratorial tone as he pointed his chin to the women behind Jason. "That is some fine female flesh behind you. The six of them will make a fine start to a great harem. I'll even throw in Katrina to make it a lucky seven."

"I won't let that happen," Jason said. "You're nothing but a loser."

When Jack attacked, he faked with his left fist, and then arched the knife toward Jason's head. Jason was ready for it, he stepped forward, and blocked with his left forearm, the one with the steel hammer's handle lying against it. Jason didn't stop, or hesitate, but drove his right fist into Jack's solar plexus with a twist of his hips.

Jack's cry of shock and anger at being blocked was soon replaced by a breathless wheeze of pain from Jason's driving fist. Jack involuntarily stepped back from the force of the punch, but used it as a ploy, as he attacked again with the knife, this time with a backhand swing. Again, Jason stepped into the attack, and bent his elbow so that his forearm was parallel with his body, fist pointed toward the sky.

When their arms met this time, Jason yanked the hammer down hard toward the ground and let the claws of the hammer dig into the tender flesh of the inside of Jack's forearm, leaving twin bloody furrows. When Jack grabbed at the injured part of his arm with his free hand, Jason again hit him in the solar plexus, this time with a palm strike.

The voice of Jason's Tae Kwon Do instructor filled his head, "Class, it's important to develop many striking tools with your body. If one becomes injured, then you move on to another one. Besides, anyone who's been in a fight can tell you if you use your fists to strike your opponent in the face, your fists will become bloody and hurt after two or three punches."

Jason didn't stop, he released his grip on the hammer head just enough to let it spin in his hand and swung the handle of the hammer around, making it a striking weapon, and hit Jack a solid blow on the back of his head. Jason knew a blow like that would put most men down and out.

Jack went down, but wasn't knocked unconscious. Jason stepped up and prepared to deliver a life threatening kick to Jack's head. Jason knew he had made a mistake when Jack caught his foot with both of his hands, twisted it, then shoved it away.

Jason went down and rolled. When he looked at Jack again, Jack was getting to his feet, looking right at Jason, grinning, and showing Jason his glowing red eyes. Jason scrambled to his feet, he had lost his hammer somewhere, but there was no time to look for it. Jack was approaching, and he didn't look happy. Jason fought down his fear and panic. More adrenaline was being pumped into his system. The headache and shakes he would have after this was over were the least of his worries right now, provided that he lived through this.

When Jason had taken Tae Kwon Do classes, the free sparring was his favorite part. He took advantage of learning all he could when he was paired against someone taller, quicker, heavier, or more experienced than himself. He learned many tricks, some dirty, in how to combat those individuals, and now he would need to use some of those tricks. He let the adrenaline be his friend now and let it flow. He set his feet about shoulder width apart and put his hands up in a defensive posture.

When he was in range, Jack faked a right-handed punch and threw a left hook. Jason dodged out of the path of the first punch, and into the path of the second. He went down and saw stars, not necessarily in that order. He felt the skin at his temple split as a result of the punch and felt the blood, as well as smelled it, run down the side of his face. He heard shouted encouragement from Diane, Dixie, Christine, Megan, Selena, Keith, Tom, and the redhead. Who was she? Jason shook his head to clear it.

Jason was still on the ground when Jack stepped into range again. Jason swung his leg out in a sweep, but Jack jumped over it. Jack's feet no sooner touched the ground then Jason, who had continued his motion, knocked Jack's feet out from under him with a second, follow-up sweep with his other leg.

Jack crashed down hard onto his back. Jason moved fast, he got to one knee, and put all of his body weight and strength into a downward punch toward Jack's face. Jack rolled away, and Jason pulled the punch, not wanting to bloody his knuckles on the pavement.

They were on their feet again, they circled each other, and watched for an opening. Jack lunged toward Jason a couple of times, but Jason held back. When Jack glanced down at a pebble he had stepped on, Jason attacked. Jason connected with a left jab to Jack's nose, then stepped wide to the left and hit Jack with another hard punch to the face. Jason then picked up his right foot, pivoted on his left foot, swinging his right foot behind him, and delivered a solid, spin-away hook punch to Jack's temple.

When Jack grabbed at his temple, Jason swung his right foot out, pivoted on his left again, reversed his momentum, and kicked Jack in the stomach with a round kick. Jack clutched at his stomach and bent over. Jason pulled his leg back, chambered it again, readjusted his weight, lifted his right leg above Jack's bent-over form, and kicked Jack on the back of the head with his right heel with an ax kick. When Jack didn't go down, Jason pulled the same leg back once more, readjusted, and kicked Jack with a solid side kick to his exposed ribs.

Jack went down that time. He fell onto his back and lay still for a moment. When he got to his feet, Jason saw murder in Jack's eyes. Jack rushed forward, and Jason tried to evade by spinning away, but Jack still connected with a punch to Jason's jaw. Jason went down again but caught himself on his hands and knees.

Jason got to his feet and met Jack's next attack. Jack threw a left jab, then a right hook. Jason evaded both this time. When Jason threw a counter punch, Jack blocked it, and grabbed Jason's wrist in a two-handed grip. Jack twisted Jason's arm, pulled Jason next to him, and hit Jason with a downward swinging elbow. Jason stepped in front of Jack, and delivered a nut-cracking upper cut to Jack's crotch. Jack let go of Jason's arm and grabbed for his injured parts.

Jason was still bent over, he lowered his rump, got his legs under him, and sprang upwards with another upper cut, this one connected with the underside of Jack's jaw. Jack's head snapped back, and he stood straight up. Jason bent his knees and jumped straight into the air, slightly toward Jack. When Jason was within range of Jack, he uncoiled a flying side kick that connected with Jack's sternum. Jack fell back against the grill of Jason's truck, and when he bounced off, Jason was waiting for him.

Jason set his feet wide in a horse riding stance, feet about two shoulder widths apart, feet parallel to each other, knees bent and toward the outside, like riding a fat horse. When Jack was in range, Jason unleashed with half a dozen alternating punches to Jack's ribs. Jason was rewarded with groans of pain from Jack, and the sound and feel of breaking ribs.

Jack reached for Jason, but Jason stepped to his left by sliding his right foot closer to his left one. Jason exploded with power again as he brought his right foot and leg across his own body in a swinging, rising arc, then reversed its direction, and kicked Jack on the side of the head with the outside edge of his foot, a crescent kick. Jack spun a 180-eighty degree turn, then turned to relocate Jason.

Jason was waiting for him, and when Jack turned to face him, Jason leaped into the air again. This time, he did a 360-degree spin in midair, and kicked Jack with a jump, spinning crescent kick. Jack went down hard, but jumped right back up, and charged at Jason again, roaring at the top of his lungs.

Jason adjusted his stance, and again his Tae Kwon Do instructor's voice sounded off in his head, "When you're faced with a charging opponent, you have two options: Option A: the best way to avoid a speeding train is to step off the tracks. Or option B: the Spanish bullfighters will step out of the way of a charging bull, then stick it with their spears." Jason chose option B.

When Jack came within range, Jason sidestepped ever so slightly, started to spin a 360-degree turn, and cocked his left leg for a spinning hook kick. As Jason completed his spin, he had his leg up, and at the last moment, pulled his heel to his buttock, but before his heel met his buttock, it connected with the back of Jack's head, and Jack went face first onto the pavement.

Jason straddled Jack, who was still facedown, and gripped Jack's shirt collar at the nape of his neck with his left hand. Jason lifted Jack's head off the pavement, and punched down hard with his right fist to the back of Jack's head. Jack's forehead smacked against the pavement. Jason drew back and punched again, this time faster. Jason kept punching Jack on the back of the head, and each time Jack's forehead made the sick, thumping noise when it smacked onto the pavement. Jason didn't register the pain screaming through the knuckles of his right fist, the anger and adrenaline had taken over.

"Do it! Do it! Do it!" voices chanted at the very edge Jason's conscious mind.

After about the sixth or seventh punch, a scene from a movie popped into Jason's head. The scene in Return of the Jedi, where Luke has Darth Vader beaten down against the railing, and Darth Vader is almost lying on his back, and doing all he can to defend himself. The look on Luke's face is pure anger and hatred as he beats blow after blow down onto Darth Vader's light saber with his own. Then after Luke cuts off Darth Vader's hand, and realizes what he's done, and what he's destined to become if he continues down the dark path, he hears the Emperor laughing and applauding behind him. Luke throws away his light saber and calmly faces the Emperor. Jason heard a laugh very similar to that in the back of his mind.

Jason stopped punching, let loose Jack's shirt, and started to walk toward Diane. Jack pushed himself to his knees.

Jason saw Joe, Megan's husband, standing a few feet in front of him, legs and feet braced in an archer's stance, with an arrow notched, feather to cheek.

"Down!" Joe yelled to Jason, who went down, and turned his head to look behind him, and saw Hector racing toward him. Jason saw the first arrow, a broad head, find its mark. The shaft sunk itself into Hector's chest to the feathers.

As soon as Joe had released the first arrow, he notched a second and let it fly toward the same target. Hector was still charging toward Jason at full speed, eyes glowing fire red. The second arrow found its mark, next to the first. Joe let a third arrow fly, as Hector was yelling with rage and still advancing on Jason. The third arrow did it, and Hector went down like a felled tree, three arrows sticking out of his chest.

"I'll never stop!" Jack yelled at Jason, his face bloody from his head smacking the pavement. "I underestimated you, but it won't happen next time! You should've killed me when you had the chance! "

"That may be, but your life is not mine to take," Jason said, he had stopped, and turned to face Jack, then turned and continued walking toward Diane's open arms. He saw the look of relief on her face turn to a look of horror. Jason once again turned to face Jack.

Jack was still on his knees, his arms outstretched at his sides, his head tilted back, face pointed toward the sky, and he was screaming as loud as he could. Jason was paralyzed by the scene that unfolded before him.

Something stepped up, out, and behind Jack, whose body posture changed. He hung his head to his chest, his arms fell to his sides, and his torso went limp, but he also watched the scene in front of him.

The thing that had stepped out of Jack looked like a living shadow to Jason. Then as it stepped around Jack, and headed for Jason, its form morphed to a more solid manlike shape, and its color changed to a red glowing shade, with blue shimmering highlights.

"Sultry! No!" Jason heard Jack call out. Jason looked around for a place to run, or hide, but saw nothing. He didn't want to run to Diane and take the chance of having this thing hurt her. He looked at Diane, her daughters, and the small group of friends surrounding them, and just as he was about to look away and charge at this thing advancing toward him, the night sky seemed to be split open by an invisible hand, and a form of pure white, blinding light streaked from it. The light was so blinding and great that it knocked Jason to the ground.

Jason had been raised in a religious home and believed in God and his angels. He never in his life imagined that he would ever see one like this. Jason assumed it was an angel, and kept his head covered with his arms and hands as it flew with sonic speed inches above his head, and clashed with the advancing red and blue demon. When the angel and the demon locked up, there was a small explosion and a huge dispersion of sparks between them that lit up the night sky.

The speed and force of the angel took the demon off its feet, and they went airborne on a course across the night sky, the angel carrying the demon away. Jason thought he heard screams of anger, frustration, and pain as the demon was carried away by the angel.

More of the demons stepped toward Jason out of the night, but Jason stood his ground. He was scared out of his mind, the terror he felt sent more adrenaline coursing through his body. The demons eyes flashed as they focused on Jason, and he thought he saw what could pass for evil grins on their faces. They advanced toward Jason, and it took all of his strength, and faith in God not to run from them.

"Jason! Duck!" He heard Diane call to him from behind. Jason turned as he went down, and saw an unbelievable sight. Hundreds of angels were streaming through the slit in the night sky. The demons stopped in their tracks, then turned away and started to flee, but the angels were too fast for them. The angels flew close to the ground and snatched the demons off the ground, looking much like eagles picking off field mice. The demons that had taken flight were no match for the angels either. The angels zeroed in on the demons, and after encasing them in an unearthly grasp, flew off with them into the night sky, as the demons screamed and pleaded not to be taken to a dark abyss. Jason and the small group behind him could tell when an angel caught a demon because of the explosion of sparks that resulted.

When Jason looked at the slit in the night sky where the angels had come through, he saw it was closed. Jack still sat on his knees where he had through the whole ordeal, and Jason could hear him weeping. As Jason started to walk toward Diane once more, Dixie and Tom walked passed him, each patting him on the back.

"I love you," Jason and Diane said simultaneously as they embraced.

Sirens from ambulances and police cars could be heard as the flashes from their emergency lights danced across every surface around the small group on the Blanket Transportation parking lot. Whatever bubble or umbrella they had been under had obviously been lifted when the angels showed up. Officers from the Strafford Police Department, deputies and detectives from the Greene County Sheriff's Department, as well as patrolmen and detectives from the Missouri Highway Patrol surrounded Jason, Diane, Christine, Megan, Joe, Selena, Keith, and Marcia the redhead.

Two EMTs looked at, medicated, and bandaged Diane's wound. "When was the last time you had a tetanus shot?" one of them asked her.

"I don't know," Diane replied. After a nurse on the ambulance staff conferred with a doctor on call at a local hospital via telephone, she gave Diane the shot. They wanted to take her to the emergency room, but she steadfastly refused, telling them she was fine.

Two more EMTs insisted they examine Keith, who gave a heavy sigh of resignation. Once they were satisfied that Keith was all right, they turned their attention to Jason. They wrapped Jason's right hand in a bandage which had already begun to swell up.

Jason insisted Diane sit on a bench in front of the dispatch office. He sat beside her and wrapped an arm around her. Christine sat on the other side of him, and insisted that Jason put his other arm around her as she snuggled against him.

"My hero," Diane told him with her 1-900 voice, and she put her head on his shoulder.

"Mine too," Christine kissed him on the cheek, put her head on his other shoulder, and snuggled in more. Joe and Megan stood close, Megan next to her mother, and Joe behind the bench, next to Selena.

"Thank you, Jason," Selena said from behind them, as she put her hands on his upper back.

"You're welcome, Sal, I wouldn't have done that for just anyone, ya know" Jason said. Selena gave him a playful, but heartfelt squeeze as they watched Keith, Tom, Marcia, and Dixie walk up to them.

"I can see I don't have to ask how you're doin'," Dixie said to Jason.

"Yeah," Keith said with a sardonic grin. "I've waited a long time to turn your little joke around on you."

"What joke?" Jason asked.

"The one you always tell me about how it's an unwritten law in the state of Missouri that the ugly guys always end up with the best-looking women," Keith said, the glee and gleam shining in his eyes. Everyone else laughed. Tom gave Marcia a mocking frown as he looked at her, and nodded his head several times.

"You're all free to go home," Dixie announced. "Even you, Selena. I called Leonard Blanket, and he said for you to lock up and go home. Jack is in custody, under heavy guard, and on his way to the emergency room. That beating you gave him, Jason, will keep him moving slow for quite a while. I have all of your statements, and have cleared you with the local authorities."

"Will you be coming home with us?" Diane asked Dixie. Jason released her when she made it known to him that she wanted to stand. Diane embraced Dixie and held her for a long time.

"Not just yet," Dixie said to her. "I have reports to make, and a phone call to the deputy director to make that will probably take a while."

"You go make your phone call, I'll take care of the reports," Tom said, then insisted by pointing a finger at Dixie, "You need some time off."

"Okay," Dixie smiled at everyone there, then said to Diane, "I'll come to your—I'll be home in a couple of hours."

"Just think about it," Tom said to Joe, as he handed him a business card.

Chapter 33

Katrina Doyle rolled over in bed, and reached for her husband, only to find Keith gone. She propped herself up on one elbow, rubbed the sleep out of her eyes, then swung her feet to the floor. It had been a rare treat to have him home these last couple of days. Her nightmares had finally stopped plaguing her, and she was able to revel in his company—and his arms.

Not finding him in bed next to her was still a major concern for her. Ever since he had told her about his encounter with Jack in the Nevada desert, the dreams of his fallen comrades still haunted him.

Katrina rearranged her nightshirt when she got out of bed. She padded barefooted out of the bedroom, and headed for the kitchen. She smelled brewed coffee and had a pretty good idea where she would find Keith. She saw Keith sitting on a lawn chair on the rear patio, just outside the sliding glass patio doors. She poured herself a cup of coffee, then joined her husband out there.

"Are you all right?" Katrina asked. She sunk one of her hands deep into the locks and tangles of Keith's long hair. She loved the feel of his shoulder-length hair.

"Yeah, I'm fine," Keith answered her with a long slow exhale. He reached for her, placed one of his bruised, swollen, and hurting hands on the inside of one of her thighs just above the knee, and squeezed. He knew this was one of her erogenous zones. He felt her step closer to him, and smiled slightly to himself when he felt her shiver and the subsequent goose bumps that appeared.

"Anything I can do for you?" she asked, the concern in her voice genuine.

"You're doin' it," Keith answered as he looked up into her face. Her emotions for him swelled when she saw the haunted look of despair, grief, and pleading in his eyes.

"Your Seal buddies again?" Katrina asked, she pulled her hand from his hair, and wrapped her arm around his shoulder.

"Yeah," Keith drawled out the word, took a sip of his coffee. "I just can't seem to let them go this time."

"I can't imagine what this must be like for you, dreaming of friends you saw die in front of you," Katrina said, she stroked his long hair again.

"Cal and Jerry's families never blamed me for their deaths that day, but I'll always feel responsible," Keith said as he squeezed her leg again.

"Are the dreams the same as they've always been?" she asked. The sensation she was feeling from his touch made her want to climb onto his lap.

"No, in these dreams, the situations leading up to their deaths are different, but no matter what I do, I can't change the end result, and they still die," Keith confided. "I just wish I could make up for that in some way."

"Honey, I'm sure if you asked Diane, you more than made up for it the other night," Katrina said, she bent over, and kissed him on the cheek.

"Do you really think so?" Keith asked, his eyes sought hers for confirmation. The haunted look in his eyes made her want to weep for him, but it also made her want to hold and comfort him.

"How many lives did you have a hand in saving the other night?" she asked. It was a rhetorical question, but she wanted him to ponder it.

"I really didn't do anything, Jason is the one who put Jack down," Keith said, his hand was still holding her leg.

"Really?" Katrina asked. "Then why did Diane, Selena, and Dixie call last night to check on how you were doing? And Jason told me over the phone that if you hadn't intervened when you did, that none of them would be alive right now. He said you were as much responsible for putting Jack down as he was."

"When did they call?" Keith asked, his grip on her leg tightened ever so slightly.

"Within minutes of each other after you had gone to sleep," Katrina said, reached for Keith's hand, and pulled it a little higher to mid-thigh. She saw the haunted look had left his eyes to be replaced by a questioning look. "I'm being selfish today," Katrina explained. "I want you all to myself, and I don't want to have to share you with anyone, not even Jason today."

"It's Dixie who wants us there today," Keith said, he took another sip of coffee, and slid his other hand a little higher up Katrina's leg.

"You seem to be feeling better," Katrina tried to stifle a giggle, and she squirmed as Keith's hand found a resting place just below her buttock.

"Being with you is the closest I've ever come to being able to deal with their deaths, and for that I will always be grateful," Keith told her as he looked into her eyes.

"You mean even more than Jason?" she asked, and Keith saw the playful sparkle glint in her eyes.

"I would dare say that Jason would never have let my hand get this far up his leg," Keith tried to look serious.

"Is that the voice of experience talking there?" Katrina asked, she was trying to get Keith to move his hand a little higher without reaching down and moving it herself.

"You are the only one I want to touch like this," Keith said, it was hard for him to maintain a straight face with her making those small gyrations under his hand.

Katrina stopped moving, bent forward at the waist, and kissed him on the mouth. As her lips found his, she let out a small moan, as his hand found the spot she wanted him to find.

"Come on," Katrina whispered to him when their kiss ended. She straightened up and offered him a hand. Keith stood with a groan of his own. It would've been easier to count the spots that didn't hurt as opposed to those that did.

"The only part of me that doesn't hurt on me is the part I want to use on you, but the parts that do hurt may keep me from using that part," Keith scoffed as he did a slow shuffle, stagger, drag mummy two step toward the patio door.

"Come on, you big bad Navy Seal, grin and bear it," Katrina giggled as she waited for him at the patio door. "You know, I will be there to help you use that part on me."

"In that case, there'll be a whole lot of grinning on this end," Keith said as he stepped past her and into the house, then gave a surprised yelp as Katrina gave him a playful pinch on the rump.

Afterwards, Katrina lay in Keith's arms, listening to his deep breathing and small cat-like snores. She had always enjoyed making love with him, but this time had been extra special. With all of his injuries from his last fight with Jack, Keith had had to move slowly in their lovemaking. Then when he had surprised them both with an unexpected encore, she surprised him by taking charge and climbing on top.

There was no doubt that she loved this man. She had never met any other man who would come close to measuring up half as much. She snuggled in closer to him and splayed her hand throughout his chest hair. She moved closer to him and kissed him on the cheek. She saw him smile at her kiss and was glad she had that effect on him. She nestled her head next to his and was glad in the knowledge that she had eased his pain over his dead friends. She took a deep breath and drifted off to sleep herself.

The phone call Dixie made to the deputy director was more scathing than the last one she had made. The fact that she had allowed a civilian to risk his life in a deadly battle so she could apprehend a suspect in a federal case did not sit well with him. Also, the fact that she had apprehended the suspect did not sit well with him.

"I did not send you there to make an arrest, Special Agent Crenshaw! I sent you there to investigate, in the role of a profiler, yet you made an arrest!" he all but yelled at her.

"It was an on-the-spot decision," Dixie responded.

"What's happened to you?" the deputy director accused. "I sent you there because I thought you had a good head on your shoulders. Now I hear you've been hanging around truck drivers. I guess I should have sent another agent who's a lot smarter than you."

"Believe it or not, truck drivers are people too," Dixie said without a moment's hesitation, her tone firm.

"How about I give you a two-week suspension, Special Agent Crenshaw?" the deputy director challenged, his patience lost.

"Can I pick which two weeks?" Dixie asked sarcastically.

"Make it four weeks, no pay, effective immediately! I'll have you brought before the Office of Professional Responsibilities, and recommend you receive a Letter of Censure!" he shouted into the phone before he slammed it down.

Dixie took it on herself to perform a little PR work. She went to all of the heads of departments of local law enforcement and thanked them for their hard work and their cooperation. She started with the chief of police of Springfield, then moved to the sheriff of Greene County, and the sheriffs of Taney, Stone, and Christian Counties. She also expressed her thanks to the Missouri Highway State Patrol's Office. She felt like she had made friends here.

Jason and Diane were in the kitchen cooking together. Dixie had called and asked them to meet her at Blanket Transportation later that day. She hadn't told them what she had wanted them there for, but they both agreed to go.

Jason and Diane had thought Dixie had handled herself quite well at the press conference the day following Jack's capture. She had argued that she wanted the local law enforcement to hold the press conference as they always had throughout this investigation, but they all agreed that it was time that the people of the Ozarks got a good look at her. After the press conference, she felt at home here.

Jason and Diane were listening to the radio station that they compromised on as they prepared the meal for after whatever Dixie had in mind for them. Diane had potatoes boiling on the stove and was preparing the rest of the ingredients for her famous potato salad when 'I'd Love You to Want Me' by Lobo came on the stereo. Jason dropped the knife he had been chopping lettuce with on the countertop, and grabbed Diane around the waist.

"What are you doin'?" she asked with a giggle, after she had let out a 'yip' of surprise.

"When I saw you standin' there, I 'bout fell off my chair," Jason sang to her as he led her in a slow, swaying, stepless dance.

"We won't get this done if you keep this up," Diane protested half-heartedly.

"And when you moved your mouth to speak," Jason sang, then interrupted himself, and kissed Diane long and sensually on her mouth. She forgot her protest and returned his kiss, holding him as tightly as she dared. Like Keith, Jason wasn't moving to quickly these days. Jack, of course looked far worse than Jason, but Jason still had a lot of bruises. Jason broke their kiss and placed his hurting, bruised hands on either side of Diane's face.

"I would do it all over again, just for you," Jason told her as he looked into her pretty blue eyes. Diane closed her eyes and leaned into him. The knife wound in her shoulder still hurt, but Jason was taking her mind far away from that. She smiled the smile of loved contentment as she moved against him and with him in their swaying dance.

"I love you," she whispered into his ear and was rewarded when she felt his arms tighten around her ever so slightly.

"I love you, too, Diane," Jason said. She laid her head on his shoulder and let the tears of joy leak from her eyes. She tightened her own grip on him when he started to sing to her again. She didn't know what turned her on more, the sound of his low voice singing to her, or feeling the vibrations from his chest onto her chest with each word he sang. She couldn't decide, and so she just enjoyed the moment.

Later that day, Dixie called a meeting with Jason, Diane, Keith, Katrina, Selena, and Tom in the same room at Blanket Transportation, along with Leonard Blanket, and Clifford Strokes.

"Thank you all for coming," Dixie told them. "The Bureau wanted me to pass on its gratitude for your assistance in this case." Dixie told them no lie, the deputy director had called her back after he had cooled off a bit, and asked her to perform this task but stood by his decision on her suspension and reprimand.

Then she turned her attention to Clifford. She stepped up beside the seated form of Clifford, and nodded to Tom, who took a seat on a chair directly across the table from Clifford. Dixie laid her Sig Sauer and badge case on the table beside Clifford, and shoved them to Tom, who let them set there directly in front of him, while he grinned at Clifford.

Dixie said to Clifford, "The last time we all were in this room, you told Jason that truck drivers like him are a dime a dozen. Well, Mr. Strokes, there aren't enough dimes in the world to pay for the service people like these two truck drivers provide. I want you to think about that the next time you're in a grocery store, or buying clothes, or shopping for a new car. Without men like these, those things wouldn't be there for your convenience." She waved a hand toward Jason and Keith.

Clifford squirmed in his seat, glanced tentatively around the table at everyone there, and rested his gaze on Leonard, as if asking for support. There was none there. Leonard sat in his chair, arms folded across his chest, head lowered, lips pursed.

"I suppose people like you think those goods could be delivered by air or freight train," Dixie said to the side of his face. "I want to be at the first place that lands a helicopter on a grocery store parking lot or drops its delivery at the end of a parachute onto that same parking lot. People like you have a hard enough time driving around a big truck, let alone trying to drive around a food drop, or a landing helicopter. How would you like to have to cross a set of railroad tracks at almost every city block while trains make deliveries to individual stores."

"Agent Crenshaw?" Leonard Blanket spoke up, only to see a hand raised from Tom for his silence.

"People like you start organizations protesting big trucks and their drivers, but those same people will be the first ones to bitch when goods aren't delivered on time because of laws they push to be passed to hinder truck drivers." "I—" Clifford started to say, only to be cut off by Dixie.

"Let me point out something to you, Mr. Strokes, you work at a trucking company," Dixie spoke more slowly and more loudly. "Do you think the money you receive each week at payday miraculously appears out of thin air? It's generated by people like Jason and Keith here who sacrifice time from their families to perform a service no one else wants to do."

"The law is the law!" Clifford snapped, he had finally found his voice. "They get no more special treatment than anyone else, they must be held accountable for breaking the law!"

"I'm not condoning law breaking on their part," Dixie smiled at him, looking into his challenging eyes, "but the laws regarding commercial big trucks are lopsided as opposed to personal vehicles. I would think with you being in the position you are in, you would be willing to help people like Jason and Keith as opposed to hindering them."

"I don't hinder them!" Clifford was indignant.

"Really?" Dixie challenged. She reached inside one of her jacket pockets, and produced a slip of paper. She laid it on the table in front of Clifford for him to see. Their eyes met, and Dixie saw the questioning look in his eyes change to an anguished look, then she said. "I did some checking this morning after I was reinstated just for this meeting. I thought it strange that a scale house would do to Jason and me what the one in Arkansas did that night. A phone call was placed to that scale house about thirty minutes before we got there. I think you'll recognize the phone number from where the call was made."

"What?" Leonard Blanket snapped.

"Don't worry, Mr. Blanket, Mr. Strokes didn't call from here, using a company phone, he called using his own cell phone," Dixie informed him. She held up a hand, as if asking Leonard to remain silent, then said to Clifford, "The only reason I don't bring charges against you for impeding a federal investigation is because Jason asked me not to."

Clifford shot a questioning look at Jason, then to Dixie, and finally to Leonard, who returned his look with his own look of anger.

"I think you owe Jason a word of thanks, and I think you owe Jason and Keith an apology," Dixie stated. She never took her eyes off Clifford.

"I don't want an apology from him," Jason said and stood up. "I want to stay pissed off at him for talkin' to Diane the way he did." Diane and Selena stood with him.

"Me too," Keith chimed in as he and Katrina also stood, followed by a laughing Tom, who scooped Dixie's Sig Sauer and badge off the table. They all turned to exit the room. Dixie left Clifford sitting alone with Leonard Blanket, as she linked her arm through the one Tom offered her, and together all seven of them exited the room.

"I think that went well," Dixie told the group with a beaming smile after they had left the room.

Chapter 34

"I wish the two of you all the happiness in the world," Dixie told Marcia. They were standing on Jason and Diane's carport. Although both Dixie and Marcia weren't heavy drinkers, they both sipped at bottles of light beer.

Marcia leaned close to Dixie and said in a conspiratorial tone, "He's a great guy, and everything I asked for."

"He may be a little more than that," Dixie said. "He deserves to be happy."

"I'll do what I can," Marcia said, and the two women exchanged knowing smiles.

After the meeting at Blanket Transportation, the small group of friends met at Jason and Diane's house for a potluck victory celebration. Everyone was there, Diane's brothers were famous for their barbeque, and had came early to get things going. There was a ton of food as everyone there had brought something. Jason and Keith had struggled with throwing two sheets of plywood over four sawhorses to provide tables large enough to accommodate all of the food.

"I thought you Navy Seals were supposed to be just a step below Superman," Jason chided Keith as they both struggled with their ends of the sheet of plywood. To everyone there watching these two, it looked like a tag team wrestling match gone wrong, it also looked like the plywood was winning.

"Who told you that, a damned black belt in Tae Kwon Do?" Keith grunted.

"Hey, watch it," Selena laughed.

"My apologies, ma'am," Keith winked at her.

"This plywood is heavy enough without having to carry you, too," Jason got another jab in on Keith.

"Well, if you were any kind of a black belt at all, you could break this sheet in half, and make it a lot easier to carry," Keith shot back, as they finally managed to get the first sheet into place.

"Hold on," Tom spoke up when Jason and Keith went to get the second sheet of plywood. He motioned to Kyle, who stepped up to help Tom with the second sheet. They had the second sheet in place in half the time it had taken Jason and Keith.

"Story of my life," Keith said, "green berets and marines always trying to show the Seals up."

"What happens now?" Jason asked. Everyone had gone except Dixie, Kyle, Tom, and Marcia.

"Jack is finally ready to move to a more secure location," Dixie said. "The hospital staff will breathe a little easier when he's gone. No one there really wanted to work on him."

"I can't blame them," Diane said. "I wouldn't want to help him either."

"The general consensus among the OR personnel was to leave him to work on last," Tom said "We almost had to make them patch him up. The beating Jason gave him did quite a number on him."

"I still have a hard time believing that he was the guy you were after," Marcia said, shaking her head slowly. "Of everyone here, I was around him the most, but probably knew him the least. I hate to think about what would've happened if I had gotten involved with him."

"It's hard to say. Serial killers differ in that some practice killing until they kill the person they're really after, like their own mother. Others kill only people they barely know, or don't know who have similar traits, but rarely kill their own family members," Dixie explained. "We may never know why he targeted you. It could be that in his particular case, he actually wanted some companionship, someone who could take his mind off of what he was doing."

"How about you, Jason? With everything that went on that night, how are you coping?" Tom asked.

"You mean the thing that came out of Jack? The demons? The slit that opened in the sky? The angels?" Jason asked.

"Yeah," Tom prodded.

"In a way it seems unreal, like it never really happened, but I know it did, we all know it did," Jason said, as he looked at Diane, Dixie, Kyle, Marcia, and Tom. "I'm just glad they were on our side."

"What are you gonna do now, Dixie?" Marcia asked, she had a hold of one of Tom's arms and was squeezing in close to him.

"Jason here has graciously agreed to further my education in truck driving," Dixie said with a wide smile.

"I tried to get her to come away with me for a mini-vacation," Kyle spoke up, "but Dixie says Jason's truck is bigger than mine."

"You are such a liar, I didn't say that, " Dixie accused, laughing, and playfully slapped him on the arm.

"Are you sure you want to be alone with her in a truck?" Kyle asked Jason, rubbing the spot on his arm where Dixie had slapped him.

"We all have our crosses to bear," Jason grinned at Kyle.

"You two are just alike," Dixie shook a finger at Jason.

"Don't let him kid you, Dixie, he's gonna need your help," Diane confided. "He's still pretty stiff and sore. I wanted him to take some time off, but he insists on running this week."

"The truck won't make us any money sitting here in the driveway," Jason said, wrapping an arm around her.

"I know, but I don't have to like it," Diane stuck out her bottom lip in a mock pout.

"What are you going to do now?" Dixie asked Diane.

"I'm going to take some me time," Diane beamed at everyone. "I'm going to spend some time with my daughters. Then, when you get back off the truck, I'm going to mother you."

"I look forward to it," Jason said.

"I meant Dixie," Diane said and jabbed him in the ribs with her elbow.

"I really look forward to it," Dixie said, shouldering her way between Jason and Diane.

"Hey," Jason said in a tone of mock frustration, "we already have one daughter here that does that kind of thing."

"Well, now you'll have another one," Dixie told him. Then catching each other's gaze, they cued each other and gave Jason a tandem Miss Piggy "harumph" in stereo. Jason gave them a sidelong look as everyone there laughed. Jason then grabbed them both around their necks with his sore arms and took turns kissing them, Diane on the mouth and Dixie on the forehead. They both halfheartedly tried to squirm away from him.

A few days later, Dixie was in the driver's seat of Jason's Peterbilt. It was night time, and she was cruising at a speed of eighty miles per hour along I-40 eastbound in Arizona. She had been talking on the CB with two male truck drivers going the same direction.

"Hey, westbound, you got three bears sittin' in the middle shootin' you in the face," said a voice over the CB speaker.

"Are they sixty-ninin'?" Dixie asked into the keyed CB mic.

"Well, I don't know about that," said the same voice over the speaker, with a chuckle. "There are three of them."

"Oh, a threesome or an orgy," Dixie was having fun.

"I think they're looking to write some tickets," said the same voice, he was all but laughing now.

"Oh, I see, a bear hunt. Wait! Wait! Let me find my switch," Dixie said into the keyed mic. She could hear Jason laughing from the sleeper.

"Are you a woman big enough to go bear huntin' with a switch?" asked one of the drivers Dixie had been running with.

"No, driver," Dixie replied. "I'm not that big, but I'm pretty mean."

"It must be the full moon out tonight," said the voice of one of Dixie's running mates over the CB speaker.

"It's not a full moon out tonight," said the voice of her other running mate.

"Are you sure?" asked the first.

"Yep, I sure am," said the second. "If it was a full moon, you could see my ex-wife flying around it on her broom."

Dixie's cell phone rang. She had it hung in a hands-free device mounted on the console of the truck. She looked at the caller ID and saw it was her boyfriend Kyle. She pushed the button on the phone to deactivate the speaker option and plugged in her earpiece. Jason climbed out of the sleeper and into the passenger side seat.

"I'll be right back, I have a phone call," Dixie said into the keyed mic of the CB.

"Ten-four," Dixie's running mates' voices responded over the CB speaker, one after the other.

"Hello," Dixie greeted with a pleasant tone, then Jason saw her facial expression change. He could tell she was concentrating on what was being said to her.

"Damn," Dixie breathed. "Are you all right?" She listened for a moment, then said, "Kyle, I love you. See you soon. Bye."

"What's up?" Jason asked as Dixie's cell phone rang again.

"Hold that thought, this ought to be good," Dixie said as she looked at the caller ID and saw it was the deputy director. She unplugged the earpiece, pushed the button for speaker phone so Jason could hear as well, and said toward the phone, "Hello, sir."

"Hello, Special Agent Crenshaw," the deputy director said, his voice from the cell phone filled the cab of the truck. "I understand you are on the road again."

"Yes sir," Dixie said. "I'm making the most of my suspension."

"I see," responded the deputy director. "I guess you've already heard what has happened."

"Yes sir," Dixie said. "I just received that news."

"Well, Special Agent Crenshaw, I need you on this case. You are the one person who knows what this person is capable of, and knows how he thinks," the deputy director said. "I will reinstate you for this case, then afterwards you can finish your suspension."

"Sir," Dixie kept her voice calm and spoke slowly, "with all due respect, why don't you send one of those agents who's supposed to be so much smarter than me?" Dixie then pushed the disconnect button and hung up on the deputy director. She looked at Jason and gave him a wink.

"What's goin' on?" Jason wanted to know.

"The U.S. Marshals were moving Jack to a more secure location when he escaped," Dixie told Jason in one breath.

"Shit," Jason swore. "You know the deputy director is right, you should be in on his recapture."

"I know," Dixie said with a wry smile. "I'm gonna let him stew for awhile. After all, there is the matter of the Letter of Censure, and the Office of Responsibilities he threatened me with."

"I think I've created a monster," Jason said with a wry smile of his own as he pointed a finger at Dixie.

"Yep, you sure have," Dixie confirmed with a beaming smile, "and I thank you for that."

Jason grinned, stood up, and headed back toward the sleeper wondering if he had made a mistake by not killing Jack when he had had the chance. He wondered how drastically all of their lives were going to be affected. He lay down on the bottom bunk, painfully flexed and unflexed his right fist, then grinned again when he heard Dixie key up the CB microphone.

"All right, you two outlaws," Dixie said into the keyed mic. "I'm stopping up here at exit sixty-six, who's buying me breakfast?"

"I'll never stop! You should have killed me when you had the chance!" Jack's words resounded in Jason's head. He had lain back down and had been laughing at Dixie's antics with her two running mates.

"Shit!" Jason all but yelled as he sat straight up in the bottom bunk.

"What's wrong?" Dixie asked, she was serious now.

"Diane!" Jason exclaimed. "Jack'll be going after Diane."

Dixie pulled up Tom's cell phone number and punched the automatic dial button.

"Hello, Dixie," Tom's voice filled the cab of the truck from the speaker option of her cell phone.

"Tom, is Diane okay?" Dixie asked without a greeting.

"I'm sorry, Dixie, this must've been the first place Jack came to," Tom's voice said.

"Is she—" Dixie couldn't make herself finish the question.

"She's gone," Tom's voice said simply. "We got people over here as soon as Kyle alerted us as to what happened. It looks like Jack kicked the door in and took her right out of her own house."

"Tom—" Dixie started, then stopped as her throat threatened to close up on her.

"I know, I'll do everything I can," Tom's voice said, then asked. "Is Jason handy?"

"Right here, Tom," Jason said, standing between the seats of the cab of the truck.

"Remember the night the angels slit open the night sky?" Tom's voice asked.

"Yeah," Jason said.

"Remember the burn marks that were left on the pavement where it looked like the demons had appeared and disappeared?" Tom's voice prompted.

"Yeah," Jason said again, a bit impatient.

"We found a mark like that on your garage floor tonight," Tom's voice said.

"What do you make of that?" Jason asked.

"I don't know what to think," Tom replied, "but it sure would explain a lot of the things the lab personnel were trying to tell us about Jack."

"Yes, it would," Dixie agreed. "Tom, we'll be home as soon as we can. I know I don't have to tell you how to proceed."

"Consider it done. I just cancelled my retirement. Jason, I'm really sorry, and I'll do all I can to help get her back," Tom said over the cell phone speaker.

"I know you will. Thanks," Jason said. He eased himself back into the sleeper and slumped down on the bottom bunk.

"Red Eye, Homespun," Dixie said into the keyed mic of the CB "There's been a change of plans, and I won't be stopping for breakfast."

"What's up?" Red Eye's voice asked over the CB speaker.

"I've got a family emergency at home, and we're gonna kick it on in from here," Dixie said.

"We'll tag along as far as we can," Homespun's voice said over the speaker.

"After I make this next phone call, I'll probably be reinstated back on the case," Dixie said into the keyed mic.

"What are you talkin' about?" Red Eye asked.

"I'm a special agent with the FBI," Dixie said into the keyed mic and braced herself for the chiding she felt sure would follow.

"Yeah, right," Homespun's voice said with a laugh over the CB speaker. "What case?"

"The Jack the Scalper case," Dixie said into the keyed mic. There was a slight silence.

"You're Agent Crenshaw? The FBI lady who caught him? No joke?" Red Eye's voice came over the speaker.

"Yes, I am," Dixie said into the keyed mic.

"Good night, Irene. Yer famous. That press conference you held was telecast nationwide," Red Eye said. "I'll do anything I can to help."

"I appreciate the offer," Dixie said, "but this is gonna be a non-stop flight. When I use up my hours, my partner will take over."

Jason half heard the conversation Dixie was having with Red Eye and Homespun. He reached onto the top bunk, pulled the pillow off the bottom of the stack, laid it on top of the pillows in the bottom bunk, and laid his head on top of it. The scent of Diane's shampoo and perfume still lingered there, and he breathed it in. Deep down he knew Diane's scent on this pillow would eventually fade away and be gone forever. He wanted to seal it in an airtight bag, and save it, preserve it forever, but he also wanted to be close to Diane, and this was the best he could do right now. Tears filled his eyes as he savored the scent of her. He and Diane had often fantasized together what it would have been like if they had met earlier in their lives. Now Jason wished he could go back just a few days and hold her once more.

THE END